I0527825

Connie glanced at her watch. They had separated nearly an hour ago. Joy should have come around the corner by now.

"Joy, you know how much I hate waiting," she voiced aloud through gritted teeth. Anxiety and frustration pulled at her like a taut rubber band. Perhaps her sister wasn't as physically fit as she looked. She was in her late 30s after all. What if she pulled a muscle? What if she had fallen?

A sudden ripple of apprehension rushed through Connie. Something terrible, beyond definition. Beyond simple physical fitness fears. It was like a cry only she could hear.

With a groan, Connie lurched to her feet, stretched aching muscles and shuffled to the jogging path. More than the pain in her lower calves nagged at her.

Had something happened to Joy?

Praise for Rebecca Grace

"THE PROBLEM by Rebecca Grace is well written, full of emotional twists and turns. The characters all seem real and the setting is so vivid I could see and hear it all. I was charmed by this story and will definitely read it again. Very well done and highly enjoyable."

~The Long and the Short of It Reviews

"I loved the way each character [in HOME FIRES BURNING] saw each other's perspective when it came to life. The book was gripping from beginning to end [and] incorporated conflict and emotion. Ms. Grace has a style of writing that draws the reader deep into the story. She writes with emotion and tenderness straight from the heart."

~Coffee Time Romance (rated 5 coffee cups)

"Both main characters and all the supporting characters [in HOME FIRES BURNING] make you want to 'pull up a rocker and set a spell.' This is a very comfortable tale of romance and remembering where your heart resides. I found myself completely charmed."

~Ecataromance (rated 4 stars)

"LOVE ON DECK is an inspiring story about learning to believe in yourself and following dreams, even when the odds are not stacked favorably. A refreshing story with characters whose chemistry ignites sparks."

~Romantic Times (rated 4 stars)

"LOVE ON DECK" is a modern story where the characters come alive with believable interplay and dialogue. This very original story will captivate readers with its consistent characters and well-developed plot…a fun and moving story."

~Ecataromance (rated 4 stars)

Deadly Messages

by

Rebecca Grace

This is a work of fiction. Names, characters, places, and incidents are either the product of the author's imagination or are used fictitiously, and any resemblance to actual persons living or dead, business establishments, events, or locales, is entirely coincidental.

Deadly Messages

COPYRIGHT © 2009 by Rebecca Martinez

All rights reserved. No part of this book may be used or reproduced in any manner whatsoever without written permission of the author or The Wild Rose Press except in the case of brief quotations embodied in critical articles or reviews.
Contact Information: info@thewildrosepress.com

Cover Art by *Kim Mendoza*

The Wild Rose Press
PO Box 706
Adams Basin, NY 14410-0706
Visit us at www.thewildrosepress.com

Publishing History
First Crimson Rose Edition, 2010
Print ISBN 1-60154-642-4

Published in the United States of America

Dedication

To my sister, Lillie,
who always made me want to write;
to Ron,
who re-inspired my writing and gave me the idea
for this book;
and to John and Shannon,
who give me a reason to write.

Chapter One

"Joy, where are you?" Connie Romero muttered as she slumped on a park bench, rubbing the back of her aching calf. Wincing, she raised her eyes to search the jogging path that hugged the sea wall in Vancouver's Stanley Park, seeking her sister's silver and blue running suit. A line of Douglas Fir trees cast towering shadows across the winding walkway. The growing shadows coupled with a layer of fine mist made it difficult to distinguish anyone from a distance.

Why had she let Joy talk her into this jog? Connie could run two miles without much discomfort, but what possessed her to try for six? Joggers in bright nylon sweat suits and bikers in neon-bright spandex jockeyed for position on the path, but Joy was not among them as they drew closer.

Connie hadn't expected her sister to beat her to their pre-determined meeting spot. Joy chose to follow the walkway that snaked around the outer end of the park, while Connie limped across a grassy shortcut that allowed her to rejoin the path farther along.

Her gaze venturing from the path, she looked across the shimmering blue waters of Burrard Inlet. The downtown high rises of Vancouver sparkled like jewels in the late afternoon sun. Overhead, seagulls circled, emitting plaintive cries. What a perfect day to start their mini family reunion. Now, if only Joy would jog around the corner so they could sit, enjoy the view, and chat for a while.

A sudden electronic song rang out, and Connie fumbled for the cell phone on her belt. Hopefully Joy had taken a cell phone with her, and this wasn't a frantic call from the television station telling Connie she needed to give up her short vacation and get back to work. It was neither. The number on the digital read-out belonged to her younger sister, Lisa.

Connie smiled as she tapped on the phone. The third member of the sisterly reunion had been unable to get away early and planned to meet them in a few hours. Maybe she was already in Vancouver.

"Hi, Lise, where are you?"

"Almost there," Lisa chirped. "Just crossed the border. We are now all in Canada, so let the reunion of the Romero sisters officially begin. How's everything going so far?"

Not wanting to worry her sister, Connie avoided the question. She kept her voice light as she scanned oncoming joggers. "This was a great idea. I'm so glad Joy suggested getting away from her family for the weekend and coming up here. We don't see each other enough. I feel like I haven't spent any time with her in ages. The kids or Ralph are always around. From our brief conversation so far, she has plenty she wants to tell us."

"That was the feeling I got last time I talked to her. I should be there in about an hour. Shall I meet you at the hotel?"

"Might as well. I suggested a walk, and big sister decided to jog around Stanley Park. It's six miles, and I'm dying."

"And Joy isn't?" Lisa's voice filled with surprise. Joy had always been the least athletic of the trio.

"Wait until you see her," Connie responded with a laugh. She hadn't seen Joy in months, and the transformation had been shocking. "She may be five years older than I am, but she's gotten herself into great shape. She's lost weight and gone from pudgy mother of two to sleek athlete. I hardly recognized her. She'll give you a run for your money, Miz Marathon Queen. She's wearing me out."

Lisa's familiar laugh came across the line. "I may run, but you're the energy queen. I never thought I'd see the day someone could wear you out."

"I feel more like a drained battery at the moment. I could use a re-charge. Joy is still running, and I'm sitting on a bench waiting. If I collapse on the way back, I'll call, and you can pick us up."

"Sounds like a plan. I'll call when I get closer."

Snapping off the phone, Connie inspected the latest group of joggers headed in her direction. Still no sign of Joy. Her eyes searched the paved walkway all the way to where it disappeared around a sweeping bend, but she still did not see her sister.

Connie glanced at her watch. They had separated nearly an hour ago. Joy should have come around the corner by now.

"Joy, you know how much I hate waiting," she voiced aloud through gritted teeth. Anxiety and frustration pulled at her like a taut rubber band. Perhaps Joy wasn't as physically fit as she looked. She was in her late 30s after all. What if she pulled a muscle? What if she had fallen?

A sudden ripple of apprehension rushed through Connie. Something terrible, beyond definition. Beyond simple physical fitness fears. It was like a cry only she could hear.

With a groan, Connie lurched to her feet, stretched aching muscles and shuffled to the jogging path. More than the pain in her lower calves nagged at her.

Had something happened to Joy?

****

"I need your help."

Inspector Mitch Weldon stopped tapping a

3

pencil on his desk and relaxed back on his chair as the sound of Connie Romero's voice brought a quick smile to his face. Calls from Connie always perked him up. Even his partner said so. Her immediate, breathless demand didn't surprise him because she only called when she needed something.

He tried to think of a quick quip because she usually followed her initial requests with some sort of teasing innuendo that left him searching for a witty reply. She was the only woman he knew who could make him blush and leave him flustered. Before he could come up with anything beyond a tentative, "Yes," her anxious voice froze him.

"Please, Weldon. I'm here in Vancouver, and my sister has disappeared."

No blushing today. This sounded serious. "Have you called police?"

"I called you," she said in an accusing tone, choking with emotion.

He drew a deep breath, jerking up to a rigid posture, all senses on alert. "I'm not in the habit of taking missing person reports," he replied, pulling open a desk drawer to get a note pad to write down the details. "That's not what Canadian Special Investigations handle, but if you give me the information, I can call Vancouver Police to help you. It's their jurisdiction."

Around him the cramped squad room bustled with activity. The air buzzed with ringing phones that competed with the voices of fellow detectives. Near the main door, Bernie Kline gestured at him. His partner must have some place for them to go, which meant Mitch couldn't talk to Connie for long. He was used to her frequent, quick calls. They were usually questions about Canadian procedures or requests for information on drugs or smuggling. She always needed answers immediately, and he'd grown used to putting her off or speaking abruptly because she was normally in a rush. This sounded like a personal predicament, and he couldn't help her at all.

Her voice filled with frustration. "Some help you are!"

"How long has she been gone?" he asked calmly.

"More than an hour. We were running around Stanley Park. I took a shortcut, but she never showed at the spot where we agreed to meet and now the sun is going down. I'm sorry to bother you, but I don't know anyone else here, and my cell phone is almost dead."

They didn't know each other that well. Mainly she was an intriguing annoyance. Even Bernie joked about his "pushy American girlfriend." She first called him while researching a television report on his unit's role in solving a string of drug related murder cases in the Northwest. Since then, he had given her a couple of on camera interviews and answered her questions. No use upsetting the American press, his captain told him. He liked listening to her voice go from rapid-fire to cajoling and watching the lights dance in her brown eyes when she got her way.

Bernie waved across the room and Mitch nodded as he dropped his pencil and stood beside his desk. He grabbed his jacket from the back of the chair. "Maybe she stopped at a snack bar." He needed to get going.

"Why would a runner stop at the snack bar, except for water, which she carried on her strap-on belt?" Connie sounded irritated. "She could have stopped for a five course lunch and still made it here by now. Besides, Joy would not do that without letting me know. She's the ultimate dependable person. You can set clocks by her. I think something might have happened."

"All right." His tone was abrupt, hurried.

"Exactly where are you in the park? Have you checked back along the walkway?"

"I walked back to where we split up, and now my other sister is walking all around the other side of the park, but she hasn't found her either."

Mitch grimaced. If he had the time, he might try to help her, but Bernie had stopped gesturing and now stood with an anxious look. Whatever he needed was pressing.

"Why don't you call Vancouver P.D.?" Mitch suggested, waving at Bernie who was now walking toward him. "There's a station near the park and I know they can help you. I'll call them too, if you want. Where are you staying? I'll call you later."

The line went dead. He didn't know if Connie was angry, or if her cell phone had died. Mitch started to speed dial Vancouver Police, but Bernie leaped forward to push down the phone button, cutting him off.

"They've just spotted our guy down by the docks. We have to move, now."

****

Connie shook the cell phone as though that might get Weldon back, but the low battery light on her phone glared red at her with accusation.

Damn, damn, double damn! Triple damn!

She hated asking for help like that. Or sounding helpless or feeling helpless in general. She limped back to the bench where she'd waited earlier to meet Joy. She shivered slightly as the dampness of the afternoon chilled her through her jacket. Maybe it was the dread chilling her. She'd checked every bench in her journey back along the walkway to where she and Joy separated and found nothing.

She hadn't gotten the chance to tell Weldon that she had called Vancouver Police, but it had gotten her nowhere. They treated her as though she was an overly distraught woman.

And she was.

Joy was not the sort to simply wander off. Even the call to Weldon had not helped, not that she expected him to drop whatever he was doing to rush out and search. She'd hoped he might provide assistance by lighting a fire under the police. She didn't know Weldon that well, except that he was part of an elite Special Canadian Police Unit, but she did know that Weldon was the sort of man who could be trusted to solve huge cases. He should be able to help find her missing sister. He'd helped her on her report about a string of drug related murders in the Northwest. She called him every time she needed Canadian information. He not only assisted her, but he called her with tips from time to time.

Usually she looked for a reason to call him because she enjoyed bantering with him. Sometimes she wondered if the man might be a specially built robot with human features, which was why she usually tried to get a reaction out of him and started off conversations with innuendo. She normally liked his surprised or uncertain reaction. She had no time for such games today, nor had she enjoyed making the call.

Naturally he would think instead about things like "jurisdiction." She might have stamped her foot similar to a disappointed child used to having her own way, except her leg muscles hurt too much. And then her phone went dead.

So now what?

Beyond the choppy waters of the inlet, lights popped on in the city skyscrapers. The sun was dropping quickly, bringing a cool dusk to the park. The temperature of her insides plummeted along with the sun. Night was coming, and it wouldn't be long before darkness overtook the walkways. Even the groups of joggers had diminished.

A fog bank moved over the water of the inlet,

creeping closer to enclosing the shoreline and the jogging path. Tears of frustration stung Connie's eyes. She couldn't remember ever feeling so helpless, but she wasn't going to let it defeat her. She lurched to her feet, summoning all her remaining energy, as Lisa's yellow jacket appeared out of the darkness jogging toward her. The distraught look on her face when she spotted Connie sitting alone said it all.

****

Such an ordinary day. More rain. Another murder.

Fighting hypnosis from the swishing windshield wipers, Inspector Mitch Weldon sat in his parked car watching joggers splash along the path that led around Stanley Park. The steady rain thumped against the roof of the sedan. Every so often he turned on the engine to allow the wipers to clear off the windshield and to heat up the interior. Not many people jogged along the asphalt path. Only a few hardy souls in colorful nylon suits that covered them from head to toe had ventured out to brave the elements.

Dark, low clouds hung like menacing gods overhead. The waters of Burrard Inlet were choppy, a murky blue-gray topped with small whitecaps. Heavy fog clung to high rises on Vancouver's North Shore, hiding the homes behind them from view. What a cold, depressing day.

Perfect for murder. And that was exactly what brought him here.

Fortunately the rain had not started until after Mitch had a chance to survey the scene. This steady rain would wash away evidence. All he could hope for was that crime scene technicians had been thorough, and the pictures taken earlier by the photographer would hold clues that might get flushed by the rain. Even a tent over the area would not be enough.

Why he lingered after everyone left was beyond him. This would not be his case. Jurisdiction belonged to Vancouver. Two patrolmen had been left to watch over the scene. They disappeared into the thick brush.

A short figure in a black raincoat at the edge of the path drew his attention. The woman approached the crime scene tape and stopped at the marked perimeter. Rain beat down on her dark, uncovered head. She surveyed the area, oblivious to drops that bounced off her drenched hair and ran down pale cheeks. As she turned from the scene, he recognized Connie Romero.

Instinct kept Mitch at the scene. Now, curiosity drove him from the warmth of the car. Somehow he had known that the murder victim discovered by an early morning jogger was her sister. Turning up his collar around his ears, he walked toward Connie, hands shoved in his pockets.

The pelting rain hid the sound of his approaching footsteps. Apparently not seeing him as he marched toward her, Connie lifted the tape and scooted under it.

"Connie!"

Startled, she jumped and turned, dropping the tape so she was inside it. Short, dark hair plastered about her head like a skullcap. Her normally expressive eyes were the dull color of a muddy river. Shoulders hunched together, her body trembled.

"I didn't see you coming," she apologized with a shrug.

"Obviously," he retorted, gesturing at her. "Get out of there. What do you think you're doing?"

Connie pressed her lips together and looked longingly back toward the thicket where a tent covered the scene. With an annoyed twitch of her lips, she shoved up the tape and slipped back under it. She stumbled as she stepped through the brush.

"Damn tree roots," she muttered.

Mitch reached out to catch her in case she fell. He normally wasn't given to physical contact, but her look of despair drew him. Her fingers were almost as cold and clammy as a corpse as he brushed them. She righted herself and jerked away from his touch, facing him with fierce eyes that said, "Hands off." Was she angry over his inability to help her the previous day?

"Let's sit in the car," he offered, pointing toward it. "Or would you like a cup of coffee? We can talk."

Connie wiped at her face, as though afraid she might be crying. It was wet from the rain, or perhaps those were tears that rolled down her face. Without makeup and with hair hugging her skull, she resembled a lost, confused child. Casting another sorrowful glance at the thicket where her sister's body was found, she nodded and followed him.

Her teeth chattered as she closed the car door so he flipped on the ignition and turned on the heat. Again he had to force himself to refrain from touching her. Grief etched fine lines on her young face, and more guilt washed through him. He should have tried to help instead of going off on a wild goose chase. His partner had received a tip about a drug investigation, but it turned out to be false. Instead of assisting Connie Romero in the search for her missing sister, he'd spent four fruitless hours combing the docks for a non-existent suspect.

Connie leaned forward, holding out shaking fingers toward the heating vents, and Mitch studied her profile. Her looks had always struck him as unique and arresting. Keen at noticing physical features, if he had been describing her as a suspect, he would have written down that she had olive-shaped eyes beneath dark, sweeping brows, full lips, and a small straight nose set in an oval face. Today the lips quivered—whether from the cold or from personal pain, he didn't know.

Mitch maintained an impersonal attitude around grieving relatives, but Connie's sadness cut through his detachment. He could feel her grief, like a cold knife pressed against his throat.

This grief-stricken woman was barely recognizable. Connie reminded him of a human bundle of energy, unpredictable but also unflappable. Today that sense of energy was missing, as was her engaging smile and the quick brightness of her eyes. Her normally rosy cheeks were a pasty shade of pale, and water dripped from the melded tips of her hair. For the first time since he met her, Connie Romero was a woman in need.

He wanted to reach out to her, but he wasn't certain how. Besides her flirtatious quips, he didn't know much about her personally, and this wasn't the time to start thinking of her as someone other than a murder victim's relative. Still, watching her cold, shaking fingers, he found he couldn't help himself. He reached out and grasped her hands, gripping them.

To his surprise, this time she didn't pull away. Her frigid fingers clung to his and he could feel the tension in her body as it shook slightly. Her hands were small, nails cut blunt, unpolished. They gripped his hand with surprising force. For a couple of minutes their hands remained joined, neither speaking. The only sounds were the thump of rain on the roof of the car, the steady thwack of the windshield wipers and the hum of the car heater. A sudden sensation of tenderness shocked him, and he cleared his throat. "I'm sorry about your sister. I know this is difficult."

At his words, Connie withdrew her hands and the spell broke. She shoved her hands into her pockets and turned to stare out the window. "I walked by there twice. Only yards from her."

He started to touch her again, but stopped himself. This wasn't right. What the hell was he thinking—touching her like that! He threw the gear into reverse. "Let's get some coffee and warm up. You're drenched. There's a blanket in the back seat if you want to dry out."

Connie sniffled, and her glassy eyes flickered down to her wet coat and soaked legs and boots like she was seeing them for the first time.

"It was my idea to take the walk," she said in a lifeless tone as the car splashed along the rain-swept road. "I shouldn't have let her go on her own. I should have stayed with her."

Perhaps if he'd responded to her summons, things might have turned out differently. He forced that idea away. This was merely a case of a grieving relative. He was accustomed to incoherency or feelings of guilt. Her situation was no different. The plaintive sound of her voice touched him, but he could not become personally involved. He kept his voice reserved.

"It wasn't your fault. You had no way of knowing what might happen."

She drew up her shoulders, and her voice became stronger, filled with determination. "I'm going to find out who did it."

"That's the job of the police department," he said, though her words didn't surprise him. This was a normal reaction.

She clutched her shaking hands together, wringing them. Her voice trembled as she spat out words. "The police department? They wouldn't help me. No one would help me when I needed them. Well, forget them! I won't let whoever did it get away with it. I'll find the monster myself, and make him pay for what he did to my sister."

While he had heard similar promises through the years, Mitch knew that such a vow would be useless. "Your feelings are understandable, but the police will do their job. They are quite capable of solving this. I am sorry I couldn't help you yesterday."

"Do you suppose she was already dead?" she asked.

Mitch inhaled sharply. "Possibly."

"He could have been any of those people who came jogging by me while I was sitting there waiting for her." Connie shifted, wet coat rustling on the seat. She faced him, her face filled with misery, tears streaming down her face. "It could have been me instead."

This time her plaintive voice reached inside him, tightening his throat, making him physically ache. Mitch pulled the car over and turned to her. He reached out and touched her cheek gently, wiping away her tears with his hand. "Don't think that." The tightness that gripped his throat surprised him.

Her fingers grasped his hand and again he squeezed them.

"The police will find whoever did it," he said emphatically and immediately let go of her fingers. Holding her hand was bad enough but this contact was much too personal. "Sergeant Frank Case is in charge of the investigation, and he is very thorough."

"I told him I'd help any way I could," she said softly with a nod of her head. "I have investigative skills, you know."

Television news research skills hardly qualified as investigative, but he wouldn't burst her bubble at an emotional time like this. Mitch snapped back into his professional demeanor. There was a job to do, even if it wasn't his jurisdiction.

"Maybe I can help," he offered, putting the car back into gear. Turning back into an investigator took his mind off personal feelings. "I know this is a bad time, and you spoke to Frank, but why don't you tell me about it?" It was a long shot, but perhaps she would remember something he could pass along to Frank.

Her chin quivered, and she bit down on her lower lip before speaking. "I don't know what to tell you. I didn't see anything."

"We'll just talk. Something might shake loose." He hated this part of the interrogation with the family, but he knew that after the initial trauma, they often recalled forgotten details.

She drew up her head, eyes focusing somewhere outside the rain washed window. "My sister, Lisa, and I walked around the park until it got dark. Then we drove around the park most of the night. We checked back with police, but they kept saying she would turn up. I knew they were wrong." Her voice shook, and she put her hand to her forehead as she paused. "I tried calling your desk again, but my cell phone kept dying."

He had wondered what happened to her. He attempted to call her cell phone once when he returned to the office but was directed to her voice mail. "I am sorry."

Her sad face hardened. "Stop saying you're sorry. That's what the police officer said who came to the hotel room this morning. He was sorry. Everyone's so damn sorry. No one did anything, and now my sister is dead!" Like the promise for revenge, her anger did not surprise him. He expected it more than her show of vulnerability.

Some color had seeped back into her pallid cheeks, and she squirmed to sit up straighter. "The thing that's so strange is...well...it's murder. An accident I could understand, like getting hit by a car. But when they told me they found her body a few yards from the road...with her throat slashed...well, that seems incomprehensible."

"I understand." He steered the car into a

parking lot beside a coffee kiosk at the edge of the park. The refreshment stand and an adjoining gift shop were a prime stop for tour buses so both remained open during the rainy season.

"How do you like your coffee?"

"Black," she replied, as though describing her mood.

Her bleak visage again touched him, and he wanted to say more, but he didn't. Leaving the heater and the motor running, he splashed through the rain toward the shelter of the coffee bar.

****

The thought of hot coffee sounded good, but Connie doubted it would make her feel any better. She wrapped the coat tighter around her, despite forced air pouring in from the heater. Would she ever be warm again? Her skin was so cold, while her brain and heart seethed with a boiling cauldron of emotions.

She watched the lanky inspector lope away through the driving rain. Weldon—that was what she always called him—was trying to be nice, but it was too late. She'd asked him for help, and he'd put her off. Now Joy was dead.

No, it wasn't his fault. He sounded sincere in his wish to help, almost like a friend. He'd even touched her, an action that surprised her, as much as it obviously did him from his quick reaction. Normally she might have taken advantage of his slight venture from his normal chivalrous, though starched behavior. Maybe she should have teased him about it. She usually liked to watch his chiseled, serious face turn a light shade of pink or to hear him search for words on the phone. But today she had no energy to try to bring a smile to his dour demeanor. Still, the touch had been soothing. Under other circumstances, she might have even enjoyed it.

Connie pressed her palm to her cheek, recalling

the sensation of his fingers on her skin. Such a gentle gesture—the sort a man might give a lover. She shook her head. No, that was crazy. She'd never thought of him that way.

Now she watched him in the distance, standing in the coffee line. Why had she never thought of him romantically? Well, for one, the man never revealed emotion. He stood straight, calm, precise. That robot clone. Turn him on, and he investigated. His clear green eyes seemed to be always searching for something. And analyzing it? Yes, he was the perfect investigator. Too bad he wasn't on this homicide case.

Homicide. With a gulp of emotion, she turned away from her study and fanciful thoughts of Weldon, staring at the dashboard of the car.

Homicide. The word seemed to trace itself along her line of vision, no matter where she looked and now it traced itself along the dashboard, blotting out the dials and controls.

Homicide. It was such a foreign word to apply to Joy and it didn't begin to touch the ache that gnawed at her insides. She wanted to yell at someone. If only police had listened when she called! Connie took a deep breath and put frigid, numb fingers in front of the heater vents. She wanted to yell at Weldon, and she might have, if she wasn't hurting so much.

The sudden opening of the car door made her jump. Weldon handed her a steaming cup of coffee. Connie cupped her hands around the warmth. The chill that held possession of her body lessened slightly.

"How's your other sister doing?" Weldon asked as he slid back into the car.

"Lisa's back at the hotel, making phone calls." Ever practical, Lisa wanted something concrete to do, so she was making arrangements. "Lisa's the sister who gets things done. Joy was always the motherly one."

"And you?" he asked and at her quick glance of surprise, he attempted a slight smile. "Which sister are you?"

Connie forced a smile across her numb lips. What the hell? That remark almost sounded flirtatious. For once, she felt flustered, but she answered honestly. "Me? I'm the flighty sister. I arrange the parties and play time. Like this trip. If we hadn't come up here, Joy would have been home with her kids and husband today, instead of laying in that cold, ugly..." she stopped, nearly choking. She couldn't bring herself to say the awful word.

Both sisters had gone to the morgue for the identification, hoping against hope the body would not be their sister. After the horrifying process that Connie knew would always haunt her, and the terrible call to their parents, Lisa returned to the hotel, while Connie remained to talk to police. All the while, she'd wanted to shout at the officers for not helping her when she first asked. After the grueling hours at the police station, Connie took a cab back to the scene of the crime. A mass of conflicting emotions competed for attention in her troubled mind.

Who had killed Joy? Why Joy and not her? Could she have prevented it? Had the killer seen her and still chosen Joy?

The questions buzzed through Connie's head, a refrain that refused to end. Even the hot coffee that burned her tongue did little to erase them.

"Vancouver Police will find the person who did this," Weldon said quietly, his green eyes grave over the top of his coffee cup.

After her experience the previous evening, Connie wasn't so certain. She took another sip of coffee, and a sudden feeling of anxiety rippled through her. Something foreign. Something frightening. Like the day before when she'd known there was a sinister reason Joy had not shown up at their meeting place.

Connie shuddered. "Thanks for the coffee, but will you please take me back to the hotel?"

Suddenly she wanted to talk to Lisa. She needed to see her younger sister.

****

Connie tried to pretend she wasn't in a hurry as she quick-stepped down the hall to the suite she and her sisters had rented. Why was she worried that Lisa might be in danger? Joy's husband, Ralph, was probably with Lisa. He'd come up early in the morning, as soon as he could get a sitter for Joy's two children, who still didn't know about the tragedy. Why hadn't she told Weldon about her sudden bout of fear before he dropped her off? Because he had not believed her about Joy?

Her fingers shook as Connie fumbled to slide the plastic key into the door. It swung open and she called out.

"Lisa?"

No answer. An eerie stillness issued from the gloomy room.

"Lisa? Ralph?"

As she moved passed the wall where the hall opened into the main room, she sensed a quick movement. As she turned, Connie felt a strong push, and she stumbled toward the wall. Something thumped hard against her head, and then there was only blackness.

Chapter Two

"Connie?"

Troubled green eyes stared down at her. Above them, a deeply furrowed brow and above that, a very short, neat head of hair.

Connie blinked. "Mitch? Weldon?" Her voice came out as a croak.

The eyes softened, turning a brilliant emerald. "Are you all right?"

That was when she realized she wasn't on her feet. Felt the strong support behind her back and under her knees. Holding her up. Holding her against his body. A very hard, strong body. "What—"

"Are you sure you're okay?" The loud voice came from beside him and belonged to Lisa as he lowered her to something soft.

Too quickly the arms and the heat from the hard body were gone from her as he drew back and knelt beside her. She felt as boneless as a filleted fish or she might have reached out to hold onto him. Quick, nimble fingers undid her coat buttons and gentle hands helped her remove her coat.

She attempted a grateful smile, but he was gone from her immediate vision and her gaze swam.

"Hey, babe, are you all right?" Lisa's solicitous face appeared in front of her as she sat on the edge of the bed.

Connie took quick stock of herself. She was stretched out on the bed, raincoat removed. The back of her head throbbed and she reached around to touch it. She struggled to sit up, but the room pitched sharply, and she settled back onto the pillow.

"Did you hit your head when you fell?" Lisa asked.

Connie blinked again. "He hit me."

"Who?" Lisa asked, new concern filling her voice.

"I don't know. Someone." She made another attempt to rise and this time she managed to reach a sitting position. Mitch appeared again, carrying a blanket and Lisa stood and stepped away so he could move to the bed.

"What...what are you doing here?" she asked.

"You left your cell phone in my car. It must have fallen out of your pocket." He leaned over to cover her with the blanket, eyes grave as they surveyed her. "Tell me what happened. Did you say someone hit you?"

"I thought you fainted," Lisa said in a high voice behind him, brushing back a short lock of thick, black hair. "When I got here, the door was open, and I came in and found you slumped on the floor. I figured you hadn't eaten all day. You haven't, have you? It's a good thing Inspector Weldon came up when he did. He had to carry you to the bed."

Weldon shifted as though the thought made him uncomfortable. A sudden vision of him huffing and puffing to lift her struck Connie. She could picture a grimace on his angular face. Had he noticed the extra ten pounds she was carrying around?

Gingerly she touched the back of her head again as Weldon moved to sit beside her. He reached over and his nimble fingers displaced hers.

"You've got quite a knot there," he said as she winced, aware of how close he was to her. He was so near she could smell the fresh scent of his shaving lotion. Something spicy.

She blinked, tossing away personal thoughts as her eyes met his and a disturbing thought hit her. "Do you suppose...it was the killer?"

Across the bed, Lisa gasped. "What?"

His teeth clicked as Weldon's jaw clamped shut with disapproval. "Don't jump to conclusions. It was most likely an ordinary thief you surprised. Some of these big hotels have had robbery problems." His sharp gaze scanned the room, and he motioned toward Lisa. "You might check to see if anything's missing or if someone went through your things."

Connie attempted to get up to help, but the room swam. Weldon caught her as she swayed on the edge of the bed, his arm circling her shoulder to steady her.

"Whoa, take it easy there, eh?" His voice was surprisingly soft. So was the gentle touch that sent a slight tremor through her. "Perhaps you should see a doctor."

"I'll be fine," she said. The skin wasn't broken and except for the knot, she didn't think she'd been hurt. Her eyes swiveled to meet his as Lisa stepped around the room to check their belongings. "It could have been Joy's killer, couldn't it?" she repeated in a low voice so her sister couldn't hear.

He tilted an eyebrow, skepticism visible. "How would he have known her room number?" He picked up Connie's plastic key card which was on the bed beside her. It contained no number.

"Joy checked us in. Maybe she still had the card folder with the number in her pocket. Maybe he even took her key card. Was it in her clothes?"

"I'll check," he offered with a quick nod.

Had she run into the killer? What had he been doing in their room? Would he have killed her if there had been time?

"Weldon," she said in a sudden frantic whisper as a terrible thought struck her. "What if she wasn't the intended victim at all? What if he meant to kill me?"

"What kind of silly theory is that?" he asked,

irritation flickering across his face.

"Well, I did that investigative series on drug smuggling."

He looked at her for a long moment, and something seemed to awaken inside her. Normally aloof, Weldon was showing unusual concern for her. What would it be like to have more than impersonal interest in those emerald eyes of his? In his gentle touch? Something told her he was a man who would take good care of a woman if he chose to.

Almost as though he guessed her improper thoughts, he pulled away and rose to his feet, running a large hand over his short sandy hair.

His departure from her side left a coldness she hadn't noticed before. Her raincoat was gone, but her clothes were damp, and her skin was chilled and clammy. Connie quavered as Lisa concluded her search and came back toward the bed.

"Is anything missing?" she asked Lisa.

"I don't see anything, not that I was carrying anything valuable. All our clothes are just as they were, and our bags are where we left them this morning." Lisa frowned as she walked back toward the bed. "Con, you need to get out of those wet clothes. I'll run you a hot bath."

Even a hot bath wouldn't warm her, but she did want to get out of the clothes. Maybe once Weldon was gone.

"What about your sister's things?" Weldon asked.

Lisa shook her head. "They're gone. Her husband, Ralph, packed all of Joy's things when we came back from the police station and took them. He wanted to get back to Bellingham so he could tell the kids himself."

Connie's eyes swept across the room. "Wait! My laptop," she said in a hoarse whisper. Her fingers stabbed at the empty desktop near the window. "My computer was sitting over there."

Weldon moved to the desk with the grace of an athlete. He pulled open the center drawer. "Did you have anything else here? CDs? Flash drives? Things like that?"

"I had an extra battery in the computer case on the floor by the waste basket."

He lifted the basket to show an empty expanse of gray carpeted floor. "No case. It's gone." He reached into his jacket pocket and pulled out a cell phone and began punching in numbers.

While he spoke into the phone in a low tone, Lisa sat on the bed, large brown eyes filled with fear. "Do you think it was the killer?"

Connie had no idea what to think. She didn't repeat her concern that the killer might have been after her, but the disturbing thought was taking root in her mind. Her drug smuggling story hadn't put anyone in jail, but its revelations had made things uncomfortable for some of the drug dealers who worked a Seattle-Vancouver connection. She had received a couple of anonymous phone calls and strange emails that appeared to be veiled threats after the series aired.

She didn't want to think that her work might have been responsible for what happened to Joy. Why would the killer go after Joy if she was the target? They had separated so the killer should have followed her. Unless he thought she would come back and look for Joy and he might capture her then. The disturbing thoughts grew and now swirled through her brain like smoke filtering through an empty room, dancing in whirling wisps.

"I want to get out of here," Connie said with a shudder. The thought of remaining in the room which had been invaded by a stranger troubled her. A sinister presence lingered over the space that even the colorful burgundy and gold furnishings couldn't overcome.

"That's a great idea," Lisa agreed with a quick nod of her head. "Why don't you change into something dry while I pack? We can go to Bellingham to Mom and Dad's, unless you want to go home to Seattle."

"I'm not going home," Connie announced. "I want to stay in Vancouver for a while. I just don't want to be in this room."

"You can't stay here anyway," Weldon said, walking toward them as he put away his phone. "I've called for a crime squad in case there is a connection. It could be innocent, but I don't see why we should take the chance. I can arrange a new room for you."

"I don't want to stay," Lisa protested. She turned to Connie, eyes filled with sadness and more than a little determination. "You shouldn't stay by yourself either."

Connie was used to her overly cautious sister, but she had faced more dangerous situations than staying in a hotel room alone. "I'll be fine. I can take care of myself."

Lisa drew back, shaking her head, dark shiny hair bouncing around her face. "Right! You always say that, and then something happens. Look at you. You're shaking from the cold. You have a bump on your head, and you haven't eaten all day. You definitely cannot take care of yourself. Don't you agree, Inspector? She needs to come home."

Weldon looked from one to the other, but he showed no inclination to get into the middle of a sisterly disagreement. Connie only knew that Joy was dead, and it might be her fault. She needed to act. She wanted to find out what had happened to Joy.

"I'll be fine," she said, though she wished she could muster more conviction into her voice. She knew what her sister was thinking—this was flighty

Connie going off into uncharted territory with no idea what was ahead.

"What about Mom and Dad?" Lisa wailed with a wave of her hand. "They're going to need us right now, and they'll be scared to think of you here by yourself. We need to hang together right now. If you want to come back later, fine. But now we need to go back."

Connie grimaced. Her sister was right. With Joy a murder victim, her mother and father would be concerned about the safety of their other two daughters, even if they were grown women. She would only contribute to their pain if she stayed. Maybe they viewed her as rash at times, but she had never carried it to the point of being selfish and inconsiderate.

"Your sister is right," Weldon agreed. "I'm certain there will be arrangements to be made."

Arrangements. How bland that sounded. He meant funeral plans. But Ralph would take care of that.

"You can come back later," he continued in a low, urgent tone. "We may need to talk to you again anyway."

Connie eyed him skeptically. She didn't want to answer questions. She wanted to find Joy's killer. She intended to face the creep and ask why he would kill such an innocent, kind soul. But grim reality hung around her like the low, gray clouds outside. Weldon and Lisa were both right. With a sigh, Connie nodded, but she made a silent pledge to herself.

She would be back.

****

A soft mist dusted her shoulders, as Connie emerged from the church after Joy's memorial service. Dense clouds scudded low on the horizon, setting a somber tone. She stood in a receiving line

25

with Lisa, their parents and Joy's family accepting condolences. She shook hands with cold fingers, while her other fist clutched a damp ball of tissue. Her stinging eyes peered into the distance, toward the choppy waters of the Puget Sound, barely visible through the fog. Beyond the Sound, the Olympic Mountains normally provided a magnificent backdrop for Bellingham, but they remained hidden behind the veil of fog. How Joy had loved so sit on her porch and watch the jagged, snow-covered peaks on a clear day. She always joked about her soul flying to live in the majestic mountains when she died. Was she there today? Connie liked to think so. She stared into the mist, seeking for a sign. The truth was she wanted to look anywhere but at the group beside her.

Her grief-stricken parents were bad enough. New wrinkles had appeared on their dark, haggard faces, as though they had evolved from middle age to senior status in one week. Ralph's round face resembled a deflated volley ball. His blue eyes were sunken and red-rimmed. She understood his shell-shocked reaction. Stabbings, mutilations happened to other people, not Joy.

A sudden gust of wind tore at her and sent umbrellas flapping. Connie gripped her wide-brimmed hat and pulled her black cape tighter around her. She glanced around at the large group, dressed in their somber colors, speaking in low voices.

The size of the crowd did not surprise her. The Romero family had lived in Bellingham for years, and Joy never lacked for friends. Many of the sad faces Connie recognized. In addition, Ralph had his own share of friends. The unfamiliar people Connie put down to business, either on Ralph's part or the new contacts Joy had made as a real estate agent. Connie's eyes scanned the crowd, nodding to people she knew.

Her gaze finally swung around to rest on her parents. Her mother's soft, round face was stoic, but Connie knew it hid heartbreak that reached to her very core. Seeing her father's long, haggard countenance was difficult too. Their black hair seemed to have turned grayer overnight. Even worse was seeing her niece and nephew, Joy's twelve-year-old son, Jeremy, and ten-year-old daughter, Mindy. The thought of them without their mother tore at her. If only the killer could see the pain his actions caused.

The killer wouldn't get away with it. She would see to that.

She picked out the tall, straight figure of Inspector Mitch Weldon among the large crowd of mourners and her heartbeat quickened as it had when she first noticed him. She'd been surprised to see him and a little shocked at her own suddenly racing pulse. Had he come officially or out of curiosity? Or maybe he wanted to see her? She knew he was not handling the murder case. She'd been in touch with the Vancouver sergeant who was leading the investigation.

No, he wouldn't have come for personal reasons. Not Inspector Mitch Weldon. It had to be the case, she told herself. Police work. While Connie appreciated what police were doing, she was pushing forward on her own as she had told Weldon. As an investigative producer, she was known for digging and getting answers no one else could. She intended to use those skills to solve this case. As the crowd separated like a parting wave, Mitch approached her.

"Connie?"

She gave him a curt nod, though her senses heightened and she was suddenly aware of everything around her. Memories of their time together in Vancouver brought a hint of embarrassment. Numb with pain, she had spaced out like a zombie at the park. The attack in her hotel had her acting like a damsel in distress. It bothered her that he had seen her in such unflattering circumstances. Was it pity she saw in his sea green eyes?

He extended his large hand. "I wanted to say how sorry I am."

His grasp was strong, and his grip lingered. Connie wanted to thank him for his thoughts, but her emotions swirled with confusion. Part of her recalled how kind he had been at the park and in her hotel room, but part of her also held him and police responsible for Joy's death. She might have been saved if Weldon had come to the park or forced the police to help.

Stifling frustration at her warring thoughts, Connie adopted her most proper behavior. "You've been very kind," she said stiffly. "I didn't properly thank you for helping me at the hotel when I was attacked. Thanks for getting police to act so quickly."

His eyes were grave. "How are you feeling?"

"Fine, except for an occasional headache."

"If there's anything else I can do..." His voice trailed off.

"Nothing, unless you want to help me find the killer," she said, her voice hardening.

A quick look of disapproval flashed across his face and his lips pressed into a thin line. "Frank Case is a top Vancouver homicide investigator. He'll find the killer."

"I've talked to him several times," she acknowledged.

"Then you know the case is in good hands," he replied curtly. "I'll check in with him and keep you up to date on the investigation if it makes you feel better."

"Thank you." Connie wanted to ask why he would go out of his way to keep her informed. Joy's death was not his responsibility. But then why had he been at the park the morning her body was found? Did he blame himself? Perhaps he was driven by his own guilt.

"I've spoken to the officer handling the break-in at your hotel," he said. "He has concluded it was a simple burglary. You said your computer was insured?"

She nodded. That was nice of him to keep track of what should have been a small case. Some of her anger dissolved. "I appreciate all you've done, and thanks for coming today. Will you join us over at the hall for refreshments?" It was the least she could offer.

He seemed surprised, but then nodded. "Thank you. I would like that."

Connie studied Weldon as they walked toward the church hall. Even if she had not known his job title, she could have guessed it. Mitch had the straight, upright look of a police officer. His shoes were always polished to a high shine. His sandy hair was not quite a buzz cut, but it was clipped so short it rarely fell out of place, despite any breeze.

Like his appearance, his stiff demeanor telegraphed a man who walked a straight and narrow path. In her experience with him Connie had discovered that he was quick-minded, thorough, and extremely logical. He wasn't her type of man, but she had thought of trying to line him up with Lisa. With their practical outlook, they could be soul mates. But as the thought rushed across her mind, a sudden jolt hit her. Was that what she really wanted?

Ralph, Joy's husband, approached them. Her brother-in-law was normally stalwart and steady through family ordeals, but the burly man slumped today, beefy shoulders bent forward.

"Are you investigating?" Ralph asked, his forehead furrowed, ruddy face drawn and taut with concern.

Weldon shook his head, his voice cool and level. "I know this is a difficult time. I came to talk to Connie."

The damp air sizzled with tension. To Connie's surprise, Weldon stared at Ralph as though the bulky man had done something wrong. Ralph appeared ready to ask Weldon to leave. What was happening? What was this about talking to her? Weldon had not indicated that. A small tingling rippled through her. Could that be true? The inspector had come to see her? Was it personal or about the case? Her pulse quickened again.

Ralph walked away, and she and Weldon joined the group entering the church hall. Connie unfastened her black cape, and to her surprise, Weldon helped her remove it. The unexpected gallant gesture sent a fresh wave of awareness through her. The men she knew wouldn't have helped her if she'd been strangling in it. Weldon hung the cape and his own overcoat on a row of hangers just inside the door.

Normally the scene of festive occasions, the big room was drab as the day outside and nearly as quiet as the church had been. Rows of folding tables had been set up with paper cloths covering them. Tables filled with food and drinks stretched down one end of the hall and a line formed by the first table. Women from Joy's church had cooked and were serving. Connie was curious about Weldon's comment that he had come to see her, but she felt a responsibility to assist with the food. She told Weldon to get a plate, and she would get back to him.

Connie approached the food table and began to

uncover dishes of sandwich makings, pasta, and potato salad. Her movements were mechanical. These days it was easier to perform tasks without letting outside thoughts invade her mind.

"Did they find out who hit you?" Lisa asked, standing beside Connie and uncovering a salad. "Is that why the inspector is here? I didn't think he was investigating Joy's death."

Her sister's concern was etched on her pale face. Small, but muscular, Lisa showed little of her normal strength. Her petite frame appeared on the verge of collapsing. Her gaunt cheeks and the lack of makeup turned her porcelain skin almost translucent. Her black suit hung on her as though it was a size too large.

Maybe it was time to lighten the somber mood. Or get rid of this sudden growing awareness of Weldon. Or at least see if her sister was having the same sort of stupid, giddy reaction to the handsome inspector. Connie summoned a playful smile as she carefully placed serving utensils beside a bowl. "He told Ralph he's here to talk to me, but maybe you should talk to him too. And not about the case."

Confusion crossed Lisa's brown eyes, as Connie winked. Her sister's dark brows lifted in surprise, and her chalky cheeks flushed. "Why would I want to talk to him?"

Connie leaned close to her sister and added in a loud whisper. "I was thinking about setting you up with him." As she said it, another voice inside her head was yelling, "No!"

Lisa's lips curved up in a half smile as she glanced across the room. She slapped playfully at Connie's wrist. "Why would you do that?"

Connie tried to make her voice sound matter-of-fact, though her stomach muscles tensed as she realized she was curious about what her sister thought about Weldon. What if her sister was interested in him? What if he discovered how much alike they were? "The two of you have a lot in common."

Lisa's chocolate eyes widened, but there was a little life to them. "Don't you dare play matchmaker. Not when you keep telling me you're too busy to date."

"He's a nice guy," Connie continued, pleased to be thinking of something other than murder. "He's quiet, a loner set in his ways. I don't know him well, but I can tell that much. He's one of those guys who likes everything in its place, all loose ends wrapped up. Kind of like...well, you."

Lisa shook her head. "Too intense for me. Why don't you go after him?"

Connie let her gaze slide over to where Weldon stood beside a table, filling a plate. Why indeed?

Physically, he had the build of a football quarterback—big but not too brawny, with wide shoulders and long legs. He wasn't bad looking. His lean face with had a strong jaw below a pair of deep-set eyes. She could imagine criminals squirming under that hard green gaze. His lips were nicely formed, but normally were drawn in a tight line. His natural demeanor seemed to be hard. Only when he smiled did Weldon show even a hint of soft edges.

She hadn't really witnessed those soft edges until that day in the park when he'd taken her hand, and the more she witnessed the more this crazy awareness seemed to take possession of her. Maybe it was the emotion and shock over Joy's death, she reasoned.

"He's not my type," Connie said, jerking her gaze from him. "I like those off-the-wall, seat-of-the-pants guys. The ones you can't count on, but who add excitement whenever they're around. Guys who enjoy clever repartee and make you think you're the only woman in the world until they leave the room and forget your name."

Sadness vanished from Lisa's normally expressive eyes, and they began to dance. "You think I would enjoy someone who is Mr. Boring?"

"I think you would like someone up-front, honest, and who does things by the book. Like Weldon. He'd arrest me after getting to know me."

"I don't think so." Lisa said with a laugh that sent her short black hair flying about her head. "I think he likes you. He was very sweet the other day when we thought you fainted."

"You girls shouldn't have to do this," their Aunt Mattie scolded, stepping up behind them and interrupting their conversation. "Let me and the others take care of setting up and serving. Get your food and go sit down."

Connie turned to hug her, fighting tears. Joy had always been Aunt Mattie's favorite. Like everyone else, she carried the haunted look of disbelief. She wrapped meaty arms around both sisters before wiping her eyes and prompting them to join the guests.

"I'm going to find the kids," Lisa said as they stepped from the table. "You better entertain the inspector."

Connie filled a plate and glanced around the room, not certain of her next move. Finally, with her nerves on edge, she walked toward Weldon. He sat at a table alone, empty plate and cup of coffee in front of him, surveying the room with an intense stare. At the moment he focused on Jeremy and Mindy who sat close to their father.

"I feel bad for those poor kids. Who could have done such a horrible thing?" she asked as she put down her plate and slid into a seat across from him. "Do you suppose they realize the pain they caused?"

"Killers don't think about that." His eyes were the hue of a turbulent ocean as they pulled away from Joy's family and scanned the crowd carefully, like he might be taking notes in his head. He pushed away the empty plate and took a sip from the cup.

"You told Ralph you came to see me, but that isn't true, is it? You didn't come to see me," she said, nibbling on a piece of celery dunked in creamy vegetable dip. "You wouldn't admit it to Ralph, but you're here to investigate."

A grim smile slashed his face. "You have a suspicious mind, Ms. Romero."

Connie angled her head, asking the question that plagued her since first seeing him at the service. "Do you often come to funerals?"

"It's a good place to get a handle on the murder victim."

She had heard of such things, but Connie didn't know it was common practice. "Is this official?"

"I'm not involved in the case, remember?"

"So this is personal?" she pressed. Only now did she realize how much she wanted an answer to that question.

A slight smile tugged at his lips, and his green eyes glittered with a sparkle she had never seen. "Maybe."

A rush of warmth infused her, and Connie started to turn away, but then she noted the pinkish tinge that rose in his own angular cheeks before he dropped his gaze.

Was there something more to the way Weldon was treating her? Suddenly Connie was aware of how frumpy she must look with her hair pinned back in a severe bun. She owned one black dress, and its high neck and generous cut did not flatter her rounded figure. Normally she would have dressed it up with a colorful silk scarf or cinched in the waist with a gold belt.

But even as she considered his comment, Weldon took a deep breath and leaned forward, the light note gone from his tone. He resumed his normal, careful delivery. "I'm sorry. I'm being unfair. Or maybe I was simply trying to mask the truth, but I'm not good at deception. I came as a favor to Sergeant Case. He couldn't get away. Yes, I am here to look over the crowd."

Connie stopped in the process of raising a chicken wing to her lips. A ghastly fear slammed through her as the realization of what he was saying hit home. "You don't suppose he...the killer is here?"

Weldon's eyes were like lasers, pointing and picking out targets as his gaze slowly swept around the room. "If it wasn't a random killing, if the killer knew her, that could very well be."

Connie bit down on her lower lip and winced. Damn! Why hadn't she thought of that? She should have checked the crowd herself.

His voice grew chilling. "Most victims know the killer."

Horror churning inside her, Connie turned to look around the room. Could someone here have slashed and mutilated Joy? The scene was so benign. Familiar faces drifted into her view, people she had met through her sister, people she knew as friends of her parents. The thought that someone who knew Joy could hurt her was too unbelievable.

She licked her dry lips and glanced back at Weldon. "Did Sergeant Case tell you that I've asked for the police report? That is open to me, isn't it? Plus the autopsy report?"

"That's not a good idea," he admonished gruffly, eyes remaining on the crowd.

"Don't tell me what is and isn't a good idea," she argued, her voice rising.

He jerked his head back to her, pinning her with a sharp look. "Look, Connie." He held up his hand to stop her as she started to protest further. "I understand your feelings. You were there. You might even wrongly feel responsible. You want to do something to avenge her death. You don't want to feel powerless. But believe me, getting worked up is not the answer. There are other ways you can remember her. Establish a fund in her name or—"

"That won't catch the killer!" Connie interrupted. "I'm an investigative journalist, remember. I do know how to dig. Even the Seattle drug task force was surprised at some of the information I came up with during their investigation. I got a commendation."

He sighed, shaking his head. "You've been watching too much TV. You aren't a trained police officer, and your investigative background doesn't make a difference. You have no idea how to conduct a homicide investigation."

Connie wasn't going to argue the subject with Weldon. She doubted she would win. The man was too focused on the right and proper way to do things. Of course he would not approve of her private inquiry. But maybe he could help her.

"What about this crowd, Weldon? Do you really think one of them could have done it?"

Weldon hesitated, as though he wanted to say something else, before his eyes shifted back to the throng of people. "You tell me. You know them. Is there anyone here who might want to harm your sister?"

Connie again examined the mourners who were mostly seated now at the various tables. "My sister was kind, thoughtful, gentle, and that was the work of a madman."

"It's easier to get angry at someone you know."

His matter-of-fact reply sent a quiver down her spine. "That's cold. I can't imagine anyone who would want her dead."

"Tell me about her husband. Any marriage problems?"

"Ralph?" Connie laughed slightly as she picked out his large figure across the room. With his wrinkled blue jacket hanging limp around him, his shirt untucked and his tie askew, he was more to be pitied than feared. "No, he's just an ordinary guy."

"Even ordinary men are known to snap." Weldon's keen eyes narrowed as he followed her gaze to Ralph.

"Not Ralph. He adored Joy. He's the stereotypical sweet husband. Joy didn't like that he worked too much, but that was the only complaint she ever made about him."

"Any money problems?"

"You're thinking he might have killed her for insurance?" she asked.

Weldon leaned back on his chair. He crossed his legs, resting one ankle on a knee. "You're playing detective. I'm simply asking questions."

Connie eyed him skeptically, shaking her head. "You don't ask questions without a reason, Weldon. You have something in mind."

A sudden, boyish smile lit up his face. "Why, Miss Romero, are you accusing me of deception? I've already told you I'm not good at that."

Connie wondered why she had never noticed how handsome he could be. Or maybe it was because he seldom smiled like that. A sudden surge of excitement rushed through her, and she dropped her glance as she felt her cheeks grow warm. Geez, she wasn't blushing, was she?

She licked her lips and adopted a business tone as she jerked her head to the side.

"Okay, if anyone should be a suspect, consider that jerk, Dick Farley over there."

The angular man was talking to Ralph, an intense look on his narrow face. Connie had met him once in Joy's office, but his abrupt, superior attitude resulted in instant, total dislike.

"Who is he?" Weldon asked, focusing his attention on the conversation.

"He worked in the same real estate office with Joy. A real pain, I guess. The afternoon I saw her, the last afternoon, she told me he was trying to mess up one of her deals and claim it for himself."

"That would provoke him into killing her?" Weldon shook his head, losing interest. "I don't think so."

"It was a pretty big commission apparently." She balled her hand into a fist and pounded it on the table to get his full attention. "I have another idea. I was reading in a newspaper that bodies often get dumped in Stanley Park. You don't suppose she surprised someone?"

He hesitated for an instant, studying her as intently as he had been studying the room. Then he shook his head again, eyes fixated on her in a steady gaze that grew unnerving. "In the middle of the day? I don't think so. Where was the other body? For that matter, what was she doing that far back in the brush anyway? It's thick in there, and it doesn't look like she was dragged in. You say she was simply jogging around the park, but the fact is, she went into that thicket of her own volition."

A tremor ran through Connie. "You're certain of that?"

His big shoulders drew up in a shrug. "Relatively." His face hardened suddenly and he grew still. "Who's the big man in the corner?"

Connie whirled around and picked out a hulking man who stood along the back wall. In a tweed jacket over a maroon turtleneck and jeans, he looked different than the mourners in their neat blue suits. Thick, black hair brushed his shoulders, and his eyes were like hard coal as they surveyed the crowd. For an instant, his piercing eyes met hers.

A tightness closed Connie's throat. "I've never

seen him before this afternoon."

Weldon pushed his chair back, the legs scraping on the hardwood floor. "I'll find out who he is. I'd better talk to a few of the others too. Thanks for your help, Connie."

His long body unfolded from the metal chair, and he pulled a card out of his pocket. His green eyes were warmer than she'd ever seen them. "I know you already have them, but keep this with you. It has my cell number and my direct line at work. Call anytime you want."

Connie held the card tightly as she watched him walk away, approaching the hulking man. What was going on with Weldon? Could he have more on his mind than murder? Something more of a personal, or even intimate nature? Her breath quickened at the idea, but she forced away the thought and shook her head. This was no time to let her own crazy imagination get in the way of what she needed to find out.

Who was that dark-haired stranger? Why was he at Joy's memorial service?

****

Joy's house sat on a hill on the edge of Bellingham, set back in the trees off a narrow paved road. The two-story wooden house and nearby garage had once been the source of her father's pride and pain. Her parents sold it to Joy and Ralph when they retired and moved to a cabin in the nearby San Juan Islands.

Built in the 1930s, the clapboard exterior had been repainted dozens of times. The tall windows in front were ripped out for a picture window in the '60s, but a small front porch remained. Grape vines climbed the lattice work so the inside was barely visible. A veranda with a double swing wrapped along one side and around the back, giving the house the appearance of a plantation house.

Stepping inside brought tears to Connie's eyes. The interior was totally different from the house where she grew up, due to Joy's efforts. Her sister had personally stripped away years of varnish from moldings and refinished the wood to regain its natural, rich mahogany color. The furniture was over-large and overstuffed, aimed at comfort for her growing family

Connie shivered as she surveyed the gloomy interior. Normally light and sunny, the gray day outside infiltrated the house. Not even a fire in the huge fireplace at one end of the great room could infuse the place with warmth. It was as though the house knew Joy was not coming back.

Joy's two children threw off their coats in the vestibule and hopped up the polished wooden stairs to their rooms. Connie didn't try to stop them. Mindy and Jeremy had spent the past four hours dealing with adults they barely knew. They probably needed some time alone. She sank onto the sofa, while her mother headed for the kitchen to put on a pot of coffee. No matter what time of day it was, Bea Romero always kept a pot of coffee going.

As the thumping footsteps faded, Connie smiled sadly at her sister who had seated herself on a nearby chair. "Those kids are going to miss Joy."

"They don't even realize what's coming."

"Did one of you leave the back door unlocked?" Ralph asked, as he walked into the room from the kitchen. He was frowning.

A feeling of unease stole over Connie. Her gaze shot to the open door of the den. She distinctly remembered closing that door before she left. The sight of Joy's desk with its pictures of her family, bulky real estate books, neat folders of contracts, and organized notes had been too much to bear. Even a smiley face that grinned obscenely from Joy's bulletin board had brought pain, so she'd closed it.

She got to her feet as Jeremy came thumping back down the stairs. "Dad! My computer's missing. Did you move it back to the den?"

"The TV is gone," Ralph said, looking beyond Connie, and she swung around.

How had she missed that? And who had set the damn fire anyway?

Her eyes met Ralph's. Fear flickered in the depths of his normally placid blue eyes. "We better call the cops," he said but Connie was already reaching into her purse for her phone, while her other hand pulled Weldon's card out of her jacket pocket.

Chapter Three

Anticipation gnawed at Connie as she watched Weldon exchange comments with the uniformed officers who had responded to the burglary. He had been nearing the border when he got her terrified phone call and returned immediately.

A chill hung over the room despite the fire, or perhaps it simply seemed that way. The idea of a stranger prowling the house sent a shudder through Connie. Why would someone break in? In the back of her mind, the question kept repeating itself—was it the killer?

The instant Weldon separated from the two officers, Connie flung the question at him. His blank stare irritated her.

"Don't you think it's possible?" she asked.

"I suppose, but the officers repeated my first reaction. Criminals watch obituaries and take advantage of the situation. It's possible that someone read the story in the paper about the memorial service. This was a rather high profile service. I've been reading the Bellingham paper, and stories about the murder and today's service were all over the front page. Things like this happen sometimes. Burglars wait until a family is gone to the funeral and break in because they know no one will be home."

"You don't think it's strange?" Connie asked, trying to keep her voice from rising. "Our room getting robbed the day after Joy was killed? Now this?"

His angular face registered no sign of emotion.

Consulting a small notebook, he nodded and touched the top of his pen to the bottom of his lip as though deep in thought. "Do you know what's missing?"

"Jeremy's computer, stereo, TV, and it looks as though they dug through her jewelry box. Ralph says their insurance company has a complete inventory."

He drew his eyes up to meet hers with a direct stare. "Doesn't that answer your questions? They stole things which can be easily fenced. Why else would they break in, eh?"

Connie didn't agree. She tugged at a lock of hair as she thought the situation through. "Records? Something secret to do with a real estate deal? Is that possible? Dick Farley and most of the people from her work left right after they ate. I don't think Dick even stayed that long. I told you he'd been trying to beat her out on a deal."

Weldon watched her with a furrowed brow. "Don't start thinking conspiracy or anything like that," he warned.

"What makes you think that's what I'm doing?" Connie asked, though that was exactly what she'd had on her mind.

He drew a sharp breath, shifting his weight, hand on his hip. "I know how grieving relatives think, eh? It couldn't be something simple. It has to be a drug cartel or serial killer. Their loved one had to be the victim of some larger-than-life occurrence."

Connie looked away, a slight tremor shaking her. He made it sound so impersonal, even if he was right. She had come across so many theories in the past few days, all without any support or evidence, but they all had one thing in common—there was more to her sister's death than a simple explanation.

"Don't waste your time and energy spinning tales," he continued, green eyes grave. "As I told you earlier, in most cases we find the perpetrator was acquainted with the murder victim."

She recalled what he said after the memorial service and the way he keenly watched the crowd gathered at the hall. Connie did not have a chance to question him before he left to ask him if he'd spotted any likely suspects, and she didn't want to do it with her sister and parents within earshot.

Then something else hit her. "Did you find out who that strange man was? The big guy at the memorial?"

Weldon flipped through pages of his notebook. "He said he was an acquaintance."

Connie drew back in surprise, shaking her head. "I've never seen him before. How did he know her?"

"He didn't say. Apparently, he's a professor at the University of British Columbia."

Connie gulped. Her skin prickled, and bile rose in her throat. "Isn't that in Vancouver?"

"Yes. He said he had an appointment to meet Joy yesterday. When he called her office to confirm the time, he found out about her death."

A chill raced across her back. Joy had not mentioned knowing anyone in Vancouver. Why hadn't she arranged to meet the man while they were there for the weekend? The sisters planned on spending three days doing things together—shopping, taking afternoon tea, maybe going to a movie. Joy could have said she had an appointment if she needed to do business. Or was the man lying? And why?

"You look skeptical," Weldon said.

She chewed on her lip, wondering if she should tell him her fears. No, better she deal with this on her own. Connie would question the stranger herself.

Bea Romero waddled into the room. Big and friendly, with a healthy dose of wisdom to go with her hearty sense of humor, her life revolved around her family. Her round, olive face shined from lack of makeup, eyes bare of her normal black mascara and brown eye shadow. Her dark coffee-colored eyes were red rimmed. As she walked into the room, her first glance was at Connie.

"Sit down, girls," she ordered. "Let me get you some coffee. Detective?"

"Inspector," Weldon corrected. "I should be leaving. It'll be very late by the time I get back."

"Then you should stay and have dinner. I was just about to serve the chili."

Connie and Lisa exchanged glances. How like Bea to invite the stranger to stay, simply because he was there.

Weldon started to refuse, but Ralph walked into the room. "I...uh...was thinking about running into Seattle tonight. I have...an early meeting tomorrow." He looked apologetically at Bea. "You're going to stay over, right? Can you keep an eye on the kids?"

She laid a heavy hand on his arm. "You do whatever you need to do, Ralphie. The kids will be fine. We'll stay as long as you need us."

A strange look of relief crossed his face. "Do you mind? I might stay in Seattle a couple of days...at the company apartment...where I stay sometimes." His pained eyes slid around the room as though searching for someone. "I...have a hard time being here. The house is so empty."

"Maybe I'll go back with you," Lisa said, getting to her feet. She watched Ralph with troubled eyes, sympathy written in their soft brown gaze. "I should be heading back, and if you need the company, I'll be more than happy to go along."

The request surprised Connie. Lisa had ridden to Bellingham with her, and they planned on staying the night before returning to Seattle in the morning.

"No one is leaving until they eat," Bea ordered, taking Ralph's arm. Her dark eyes fell on Weldon. "That includes you, Detective. It's been a long time since we had those little sandwiches at the church. I know everyone's hungry."

Weldon mumbled a correction again, and Connie stifled a laugh. He shifted, looking uncomfortable. Here was a man not used to taking orders from a bossy woman.

Connie touched his arm gently. "Don't even argue, Detective," she said, emphasizing the final word. "She won't hear you."

A trace of a smile crossed his lips as he shrugged. "Of course I'll stay."

****

Despite his acceptance of the invitation, Mitch was ready to leave. He wanted to get back to Vancouver and go through his findings with Sergeant Case. He wasn't about to admit the truth to Connie, but she was right. Too much coincidence didn't sit well with him, and it wouldn't with Case either. Somewhere along the line, someone was searching for information, not trying to loot valuables. He would bet the person was a novice, or the culprit would realize how obvious his actions were.

Could it be Ralph? That wouldn't surprise him. He knew the family's schedule. Despite the man's affable appearance, Weldon was picking up strange vibrations. Perkins jumped and twitched every time someone spoke. He wanted to watch Ralph with the family. And he wanted to know why the big man was in a rush to leave. This was a time for the family to pull together, not to go in separate directions. Mitch had witnessed the closeness all afternoon. Except from Ralph. Certainly he was giving the appearance of the grieving husband, but it seemed too pat. Even with Connie's off-the-wall theories, Mitch clung to the premise that murders were rarely committed by strangers.

Now that the decision had been made to eat, the process moved forward quickly. Ralph and Joe

Romero carried extra chairs into the dining room, while Connie and her sister hauled dishes out of the cupboard. Mrs. Romero directed them all, carrying on conversations half in English and half in Spanish.

Before long they were seated around a large, round table on wooden chairs covered with thin, colorful pillows. Connie and her sister wore haunted looks as did Mr. Romero. Only Mrs. Romero moved ahead with purpose, serving up steaming bowls of fragrant chili accompanied by warm tortillas. Ralph huddled in his chair.

The hearty chili left a little burn on the tongue and back of the throat, but its rich flavor had Mitch savoring the taste. Still, he had more on his mind than chili. As he ate, his attention focused keenly on the people at the table—especially Ralph.

"We're going to miss Joy," Lisa said after a few silent minutes. "I feel bad I hadn't called her until two weeks ago."

"I know," Connie agreed, folding up a tortilla and dunking it into her chili. "Me, too. I should have called. I didn't know she needed someone to talk to her."

"She had the kids. She could have talked to them," Ralph said. He lifted a spoonful of chili, but didn't eat it. He dropped the spoon back into the bowl, gaze slipping toward the cuckoo clock on the wall. Weldon noted his look of anxiety. The man wanted to leave.

"I mean gossip. Among sisters." Connie attempted a laugh, but it died on her lips. She poked at her chili.

"She wasn't talking to many people," Ralph said. "She was always working on her real estate deals. She'd be on that damn computer from the time she got up until she went to bed." His voice took on a sharply accusing note and thick fingers drummed the tabletop in a nervous rhythm.

Connie nodded, dark hair bouncing on her shoulders. "She called several times. I should have caught the hint. Joy never called without a reason. I was always too busy so I'd tell her I'd call her back."

"Me, too," Lisa said glumly. "And I never called back either."

"I didn't call back until last week when we set up the weekend plans," Connie added.

Silence fell on the table, and Mitch examined each sad face, lost in thoughts of the woman who would never sit and enjoy chili with her family again. He couldn't help but notice that Ralph continued to fidget and check the clock.

"She had a good life," Mrs. Romero said and patted Ralph on the shoulder. "I thank you for that, Ralphie."

"Scared the heck out of Connie," Lisa said with a giggle.

Connie whirled to face her sister. "What do you mean?"

"Her happy home life! You were so excited by it at first and then you became totally opposed. You weren't going to let that settled thing happen to you."

"I was just different. I knew I would never be as happy as Joy. She was so content she had that *Song of Joy* on her phone."

"She had what?" Mitch asked.

"Beethoven's Ninth." Connie hummed a few bars and he recognized the tune.

"I don't know if she was still happy," Ralph said, getting to his feet, bowl of chili barely touched. He stretched, eyes sliding over the clock. "I should be going."

"Wait," Connie called. Her eyes grew wide with curiosity. "What do you mean she wasn't happy?"

Ralph shifted, leaning his arms on the back of the chair. "She was studying these mystic religions,

48

looking for some new spiritual meaning. She never went to church anymore. She was reading these books..."

The big man didn't seem to notice Connie's growing sudden interest, but Mitch could almost read what she was thinking.

"May I see them? Or borrow them?" Connie was on her feet. She glanced at Mitch as though expecting him to make the same request, but he didn't think the books had anything to do with Joy's murder. It might keep Connie occupied for a while, though. Safely occupied.

"Go ahead," Ralph said with the wave of his hand. "Take what you want. They're in a box in the den. I was so angry when I saw them the other day, I boxed them up. I was going to throw them out. Along with that damn computer."

"You can't blame the computer..." Lisa began.

"It took all her time. We bought it for Jeremy, but she was always on it, and then she wanted her own. I just spent a fortune on a new laptop for her."

That caught Mitch's attention. "Was it stolen?" he asked. No one had mentioned Joy's computer. Connie's laptop and the boy's computer were gone, but no one had brought up a third.

"It's in the shop. She wanted more memory, or some damn thing. She hadn't had it long, a coupla weeks." He turned to Connie, shoulders slumping. "You want it? Didn't you say yours was taken?"

"Yes, it was, and I thank you for the offer. I can pay you back with my insurance money. Are you certain you don't want to give it to Jeremy?"

"Uh-uh. I don't think we need a new one. Jeremy likes to play games, but I'll get him a new game system. I don't like the things kids can find on that Internet."

"I know what you mean," Lisa agreed.

Mitch tuned out of the conversation. Instead he

let his attention slide from one person to the next. Connie was fun to watch. Her animation was back, and he found himself smiling at her antics. She kept the conversation flowing. Ralph retreated into the background, but Weldon noted how many times he checked his watch. The man was in a rush to be somewhere and when he left, Mitch was going too. He was curious about where Mr. Ralph Perkins was headed in such a rush on the day of his wife's memorial service.

****

"Thanks for the lift. You're saving my life. I didn't want to drive all the way to Seattle for a few items. With Lisa going back, I wouldn't have a companion to keep me awake."

Connie gave Weldon a bright smile across the front seat. She could barely make out the firm set of his jaw and the tight-lipped expression on his face from the glow of the dashboard.

She fiddled with knobs on the control panel, seeking heat. "Is this as high as it will go?"

Weldon reached over, and their fingers brushed. "Let me fix that, eh?"

Electricity seemed to race from his skin to hers. Connie was suddenly aware of their close proximity. His male presence seemed to fill the dim interior. She noted the faint scent of sandalwood, a scent she recalled from the day in the Vancouver hotel when he carried her to the bed. Her gaze fell to his strong hands gripping the steering wheel, and again a strange awareness rushed through her. What had it felt like to have those hands touch her? Her breath caught. Enough of such odd thoughts. She had no time for designs on Inspector Mitch Weldon!

"You didn't want to bring me, did you?" she said in a playful tone. Things had happened very quickly after Ralph and Lisa left. When she heard Weldon ask for instructions to the freeway, going south instead of north to Vancouver, she jumped at the chance. This gave her an opportunity to go home to pick up a few extra clothes so she could remain in Bellingham—or better yet—return to Vancouver. He didn't seem to like the idea, though a quick plea from her mother had changed his mind. Ever since they left, he had been very quiet, and he didn't answer her question now either.

"You know the US has a speed limit," she said, noting that he was going faster than the limit. "And there are some curves until we get to the other side of the lake."

"I know the road," he said.

Darkness blanketed the night outside, headlights reflecting wet pavement. A few lights dotted the blackness in the distance. She knew what was out there. To the right, Lake Sammish stretched to a line of steep hills on its other side. A wrong slide on the wet roadway could send them plummeting toward the lake.

"Did you have a schedule to keep?" Connie asked, as he checked his watch quickly.

He drew a deep breath. "I might as well tell you since you'll find out anyway. I want to catch up to your brother-in-law. I don't believe he suddenly had work in Seattle. Something else is taking him back."

"You really suspect Ralph? But that's crazy!"

"I've seen the same pattern too many times. Victims know the perpetrator. I told you that." He grunted, and pointed. "There! There's the vehicle."

Skillfully he eased his foot off the accelerator to slow down and pulled into the slower lane. He kept enough distance between them and the other car so that Ralph and Lisa would not notice, but he could follow the tail lights.

"Vehicle, perpetrator!" she chided. "Do you ever talk like a regular person, Weldon? Why not killer or car?"

A slight smile slashed across his angular face. "Do you ever stop talking?"

"You think I talk too much? I'm simply curious. It's what makes me good at my job. As soon as someone tells me one thing, I want to know the next step or why stuff happens."

His smile widened, and her stomach jumped. Damn, she had not realized how handsome he could be. The two of them had never spent this much time together. Their talks were usually confined to the phone where he gave her lots of "perpetrator" and "victim" talk.

"You talk about my language usage, and you say 'stuff'? Is that supposed to convey some actual meaning?" he asked with a laugh.

Connie slapped her knee as she joined in the laughter. "Sorry, Inspector. And you know something else? I've never heard you laugh either, until now."

He chuckled again, but this time, she heard an edge. "I live in a world where there isn't much to laugh about."

She was getting a lesson in his world—a world of violence and a search for murderers. Perpetrators.

"I can't imagine doing that all the time, trying to find killers." She studied the angular lines of his face which had hardened into a chiseled mask. Just what kind of a man was Weldon when he was away from his job? She thought he might be a good match for Lisa, but what really existed behind the crisp, pressed suit and shirt and cool demeanor? Was there an inch of softness in there somewhere? Maybe she should try to find out—and not necessarily for Lisa. Her recent dealings with him had her thinking in a new direction.

He had not answered her comment, as though it was simply a statement of fact.

"My world can be hard-edged," she added. "In

the news business you hear about gruesome things, you report on them, but then the next day you're doing a dancing dog story."

"I thought you were an investigative producer." His face softened slightly as he cast her a quick glance.

The look was long and sent a quick surge of excitement through her. She fidgeted with her coat buttons. His long fingers turned the heater dials, taking the heat a little lower, but she doubted it would lessen the spurt of internal heat that was beginning to rush through her body like a deadly virus.

"Well, yes, but I really want a job with one of the big networks. I'd love to produce for a news magazine where you get to travel on their dime. This gig at Puget Sound News is just another step in that direction." She had never told him that, but they'd never had this much personal contact. Now she wanted him to know more about her because she was growing more curious about him.

"You need to focus on that," he said softly. "I'm certain your sister Joy would want that."

Connie chortled. "Weldon, you wily rascal! You don't miss a trick. You're worried about my investigating this case, aren't you?"

"I think it's a bad idea," he said with a shrug.

"You heard what Ralph said," she argued. "Joy changed in the past few months. I should have seen that, and I would have if I'd just talked to her. She needed my help when she was alive, and I wasn't there for her. I can't let her down now."

"Trying to find a killer out of guilt is not a good idea," Weldon said, his voice taking on a hard edge. "It puts too many emotional variables into play. This is exactly why I discourage family members from trying to solve cases. Leave it to the professionals. Frank Case is one of the top detectives in the department."

"You're not on the case, but you came to the service today, and now you're chasing Ralph. That sounds to me like you're investigating."

Another shrug. "I am simply picking up information for Frank. If I can take back proof for him that Ralph Perkins is acting in a suspicious manner, he'll take it from there."

"You both suspect Ralph?"

"Case sensed there was something wrong with your brother-in-law from the beginning. He was very edgy when he was interviewed in Vancouver. He packed her belongings that morning before he left, as though he didn't want police to have a chance to go through them. Now he tells us her computer is in the shop. It could be that he's having the memory erased."

"I think you're wrong," she said, shaking her head in disagreement. "I think you need to be thinking about what Ralph said about the spiritual areas. What if she got involved with a cult and wanted out? Or if it's someone she knew, what about that real estate guy, Farley? He looks like a real shark."

"I knew you'd jump on the spiritual issue. We'll check it out, along with her work competitors. I still think your brother-in-law is the best bet."

Connie wanted to argue further, but she held back. Now she knew more than ever that she needed to get involved in this investigation. Ralph would never hurt her sister, and if that was where Weldon was heading, he was pointing the Vancouver PD detective in the wrong direction. Sergeant Frank Case might appreciate her research when he realized Ralph was the wrong suspect.

****

"Are we there?" Connie asked, blinking sleep from her eyes. She had fallen asleep shortly after trying to convince Weldon to look at different suspects in Joy's case.

Lights flickered around the front seat. They were at a stop light. Ahead of them, Ralph's blue car had made it through the intersection and cruised slowly down the street.

"Do you know where this company apartment is?" Weldon asked, his voice tinged with irritation, the palm of his hand pounding the steering wheel in frustration.

"About three blocks from Lisa's. It's why she wanted to go back with him." Connie sat up. They were in the lower part of downtown Seattle near the waterfront. It wasn't anywhere near Lisa's apartment. Her heart began to thump with anticipation.

"He's not headed there. He dropped her off at least a mile back," Weldon said.

The light changed and wheels squealed as Weldon stepped on the gas pedal to catch up with Ralph. She craned her head to see signs. She'd visited his company headquarters too. It wasn't far from here, but it was in the opposite direction.

"What do you suppose he's doing down here?" she asked. The industrial and business section was further south. They were cruising through an area of restaurants, tourist shops, and trendy boutique hotels.

"Let's just find out, shall we?" A look of intensity settled on Weldon's face, and his green eyes sparkled as the lights hit them.

After two blocks Ralph turned his car into the parking structure beside a hotel. On the edge of downtown, the Waverly Hotel was an older building that had recently been renovated to attract the business traveler. Weldon eased his car to the curb.

"You stay here," he ordered. "I'll see where he goes."

Butterflies dancing inside her, Connie waited a few anxious moments. What was Ralph doing at the Waverly? And what was going on inside at the moment? She couldn't take it any longer. Hopping out of the car, Connie looked around for Weldon or Ralph. The sidewalk was empty, and while the lights of the hotel's front entrance cast a glow onto the damp sidewalk, she couldn't see inside. Connie began walking toward the front drive, but stopped when the lanky inspector raced out.

He nearly barreled into her as a car came screeching out of the parking structure to her left. Connie froze as headlights stroked her body and nearly blinded her. A scream of fear died in her tight throat. Before she could react, Weldon caught his balance, wrapped his arms around Connie and whirled her out of the way.

Ralph's car zoomed past her, skidded onto the street and careened around the next corner.

She stared up at Weldon in shock. Had Ralph been trying to hit her? Could Weldon be right? Had Ralph killed Joy?

Chapter Four

"Are you all right?" Weldon held her tightly, concern etched on his grim face. Gentle hands steadied her.

Connie nodded, though her knees shook. "Another rescue. This is becoming a habit." She tried to laugh, but it came out as a choking sound.

A smile crinkled the corners of his lips. "A nice habit."

Her breath caught. Their eyes held, and he seemed to realize what he'd said. Even in the gloomy light she could see his face redden. He drew his hands from her, but held them ready to catch her should she stumble. A laugh escaped her constricted throat.

He turned away, running his hands through his hair as he stared down the street. "He's getting away. Let's get going, eh?"

"Sure, Chief." Connie glanced over at Weldon as they settled into the car. Was something happening here? Was he interested in her? She'd wondered about it earlier and now here it was again. She was normally good at spotting a man's interest, but until that day at the crime site and in her hotel room, she'd never even thought of him that way. Was he having the same thoughts about her?

She studied Weldon, noting his strong hands as they rested on the wheel, examining the clean chiseled lines of his face as the car passed from light to shadows. His lips were full and strangely inviting. His broad, large shoulders looked good in his tweed blazer. She inhaled deeply, breathing in that clean scent of his cologne as she had earlier, but now there seemed more of an intimacy to their closed-in surroundings.

The car hit a bump, breaking the spell that seemed to bind her, and she jerked her thoughts from Weldon. She needed to stop that! She had to focus on what was important! Joy and Ralph. What about him? Everything had happened quickly, but was it possible he wanted to run her down? She voiced the question aloud.

Weldon shook his head. "I don't think he knew you were there. I didn't realize he would stop at the front desk and he caught sight of me in a mirror. He got a panicked look on his face and rushed back toward the car park. I don't think he was aiming at you. He was simply trying to escape me."

That was as relief. She didn't like the idea of suspecting that Ralph might harbor murderous thoughts about her—or Joy. "Ralph is not the sort to be a killer," she said.

Weldon's full lips pressed firmly together. He maneuvered the car around the corner where Ralph had disappeared. Cars lined the street, but Ralph was not in sight.

"Maybe he went to his company's main office," she offered.

"Perhaps. Where is it?"

He followed her directions and as the car turned onto the final street, they saw Ralph walk through the building's lit doors.

Weldon nodded shortly. "I'll take you home so you can get your things. How long will that take? I'm going back to the hotel to question the desk clerk."

"Who do you think he was going to meet?" she asked.

"That's what I want to find out."

"Who the hell could he be meeting?" she asked impatiently.

Weldon's face was severe, and he seemed to weigh his words before replying. "You say your brother-in-law is not a killer. You may be right, but if he didn't commit the killing, perhaps he hired someone. He would have to make a payoff."

A cold ribbon of fear and anger ran through Connie. Ralph hiring a hit man? That seemed more implausible than doing it himself. That required planning. "Ralph's not that cold-blooded."

"Perhaps, but it has to be considered a possibility," Weldon argued.

"I'll go with you," Connie said. "It will take a while to get there and back."

"This is a police investigation," he reminded her bluntly. "If you want a ride back to Bellingham tonight, you'd best tell me where you live."

Connie started to argue, but she could see the taut lines of his face. Weldon was not going to accept an argument.

"Two blocks over and turn to the right. You can let me off on the corner."

****

Sunlight danced among the clouds, lighting the kitchen through large windows. The warm scent of fresh coffee filled the air. Connie sat at Joy's kitchen table, newspapers spread around her. She'd returned her niece and nephew from a visit to their grandparents and their shouts rose periodically from the backyard as they played with friends. She sipped coffee while waiting for Ralph to return from the grocery store. Looking for something to do, she read the Vancouver newspapers she had found folded and stuffed into a magazine rack in a corner of the kitchen.

One picture that filled a fourth of one page brought tears to Connie's eyes. She had seen many photos like this and never been moved. Her fingers lightly touched the grainy gray image. It showed police carrying a body bag through a dark thicket of underbrush. How many times had she seen that sort of photo in a newspaper or viewed similar video? To others it was simply a body bag carrying a murder victim, but for once, she knew whose lifeless body was inside that bag. She recognized Weldon's stiff posture, off to the side, watching along with several officers as the body was carried out. She flipped up a corner of the newspaper. It was four days old.

Connie re-read the headline, fear dancing along her spine. "New Murder Not Latest Slasher Victim." What did that mean? She pushed her palms over the paper to straighten it so she could read the article.

The latest murder victim found in Stanley Park, 38-year-old Joy Perkins, is apparently not a victim of the BC Slasher. Canadian Special Crimes Agency Inspector Mitch Weldon, who recently took control of the BC Slasher task force, says the investigation has concluded that the latest victim may be an attempt by a copy cat killer to duplicate the murders, but there were too many dissimilarities to be the work of the madman who has claimed the lives of six women.

Anger rose inside her as Connie read the story a second time. Six women? Victims of a madman slasher? Why the hell hadn't Weldon told her? No wonder he had paid such close attention to Joy's case. He made his appearance at the murder scene and the memorial seem so coincidental. The man was conducting his own damn investigation. Why did he think Joy was not one of the victims? Didn't it make more sense that she was attacked by this crazed BC Slasher than Ralph?

The kitchen door opened, and Ralph lumbered inside, arms burdened with plastic bags. He started to smile when he saw Connie at the table, but then he noticed the papers on the table.

"What are you reading?" he asked, stiffening.

Connie held up the newspaper. "Have you been collecting the Vancouver papers, Ralph?"

He dropped the bags on a counter. "I was curious to see what they were finding out. Those damn cops won't tell me anything. It's like they're afraid I might spoil their investigation. She was my wife, dammit. I have a right to know what happened to her." His round face flushed with frustration.

"I know. Weldon promised to keep me informed, but he never calls and all he tells me when I call is that the investigation is continuing." Her gaze drifted back to the newspaper. She had an idea now of why he had been so closed-mouthed, but if he suspected Joy as a BC Slasher victim at first, why had he not been honest about it? What made him decide she was not a victim? His attitude made Connie more determined. If she was going to get answers, she'd need to dig them up herself. She drew up her shoulders and faced Ralph to make an admission that she had not even made to Lisa.

"I'm going back up there. I refuse to settle for vague phone calls. I'm going to see what I can find out myself."

Ralph stopped in the process of pulling a bag of Oreos from one of the plastic bags. "Can you do that?"

"Of course. I understand I'm allowed to read the police reports. I might not be a forensic expert, but there are things I can check that might help find who killed her."

"Is that wise?" he asked, thick brows furrowing.

"It's a great idea, especially given this." She pointed at the newspaper. "Did you read this article about the slasher cases?"

Ralph nodded. "I wonder why that inspector never told us about that." He put the cookies on the counter and reached into the plastic bags for more groceries. He removed item after item, one at a time at such a slow pace Connie was ready to take over the job.

She held back only since he knew where everything was. She lifted her coffee mug to her lips and sipped. The coffee was growing cool. "He says he thinks Joy was killed by someone she knew."

Ralph grunted and thumped the counter with his palm in frustration. "Sergeant Case said that too, but no one who knew her would want to kill Joy." His voice took on an unusually animated tone.

"Exactly," she agreed. "Besides, why do it while we were in Vancouver? They could have done it any time, any place when she was alone. I've heard of people making phony appointments to see homes and attacking real estate agents. Why not do that? There were so many other places the killer could have approached her."

Ralph didn't answer. His ruddy face had grown troubled after his sudden show of emotion, and he'd returned to his mechanical movements. Connie still didn't believe Weldon's theory about Ralph. The big, friendly man had such a benign nature and moved in such a deliberate manner that she couldn't imagine him doing anything that required quick action. And violence? It didn't compute.

Weldon never told her what the desk clerk said the night he returned to the Waverly Hotel. She still didn't believe Ralph might be meeting a hit man. Where would he find one? How could he afford to pay a big sum of money?

Lisa later admitted that Ralph appeared tense on their drive to Seattle, but he claimed he was late to meet a visiting business acquaintance. That made more sense. Perhaps when he saw Weldon he worried the inspector might ruin the meeting so he rushed to leave. She no longer feared Ralph intended to run over her. It had been an unhappy coincidence that he came roaring out as she was going in. And, he had gone right from the hotel to his company office.

She and Weldon had not spoken much on their return trip. When they parted company, he agreed to keep her informed, but she had initiated all the contact. She could not wait any longer. She was going to Vancouver. She hadn't seen the autopsy findings or police record, and since she still had time off work, she intended to make the most of it.

Ralph had started unloading the second bag, and she rose to help him. This would take forever if she left him on his own.

"Let me empty those, and you put things away." She began removing cans from a bag on the floor.

He shifted and let her take over as though used to taking orders. "Do your mom and dad know what you're doing?"

She had spent the weekend in the San Juan Islands with her parents and Joy's children. They hiked and went fishing, but sadness shrouded every move. "I didn't want to worry them."

Bea Romero had not said she feared for the safety of her other two her daughters, but she looked pained by Connie's departure, even more so than usual. Instead of normal warnings about being careful, she squeezed Connie's hand tightly, sad, black eyes filled with a mist of tears. It hurt Connie to see her naturally cheerful mother looking so defeated.

They hugged each other and clung together for a moment before Connie jerked away and hurried to the car to join Mindy and Jeremy. Another minute and she might have broken down sobbing, grasping at her mother like a ten-year-old.

As she finished pulling out groceries, the memory of those emotional moments choked her.

She drew a shaky breath and turned to fold the newspapers. Better to get answers to Joy's death instead of obsessing on sorrow.

Perhaps she should start now. She tucked the papers back into the magazine rack. "Say, Ralph, last week after the memorial, did you know Weldon followed you?"

A strange look crossed Ralph's face, and his puffy cheeks grew pink. "I saw him. I went to the Waverly Hotel to meet a client, and there was the inspector. I had no idea what he wanted, but I found out he tailed me. He considered me a suspect. Isn't that foolish?"

He lifted his face to hers, and Connie stared into his clear blue eyes. What she saw was surprise, not guilt. She nodded, reaffirming her belief in him. "You loved Joy as much as the rest of us. I don't understand why he ruled out that she could be a slasher victim. That's more likely."

Ralph's large head bobbed in agreement. "Did you know that other detective questioned people at work about me and Joy? 'How did we get along?' 'Where was I that day?' Lots of questions that has everyone looking at me funny. Some people knew that we'd been having marital problems, but everyone has troubles. They weren't serious enough to kill a person over. You understand that, don't you?" His beseeching look and tone appealed for her support.

"People have marital problems all the time, but they don't kill each other," Connie agreed, though his comments surprised her. But they gave her an opening she had not expected. "Had you discussed divorce?"

"Oh, hell no! Someone said the cops asked if I might hire someone to kill her. What kind of crap is that?"

She slid an arm around his wide back and gave

him a partial hug. "I won't look at you funny, and I don't think you hired a hit man. I know you didn't kill her. So do Lisa, Mom, and Dad. I'll make certain the cops know too. Maybe I can give them other options."

His smile was so thankful it almost brought tears to her eyes. "Do you think you can find out anything?"

"Who knows? But if police focus on you, then they're not looking where they should be. Do you know if they talked to people where she worked? Or Dick Farley?"

His head jerked up. "Dick Farley?"

"She told me he was giving her trouble. Do you know anything about that? Maybe I should talk to him."

He shook his head vigorously and waved his hands. "Talking to him won't do any good. That's a dumb idea. Maybe you shouldn't get involved in this." He walked to the refrigerator and opened it. "I better make lunch for the kids. Do you want a sandwich?"

His agitation and sudden change in manner was a shock. He began jerking cold cuts and mustard out of the refrigerator. What was going on? Was there something to her question about Dick Farley? She didn't have time to pursue it, but she filed the thought away to ask later.

"I'll take a rain check on the sandwich. I better hit the road." She paused a minute to study his glum, haggard face as he concentrated on putting mustard onto a slice of bread and placing ham and cheese on top, moving in slow motion. Part of her ached for him. She patted his thick shoulder as she walked by. "We're going to find who did it. You mentioned books she'd been reading? May I take them?"

He pushed the sandwiches aside and wiped his

pudgy hands on a paper towel. "I'll get them and give you her laptop too. It came back from the shop yesterday."

By the time Connie was ready to leave, she was loaded with a box of books and a black bag containing Joy's laptop.

"I feel bad about the computer," she said as she hooked the bag over her shoulder. She'd been pricing computers since her laptop was stolen. Prices had gone up since her last purchase.

Ralph shook his head and eyed it warily. "No problem. I don't want it around."

****

Vancouver sat below a thin line of low clouds that threatened rain at any moment. Connie had always loved the city, but she wondered if she would forever see it in terms of sinister shadows. A madman lurking in a dark corner, waiting to claim another victim—like Joy.

As soon as she got onto Oak Street, the long sweeping boulevard that took her into the heart of downtown, Connie called Weldon. He didn't answer. She tried the main desk, only to discover he was out on a case.

A slasher case?

The clerk wouldn't tell her where he was. It bothered her that he had not mentioned his connection to the slasher case. Joy's throat had been cut. Connie knew that much about how her sister died. Joy had been mutilated. Why didn't he think Joy was a victim of his killer? She left a message with the desk clerk, providing her cell number, though she didn't reveal where she was.

In the meantime, she would check into her hotel and begin researching the slasher cases. She had been thinking about that since leaving Bellingham. Weldon was certain Joy was not a victim. She wanted to know more.

Connie had chosen a small, stylish older hotel on the West End instead of the large glass tower near the waterfront where she, Lisa, and Joy stayed. The room was newly renovated in a Victorian theme. She unpacked Joy's computer and set it on a small writing table. Luckily the room offered a complimentary Internet connection so she could work as long as she needed.

She turned on the computer and marveled at its quick speed in booting up. Ralph might not like the machine but she wasn't going to complain. As she examined the programs and features she realized this was a top of the line model. Ralph had given her a bargain. She smacked her forehead with her fingers.

"Dummy!"

It had just hit her. She had Joy's laptop. What if the BC Slasher had not killed Joy? What if Weldon was right and someone Joy knew killed her? Could there be evidence on the computer? Police were always looking for evidence on a personal computer, and here she had it right in her hands. If she was going to look into personal connections, what better place to start?

Her fingers hesitated over the keyboard before Connie began to maneuver the touchpad. The laptop didn't appear to have much data. Joy had no email in her Outlook folder and she had not set up her calendar, nor were there any names under contacts. Connie did a quick check of Joy's documents to see if there was anything unusual, but saw nothing out of the ordinary except several files on Mystics and Myths.

Ralph had mentioned that was one of Joy's recent interests. Connie opened the files, but the information appeared to be articles or links to Internet sites. She made a note of where the files were stored. She would study them more in depth later.

Business held a couple of folders with names she didn't know. The folders appeared to have business letters, but on quick perusal, nothing appeared promising or threatening. She would come back to them later. One might be the deal that involved Dick Farley. She scanned the recycle bin, in case Joy had eliminated files. Nothing. Weldon had mentioned the hard drive might have been cleaned, but that didn't appear to be the case. There were files on it. She could have Lisa, the computer whiz kid, check later, just to be sure.

So now what? A sigh of exasperation escaped her. She scanned the icons on the computer and tapped the Online International symbol. Hadn't Joy once said she used that email service? It opened to reveal two screen names: Joy Perkins and Sexy Lady.

Sexy Lady? Huh? Connie could not imagine her staid, practical sister using such a name. Connie clicked on it, figuring Joy used her real name for business. The email account brought up dozens of new entries, but as Connie began to go through them she discovered they were mainly spam. None were dated before Joy died. Nothing was stored in the account itself.

Hell, this was a waste of time. She hit the search feature. Time to look into the BC Slasher. She did a search and came up with the Vancouver newspaper that she had been reading at Ralph's house. She copied the stories and saved them into a file. She went back a couple of days to read the older articles about the killer. The bodies had begun turning up nearly a year ago. The victims were young, mainly prostitutes or teen runaways. He apparently hit in the middle of the week, killing his victims elsewhere and dumping the bodies in Stanley Park. No wonder Weldon had responded.

Perhaps he ruled Joy out as a victim because she was killed in the park.

She went through as many of the related stories as she could find, saving them all for further study. In many, Weldon's name jumped out at her. He'd apparently been working on the case for some time.

He had cautioned her about thinking her sister might be a victim of a serial killer, as though he knew she might uncover the truth about the BC Slasher. Perhaps she needed to go beyond that. Certainly the Northwest had suffered its share of gruesome serial killings. Who could forget the frightening case of executed killer Ted Bundy? Even one of the infamous Hillside Stranglers from Los Angeles had been captured in Bellingham. Perhaps the most notorious string of murders took years to solve. The Green River killings drew national attention, when the bodies of prostitutes were found in wooded areas.

Connie had called contacts in the Seattle Police Department to see if there were cases like Joy's on their books, but like Weldon, they scoffed at her conjecture. Maybe there were other murders she could check on her own. She opened another browser so she could compare what she found. Nothing stood out except for a case in Portland from the previous spring. A woman's body had been found along the Columbia River. Like Joy, she had been stabbed while she was jogging. No arrests had been made. Connie saved that file just in case.

A ringing blasted out of the computer and Connie jumped.

NiteMan: Long time no see!

The message appeared in a small box in the upper left corner of her computer screen. What the hell?

NiteMan: Hey, babe. I've missed you. Are you coming into The Lair?

Her heart began to beat at an accelerated rate. Babe? Who was NiteMan? Why he was being so familiar and inviting her to The Lair? She started to tell him he had the wrong person, but as she typed the words, Connie realized she would not send them. Could this be another lead in Joy's case? She backspaced to erase the words she'd written and tapped out another reply.

SexyLady: I've been busy.

NiteMan: Come talk to us. We've been wondering where you were. You never told us you were taking a break. Did we upset you?

Another screen popped up. "You are invited to The Lair. Click here."

Connie didn't hesitate this time. She positioned the pointer and clicked. Immediately another screen filled her monitor. A list of names popped up to the left of the screen, together with an ongoing conversation that began to scroll by in the center. She had to read quickly to keep up. At the bottom was another box for her to write comments, together with a "send" button. She hesitated, unable to decide what to write or if she should.

DarkMaster: Look who is back.

DeadlyGhost: Sexy Lady, welcome back. We've missed you.

SkyGirl: You just come and go? Forget your friends when you feel like it?

NiteMan: Lighten up, Sky. We're glad to have her back.

The conversation rolled by so fast Connie had little time to type in more than a quick greeting. She had no idea who these people were, but apparently Joy conversed with them from time to time online. As Sexy Lady? Why? She had heard of online chat rooms but never visited them. What kind of people frequented them?

She studied the names. DarkMaster? NiteMan? Who were these people? How had Joy become involved with them? Despite the odd names, the conversation appeared benign. Someone's daughter was coming to visit. Another was complaining about recalcitrant children. Then Connie realized the conversation had slowed and someone had addressed her directly.

SkyGirl: Aren't you going to speak, Sexy? Too good? Why did you come back?

Connie typed as fast as she could and hit send as others questioned her and cajoled her to respond.

SexyLady: I'm glad to be back. My computer was in the shop. Had no way to communicate.

NiteMan: All is forgiven. You're our favorite.

SkyGirl: Watch it!

DeadlyGhost: Well, we always enjoy her sage advice and witty comments.

Sage advice sounded like Joy, but witty comments? She couldn't picture her older sister in this environment. Connie was growing weary of the chat room. It didn't offer what she needed. She couldn't imagine Joy talking to this group for long, though the thought of Joy calling herself Sexy Lady disturbed her. What was her sister thinking? Did Ralph know about the name? Was that why he didn't approve of the computer? She would have to call him and ask. Maybe she could take it up with Weldon.

LastDance: You're quiet, Sexy. Got something on your mind?

SexyLady: Just overwhelmed and pleased to be back.

Raven40: You know, I've always said that even though the computer is anonymous, you can tell something about a person simply by what they write online.

PrettyOne: Uh, oh, the great mystic has an

ax to grind.

Raven40: Just a word of warning.

SkyGirl: To who?

PrettyOne: Whom! You still have few grammar skills, Sky

Raven40: Stop bickering. We have more important things to consider.

DarkMaster: Such as? Stop being mysterious, Raven.

Raven40: We have a ringer in our midst.

PrettyOne: A ringer? How can you tell?

Raven40: Sometimes you can tell when someone is pretending to be someone they're not. Even on the computer.

Connie swallowed hard and her hand flew to her throat. She had an idea he knew she was not Joy. How could he know that? She tapped out a message.

SexyLady: You think it's me, Raven?

Raven40: Making no claims. I know who it is. So does that person. The question is why?

DarkMaster: You're toying with us, Raven. Like when you describe your mystical religions. Is this going to end in another of your animal tales?

Raven40: No. This one ends in death.

Cold apprehension seized Connie. Who was this guy and why was he doing this? She scribbled down his name on a note pad. No one else interested her, but she should find out this guy's real name. He had figured out that Connie was pretending to be Joy.

SexyLady: Is there a point here, Raven? What is it?

NiteMan: Good going, Sexy. Don't let him make his blanket voodoo statements.

Raven40: That is the point. Death.

Her breath caught. Then the little box that had popped up originally returned to the upper corner as her computer sang out.

NiteMan: Don't worry about him. You should know by now that guy is a nut case.

SexyLady: He's acting very mysterious.

NiteMan: Yep. Always got to tease us with riddles and oddball crap. He's the one guy who makes me want to break our rule.

SexyLady: Which one?

NiteMan: Numero uno, of course. There are times I want to track him down and find out who he really is.

SexyLady: So do it.

NiteMan: Uh, Uh. You know that's against the rules. I thought that was why you got mad.

SexyLady: Not sure what you mean

NiteMan: I thought you got angry cuz Sky Girl was trying to change our rules about revealing our real names. I agree with you. We all made those rules when we opened The Lair. I see no reason to change them now.

SexyLady: Maybe we should.

NiteMan: Come on. Have you been thinking of changing them just to find out who Raven is? Or was that why you disappeared? Were you afraid they were going to find you?

Connie sat back on her chair, re-reading the last few exchanges. That was yet one more element to tell Weldon. Joy apparently had been talking to an anonymous group of people on the Internet. The comment from NiteMan about their desire for secrecy also appeared to clear the group from any involvement in Joy's death. They didn't know her name, and from what everyone was saying, they didn't know she was dead either.

She gulped, and cold dread slithered down her back. That was true.

All except for one—Raven.

Chapter Five

Connie squeezed her eyes shut and then blinked. How long had she been sitting in front of the computer? It seemed like hours. Outside, the fog and gray clouds had lifted, and sun dappled the peaceful blue waters of English Bay. Two long tankers rested in the outer waters of the bay. Closer in, small knots of people in colorful garb jogged or walked the path along the edge of the water, the outer rim of Stanley Park. She should take a walk instead of sitting cooped up in the hotel room, conducting research and talking online with those strange friends of Joy's. The idea vanished as quickly as it had come. The last time she walked that seawall path, it had been with Joy. The sunlit path was no longer so appealing.

Her cell phone chirped and she grabbed it, noting a number she didn't recognize, though it was a Vancouver prefix. She tensed as anticipation rippled through her.

"Connie, what are you doing in Vancouver?"

The computer in front of her lost its importance at the sound of the perturbed voice. Her fingers seemed to lose their bone structure and she almost dropped the phone. She had to struggle to make her voice sound normal.

"Hello, Weldon. Nice to talk to you too. How do you know I'm in Vancouver?"

"Your mother told me. I thought we had agreed you would let us do the investigating. Don't tell me you're here on vacation, eh?"

The hard edge to his voice bothered her. What

had she expected? For him to be pleased she was back in Vancouver and he might see her? Whatever her hope had been, she could tell he wasn't happy, and she was growing weary of his patronizing attitude.

"I'm here to see what I can find out about the slasher cases." On the computer screen, the word "slasher" stood out like a shout from the headline of a two-month-old newspaper. The killer had apparently been around for a while. "The BC Slasher case you're investigating," she added in a hard tone.

"That case has nothing to do with your sister," he replied sternly without missing a beat. "Don't start thinking it does. I've been investigating those killings for some time."

"Yes, I know," she cried. "What I don't know is why you didn't tell me. You thought Joy's death might be part of your case at first, didn't you? That's why you were at the park."

He replied with no attempt at an apology. "I investigate every body found in Stanley Park, yes. I don't feel like I owe anyone an explanation of my investigative work. Most of it is confidential and not open to the media. Now you haven't fully answered my question. What do you hope to accomplish by coming back to Vancouver?"

Connie sighed as a wave of frustration rushed through her. "You know damn well why I'm here, Weldon. I want to see the autopsy report on Joy and any other police files I might be able to view."

"They won't tell you anything. There is no information in the police report or the autopsy that might lead an amateur sleuth to any workable conclusions. I advise against it. The report itself is rather gruesome reading. It's not pleasant for a layman."

His superior attitude grated on her. Connie had viewed gruesome crime photos in the past. She often had to decide which pictures her own network could air without offending the public. True, she was not looking forward to seeing the photos of Joy, but she resented Weldon thinking she was too fragile to look at them.

"Weldon, I saw her body. I know how gruesome it is."

"Actually you didn't see her entire body. I know you heard that she was mutilated. Are you certain you want to see the pictures that show the exact puncture wounds? Even the drawings are graphic."

"I'm not an innocent little maiden you need to protect," Connie argued. "I can handle it, or I wouldn't ask to see it. Do you think you can arrange that for me? I haven't called Case yet."

He sighed, and she again could picture his disgusted look of resignation. "You're going to have to call Case yourself. That case belongs to Vancouver Police. It is not part of my jurisdiction, nor part of my homicide investigation."

They fell silent and she waited for him to close the conversation.

"Connie, you should go home," he urged in a quiet voice.

Her heart skipped at the low, almost intimate tone. Was he making the request out of concern for her? Unfortunately she feared he was doing it more in his role of a law enforcement officer—he didn't want her getting in the way of the investigation.

"Weldon, I can't. I wish you'd told me that you were a part of the investigating team," she said, trying to keep her voice from sounding whiny.

"I told you from the first that your sister wasn't the victim of a serial killer. I ascertained that immediately. Both Frank and I agreed on the most probable direction in which to look for the killer." His voice became harder, and she knew where he was headed. "How is your brother-in-law? Is he still having clandestine meetings?"

Connie clutched the phone tightly, almost ready to tap the "off" button. "He was meeting a client that night, for your information. I've asked him about it, and he told me. I'm sure he would have told you, if you'd given him a chance."

"He had the opportunity to be honest from the beginning."

She drew a deep breath. "Look, I don't want to tell you people how to do your jobs, but do you know if Sergeant Case has investigated Dick Farley? Or that guy we saw at the funeral?"

"Will Lonetree is a respected member of the University of British Columbia teaching staff in their Anthropology Department."

"Anthropology?" Connie turned her attention back to the computer and clicked on the folder for Mystics and Myths. British Columbia tribal myths had its own folder. Connie's heart thumped as she opened it. It was empty. She frowned and closed it.

"Having spoken to Lonetree, I hardly think he would hide in the bushes to attack your sister," Weldon said.

"Anthropology could include religion. Ralph said she was getting into these mystic beliefs, like Wiccan or mythology. She was doing research, and I have her books."

"Perhaps." He didn't sound convinced

Her gaze fell on another folder she had kept on the computer desktop. The Lair. "Do you know if Case is investigating her online connections as well?"

"Online connections?" Weldon sounded surprised.

"I stumbled across some strange people in an Internet chat room this afternoon. They all thought she was still alive."

He paused a moment before answering. "That

should rule them out as suspects."

"Not quite. One person seemed to know that her account should no longer be active."

"Her account? What were you doing on her account?" His voice rose in exasperation again. "Connie, don't start playing decoy or pretending to be her. That could get you in trouble."

Naturally Mr. Straight-and-Narrow wouldn't approve. "Don't lecture me, Weldon."

"Somebody needs to," he retorted. "This whole idea of going through the autopsy and the police records is foolish."

"I'm going to do it. I'm calling Sergeant Case as soon as we hang up to make the appointment." She probably should not have childishly warned him, but she feared him telling Case she was in Vancouver so the sergeant could put her off.

"You're making a mistake," he admonished, and his voice actually dropped to a softer level. "Connie, you're too close to this case."

"I'd rather be too close than do nothing at all."

****

"Do you have a dollar to spare?" The scruffy man wrapped in a torn blanket approached Connie as she jammed coins into the meter beside Vancouver Police Headquarters. A faded cardboard sign hung around his neck. "Hungry and Homeless."

The man's sudden appearance startled her. Connie nearly hugged the parking meter as though it might serve as a defensive weapon. His bearded face was placid, his shoulders stooped. He held out a grubby, scrawny hand.

With shaking fingers, Connie fished an American dollar bill out of her purse and handed it to him. Such scenes were probably normal in this part of the city, but as he turned and walked away, she found herself looking around more carefully. All her senses were alert. The building squatted on the corner of a dingy block on the eastern edge of the downtown area. Masses of people bustled along the sidewalk as though they had some place they needed to be ten minutes ago. Despite the crowd, she felt alone and vulnerable. Several times she met the eyes of someone watching her, and it sent a quaver of fear through her. Was that person following her? When Connie almost crashed into determined, fast moving commuters as she crossed the sidewalk from her car to the front door, she had to fight quick bouts of paranoia. No one knew she was here except Weldon, Ralph, and Sergeant Case. She should not be in danger.

What was it about this city that frightened her? She'd once loved to wander along the waterfront and or stroll down busy streets to find unusual shops or colorful bistros. On this trip being out of her hotel room held little appeal.

Connie breathed a sigh of relief when she arrived inside the cavernous entry area. A grim, stocky policeman in uniform sat at the front desk directing foot traffic. A harried young woman, also in a blue uniform, worked to his right, shoving papers into bins, while several others behind the high desk answered a barrage of ringing phones. She gave her name to the officer and was told Sergeant Case was expecting her. The young female officer came out from behind the desk and led her down the hall to a wide doorway that opened into a large, open room.

Connie followed the woman through a maze of desks. The room was the size of a massive warehouse and buzzed with activity. Officers sat at desks talking to each other, some spoke on the phone, while others tapped computer keys. It reminded her of the cable newsroom where she worked.

For an instant, she felt eyes on her and glanced around. She shook her head. No, no one was looking at her. They were engrossed in their work.

She spotted Case and the thin, balding police sergeant walked forward to greet her with a toothy smile. In a spotted rust-colored shirt with a blue tie that didn't match his blue pants, he wasn't exactly the picture of sartorial splendor. Hopefully his investigative skills were more advanced than his sense of fashion.

"Miss Romero." He held out a bony hand.

She shook it and followed him to a metal desk. He gestured toward a chair and she perched on the edge. Her eyes drifted over the desk to the manila folder with Joy's name in big letters on the front.

"How may I help you?" he asked, long thin fingers tapping the folder. "You said something about viewing the police reports? Is there a reason?"

"I...want to see the pictures, the autopsy," she said, licking her lips which had suddenly become very dry. "I understand that I'm allowed."

He paused, fingers still on the folder claiming possession. His voice droned, "Yes, you are, but I wouldn't recommend it. If it's the investigation you're worried about, that we might miss something, I can assure you my men and I are very thorough."

She swallowed her frustration. "It's not that. I've been checking around on my own..."

His long face drew into a frown, and a deep furrow crossed his brow. "That isn't a wise idea."

She held up her hand and nodded. "I know. Inspector Weldon already warned me."

He attempted a smile, but it didn't reach his placid brown eyes. "Miss Romero, we'll catch your sister's killer. We have several theories we're investigating."

"Like Ralph?" She fought to keep accusation out of her tone. "He's your main suspect, isn't he?"

He sat up straight and held up a large hand. "I can't go into details of what we've uncovered, but we have reasons for our suspicions."

"I can't imagine what they are. As I've told Weldon, Ralph is no killer, and if he's the primary focus, you're letting the real killer escape. There's Dick Farley, one of her competitors at work."

Again the hand came up, like a stop sign. "Miss Romero, I'm aware of Mr. Farley, but I've found nothing to implicate him."

"But you've found reasons to suspect Ralph?" she asked pointedly.

"I'm not going to discuss evidence with you." Case's eyes narrowed, and his head shook so rapidly that strands of his plastered-down, thinning hair shifted like sticky ribbons. "When we make an arrest and the case goes to trial it will all come out."

The man was like Weldon—a by-the-book policeman. He was not going to be forthcoming about why he suspected Ralph. But she could still help her innocent brother-in-law by finding the real killer.

"I understand. May I see the pictures?" Connie looked toward the folder.

He drew a deep breath and lifted it. "I can put you into an interrogation room to view them. You're not allowed to take anything. You may see them, but we will not make copies."

"I understand. Maybe I might notice something that might help your investigation."

Doubt was written on his face, but he did not push it. Instead he lifted the folder and motioned with his head for her to follow him. He led her back down the wide hall to a narrow door. He opened it and gestured her toward a metal table in the center.

"You'll have privacy in here. It's where we normally conduct interviews. I would stay and go through the pictures with you, but I have a meeting. You can turn in the folder to the woman at the front desk when you're finished. She'll check to make certain all the pictures are there. I'll also need to give her your handbag, cell phone, and coat before you view the photos."

"My handbag…" but even as she asked and before he answered, she knew why.

"Let's just say we don't want any unauthorized photos leaving this building."

He put the folder on the table and pulled out a metal chair. It scraped eerily on the tile floor. She took off her coat and handed it to him, along with her purse. "My cell phone is in my purse."

He glanced inside and then with a final nod, he left the room.

Connie sat at the table, drew a deep breath, closed her eyes, and opened the folder.

****

Rain spattered against the floor-to-ceiling windows in torrents, hiding a view that on most days would be breathtaking. Heavy clouds and a driving rain kept visibility to a minimum. Even the choppy waters of Burrard Inlet were barely in evidence. The North Shore with its suburbs that crept up a string of steep mountains showed only as a shadowy promise.

Mitch Weldon sat in a wooden booth across from Connie, studying her. Despite his desire to keep his relationship with her totally professional, part of him ached at the sight of her vulnerable face. He clasped his hands in his lap to keep from reaching across the table and pushing away the strand of dark hair that hung across her cheek.

Large ceramic bowls of steaming soup rested untouched on the table in front of them. A basket of hot bread with small tubs of butter sat in the center. A gaunt waitress plopped down two cups of coffee on the table and vanished.

With a shaking hand, Connie lifted a spoonful of vegetable soup to her lips, but Weldon noticed she barely sipped it, as though she had little sense of appetite. After the morning she'd had, she probably didn't have one.

The warm scent of clam chowder drifted up to him and he picked up his spoon and attacked the creamy mixture. His own sense of appetite was acute. The brisk weather always seemed to do that to him.

Obviously he had been correct about her venture to look at the pictures of her dead sister. Her face was nearly the same color as the clam chowder, and her eyes were lifeless as they gazed down at the tabletop.

He had tried to warn her about the graphic pictures. He hated that the Police Department was required to allow relatives to view that sort of gory evidence if they requested. He'd viewed hundreds of similar pictures over the course of his career, but every set could leave him shaken if he didn't adopt a non-personal attitude from the start.

Joy Perkins' photos were brutal. Nothing could have prepared her for them. The memory of the color shots of blood puddled on her sister's lifeless body would probably stay with Connie for a long time. Joy's hair was matted, her bloodless face barely recognizable. Her contorted body stretched across mud and leaves in an obscene pose. The slits on her torso were jagged and obscene. How many of them had Connie viewed before giving up?

He'd arrived at the police station shortly after her, entering the viewing area beside the interrogation room. He watched her without her knowledge as Connie took one look at the first graphic picture and grasped her mid-section as though she wanted to vomit.

The shocked look on her face sent a tremor through him, a surprising ripple of sadness and guilt for letting her attempt this. He had to remind himself he had no control over her. He had tried to dissuade her. She insisted. Now maybe she would realize the futility of her proclamation that she could investigate this case.

A tear slid down her cheek and she wiped it away with fingers that trembled. This was more difficult to watch than viewing the photos. Bile rose in his throat and nausea roiled in his stomach. She turned one picture over and gasped at the next.

Oh, hell, he couldn't let this go on. As she placed her hands over the photo, he lurched out of the room and jerked open the door to the interrogation room. Big swaths of tears stained her cheeks and she looked up, pale and shocked. The folder was closed. He put his hand on her shoulder, which was shaking and squeezed it. She attempted to wipe the tears from her cheeks as though she didn't want him to see them.

"Let's get out of here," he said, taking hold of a frigid, clammy hand and helping her to her feet. For once, Connie didn't argue. She simply let him take her arm and lead her out of the room.

Shocked at his own volatile reaction to her distress, he had not known what to do as he guided her down the hall. As she had been the day he'd seen her in the park, she moved like a wispy form without substance. He sat her on a bench in the hall and brought her water and then returned to the room to retrieve the photos.

The haunted look remained when he returned with her coat and purse. She sat still as a statue, so he recommended lunch and brought her to a restaurant near the station. She probably was not hungry after seeing those horrible photographs, but his intention had been to get her away from the police station and anything that might be a memory of her sister's death.

"Feeling better?" he asked.

"A little," she said, attempting another mouthful

of soup. This time she actually took a sip.

The smell of tomatoes mixed with basil reached him. He had recommended the minestrone and this time she took a full spoon into her mouth.

"This is good. How's the clam chowder?"

He nodded appreciatively as he swallowed. "Very good. You should have tried it. Actually all the food here is very good." He tried to smile, but he didn't feel jovial and it felt stiff and forced on his lips.

Now that they were away from the police station, he realized how strained and awkward they both were. He could never have pictured himself sitting across from her on a social occasion—not that he socialized with anyone that much. Anyone looking at them might mistake this as a business lunch or perhaps something personal. She was dressed informally in a white turtleneck sweater and brown corduroy pants. Her thick hair was pulled severely into a clip at the back of her head, away from the delicate features of her sad face. He wore his normal khaki pants, a tweed sport jacket and a light green striped shirt that his sister had bought him because she said it brought out the green shades in his eyes.

Her glance traveled around the homey restaurant as though seeing it for the first time. Under other circumstances they might have enjoyed the atmosphere. The scent of frying hamburgers filled the air, though the dishes being carried from the kitchen were laden with everything from pot roast to salads. The restaurant was housed in an older renovated building along the waterfront and retained the wood floors and the high ceilings of the past. Polished wood panels came up half the wall. The tables were painted various shades of blue with sheets of white butcher paper serving as table cloths. A long counter stretched along the front, and police officers in uniform occupied most of the stools.

"I can't decide if this is a tourist trap or police hangout," she said, a touch of a smile lifting her lips.

He was pleased to see a hint of color return to her cheeks. "Both. I bring visitors for lunch and often meet colleagues here."

"Colleagues?" she said and this time she smiled fully and life leaped back into the depths of her eyes.

A sudden, sharp alarm seemed to go off inside him, as strange and unusual as the tug at his emotions when he'd been watching her in the room. He licked his lips and swallowed hard, uncertain of what to say.

"You mean, like friends?" she said and though her laugh was quick, it was a laugh.

She always teased him about being stiff and at times it grew irritating, but this time it actually pleased him.

"Well, yes," he said. Their eyes held and then she looked away, a pinkish tinge rising in her cheeks. He dropped his gaze as well, aware he'd actually been holding his breath, as though waiting for something.

For a few minutes they concentrated on their food. The soup was good and hearty, very welcome on such a cold, miserable day. The bread was warm and crusty, and a tub of soft herb butter provided a welcome addition.

Connie broke off a small chunk of bread, buttered it in deliberate motions and then lifted it to her lips. She chewed slowly as though relishing the taste. He watched her, pleased that her appetite might be returning, that she might be able to tease, even if he was to be the brunt.

A shadow seemed to cross her face as Connie put down her bread. "Tell me something, Weldon. Why do you guys suspect Ralph so strongly?"

He had just taken a sip of coffee, and he nearly

choked on the hot liquid. Why was she back to discussing the case? He had hoped she had learned why it made no sense for someone who wasn't a trained professional to get involved. "You'll have to ask Sergeant Case that. I'm not privy to that information."

"Oh, puh-lease," she said, rolling her eyes. "Like hell. You are giving me the runaround and telling me I don't need to investigate. Has it occurred to you that if you were honest with me, and told me why he's such a strong suspect, maybe I'd agree and just go away?"

He drew a deep breath. "Would you?"

"If I really thought he did it, I might." Her expressive eyes grew hard, challenging.

Case would probably chastise him for this, but perhaps she would stop this silly investigation idea before it went any further. Besides, all he had was preliminary information, the sort they used to begin a deeper investigation. "Did you know that Perkins is in trouble at work? That he's in danger of losing his job?"

Her eyes widened slightly in disbelief and then lowered, her brow furrowing as though she was thinking it through. "Joy never mentioned anything like that."

He started to say that Joy probably would not have wanted her family to know, but Connie was shaking her head.

"No, no. Last time he lost a job they took out a loan to get them through. Maybe that's why Joy was working so hard."

"Maybe this time he couldn't," Weldon said, wondering how much he should divulge. "He had not paid off the last loan. Maybe this time he took out a big insurance policy instead."

Connie dropped her spoon into the soup and it sent up small, red splashes onto the tabletop. She jerked her head up in surprise. "You can't be serious."

"Frank checked into it," he admitted.

"And?"

He put down his spoon. "I don't think I should discuss this with you. You need to drop the matter and let Frank do his job and solve this murder."

A smug smile touched her full lips, sending a small shudder of physical awareness coursing through him. He needed to stop looking at them and then her words registered.

"Oh, yeah, well, I may do it first."

As much in defense of his own wayward thoughts as her haughtiness, his face relaxed into a sardonic smile. "Really?" He left unstated the reminder that she couldn't even look at the police report without becoming ill.

Connie lowered her gaze to the ceramic bowl as though she found the carrots and pasta that floated in it fascinating, and Weldon felt an immediate pang of guilt.

"Forgive me. That was unfair," he said quietly.

Her small face grew determined, though she didn't lift her eyes. "There are ways to investigate without having to deal with grisly photos and reports."

"I suppose," he replied stiffly.

"I've investigated people and situations before. For instance I've started checking the financial records for Dick Farley. Since real estate sales and tax records are public documents, I have access to them. For instance, he owns a number of properties that he's been unable to sell and he's behind on his taxes. He's been buying and flipping houses, you know, where you buy a fixer-upper and resell at a big profit? Well, I guess his business isn't going well."

"How would that translate into a motive?"

"If she's out of the way, a good part of his competition is gone. He might pick up her listings. That would make him money. And there might be something shady to his deals that she knew about, like contractor kickbacks."

He could see that she was reaching, but he said nothing. Let her keep checking records.

"Besides," she rushed on. "There are other suspects. I told you about those strange people on the Internet."

She sounded so hopeful he didn't have the heart to burst her bubble. Anonymous computer contacts were harmless. "I thought they didn't know she was dead."

The corner of her lip twitched in irritation. "Well..."

He turned to gaze out the window to avoid her eyes. She was going to run into a brick wall with her fanciful conjectures, but that was fine. It would take time and give Frank the opportunity to complete his work. He had only one caution. "If you continue investigating that, you shouldn't pretend to be Joy. If she was a target, that person will know. It could be dangerous."

Her lips twitched, and she smiled fully for the first time since coming out of the interview room. "Weldon, are you worried about me?"

His cheeks grew hot as he jerked his gaze back to her. Normally he might ignore her teasing, but he found the sudden sparkle in her eyes a pleasant change from the earlier haunted look. Clearing his throat he attempted to keep the conversation professional. "I'm trying to keep the investigation where it belongs. In my experience, unless there's evidence in another area, an inquiry starts with the inner circle and widens from there."

"You don't think the Internet friends are any more to blame than those mystic religions," she stated.

"They're both far-fetched premises," he noted with a shrug.

"What if she met someone online who was into something kinky?" she said in a voice gone playful. "Something erotic. You know people get into strange Internet relationships all the time. Bondage, masochism, phone sex, cybersex. Haven't you ever checked out the illicit offerings on the Internet?"

Weldon blinked again, saying nothing. He could see what she was doing—baiting him—as she often did. Did she fool around like some people did on the Internet? Posting sexy photos? A sudden image of her in a filmy low-cut night gown seared his brain. Warmth rushed through him, igniting nerve endings he hadn't felt come alive in a while. Whoa!

He jerked his gaze from her and broke off a piece of bread and smeared it with butter, not bothering to reply. Hell, he wasn't certain he could.

Luckily when she spoke, all the teasing was gone from her tone. "Had you or Sergeant Case thought of that?"

He drew a quick breath, ready to go back to the discussion of the investigation. He chewed thoughtfully on his bread and then swallowed. "I can have Frank look into it. It's more practical to think if she met someone on the computer, she was leaving her husband and he refused to let her go. Perkins said she was inattentive. People in her office and his said the two were having marital problems. Perhaps she meant to share that information with you and your sister that weekend. Didn't you say that she had something she wanted to tell you?"

Her cheeks turned pink and her eyes glazed over. Guilt prickled at his insides. He had taken her light comments and turned them around. He started to apologize and then stopped. That might turn the conversation personal again. Keeping her at arm's level was safer.

"Not Ralph," she argued. "Do you really think he followed us to Vancouver to kill her?"

He flung his hands open. "What better place? It's outside the United States' jurisdiction. I'm certain he could find reasons it would work to his advantage. Perhaps he knew of the slashing cases and thought this would simply be lumped into that group."

Connie shook her head. "I don't think so. If it was someone close to her, you're much better off looking at Dick Farley."

He didn't consider Farley a suspect, but what if she unwittingly stirred up trouble by looking through the man's dealings and angered him? "Have you talked to Farley? If you think he should be a suspect, is that wise? It could put you in danger."

"Ah, worried again," she teased, a soft giggle escaping her. She put her fingers over her lips, clearly embarrassed. A soft pink flushed her cheekbones.

Weldon turned away, not answering, not certain how to answer. No wonder he was always being accused of being lacking in social skills. And this sudden turn with her from an impersonal family member to—what? Someone he wanted to get to know better? Maybe on a personal level? He shook his head as though to cast off that thought and then realized she had taken that gesture as the answer to her teasing question. The warm glow left her eyes.

"That's why I haven't talked to him personally." Her tone grew serious. "I don't want him to know I'm looking into his dealings. I have more research to do before I talk to him. Let's go back to your serial killer. What about him? Have you totally ruled out the Slasher?"

Her sudden change in direction caught him off guard, but he quickly shook his head in disagreement. "It's not the same. That madman is dumping bodies in Stanley Park. He's a coward and is not looking for victims there and certainly not in broad daylight."

"But he mutilates his victims? Isn't that his MO?" she asked.

He drew back, finding himself suddenly amused at her earnest question and attempt to use American television police jargon. "MO? As in Modus Operandi? Are you asking me as an amateur detective seeking answers on her sister's death? That question sounds suspiciously like a certain journalist I've had to deal with in the past."

A quick laugh escaped her. "Weldon, I'm shocked. You're making a joke, actually demonstrating a sense of humor."

He wiped crumbs from his hands. "That's one thing I have never been accused of having. But seriously, please don't think that my investigation—and I hate the title that the papers have given it—that it has anything to do with your sister or that I purposely misled you. I determined your sister's death wasn't part of my case, and I didn't want you to think it could be."

His admission was accompanied by a total avoidance of her eyes. He wanted to apologize for misleading her, but he had confidential information he could not reveal.

"She could still have been the victim of a serial killer," Connie protested, though not as vehemently as before. "There have been other killings. I found a jogger in Portland who was murdered. There could be others."

"More research on the Internet?"

Connie shrugged. "I'm good at research."

The thought of her sitting at her desk, researching on the Internet pleased him. It would keep her out of harm's way. "Fine, stick to that. If you uncover anything unusual, bring it to me or Case. I don't want to see you get in over your head."

"Well, goodness, Weldon, I'm beginning to think you might even like me."

Again his cheeks grew warm, and he dropped his face and lifted his coffee mug to his lips, hiding his eyes behind it.

Like her? He had always liked her, but now he was beginning to think there was more to his feelings. He had never been in this position before, and he wasn't certain what to do about it.

****

The silence hit her first, as Connie stepped from her car in the misty park. The parking spot was just above where she and Joy had parted moments before her sister met her doom. A dense fog hugged the treetops and while the rain had stopped, a thick mist dampened her skin.

A sudden cry from a seagull overhead sent her heart racing and then the stillness returned, closing around her like a compacting waste receptacle. Connie walked along the path and stepped under the shelter of the trees. The brush was trampled, but the crime tape was gone.

A thin ribbon of dread ran through her. Connie could stop, she knew. She didn't have to continue. But the pictures had defeated her. If she truly intended to investigate this crime, she couldn't be afraid to get her hands dirty. She needed to remember Joy. Thoughts of Joy jogging so happily through the park one minute and then being so brutally attacked the next were horrifying. Those pictures had been terrible. It would be a long time before she could get those visions out of her head. But they also made her more determined to find the culprit.

Connie moved forward, passed a shredded yellow ribbon that clung to a tree branch—the only evidence left that this had once been a police crime scene. Maybe she should have told Weldon she was coming here. He might not have approved, but she could probably have talked him into making the trip with her. He said he had the afternoon free.

A branch cracked below her foot, and the sound might have been a rifle burst. She paused for a second before continuing. As Connie stepped into the clearing where her sister had died, she froze. The branches on the other side of the clearing began to sway, and she heard the crackling of breaking branches as someone ran through the brush away from her.

Connie ran through the clearing, hurrying after the cracking sounds. The crackling stopped, replaced by thudding footsteps. Seconds later she reached a path through the interior of the park. Following a pair of muddy footprints until she reached the main road, she arrived in time to see a burgundy van pulling away from the curb.

The British Columbia plates started with BCE, but the van disappeared around a corner before she could memorize the rest.

Chapter Six

"Is Inspector Weldon in?" Connie hunched over her cell phone in her car, water dripping from her raincoat onto the cold skin of her hands and neck as she shook off her hood. Her hands shook wildly, and her breath came fast and uneven. She should have taken the phone with her when she went into the park. Instead she'd had to run back to her car to call Weldon and tell him about the person who had run from the site of Joy's death.

"I'll check," said the crisp voice at the other end of the line.

Rain thumped noisily on the roof of the car. Waiting annoyed Connie, but she'd received no answer on Weldon's cell. His direct line had gone straight to voice mail. The only alternative was calling the main number and requesting to speak to him.

"The Inspector has the day off," the voice said.

Frustration washed over her. "I need to reach him. Can you beep him?"

"I suppose." Now the voice began to sound irritated. "Is this an emergency? Would you like to talk to someone else?"

"No, I want to talk to the inspector. Can you beep him?" Connie read out her cell phone number and hung up before the voice could protest. She flipped the phone shut, shoved off her wet coat and sat back to watch the rain splash over the window and think about her close call in the woods.

She hadn't seen much of the man who ran away. Wait, how did she even know it was a man?

Summoning all her powers of observation, Connie ran through everything that she had witnessed since getting out of the car. Most of the time, the person had been nothing but an elusive shadow. Not even a shadow. More like a blur, always moving. The muddy footprints she'd followed had been big. Much bigger than most women's feet. The crashing through the bushes had been loud, like a larger man.

Her cell phone chirped. It might as well have been a bullhorn in the closed-in surroundings of the car. Jumping, she fumbled to find it.

"Connie? Is something wrong?" Weldon's voice sent a wave of welcome relief through her, slowing her pulse which had been sent racing by the ringing phone.

"I'm at the park where Joy died. There was someone there at the site. He took off when he saw me."

His intake of breath was sharp. "Have you called Case?"

"Well, no. I wasn't certain if it meant anything." Actually she had not even considered calling Case. Reaching Weldon had been the first thought that came into her head.

"So you called me. I'm so lucky."

His voice sounded slightly sarcastic, and normally she might have teased him for being amusing. Not this time. Only now was her breath beginning to slow.

"Where are you right now?" he added.

"I'm still at the park in the Brockton Point parking lot, just on the other side of where her body was found."

"Listen carefully. Don't leave there, but stay in your car and lock the door. I'll be there in ten minutes," he ordered in a crisp voice.

"You're that close?" she asked in surprise.

"Actually I'm on the other side of the park."

"Another slasher case?" she asked, swallowing a gulp. Visions of a new body, torn and ravaged and left in a bloody clump of leaves and pine needles raced through her head.

"I'm walking my dog. I'm off today."

"Your dog?" Connie had never known anything personal about Weldon. The discovery that he had a dog shocked her. It seemed so...well...normal, ordinary. She thought of him as a button-down, lace up the boots type of guy. Almost robotic. Turn him on, he went to work and caught criminals. The thought that he had a dog made him more human.

He did not respond to her note of surprise. He simply repeated, "Ten minutes."

Connie closed her phone. Fog formed a screen on her front windshield so that no one could see her. But it also stopped her from seeing out in case someone might be approaching. Using a tissue, she wiped the foggy front window so she could see better. The rain was lessening. Why was Weldon walking his dog in the park on such a rainy day? She had a feeling he was investigating at the same time. Maybe looking for fresh victims? Or thinking about how the slasher was able to dump his bodies without being spotted? She'd have to check on their locations when she got back to her computer.

Connie checked her makeup in the mirror, realizing she was looking forward to seeing Weldon even though she'd only left him after their lunch two hours ago. She put on fresh lipstick, dotted powder on her cheeks, and ran a brush through her hair. She wanted to look better than the sorry sight she had presented over lunch.

A slight splash of guilt washed over her, knowing that he had given up his day off to be at police headquarters when she looked at Joy's photos. Had he known how she would react to them? Thinking back, he had been very gallant at lunch, only once even hinting about her moments of weakness.

Now it appeared she was suffering from more moments of weakness in her quest to find Joy's killer. If only she'd been able to run faster she might have been able to see the man who had shown such an interest in her sister's death site. Could it have been a curious onlooker? Then why had he run when she approached? Didn't that indicate guilt?

A boxy green SUV splashed into the parking lot and pulled to a stop beside her. Weldon emerged and opened her passenger door and slid inside. He had changed from his earlier formal attire and now wore a nylon jacket, corduroy slacks, and a turtleneck sweater. On his feet he wore jogging shoes.

"Where's the dog?" she asked with a smile, stretching around to look for an animal.

His lean face was set, not in the mood for frivolity. Despite the casual wear, he was still carrying the stiff aura of officialdom. "He's in the car. Tell me where you saw this person."

Twisting toward the window, Connie pointed toward the thicket of trees where she had entered the woods. "Over there. I walked over from this side to the place where her body was found. Apparently he was parked on the other side because he ran that way. I followed him, and saw his car pulling away."

"Show me," he ordered.

She pulled on her raincoat and jerked the hood over her head as she emerged from the car. Weldon followed her lead and together they walked across the street, under the canopy of Douglas Fir trees and into the thickly wooded grove. Cold enveloped her with the force of an arctic gale as though she was walking on a glacier in a bikini. The rain had stopped, but its remnants dripped from the thick branches. Thick drops thudded hollowly on her hood. He walked slowly, head swiveling from one direction to the next as though taking it all in.

At the site where Joy died, he paused only briefly. Connie studied it again. Having seen the pictures, she knew exactly where the body had fallen among the wet leaves, shrubs, and pine needles. Her sister's blood probably still soaked part of the muddy ground.

"Where was he?" Weldon asked, turning to face her.

Connie pointed beyond the clearing and walked with him to where torn branches signaled the man's path to escape. She indicated the muddy trail and started to comment on how big the footprints were, but rain had washed away most of them. Others were smudged to her horror, by her own footprints leading away and back to the murder scene.

Weldon said nothing, though the frown that creased his lean face said it all. Again, he merely took his time, stepping around the area, eyes fixed on the path and then examining the broken branches. As she followed him, Connie caught sight of a broken branch that held two limp strands of yarn.

"Is this anything," she asked, pulling it from the branch and looking closely at the red and brown colors. She held it out to him between her gloved fingers.

He studied it, brow furrowed. He touched the branch where she had found it and shook his head. "That could have been left by any hiker going through this area." He gauged the distance from the tree to the footprints, eyes narrowing. "I doubt the man would have gone that close to the tree."

"Unless he didn't see the branch sticking out. See, this part of the branch snapped off," she pointed at the bent twig.

"Maybe." He pulled a plastic bag from his jacket pocket and slipped the strands of yarn into it.

"You keep those with you?" she asked.

"Always." His smile was grim, and then a look of surprise came over his eyes. He reached inside his jacket and pulled out his cell phone.

"Damn," he muttered as he studied the small screen.

"What is it?"

"Emergency." His face grew hard and paled slightly. He slipped the phone back under his jacket. "I have to go."

"Slasher?" she asked as he began walking rapidly back up the path toward their cars.

"Who knows? But I better get over there. I wouldn't worry about this. I doubt it was the killer returning to the scene of the crime. That's more publicity than truth. I'll take the fibers to Case. They might have been missed in the earlier sweep of the area." They came out of the underbrush and he issued a curse.

"Damn, I forgot about Bruno."

"Bruno?" She followed the direction of his gaze. His car windows were fogged over except where a dark head pressed against the back window. The dog began to bark when Weldon came into view.

"I can't leave him in the car all afternoon, and this is going to take a while." He glanced at his watch.

"Do you want me to take him home for you?" Connie offered.

He stopped as he hurried toward the car and turned to look at her in surprise. "Would you? I'd appreciate it."

"Sure."

Before she had a chance to realize the folly of her offer, or to renege, he reached into his pocket and pulled a key ring from it. He singled out a key and removed it from the ring.

"This opens the back door. The alarm is right

next to the door and I'll write down the alarm code and instructions on how to get there while you get acquainted with Bruno." He opened the back door of his SUV and the big dog hopped out as though it had been kept inside too long. It bounded immediately to Connie and sniffed at the edge of her raincoat.

She leaned over toward it, patting the top of his head and letting him smell her fingers. "Hi there, Bruno."

The dog was a brown and white Irish Setter and very friendly. Pushing back her hood, she leaned over and rubbed its silky ears. The big dog rewarded her with a wet, sloppy kiss.

"He likes you," Weldon pointed out with a soft chuckle.

"I've always been a big dog lover," Connie admitted, leaning her cheek close to the dog to feel its soft fur. "I just can't keep any animals because I'm on the road so much."

She and Bruno continued their get acquainted session while Weldon made a quick call, then wrote up a note with his address and the alarm code. Within minutes she was leading Bruno over to her car, instructions from Weldon on how to get to his house in her hand.

The dog was well behaved once it was in her car, settling onto the seat in the back while she began to decipher Weldon's instructions which had been scrawled on a piece of his police notebook.

The inspector lived on the north side, and she guided her car out of the park and onto Lions Gate Bridge, the towering structure that separated the city from the North Shore. The going was slow since the afternoon rush had started. Connie was tempted to turn around and go back through the park one more time and find out where the inspector was. He had not said so but Connie suspected he'd been called to a slasher dumping. Her curiosity was high, but she had promised to take his dog home first. She would do that.

The house was a small, neat bungalow right above Highway 1A, the main road that led north out of the city into the northern part of British Columbia. Sitting on a hill, its wide front window held the promise of a great view of the bridge and Stanley Park to the south. She parked and let the dog into the backyard. Bruno bounded away, loping across the lawn, happy to be home. Should she just leave him there?

The backyard did not have a dog house, so maybe he wanted the dog put inside in case it started to rain, or perhaps even snow. The heavy winter clouds that hung overhead could go either way. Pale light shone from a brick and glass structure at the back of the yard. Perhaps that was where he kept him. Connie walked over to it, but the door was locked. She tried to see inside the glass walls and gulped.

Several rows of brightly colored flowers lined the walls. A greenhouse? Weldon had a greenhouse? She would never have pegged him for that. Bruno whimpered and licked at her hand. He wanted to go inside so she walked back to the house and unlocked the back door. Bruno brushed past her into the house, his toenails clicking on the tiled kitchen floor.

A warning beep from the alarm system rang through the house and Connie quickly punched in the code to turn it off. Was he used to giving this out? Now she could get into his house. Certainly a police officer would be more careful than that. Did it mean he trusted her? What else could it mean? That they were establishing a personal relationship? She smiled to herself, finding she liked that thought.

Bruno whimpered and nudged her toward a plastic container with a twin set of bowls.

"Thirsty, Bruno?" she asked, picking up the

bowls.

She poured water on one side and searched the kitchen cabinets for dog food. The kitchen was well stocked, the dishes all neatly placed. She told herself she wasn't being nosy; she was searching for dog food. Connie finally found it on the lower level of the pantry that took up the corner of one wall. She filled the bowl around Bruno's head, and he began wolfing it down. Now that she was inside, her duties completed, Connie found herself looking around. Somehow she had known that Weldon would be as neat about his home as he was about his appearance. The house offered a whole new picture of the stiff, tidy man.

The kitchen was austere and spotless as a cleanser commercial. It held no wall hangings, no signs of a bulletin board with recipes tacked on it like her own kitchen, no oven mittens or kitchen towels hanging crookedly on racks. The small room appeared large and airy, thanks to a row of windows that peered into the backyard providing a view toward the mountains. A teak kitchen table and matching chairs sat in front of the window. The cabinets were light wood and the white, tiled counters were bare except for a silver coffeemaker and matching blender. She doubted he made margaritas in the blender. Probably he mixed power shakes. A door at the end of the room was open and she caught a glimpse of Bruno's large basket with a lime green blanket beside the edges of a washing machine.

Connie ventured out of the kitchen while Bruno crunched on his dog food. A modest formal dining area held a table with two silver candlesticks in the center. A large hutch took up the end of the room, and much to her surprise its glass windows showcased crystal glassware and a delicately-patterned china service. The rich maple wood gleamed, even in the dim gray light of the afternoon.

The living room looked out toward the narrow street, and if it offered an awesome view, it was hidden by the thick layer of clouds. Like the rest of the house it was spotless but plain. An entertainment center took up much of one wall and against the other was a sofa and a brown leather reclining chair that showed the only signs of wear. A lamp table with books and magazines on a lower shelf sat beside it. Several remote controls sat on the table. She had a hunch this was where Weldon spent his leisure time, if he had leisure time.

She peered into an entry way. Two doors along the hall were open. Through the first door she could see a mahogany bookcase and the edge of a desk. An office, most likely. The other door opened into a compact bathroom.

The closed door in the back drew her attention, but she wasn't going there. She guessed that was the bedroom and that was a little more than she wanted to know about Weldon. So far she had not seen any glimpses of a woman's touch in the house, except the crystal and china, and that could have been left over from a previous marriage. She knew he was single, but was he also unattached? Or gay? Why should she care?

But she knew, didn't she? While the whole morning had been cold and gloomy as the day, he had been the only bright spot, hurrying her out of the police station, providing her with soup and coffee, even if she hadn't tasted anything. Something inside her had come to life when he joked, and for once his smile had reached those bright green eyes, making them dance like sparkling emeralds. A dimple appeared in one lean cheek. The sight sent a quick ripple of awareness through her that she still felt. It had been a while since a man had raised that sort of reaction just from his looks.

Connie walked into the office. Like the living room it faced the front of the house. Painted a light gray with heavy mahogany furniture, it gave the feeling of somberness. A bookcase stood against the wall opposite the door, with a desk in front. Opposite it, beside the door was a mahogany door flush with the wall. Was it a wet bar? She was tempted to check, but the back wall drew her interest instead. Pictures, all neatly lined up, were placed above two half-bookcases. She walked over to examine them. Weldon stood beside an older man in a blue police uniform. Another showed him and several others all dressed in police blue, complete with hats and white gloves. Were they friends? Relatives?

Her fingers drifted over the book shelves. He had a taste for mystery, the Canadian west, and true crime. His small wooden desk was neat with all his papers in a bin. His computer was a laptop, similar to the one she'd had stolen. Connie touched the connected mouse and the screen came alive.

She was about to peer at it closer when movement through the front window caught her eye. A car cruised past the house at a high rate of speed. She stared at it as it barreled by. A burgundy van! She hurried to the front window but didn't make it in enough time to see the license plate. It careened around the corner and was gone.

Could it have been the same van? Had it followed her here? Would it follow when she left? Suddenly she was in no rush to leave. Weldon probably wouldn't mind if she brought in her laptop and did some research at his desk. The thought of being in a house with an alarm system was suddenly very appealing.

****

Mitch found himself smiling as he turned into his driveway and saw Connie's Honda parked in front of the garage doors. Earlier she had called to ask if she could stay and work on her computer. She said she had seen a van similar to the one in Stanley Park. He didn't know if she was imagining things, but he agreed to let her stay as long as she wanted.

He had not expected to remain working until eight o'clock, and he had not expected her to wait. Had he hoped she might? He had been thinking about her a lot when he was walking Bruno before she called. Only a busy afternoon had kept away thoughts of her.

He parked beside her car and hopped up the back steps to the house. Bruno met him at the door, and the warm, inviting scent of beef stew greeted him, making his stomach rumble. The clam chowder from lunch had long since been forgotten.

A Dutch oven sat on the stove over a very low fire, the source of the delicious smell.

"Hello?" he called, but there was no answer.

He put down his briefcase and walked into the dining room. The sight of her stretched out on his sofa brought a quick round of fear. "Connie?"

Her body jerked, and her eyes fluttered open. She had been sleeping. As Connie rubbed sleep from her unfocused eyes, his blood grew warm, and his heart rate kicked up a notch. He liked the sight of her curvy body rising from his couch, one cheek pink from resting on a cushion, eyes looking dreamy. Why hadn't he ever noticed her feminine appeal?

"Oh, sorry," she said, blinking rapidly. "I must have dozed off."

He found himself entranced with her movements. He wanted to touch her skin that glowed in the dim light like a golden bottle of ale. Silky black hair fell across her cheek and she shoved it aside. What would that hair feel like in his hands? A tremble of awareness rushed through his lower body.

"I'm sorry I'm late," he apologized, knees

growing weak. "It took longer than I thought."

"I didn't mind. It was nice of you to let me stay."

"Looks like you didn't waste your time. The beef stew smells wonderful. At least I surmised that was what you have cooking."

"You had meat that needed cooking and some aging vegetables in the refrigerator." Her face pointed down, and again his heart thumped. There was something about the way she did that—put her face down modestly—that made his insides leap.

"I don't cook very often," he admitted, shifting uneasily. There was something rather intimate about having her in his house. Even from where he stood he could smell the fresh scent of her perfume, something floral. He first noticed it the day he carried her to the bed in her hotel room. He couldn't identify it. He simply found the scent intoxicating.

She was on her feet—bare feet—he noted. "Are you hungry?" she asked.

"Famished," he admitted with a grin.

"Well, why don't you get cleaned up, and I'll dish up the stew," she ordered with a wide smile that again attacked his inner areas.

Mitch nodded, jotting down his awkward feelings to inexperience with women in his house. How long had it been since he'd been around a woman? More importantly, since he'd wanted to be around a woman?

Sudden memories of Wanda flashed across his mind. Those weren't happy memories, and he didn't want to think about his ex-wife now. Not when some other woman was going to be in his kitchen, fixing him dinner.

"You are staying for dinner, aren't you?" he asked, suddenly fearing she might leave. He felt like he was seventeen, asking the head cheerleader for a date. Why did she make him so alternately excited and then uncertain?

Her quick smile warmed him and dissolved some of his concern. "Of course. I'm in no rush to get back to my lonely hotel room or those thieves who might be lurking in the halls."

Mitch watched her walk to the kitchen, noting the gentle sway of her hips in the form-fitting pants and the tiny waist emphasized by the knit top that clung to her curves before he drew a deep breath and turned toward the bathroom.

He washed his face and hands and rubbed his palm across his face to see if he needed to run a razor over it for the second time that day. No, it wasn't that bad. While a fine line of whiskers rasped across his hand, he didn't want to take the time, and he didn't want to give her the notion that he was out to impress her.

Drying his hands on a towel, he noted that the soap bottle was freshly filled and a small bottle of daisies from his backyard greenhouse sat on the vanity by the sink. He blinked as he turned around. Not only that, his shower curtain was hung. He had hung the inner lining when he bought the set, but somehow he'd never taken the time to hang the dark green curtain itself. It had sat folded on the corner of the vanity for three months.

He felt like he was beaming as he walked down the hall toward the kitchen. He stopped when he heard her humming in the dining room. He turned in that direction. The candles that always sat on the table were lit, and another fresh vase of daisies sat between them.

His mother's china bowls, which hadn't been used since his brother visited in the fall, were on the table filled with rich, thick stew. The colorful straw place mats and linen napkins his mother had given him made for a very cheery setting.

The surprise, though pleasant, left him speechless for a moment. "This is very nice," he finally said, realizing she was watching him with expectant eyes. "Would you like some wine? I have to admit that a good bottle of red is one of my weaknesses."

A bubble of laughter burst from her lips. "Really? Wine, huh, Weldon? I wouldn't have guessed it. But then who would have thought you were a gardener. Your greenhouse is awesome." She placed a basket filled with thick crusty rolls that he bought at the local deli on the table.

Mitch's face grew warm as he leaned over the cabinet where he kept his wine supply. "I enjoy visiting wineries," he admitted. "I've been to most of the British Columbia wineries and a few in Washington. I always come home with several bottles." He examined a couple of bottles and finally settled on a BC Merlot. He took his time opening it, aware of her watching him as he removed the wrapper and pulled out the cork in a smooth motion.

"Normally, it should breathe for half an hour, but this should be fine." He poured a glass for both of them in his mother's crystal glasses and then settled onto a chair.

She gave him a wink, dark lashes sweeping across her cheek. Was it really as soft as it looked? He had never been so tempted to check. What the hell was he thinking? Certainly he had become more and more aware of her since that day she stepped under the police crime tape in the park and got into his car, but today everything had seemed to explode as he watched the tears roll down her cheeks as she viewed those terrible photos. He wasn't certain what was going to happen next or if he should prolong this contact with her. They would probably both be better off if he just sent her home. Instead he fussed with his napkin, pulling it across his lap.

"You have some very nice things," she said, sitting across from him, hazel eyes shimmering in the candlelight.

He'd never really noticed the light flecks in her eyes before. In fact he'd always considered them on the dark side. Or maybe that was usually her mood when she was dealing with him. A strand of black hair teased the front of her shoulder.

"My mother left them to me when she died," he said, lowering his gaze. He needed to stop looking at her. This was getting out of hand. "My brothers and sister were all married, and I was in the process of getting a divorce..." he stopped. Was he babbling? What was wrong with him? "You don't want to hear all my personal problems."

Her quick laugh made his stomach jump. This was getting crazy. One thing was for certain: he would never think of her as just an intriguing annoyance again. He finally admitted to himself that he'd wanted to see her tonight. He had hoped she might stay until he got home.

"I'm good at listening to personal problems," she replied with a shrug. "Lisa says it's my forte. It's why I feel I let Joy down. I listen to everyone else's problems like my producer, Sandy, Lisa, my mother, my dad. I should have had time to listen to Joy."

"You can't be there for everyone," he said quietly, lifting a spoonful of stew to his mouth. The meaty flavors blended with a rich sauce on his tongue. "You're a good cook," he said honestly.

"Sometimes," she acknowledged, her cheeks growing pink. "I don't have time to cook much, not that I have anyone to cook for."

He nodded quickly, noting from her comment that she was alone, but he kept his eyes on his bowl. He was at a loss for conversation, but the words seemed to pop out of his mouth. "Any other talents I should know about?"

"I'm very handy around the house." Her tone was light, teasing, the sound he always looked forward to when she called.

"I noticed," he replied, nodding in approval toward the hall and the bathroom beyond. "You hung the shower curtain. Thank you."

"I fixed the leak in your sink," she added proudly. "Well, it's not totally fixed. I tightened it up, but you're going to need a new seal there. You can get them at the hardware store for a couple of dollars. Just unscrew that fitting and you'll see what looks like a rubber washer. It's cracked. When you replace it, the leak will be gone for good." She stopped talking and brushed her hand across her hair and dropped her face again.

"I never realized how good it was to have you around."

Her cheeks turned a very healthy pink this time, and when she lifted her eyes to look at him, their hazel depths glimmered with sparkles in the candlelight. "You're flirting with me again, Weldon?"

A quick surge of heat ran through his middle section, settling in his loins. He smiled and attempted a nonchalant shrug. He was tired of denying it. "Maybe a little."

Her giggle was like a tinkling bell. Quick and silvery. "This is a nice change. You think I'm silly, don't you?" she asked.

"Not necessarily."

"Do you ever really smile?" she asked. Then she laughed again as he felt his face crinkle into a smile. She leaned forward, across the table. "There! I saw you do that earlier. That's not so difficult, is it?"

"No, I guess not." He attempted another smile. "Did I tell you that I frequently watch your cable network so I can see the stories you're doing?"

Connie's smile lessened, and her nose wrinkled. "You see all our fluff reports. They have us doing consumer-oriented stories, instead of crime reports. I liked them much better."

"These are useful. You must do a good job, if you're the one coming up with all the information."

"I'm good at research. I told you that."

"Did you do any other research today?" He regretted his question as soon as it was issued. Far better to tease than bring her back to thoughts of Joy and the investigation.

"Yes, I talked to those online people again, and I saved the conversation. I wanted to show it to you. It's not scary. These people just talk, but the names are strange. One of the guys told me that they made a pledge never to try to meet each other or figure out each other's real names."

****

"See, here it is," she said, pulling up a file on her computer. Mitch leaned close to her, aware of her warm, floral scent. The sight of her sitting in his executive chair was something he could get used to.

He picked up his glasses from the desk and put them on as the screen lit up with a page of names and a computer chat room conversation. He read over it slowly, trying to see why it fascinated her.

Judy1975: Let me have it for going back to him.

DreamBaby: You're making a mistake. Men are jerks!

NiteMan: Don't talk in generalities.

DreamBaby: Men should be shot!

DeadlyGhost: Violence never solved anything, ladies.

DreamBaby: I'd shoot my husband if he was screwing around.

NiteMan: You're quiet, Sexy. No opinion?

DreamBaby: Sexy kowtows to her husband.

PrettyOne: You can't hate all men, DreamBaby.

DreamBaby: Not all, but I haven't met many worth my time.

LastDance: Let's focus on Judy, gang.

SkyGirl: Right. We tried to tell you he was no good. Now you see we were right.

LastDance: Don't worry, Judy. You're among family.

SkyGirl: The best kind of family.

NiteMan: We haven't heard from Sexy.

SexyLady: Sorry. I was distracted.

SkyGirl: You're so self-centered. You never help anyone.

Weldon glanced at Connie who read with avid interest. "What's the significance?" he asked, feeling confused. "People have these sorts of conversations all the time and names don't mean anything. My brother calls himself Dark Crusader. My sister is Hot Mama, and she's a 42-year-old grandmother with a weight problem."

"The really strange guy, Raven, wasn't there today."

"Who were you?"

"Sexy Lady." She pointed at a line. "I'm not very fast. These people are quick."

While the conversations might indicate her sister's disconnect from her husband, he doubted it led to her death, but he wouldn't discourage Connie from pursuing it. She appeared blind to Perkins' shortcomings, and what if she uncovered some ugly truth before she realized what she was doing? What if the man could fly into murderous rages? The Internet investigation was safer.

She closed the file and shut down the computer, hiding a yawn. "I guess I'll go back to the hotel."

Before he could respond, Connie stood, and their bodies collided awkwardly. Mitch grabbed hold of her arm to steady her, and their eyes met. Her hazel eyes were so clear and filled with...what? Questions? Fears? He didn't know. It had been too long since he had been this close to a woman he was attracted to.

Her warm scent intoxicated him more than the wine had, and for an instant dizziness swamped him. He could feel her breath on his cheek, and her pink, plump, inviting lips were only inches away. A spark of electric want sizzled between them.

With a groan, he leaned toward her, and he heard her quick intake of breath. Her lips brushed his and he didn't know if he'd made the move toward those tempting lips or she'd reached up to meet his. It didn't matter. Closing his eyes, he lost himself in the sweet sensation of her warm, pliant mouth.

Her lips opened wide beneath his, kissing him back. Her searching tongue thrust into his mouth, meeting his. His arms wrapped around her, pulling her close to him, hands searching over her curves.

She moaned beneath him and he felt her fingers touch his hardening body. The gesture sent ripples of delight through him and he shuddered.

He wanted her so badly he hurt, but even as the realization hit his foggy head, he knew he couldn't go any farther. He grabbed her hand to stop her fingers from their delightful search, and drew back from the lock of her kiss.

"Wait."

Her moan of response only made the aching in his lower body more intense.

"Connie, wait," he repeated, taking both her hands into his. They were both breathing heavily, and as he looked down he could see the outline of her hard nipples through her clothes.

He lifted his head and rested his chin on her head.

"Mitch," she murmured in a voice filled with wanting.

"I'm sorry," he said gently, releasing his hold on her. This couldn't go anywhere and it wasn't fair to let her think it might. In her current emotional state as she dealt with the loss of her sister, there was no telling where Connie might reach for help. She needed something, but it wasn't him. He had a crazy physical attraction to her, but he could not let her vulnerability and that attraction get them into trouble.

Her eyes were dreamy and she rocked back, away from him. She smacked her palm across her forehead. "Oh, hell," she said with a shaky laugh.

He wanted to laugh too, but instead jerked back, turning away from her so that the temptation to reach for her again was over. "I'll walk you to your car," he said, inhaling sharply.

Chapter Seven

"Connie? Hello, earth to Connie? Did you hear me?"

"Huh?" Connie jerked her eyes from the view of Puget Sound and her thoughts from the kiss she had shared with Mitch Weldon. Her cavernous loft was growing gloomy and in the distance, lights along the Seattle waterfront blinked on. She turned toward Sandy Sinclair, her associate producer, who sat nearby reading a sheaf of printed pages.

"Even with this desk lamp, it's getting too dark to read. Could you turn on a light or two?"

"Oh, sorry." Connie rose and flipped on the floor lamp beside her desk where Sandy sat.

She had come by after work because Connie had material she wanted to share. The pages were from the diary of a woman named Naomi, who had deserted her family to join a religious commune. She'd married another member and had a daughter, but when she and her child wanted to leave, they'd become virtual prisoners at the compound in eastern British Columbia. She escaped but had gone into hiding, fearing for her life and her daughter.

Sandy resumed reading while Connie walked around the room. Her loft was as big as Weldon's small bungalow, but the space was mostly contained in one large room. It stretched the length of one quarter of the fifth floor of a refurbished warehouse on the southern edge of downtown Seattle. The room was sectioned off by furniture and Chinese dividers. The only closed-in areas were a closet, dressing room, and the bathroom. The walls were exposed brick punctuated by small areas of glass brick and a huge expanse of windows facing west. The kitchen and her office area lined the back walls. A tiled counter and bar separated the kitchen from the rest of the room. Connie stopped in the kitchen long enough to fill a tea kettle with water and put it to boil.

As she'd done ever since her return to Seattle two days ago, Connie felt her thoughts drift off. To Vancouver. To Mitch. To that magic kiss they had shared. Who knew that stiff man could be so good at romance? No, not romance. A physical sensation. That's all it was, she kept telling herself. A physical reaction to the tension around them. Still, her breathing quickened just thinking about it.

"This is weird," Sandy said.

Again, Connie had to force her attention back to the present. She had to stop slipping off like that. She turned toward Sandy. "What?"

"You wouldn't think this sort of thing could happen in this day and age." Sandy pushed her glasses up her freckled nose. "This group sounds peaceful on the surface—the Assembly for Truth and Spiritual Re-awakening. She makes it sound like they've killed people who try to leave them."

"I know." Connie moved to her printer and removed several additional pages. "These are the emails I was telling you about from Joy's computer."

"Where did you find out about this?" Sandy asked.

"One of the books Ralph gave me was the spiritual teachings of their founder, Ray L. Lincoln. It looked pretty well-read, and then I found those emails on Joy's computer so I googled the name and one of the entries was Naomi's diary." The research had taken up all her time since her return from Vancouver. It had been a relief to spend her days digging online and reading. Researching was a job

117

she knew.

She pointed to the email sheet. "The thing I found interesting was their request for a donation when Naomi first met the group. Joy has an email asking for that same sort of donation."

Sandy scanned the pages. "Do you suppose Joy got mixed up with these people?"

"I don't know. I've been thinking of emailing them as an interested party and not mentioning Joy. Maybe I can get in touch with disgruntled ex-members that Naomi mentioned."

A sharp whistle went off and Sandy jumped. "Yikes!"

"Tea's ready," Connie said with a smile. She wasn't skittish as she had been during her visit to Vancouver. She put it down to Joy's death, the pictures, and that strange incident in the park. Still, she felt more comfortable sitting at her computer, digging for information.

Leaving Sandy to finish reading, she walked to the kitchen, put teabags into a teapot, and filled it with the boiling water. As she finished, Sandy put down the papers and came over to join her. Her normally bubbly friend's silence surprised her, and she grew aware of close scrutiny.

"Be honest. This stuff is interesting, but how are you holding up, babe?" Sandy asked.

"Okay, I guess. This gives me something to do." She took plates out of the cupboard and opened a brown bag Sandy had brought. She removed two pieces of cheesecake from the bag and put them onto the plates. "Thanks for bringing dessert. I've been dying for cheesecake."

"When are you coming back to work?"

Part of her wanted to be back at work, digging into a hot story about human smuggling, drug trafficking, or terrorist cells in the Northwest, but her unit wasn't working on stories like that. They'd been assigned consumer-friendly stories—where to get the best bargains and how to keep from being ripped off by Internet auctions.

"I still have a few days off before I have to go back," she said as she placed the plates and mugs onto the counter. She and Sandy climbed onto stools and dug into the cheesecake. "I'm glad you came by."

The two were not only co-workers, they were friends. Sandy was a petite ball of energy, always on the move. Smart and ambitious, she made no secret of her desire to become an investigative reporter. Her young appearance held her back, but a mass of blonde, curly hair and pert good looks pointed toward a promising future. Her personality radiated charm on camera, though even a generous supply of makeup couldn't hide the scattering of freckles across her cheeks and nose. She was one of the few people to whom Connie had confessed that she was conducting a search for Joy's killer. So far her research wasn't producing many results.

"What else?" Sandy questioned as she lifted a forkful of cheesecake, young face earnest. "What happened with that serial killer information?"

So far Connie had found only the Portland death. Nothing else was remotely similar. She intended to expand her search to include the rest of the western states.

"I'm afraid it's leading to a dead end," Connie admitted with a sigh. "What's happening at work?"

Sandy's nose wrinkled. "I set up that Internet story we were assigned on finding bargains. They want it next week so I'm under the gun. Wait until you see what they've got us doing."

As associate producer, Sandy did the preliminary research. Connie sorted through the material, and together with the reporter, selected interview subjects and determined how to put the story together. Sandy played backup, while Connie conducted the majority of the interviews along with writing and supervising the reporter and editor on the final product.

Connie rolled her eyes at the thought of doing puff pieces. "That's why I'm not rushing back. I prefer hard news."

She knew the managers were angry over their series on drug running. It had not garnered the ratings they wanted, and they'd been threatened with lawsuits. Now the investigative team was being "consumer friendly." She hated the new direction. Not to mention she no longer got to call Weldon for information.

Weldon. Now there was a topic! She longed for a reason to call him, but after that kiss, she didn't want it to seem like she was chasing him. Oh, for a good drug smuggling story!

As though she guessed what Connie was thinking, Sandy leaned close to her. "You told me about the investigative part of your trip to Vancouver, but I get the feeling you didn't tell me everything about meeting up with your inspector."

Sandy had met Weldon once and they'd shared the details of Connie's teasing infatuation with him. She licked her lips, recalling the touch of his lips against them, debating how much to tell Sandy.

"You're blushing!" Sandy howled with laughter as she watched Connie eagerly as though she guessed something juicy was to follow.

"He...um...kissed me."

"What?" she shrieked. "You've been back how many days and you never told me? Did you want him to?"

"I almost grabbed him by his ears." The memory could still turn her stomach into a vat of butterflies. He had been so close to her and she could feel his breath on her cheek. She had been aware of his strong, taut body, the sheer male power of him, and for a moment time stood still while she waited. She feared he would turn away, and she still didn't know if she reached for him or he leaned closer to her.

Whoever made the move, it had been magic. Pure, joyful, firecracker magic. She had replayed it in her mind like rewinding a tape, over and over, savoring the sweet sensation. She could taste him, feel the pressure of his tongue against hers, the hardness of his body.

"You want him!" Sandy squealed with delight, blonde curls bouncing. "Or did you..."

"Nothing happened," Connie said quickly. She sighed, as she had been doing when she thought back on those close moments. "Nothing. We just stopped. When I thought about it later, I decided it wasn't a big deal. It's not like anything will happen beyond that kiss. He's not my type, and I doubt I'm his either." But he had wanted her. She'd felt that. Maybe she shouldn't have touched him. Thoughts of her forward behavior made her cheeks warm. She couldn't admit her aggressive move to Sandy.

Sandy's look of disappointment mirrored her feelings. "Who cares about types? I think he's cute, and you do too. Next time you better let him know it."

The thought made her tingle, but she shook her head. "It's not likely there will be a next time. I think he just got carried away."

"Uh-huh," Sandy said in a knowing voice and then burst out laughing.

"Anyway, after that close call he couldn't wait to get me out of town," Connie said, regret echoing in her voice. Should she have called him the next morning before she left?

"Are you going back?"

Connie stared at the windows and the sparkling lights beyond. The familiar view seemed so safe, while Vancouver could hold danger. And it went beyond the killer lurking there. Was she ready for a relationship? No! Hot sex? Maybe. Well, yes. But something told her Weldon was not the sex-for-fun type. He'd want—no, expect—something more. "I'm not sure I have any reason to return."

"Besides the inspector?" Sandy joked.

What could she discover if she went back? Weldon didn't think the BC Slasher was to blame and she respected his judgment. She could go through the police report, but he'd been right about that too. She had no technical expertise to judge what she was reading. There was that weird dark guy who had been at the memorial. She'd called the University before she left Vancouver, but he was out of the office. Connie declined the opportunity to leave her name. She wanted to talk to the man face to face. So what else was in Vancouver besides exploring this strange new feeling about Mitch Weldon?

"Forget the Inspector," she said with a shake of her head. "I need to concentrate on finding Joy's killer."

"Do you think this cult thing might be the answer?" Sandy asked.

"Perhaps. It's a lead at least. I'm also going to look deeper into the financial records for that guy in her real estate firm. Weldon and Case say it might be someone close to her."

"That's frightening. I've heard police say the same sort of thing, but to think that you know a killer..." Sandy shook slightly as her young face turned somber.

Connie began picking up the mugs and plates. "There is one other thing. You said something once about connecting with a guy on the Internet. How does that work?"

"What do you mean?"

Connie placed the dishes in the sink, gauging

what she should admit about her online chat research. "I was talking in a chat room to these people..."

Sandy's face lit up in a smile. "You mean like Joy?"

A knot twisted in Connie's stomach as she whirled to face her friend. "What do you mean 'like Joy?'"

"When she visited a couple of months ago, we talked about chat rooms and she said she was talking to these people. She was curious about meeting someone and whether it was safe. I think she mentioned it to me because she overheard us talking about my going out with that guy I met online."

"She was curious about meeting someone from the Internet?" Neither Joy nor Sandy had ever mentioned this particular conversation.

Sandy's freckled face grew animated. "We talked about how much fun it was to chat online. I told her I was always visiting rooms like 'Seattle's Single Scene.' She was curious about whether people ever met in person."

Connie digested the information as she walked toward the office area. Sandy had appeared bored by the cult information, but Connie sensed her growing enthusiasm as she dug through her piles of folders looking for the pages of computer conversations. "Let me show you something."

"You don't suppose she met someone online?"

"It doesn't sound like something Joy would do. She was the settled one, the happily married Romero sister. Why would she be chatting with men online?" Given Ralph's comments, she was beginning to wonder, but none of the men online had shown an interest in Joy.

"Maybe she chatted with them because she was the happily married sister," Sandy said. "You don't meet the guys, but they talk to you as though you're a woman. You can pretend to be a sexy chick, no matter what you look like."

The thought of practical Joy pretending to be someone else surprised her, and yet there was that name, Sexy Lady.

"I'll bet she didn't go into those single pick-up rooms. I don't remember ever seeing her there."

"How would you know who she was?" Connie looked up from her search through the folders.

"She told me she normally used the screen name JoyfulP in chat rooms."

Connie shook her head as a small ribbon of relief rushed through her. "I didn't see that name on her computer."

Sandy shrugged. "Names can be changed at the drop of a hat. Maybe she changed it."

"Is there any way of finding out who has what screen name?" Connie asked.

"Ask Lisa. She's the computer whiz, right?"

She had not thought of involving her young sister, but Sandy was right. If anyone could work through secrets on a computer, it was Lisa. Maybe she could find out the real names of visitors to The Lair.

"I love chat rooms," Sandy said. "I enjoy talking with people from all over the country, and there's something liberating about being anonymous. You should join me in Fun and Flirty. We'll come up with a good name for you."

"What if I said I was SexyLady?"

Sandy's eyes grew wide in surprise, but she giggled. "Wow, there's a side of you I haven't seen. It would fit perfectly into Fun and Flirty."

Connie had never considered herself a flirt, let alone a sexy lady. She liked to tease Weldon, but otherwise, she wasn't much in the man-chasing department. She didn't understand why Joy used that name. She pulled out several folders from her stack and put them on the desk.

"Take a look at this and tell me what you think."

****

"They seem pretty normal," Sandy said, looking up from the printed pages, glasses sliding down her freckled nose. "A bunch of married people sharing their problems. Did Joy belong to this group?"

Connie nodded. She wasn't certain how much to tell Sandy. Her friend's tepid reaction was similar to Weldon's.

"We should go online and join in. Do you suppose they're on right now?" Sandy asked, looking toward Connie's computer.

"Probably. They get together in the evenings."

"Let's do it."

Connie signed on and brought up the page for The Lair. She typed in a greeting.

SexyLady: Hi All. Sorry I haven't been around more.

SkyGirl: Oh, look who is gracing us with her presence again.

LastDance: Sexy! Good to have you back. Leave her alone, Sky.

Judy1975: Maybe she's been busy.

SexyLady: Yes, I have been very busy.

LastDance: What have you been up to?

Raven40: Maybe she's been up to no good.

"Hey! What does he mean?" Sandy asked.

"This guy is strange," Connie said, pointing her finger at the screen name. "Pay attention to what he says." Her skin prickled. He had not been around the past couple of times she'd been online, but it was obvious he was picking up where he left off before. He knew she was not Joy.

NiteMan: What the hell does that mean? Don't play games, Raven. You haven't been around either.

Raven40: Been working out of town.

LastDance: We're glad to have you back, Sexy. Raven, I'm not so sure about.

PrettyOne: Is there a problem, Sexy? Some way we can help?

Connie typed out a reply and cleared it before she could hit the send button.

"Damn," she muttered.

"Let me do this," Sandy offered and scooted toward the desk, positioning the keyboard so she could reach it. She scrolled back over previous messages. "Let me see what I can find out."

SexyLady: I have been having trouble.

DreamBaby: See? There's an answer to everything. Can we help?

Judy1975: That's what we're here for.

PrettyOne: Is it man trouble, hon?

SexyLady: How did you guess?

Sandy typed quickly, much to Connie's surprise. She kept up with the conversation better than Connie ever had.

SkyGirl: Is it that rat of a husband again?

"Rat of a husband?" Sandy glanced up. "What have you been telling these people?"

Connie grimaced, tapping her fingernails on the desk. Time to be honest. "Actually that's Joy's account. I've been talking to them as, well, Joy."

"How could that be?" she asked, brow furrowed in consternation. "Don't they realize..."

"They don't know Joy is dead. I was trying to find out if Joy had told them anything, you know, like about her marriage."

Sandy's blonde head bobbed up and down. "That changes things." She pulled the keyboard closer to the edge of the desk and tapped on the keys.

SexyLady: How did you guess?

NiteMan: You should leave him. I told you that last time.

DreamBaby: Men are all rats.

DarkMaster: We're trying to help, Dream. Can't you leave your prejudice for once?

SkyGirl: She comes back when she needs help. The rest of the time she ignores us.

"This SkyGirl doesn't like Joy," Sandy said with a laugh and typed again. Connie leaned over her, watching the lines unfold. Sandy was quick with her responses. She kept up with the comments and responded in time for her answers to make sense. Connie doubted she could ever do that.

SexyLady: You're supposed to be my friends.

Judy1975: We are.

NiteMan: I'm here for you.

PrettyOne: So am I.

LastDance: You know I've always been here for you.

JustMelvin: Me too.

DreamBaby: Melvin, go away. I thought we tossed you out

NiteMan: This isn't the room for you, Melvin.

JustMelvin: That's not fair. Were supposed to be a group. Remember?

DreamBaby: You're too young.

JustMelvin: How do you kno? Your not supposed to know.

DreamBaby: Your grammar and spelling tell me.

LastDance: Let it go. We're helping Sexy Lady.

Judy1975: That's right. Tell us your problem.

SexyLady: It's the same one, my husband. Maybe I'll leave him.

Raven40: Maybe you've left more than that.

"Whoa!" Sandy's head jerked up, her face puzzled.

"You see? This guy is strange. He said stuff like that last time. Like he knows I'm not Joy and she's dead. How could he know? NiteMan told me they're not supposed to know each other's real names or where they're from."

"Okay, that makes sense."

"Does it?" Connie asked. "Have you heard of such a thing? Where the group doesn't want to know real names?"

"We do it in Just Plain Folks. The idea is you don't have preconceived notions of who everyone is. Everyone's equal and we just talk. For a while we didn't even admit where we were from. I never give my real name, even in regular rooms."

"That sounds odd," Connie mused. "You don't know who you're talking to."

"It's not like you're going to meet these people. You're exchanging ideas, but you don't have the old guys hitting on young girls. The only problem is someone like JustMelvin." She pointed at the conversation. After Raven's comment, JustMelvin had told him to leave her alone and the rest of the group had turned on Melvin again. "Judging from his spelling and grammar, I think he's in his teens and they sense that so they're trying to get rid of him."

"Forget that. I don't think they had anything to do with Joy's death."

"Aren't you curious about why they called her husband a rat? It sounds like she told them she had problems with Ralph."

Connie thought of what Weldon had said. Her co-workers knew Joy and Ralph were having marital difficulties. Why had Joy never shared that with her? Connie prided herself in being available to her friends. She should have been available to her sister so she didn't have to turn to this group of strangers.

"I don't know, Sandy..."

"Just let me just see what I can find out." Sandy turned back to the keyboard.

SexyLady: Getting back to my problem. You think I should leave him?

DreamBaby: Is he still seeing that woman?

SkyGirl: I'd ditch him unless he gets rid of her.

DreamBaby: I'd ditch him anyway.

Judy1975: It's not always that easy.

LastDance: Maybe she loves him still. Ever think of that, gals?

DreamBaby: Don't call me a gal!

SexyLady: I don't know if he's still seeing her.

Connie gulped as she read the comments. "What? Seeing another woman?"

"Do you know anything about that?" Sandy asked, eyes still on the screen.

Ralph and another woman? The idea was incomprehensible. What if Weldon or Case found out? Or did they suspect it already?

"Get off of there," Connie urged again as a chill ran through her.

"Just a sec," Sandy said, typing in quick motions. Connie leaned close to see what she was saying.

SexyLady: Maybe I'll leave. I'll sleep on it. I'll let you know my answer.

DreamBaby: Don't sleep. Take the kids and go now.

Judy1975: Let her think it over.

PrettyOne: Just don't take too long like Judy did.

SexyLady: Thank you for the help. May I ask another favor?

NiteMan: Always.

LastDance: We're here for you, babe.

SexyLady: May I invite one of my other

friends to join us? She needs help.

PrettyOne: No!

SkyGirl: We agreed no new people.

LastDance: It might be a good idea. Little Bird is gone, why not replace her?

DarkMaster: Replace Melvin.

JustMelvin: That's not fair

SkyGirl: I vote no. She would know who that person is. We'd be at a disadvantage.

PrettyOne: I agree.

Raven40: I say yes. I'd like to know about Sexy's friend.

The other men joined Raven, inviting in the new participant and finally, victory on her side, Sandy signed off.

"Why did you do that?" Connie asked.

"I might go back. Didn't you say you didn't feel like talking to these people?"

"I'm not sure that's a good idea." Much as she appreciated Sandy's help, she wasn't certain she wanted her friend to get involved.

Sandy waved aside her protest. "This is a mind game, and I enjoy matching wits with people. I guarantee that within a few days I'll find out exactly who everyone is and their relationship with Joy. I may even find out about that other woman."

Chapter Eight

"I don't believe it," Lisa said, shaking her head as she stared out the window of Connie's car. "Ralph and another woman? No. Never."

They were driving north toward Bellingham. Lisa had promised Ralph to clean out Joy's closets and give her clothes to a battered woman's shelter. Connie invited herself along when she found out about her sister's mission, but she purposely waited to tell Lisa about what she and Sandy discovered until they were in the car headed toward Bellingham.

"That was my first reaction too." The thought of Ralph cheating on Joy stayed with Connie after Sandy left. She had paced her condo, glass of sherry in her hand, slippers padding on the hardwood floors as she walked from one end of the loft to the other. Had Ralph been having an affair? Had Joy known? Ralph confessed to being inattentive, but was it more than that? Did Weldon or Case know? Was that why they focused on him as a suspect?

Her concern had been followed by the fear that Joy shared the information with Lisa but not her. Lisa's vehement reaction indicated she hadn't known either.

"Ralph has trouble picking out a clean tie without Joy telling him what to do. I've never seen him flirt with a waitress or look at another woman. Can you see him trying to pick up someone?"

Connie chuckled at a mental image of the heavyset man with his unkempt appearance making an advance on a woman. "I know what you mean.

And why now? I mean, Joy never looked better. She had lost weight and was getting into the fitness regime."

Lisa jerked her face to Connie, alarm written on it. "You don't suppose that's why she decided to lose weight, do you? Ralph was looking elsewhere and she wanted to get him back?"

While Connie had not considered that, it made sense. "He mentioned that he and Joy were having marital problems last time I saw him, but he made them sound minimal. I would never have guessed another woman."

"Why don't we just ask him?"

The ever-practical Lisa. Connie was conducting secret online investigations but Lisa was straightforward. Just ask. It was like this trip. Leave it to Lisa to take a realistic approach. Her dead sister's closet needed to be cleaned out and battered women needed clothes. They were donating Joy's old clothes to a battered women's shelter.

"Do you think he'd be honest and come right out and say, 'oh, yes, I was having an affair?'" Connie shook her head. "I doubt he'll tell us the truth if he was playing around."

"Ralph is not a good liar. I think we could tell."

"True," she agreed. Lisa was probably right. Joy had always talked about how honest he was. "I would like to be able to put that whole issue to rest with Weldon."

"How is the handsome inspector?" Lisa asked, her voice taking on a teasing note, much as Sandy's had.

Was she that transparent when she talked about him? A long, loud sigh escaped Connie. "Handsome. And a lot more appealing than I want to admit."

"Ah, do I detect interest?" her sister teased.

Connie had not told her sister about kissing

Weldon. She sighed heavily. "I don't know and that's the worst part. I really—oh, hell." She turned the steering wheel as a big black piece of rubber materialized on the roadway.

Thunk!

The car shuddered as something hit the left side.

"What the hell was that?" Lisa asked, but Connie was already maneuvering to dodge another part of shredded tire on the pavement. Even though she missed it, the car shook again.

"Damn, I wonder if that thing hit something underneath."

"The rest area is coming up. Pull over," Lisa urged.

Connie checked her rearview mirror. She was traveling in the fast lane and luckily the freeway was empty. There was nothing behind her except for another car in the right lane farther back. She signaled and pulled into the right lane and onto the off ramp. The rest area was deserted, but they weren't far from Bellingham. If the wayward tire had damaged anything they could get a tow truck and have someone pick them up.

She slowed the car, waiting for another shudder. She glanced at Lisa. "Feel anything?"

"No, but we should check to be sure."

Connie stopped in the parking slot and they both got out of the car. Connie walked around to the passenger side and fell to her knees. Thank goodness she'd worn jeans instead of nice slacks, like Lisa.

"Anything there?" Lisa asked.

"I'll need to look underneath." Connie twisted her hair into a knot so it wouldn't drag on the ground and bent over far enough to look up at the undercarriage of the car.

"Do you know what you're looking for? I know you're Ms. Mechanic Fix-it, but will you know if there's a problem?"

"I can see if there's something stuck under here," she replied.

In high school Connie had taken shop and auto mechanics, mainly to prove a point about being able to do anything she wanted, but over the years those skills had come in just as handy as her journalism or history courses. Like the day she spent fixing Weldon's leaky faucet and hanging his shower curtain, she'd become very adept at making minor home and auto repairs.

"I'm going to run over to the shelter and get a soda," Lisa said. "Do you want anything?"

"We'll be in Bellingham in a few minutes. I'll wait."

She finished her search, finding nothing. The underside of the car looked perfectly fine, from her vantage point. Perhaps the errant tire had gotten caught underneath for a couple of rotations before falling away. They weren't far from their destination. If something truly was wrong, she'd simply keep her speed low until they reached the outskirts of the city.

Lisa arrived back at the car as she got to her feet and brushed the pebbles off her hands. "That was quick."

"It looks okay and we're almost there."

They climbed back into the car and Connie concentrated on the way the car handled as she drove forward, going steadily faster until they re-entered the freeway. Whatever had been the problem appeared to be gone.

"Damn!" Lisa said in a hoarse whisper.

"What?" She realized Lisa had been twisting in her seat since they got back on the road.

"Is that car following us?" Lisa twisted around to look behind them. "That car back there was at the rest area. It pulled in right after we did. I didn't see anyone get out, which I thought was strange. Now it's behind us again, so it must have come out of the rest area right after us."

A thread of fear shimmied down Connie's back. She jerked her gaze to the rearview mirror. There were at least three cars behind them now. "Which one?"

"You can't see it. The black car pulled in front of it. Why are you slowing down? It's going to catch up with us."

"I want the black car to pass. I want to see that other car. Did you see what color it was?" She hadn't told Lisa or Sandy about the burgundy van.

"The car was dark, but I couldn't really see it through the trees. I thought it was odd that it pulled up to the rest area on the truck side and simply sat there. I mean, why stop at a rest area if you're not going to get out of the car?"

Why, indeed? "Was it a van or a car?"

"Van, like an SUV? Well, yes it was an SUV as opposed to a car, if that's what you mean."

The black car signaled to pass and came around them on the left. Connie glanced at the mirror, but the freeway was curving around a hill. She slowed again, hoping to catch a glimpse of the car. Could it be the van following her? Or was she becoming paranoid?

She checked in the rear view mirror again, but saw no sign of a van. The two cars that came around the curve behind them were sedans, one white and one gray.

"Is it back there?" she asked, trying to keep the alarm from her voice.

Lisa shook her head. "It's gone. Maybe it pulled off. We're being silly, aren't we? Maybe the car hit that shredded tire too so they stopped to check. Pure coincidence."

"Maybe," Connie agreed, but she kept checking

the rearview mirror anyway.
****

Ralph greeted Connie and Lisa at the front door with a sad, but grateful smile. "Thanks for coming."

The two sisters traded quick, questioning glances. Connie thought Ralph looked bad when she saw him several days earlier. Now he wore a haunted look like a funeral suit. His blue eyes were dead and lifeless. His stained dress shirt was wrinkled and his tie hung loosely. His black pants looked as though he had slept in them. His round face was unshaven, and his thinning hair hung in greasy strips.

Tears stung her eyes. Seeing his physical and mental deterioration, Connie could not imagine her stricken brother-in-law would have anything to do with his wife's death, even with the talk of marital infidelity swirling around.

Connie hugged him quickly. "How are you holding up?"

His lip twisted, and he lifted a heavy shoulder. "Surviving. Thanks." He stood aside for them to enter. "I appreciate your taking care of this. Sometimes I feel so lost. I started to go through the closet, but it's so sad. I think of her in certain dresses..." he stopped, swallowing hard, and his eyes grew watery. For an instant Connie feared he might break into tears.

"It's no problem," Lisa said, taking his arm and hugging his large frame. "It's a big help to the shelter."

Connie stepped into the front hall. Like Ralph, the house appeared incomplete and unkempt. The wooden furniture and normally gleaming surfaces carried a fine layer of dust. Coats and shoes cluttered the hall, as though waiting for Joy to come home and put them away.

"Would you like coffee?" he asked, turning

toward the kitchen.

"Sure," Connie said as they followed him to the kitchen.

Unlike when she dropped off the children, the kitchen was a shambles. Dishes littered the sink, and cabinet doors hung open. Settings from the night before were still on the table, the food hard and congealed. Connie crossed to the coffee pot and discovered it was half full, but cold.

"I was just going to fix some," Ralph explained with a shrug.

"I'll do it," she volunteered, picking up the pot to dump its contents and wash it out. "Lisa will keep you company." Giving him a gentle shove toward the table, she turned back to the counter.

He sat across from Lisa, head lowered, eyes studying the messy table as though uncertain what he was viewing. Ralph resembled a zombie, moving from one place to the next with no goal in mind.

Lisa put her hands on his. "It'll be okay, Ralph."

Connie knew where everything was, and she worked efficiently to wash the pot, get fresh coffee, and get the coffeemaker going. While it brewed, she began rinsing the dishes in the sink. She opened the dishwasher door to load it and discovered the racks already full.

"Let me unload it," Ralph offered, getting to his feet.

Lisa caught his arm and pulled him back to his chair. "Let her do it. You need some help, and that's why we're here."

Ralph's lips lifted in half a smile. "Sometimes it's difficult to function."

"We understand." Lisa's tone was soothing. "We all miss her horribly, and I didn't even see her that often. I can't believe how much I miss knowing she was there if I needed to talk. No matter how busy she was, she was always there for me. I wish I could have helped her…"

"How are the kids doing?" Connie interrupted. She could see tears edging into her sister's eyes, and Ralph was one step away from blubbering.

"They went back to school yesterday," he said with a grimace. "They try to help, but they don't know what to do and I hate to force them. She did everything for us."

"You ought to get a cleaning woman or a nanny," Connie suggested as she tapped her toe on some sticky foreign substance stuck to the kitchen floor. Then she thought about what Weldon had said about Ralph's money problems. If he was as distracted as he looked, his work situation had to be getting worse instead of better. He probably couldn't afford to hire a nanny. "Mom could come over and stay for a while," she volunteered.

"We'll be all right," he said, taking a big gulp of air, as though he was fighting back tears. He leaned his elbows on the table, and rested his chin on his fists, his face a picture of dejection.

"Well, don't worry about her clothes," Lisa said. "We'll get that cleaned out for you. I'm sure it's hard to have them all there as constant reminders."

"If you need anything else, like money…" Connie offered. "I'm going to pay you for that computer, Ralph. It was expensive. When I get my insurance check, I'll give it to you."

He shook his head. "You don't need to pay me. Money's short right now, but she did have insurance and I don't want payment for that damn thing. I'm just glad it's gone."

"Why do you hate that laptop so much?" Connie asked. She started to make a joke of it, but his head jerked up and a hard look came into his blue eyes. When he'd first demonstrated a dislike for it, she'd thought it was because Joy was working on it so much. Since she'd met the people in The Lair, she wasn't so certain. She had told Lisa a little about the strange group during their drive, but like the others, Lisa didn't think it meant anything.

"That damn computer was a menace," Ralph said, facing growing red. "She was on there all the damn time. First thing in the morning. Last thing every night. Like a damned addiction."

"I know she was working hard," Lisa said.

He shook his head and his voice turned hard. "I don't know what the hell she was doing. Once she got that computer all she did was sit on the damn thing—day and night. She forgot the rest of us existed. That damn thing was the reason for all our problems."

"Problems?" Lisa repeated in a quiet tone, her gaze darting to Connie's.

Connie nodded slightly, urging her to continue the questioning, but he shook his head and lurched to his feet.

"Thanks for going through her closet. Keep anything you want and give the rest away. I'm gonna take a shower and go downtown for a while."

"Whoa," Connie said, as the sound of his footsteps died on the stairs. "It sounds like he blames the computer for everything."

Lisa's eyes were on the door, and she shook her head. "Whatever problems they had, I still don't think he hurt her."

Connie agreed and went back to work while Lisa cleared the kitchen table and tidied up the counters. After stacking the dishes and reloading the dishwasher, she took a mop to the sticky floor. By the time she and Lisa went upstairs, the kitchen was clean.

The master bedroom was as messy as the rest of the house. Ralph's clothes were strewn about, as though he had not hung up anything since the murder. A layer of dust covered the walnut furniture. The king-sized bed was unmade, pale blue sheets spilling onto the floor.

Two empty boxes sat by the closet, evidence that Ralph had made an attempt to clean out his wife's clothes and then abandoned the effort. Together Connie and Lisa began going through the clothes and taking them off hangers. They carefully folded them to put in the boxes. Joy had never made clothes or shopping a priority, so Connie was surprised as she pulled out several tailored suits. They carried designer labels. Her sister had always shopped at discount stores and teased Connie for her attention to fashion. Now Connie admired the suits. Even if they were on the conservative side, the price tags would be expensive.

"Very nice," she said, running her hand along a cashmere dress. "I guess she was getting a new wardrobe now that she'd lost weight."

"Look at this." Lisa pulled out a black silk dress with a low cut neckline in a see-through plastic bag. "Did you ever see her wear this? Or this?"

The second dress was a soft pink and smaller than the other. Connie started to say it was probably an old party dress, but then she saw the tag dangling from the neck.

"Check out the price of this," Lisa said in a shocked tone.

Connie lifted the tag and whistled. "More than three hundred dollars? Since when did Joy spend that much on a dress? This doesn't look like our sister. I was going to say that about the suits, but I thought maybe she bought them secondhand. Now I'm wondering. Was this all because she had lost weight? Do you suppose this is why they were having money troubles?"

"Look at these sandals. Wow!" Lisa lifted a pair of stiletto heels. They looked totally impractical for their staid older sister. "Manolo Blahnik? Don't they cost a lot? They're new."

Joy had always enjoyed shoes so they weren't surprised to find that the whole back of the closet was lined with shoe boxes, but Connie knew the price of the designer shoes and there appeared to be a whole row of them.

"I wish I wore her size," Connie lamented, opening another box. "I might not mind wearing these pumps." Her fingers skimped over the buttery soft leather and she turned them over. "They don't look like they've ever been worn. Maybe I'll take them to Sandy."

"Sure." Lisa pulled out more boxes and opened one. "Hey, they're not all shoes. What the hell are these?" She lifted a folded pile of papers that had been jammed into one of the shoe boxes. She unfolded them, brow wrinkling quizzically. Then she giggled.

Peering over Lisa's shoulder, Connie examined the pages. "What?"

"They're her stories! Remember how she wanted to be a writer before she met Ralph? Look at these—typed and printed on that old word processor Dad bought."

"Sometimes I think that's why I was so determined to go to college," Connie admitted. "Joy was so convinced she'd be a writer and then she gave it up to get married." She sighed and shook her head as she put the pages back into the shoebox.

"I'm taking these," Lisa said closing them up. "I'll save them for Mindy when she's a teenager." She opened another box and frowned. "Wait. These are new."

Connie glanced at the printed pages and then reached for them. They were filled with computer conversations. Why would Joy have kept those pages? She perused the names. One of them was Sexy Lady.

"Those are her computer conversations," Connie said in surprise.

"Why would she save them?" Lisa asked, holding up the pages, sifting through a couple.

"I have no idea, but I want to look them over. Save that box." The next box held more printed pages. She noted only two names on it, Sexy Lady and Mike7445. Who the hell was that? She'd never seen him in The Lair. The surprises seemed to go on and on. What the hell had been going on with Joy?

****

Rain dripped from the overhang and fell in windblown torrents. Connie watched the storm gather fury from a chair at the kitchen table. The gentle scent of fresh brewed coffee permeated the air. The view and smell brought back memories of mornings in this same kitchen.

Tears stung her eyelids as she and Lisa relaxed with an early afternoon cup of coffee and talked about the past. The cardboard boxes they had filled with Joy's dresses, coats, and shoes were stacked in a corner. The computer conversations were in three shoe boxes in a plastic bag beside them, along with several pairs of new shoes that she was taking to Sandy. Ralph had not returned. The two sisters were waiting for the rain to subside so they could pack the car and drive back to Seattle.

"Remember the three of us sitting in that old car?" Lisa asked, dabbing at her eyes before taking a sip of coffee. She pointed outside the window to the rusted hulk of a Plymouth, near the garage. It had once belonged to her grandfather, and it was left at the house when he passed away. Her father always planned to restore it, but somehow he never got around to it. Joy kept threatening to have it taken to the junkyard, but it still remained in its corner.

Perhaps she let it stay because it reminded her of their childhood. As girls, Connie, Joy, and Lisa claimed the Plymouth as their own magical spot. They turned it into their private fantasy world with Joy making up adventures for them to pursue. The backseat transformed into fabulous homes for their dolls and the sisters made up glamorous lives for them all. Joy's stories centered around a fabulous career, one in which her doll became a best-selling writer, while Connie's wanted to travel.

As they grew older, they stopped playing, but the car was where they exchanged dreams, shared secrets, and planned for the future. When they needed privacy, the sisters escaped to the Plymouth. Joy described her first kiss to Connie in that car and confided her decision to forego college to marry Ralph. Connie revealed her plans to attend college out of state.

"Wouldn't it be nice if we could turn back time?" Lisa asked. "Like we used to pretend in that car? Drive into the past? Even a couple of months would work. While I was glad she and Ralph took the kids to Disneyland for Christmas, now I wish we'd had that last holiday together."

Connie knew what she meant. For an instant, she was tempted to run out to the car, despite the thumping rain. Escape and try to recapture those moments from the past, a part of Joy she'd missed or lost. "Maybe it's that car that is driving me so hard to find out what happened to Joy. Maybe if we could have spent the afternoon sitting in that car talking, instead of going to Vancouver, I could have found out what she was thinking. It was great she lost so much weight, but now I'm wondering why she was doing it after all these years. Or did other things start happening because she was looking so good? See what I mean? Maybe...oh, hell..." She swallowed hard in an attempt to bite back tears.

Who was she kidding? The magic of the old car was gone. Its white paint had turned a sickly green

143

with moss. The bumpers were rusted, the tires gone. It sat on four wooden blocks. The windows had long ago been punched out, so the interior was rotted.

Lisa patted her hand and sighed wistfully. "Do you think it's possible Ralph could have done it?"

"Of course not." Connie's sudden bout of tears disintegrated. "Did you get a look at how devastated he was this morning? The man is losing it. I feel sorry for him. As for him having an affair, can you imagine a woman wanting to be involved with him?"

Lisa shook her head and laughed, but then her eyes sobered again, and her face regained its somber concern. "Then who? The police say it was someone who knew her, but who would want to kill Joy?"

"I wish I didn't have to go back to work this week. I think I could figure this out if I had more time to work on it. I feel like I'm going in circles. I have lots of theories and no proof of anything. I have information on a jogger in Portland who was stabbed and mutilated, and one in Scottsdale, Arizona. I'm also looking into that religious cult and I found out there might be a branch in eastern Oregon. I've put in calls to reporter friends who work in Portland, and they're working on it for me. I have Sandy working on some leads too."

Lisa sipped solemnly at her coffee. "You're making me feel guilty. I'm not convinced you should be investigating, but you have reporter friends in other states helping to solve our sister's murder. Even Sandy. You're starting to make me wish I could help, though I can't imagine studying police reports or reading about serial killers."

Remembering her experience with the photos, Connie nodded. "There is something you could do. I told you about that strange Internet bunch in the chat room. If I give you the names, is there a way to find out who they are? None of them have profiles in the main file."

"Why would you care about that?" Lisa asked, making a face.

"Joy told them about her marital problems. Why would she tell them and not us?"

Lisa's brows drew together, eyes growing grave with thought. "Maybe she made up the marital problems, so she'd have something to say to those Internet friends. The thing I've discovered about chat rooms is that they allow people to be creative about their lives. Everyone is a model, lawyer, or Air Force pilot. Maybe that's why she kept those papers, to know what lies she was telling. You know how Joy loved to make up stories. Maybe she saw that as a chance to do it."

Connie hadn't considered that possibility. Perhaps Joy manufactured the problems with Ralph as a way of making her life appear more dramatic. Most of the women in the group had been supportive. She shoved her empty cup aside and peered out. "The rain's letting up. We'd better get those boxes loaded and get going before the rain comes back."

"Good idea," Lisa agreed.

They carried the boxes through the rain which had turned to a fine mist. Connie popped open the trunk to reveal a box of books in the center.

"Hell, I forgot I had more books Ralph gave me." She pushed the box to one side. She'd grabbed two of the books on top and found the reading about Naomi and her cult experiences so fascinating she'd never gone back to the others. She needed to go through them. There might be others about the Assembly for Truth and Spiritual Re-awakening. Perhaps one had information about the Oregon arm of the group.

Lisa picked up a book. "Myths of the Northwest Tribes? The World of Angels? This was what she was reading?"

"I told you about that strange religious group

she was getting involved with recently. I guess she was looking at a number of different angles."

"Do you want me to look through these?" Lisa asked. "I'm no investigator, but I'd like to know what she was thinking." She looked toward the back yard with its old rusted car.

"Sure, go ahead. I have to go back to work, so my time is going to be limited."

They moved the box to the backseat and went back to loading clothes. As they were stuffing the last box into Connie's trunk, Ralph's car skidded up the lane.

"I'm sorry I was gone so long," he apologized. "I went over to the Muddy Hen, and lost track of the time."

"No problem," Connie said. "We're done."

"Did you get her jewelry?"

"Don't you want it?" Connie asked. "You should save it for Mindy when she grows up."

"You can give it to her. Joy didn't have much good stuff, but I worry someone might break in again. They didn't get it in the last break in, but you never know. I guess I could get a safe deposit box, but it seems so much trouble…"

Lisa and Connie exchanged glances and followed him back to the bedroom. He lifted a painted, scarred wooden box they both recognized. It once belonged to their grandmother. Tears filled Connie's eyes as she took it. She remembered the day of Joy's graduation when their grandmother had given it to her. He was right—she and Lisa should pass it on to Mindy.

He picked up a manila envelope from the dresser and held it out. "Take this too. I kept her wedding ring, but the police said this was the jewelry she was wearing."

Mist filled his eyes, and Connie swallowed hard, fighting the choking sensation that gripped her throat.

Lisa took the envelope and patted his arm. "I'll take care of that."

They walked back to the car and after trading hugs, Connie guided the car down the lane.

"I have a safe deposit box," she said as they drove away. "We can put her things there to save for Mindy. What's in the envelope?"

Lisa pried it open and slid the contents into her lap. Inside was an antique gold watch that once belonged to their grandmother. It was passed on to Joy the same day she received the jewelry box. Along with it was a thin gold bracelet with a small round pendant that said "Joy."

"What's this?" Lisa lifted a final item. A small gold pin rested in the palm of her hand,

Connie craned her neck to look at it. "I've never seen that before."

"Neither have I. You didn't notice her wearing it the day she died?"

"She was wearing a jogging suit. Seems like I would have noticed that."

"I wonder if police made a mistake." Lisa turned it over in her hand. "This doesn't look like something she would buy, but it's fourteen-carat gold."

"I'll ask Weldon next time I see him."

Lisa handed it to her, and as she stopped at a red light, Connie studied the pin. She had never seen anything like it and never on her sister. About the size of a thumbnail, it was heavier than its fragile look. The gold pin was the shape of a bird with open wings and tiny feet. She slipped it into her pocket. This would give her an excuse to call Weldon.

"Hey," Lisa called, pointing to the right as the light turned green and Connie maneuvered the car toward the freeway onramp. "Let's stop at the Muddy Hen and get a hamburger and fries to go.

Ever since Ralph mentioned he'd been there, I've been thinking about their French fries. They still use fresh potatoes. You can't get any like that in Seattle."

Connie would have argued, but her stomach was beginning to rumble. They had not eaten since downing muffins early that morning when they set out from Seattle. She pulled into the Muddy Hen's gravel lot. "Why don't you go in and get the order? I want to check voice messages."

With Lisa gone, she stared hard at her phone and then with shaking fingers, she tapped in Weldon's cell number. Finally she had a reason to call him. Anticipation gripped her momentarily, but it turned to frustration when there was no answer and it dumped to voice mail. Still, the mechanical sound of his voice increased her pulse rate. She left a message, all her senses alert, and a feeling of awareness tickling her stomach as she spoke.

That task handled, she checked her voice mail. Among them was a giddy message from Sandy, giggling about her online research. Connie had just finished, when Lisa returned. Her sister wore a shocked look as she shoved the grease-spotted bag onto the console between them.

"What's wrong?" Connie asked.

"I mentioned that Ralph said he'd been here drinking beer, and the bartender said he hasn't seen Ralph in two months. He's been here all afternoon. Connie," she cried, her face pale and filled with doubt. "Ralph lied to us!"

Chapter Nine

NiteMan: Good Morning!
Searcher: Hi there. You're up early.
NiteMan: I just got home from work.
Searcher: I'm just starting work.
SexyLady: Good morning!
Searcher: Sexy Lady, I've been wondering where you've been.

Connie frowned at the screen. Who was Searcher and why was he wondering about her? She'd never seen the name before. She lifted a steaming coffee mug to her lips and sipped from it slowly, debating how to answer. Coffee was a necessity this morning, and she'd made it extra strong. She'd gotten back to Seattle late the previous night almost too tired to sleep and she still felt groggy.

Sexy Lady: I've been out of town. How is everyone?

Her question elicited replies from others so Connie leaned back on her leather chair, putting her feet on the short cushioned bench under her desk. Her office area was normally her favorite spot in the loft. Since most of her time at home was spent there, it was arranged for maximum comfort. Tall bookshelves lined the wall behind her while her desk faced the row of windows and a magnificent view of Puget Sound. Today was clear, and beyond the windows, the water glowed in a vivid azure hue that she'd never seen any other place. Sailboats dotted the water, and a green and white ferry glided toward the city.

Nothing could beat a beautiful Seattle day when the water was that deep, perfect shade of blue. Across the water, the rugged peaks of the Olympic Mountains stood proudly outlined in snow against a pale blue sky. The lure of the outdoors was strong. Not many January days dawned with such promise. Despite the sun, Connie fought the urge to go out— she had too much work to do.

In one corner of her work area were the papers from Joy's shoe boxes. She wanted to leisurely look through them. From the moment she had returned to work the previous Monday she had been on the go and unable to continue her investigation. A fishing boat disaster on the coast had kept her occupied and far from thoughts of Joy's death. She didn't go out in the field for breaking news very often, but when an emergency hit, Puget Sound News marshaled all its resources. The crisis required several field producers. Her job had been to coordinate live reports for three reporters and to see that their stories got edited and fed back to the newsroom. From the early morning newscasts through the late program, she had been on the phone, making calls and editing tape.

Now that she was home, she felt remiss about ignoring her investigation. She needed to get back to the questions of Joy's death. The discovery that Ralph had lied and that Joy was buying expensive clothes and hiding computer conversations shed new light on the possibility of marital problems.

She had tried to call Weldon and Case, curious to see if they would talk with her about the marital problems, but her personal cell service was hit and miss on the coast. She'd been using a work cell phone, so she couldn't make what amounted to international calls to Vancouver. She'd left messages and hoped to find a return message at work or on her cell once she got back within range.

Neither had called, so she was back in the chat room. How much had Joy told these people? Could she have been making up a story as Lisa suggested? Connie wanted check out who was in The Lair, but she was curious about this Searcher person.

SexyLady: Not much happening this morning. Where is everyone?

NiteMan: You missed a late night.

Searcher: They helped me with a problem.

SkyGirl: You'll be fine. We all have our problems, don't we?

NiteMan: Always ready to help.

JustMelvin: So am I

SkyGirl: Get lost, Melvin!

Searcher: Let him stay. I enjoy his company.

An instant message box appeared in the upper corner of Connie's monitor and her computer rang with a familiar tone.

Searcher: Hey, Con, it's Sandy.

Relief rushed through her. No wonder she had never seen the name. Sandy had set it up to get into the group the night she'd been online as SexyLady. From the friendly way NiteMan and even SkyGirl greeted her, it appeared to be working. Letting the other conversation between NiteMan and Melvin go, she responded to Sandy.

SexyLady: Thanks for letting me know. I was a little worried.

Searcher: Our secrets are safe, but I have tons to tell you. Lunch?

SexyLady: Why don't you stop by?

Searcher: Righto!

Connie went back to watching the conversation swirl past. She had trouble keeping up, and the talk was going nowhere. She signed off, checked her phones to see that both her home phone and cell were working and then picked up Naomi's diary. She'd been reading it in her spare time while she was on the coast, fearing it might have contributed to Joy's marital problems. Naomi had shut out her family as she became more involved with the cult. Perhaps it held clues to the final days of Joy's life—or her death. Connie turned to the page with the picture of R.L. Lincoln. Just who was he? Maybe it was time she did more investigating into this man.

****

Mitch told himself he was simply being polite as he picked up his phone and tapped in Connie's phone number. She had left several messages during the past week. He had debated most of the morning if he should call. He didn't like that uncertain, uneasy, queasy sensation in his stomach each time he'd called her phone and an impersonal voice said she was out of range or service was off. It reminded him of the waiting he'd once been forced to endure whenever his father was missing for hours on end.

No, this wasn't like that. Connie was simply part of a case, he reminded himself. Not even that—she was simply an acquaintance he was assisting.

"Yes, but you're assisting her to protect her," he'd muttered to himself. And he didn't kiss acquaintances. Or fantasize about them. "You're calling her from home on your day off. That sounds personal to me. Damn personal! You should be out in the greenhouse." He was about to put down the phone and grab his gloves when she answered, sending a wave of relief through his body, followed by a searing awareness.

"Hello?" she said again when he didn't reply, irritation in her voice.

"Connie? Miss Romero, I'm sorry. It's Inspector Weldon, returning your calls." He slid onto his chair, sitting straight up, hoping the rigid stance would help him adopt a professional attitude with her. His thoughts about her were growing more and more unprofessional.

"Weldon! Did you get my messages?" Her voice came to life.

"Yes, and I'm sorry I couldn't get back to you sooner. I was in Blackhawk much of the week. I tried calling you, but your phone went right to voice mail." He didn't add that small twinges of uncertainty had pricked at him when she didn't answer. Or that he'd finally called her office and asked directly where she was. He'd been surprised at how relieved he was to learn she was on assignment and would return at the weekend. At one point he feared she might have uncovered something and sent Ralph Perkins over the edge. Just hearing her voice now soothed his frazzled nerves, even as it pumped excitement through his veins, an unusual feeling he didn't particularly want to experience.

"Blackhawk? Isn't that a primo ski area? Don't tell me you took the week off?" she asked, her tone light.

He grunted, though his lips turned up in a small smile. "Quite the contrary. I was on a case that took me into the mountains on the other side." Why was it that anonymous tips always had to be some place far away, and why did they turn out to be wild goose chases more often than not? Still they needed to be investigated, and he didn't trust anyone else to do that investigative work. They might miss something valuable.

"Joy's case? The Slasher?" she asked, sounding interested.

He hesitated, staring down at the floor. Naturally that would be foremost on her mind. "I can't discuss it with you."

"Like you didn't the last time I saw you?" Her voice turned cold and accusing as quickly as it had become flirtatious. "Don't think I didn't notice how you danced around talking about that. You talked about everything else except what you found in the park that afternoon. I had to read about it later in the paper."

He drew a deep breath and cleared his throat. He should have known she would see it and probably misinterpret it. Still, it was better to keep this impersonal than let it go in another direction. "Is that why you called?"

"I called about Joy's possessions, the ones in the envelope that Sergeant Case gave Ralph?"

That surprised him. "What about them? Those were her personal possessions that she had when she died. We return them unless they're evidence. Was something missing?" Why had she been trying to reach him about her sister's property? Why hadn't she called Case? His tense muscles relaxed and a smile tugged at his lips. Maybe she had used it as an excuse to call him. That thought pleased him.

"I think the police made a mistake," she said. "There was a pin in the envelope, shaped like a bird. My sister and I agree it didn't belong to Joy."

"I don't know what you mean, but I'm not familiar with what was in the envelope."

"Well, it looks valuable so we should return it so you can find the proper owner."

"Did you ask Case about it?" he asked.

She didn't reply, and his senses became alert as his breath quickened. He'd been right. The jewelry had nothing to do with her phone call, other than providing an excuse. A sudden lightness burst like exploding fireworks within him. "Admit it, you just wanted to call me," he said.

Her laugh was quick and vaguely unsettling. "Weldon, you devil, you're flirting." Her voice sounded like a high-pitched teenager.

"To be honest, I don't know what I'm doing," he answered with a chuckle, his smile widening.

"Maybe I should come back to Vancouver more often."

"No!" The response was quick, his voice taking on his hard, official tone. He had no time to deal with a bout of teenage wistfulness.

"Then maybe you should come see me."

Her tone was soft, intimate. He blinked and looked down at his chest, aware his heart had begun to beat faster and his breathing had quickened at her response. He cleared his throat to keep from sounding too eager. "Maybe."

What the hell was happening between them? She had called him about the pin, wasn't that what she said? But was this mild flirtation better than discussing murder cases with her? He visualized her dancing eyes and that silky black hair he'd wanted to touch. For an instant his mind flashed on the soft curves against his body, the warmth of her lips and her searching touch... Oh, damn, he was getting hard just at the thought.

"I could cook you dinner," she continued. "You could bring one of your special bottles of wine."

"Maybe," he repeated. Was he breathing so hard she could tell it on the other end of the line? His lips were dry, and his throat grew tight. He grabbed a bottle of water at the edge of his desk.

"You say when," she said in a light tone.

"Maybe...next week." He sipped from the bottle. He felt like he needed to drench himself with it. If this kept up, he'd need a cold shower when he got off the phone. As he started to put it down, he noticed the folder with Joy Perkins' photos at the edge of the desk. He picked it up and rifled through it. The grim pictures had the effect of a shower. "Wait, she was wearing the pin."

"What?" Connie asked, sounding confused.

"Your sister had it on when she was killed. It was pinned to the collar of her jogging suit."

"I don't think so. Joy debated if she would wear her rings because her fingers swelled. Is there a way to be sure?"

He checked several other pictures, and it was visible on all of them—a tiny light-colored pin. "It's in the photos," he said grimly.

"What?" A croaking sound came across the phone line. "How do you know?"

"I have a picture in front of me." He continued to sift through the pictures, trying to find one that had a closer view of the object. It did look out of place on the informal sportswear.

"You're at work on Sunday?"

"Actually Bruno and I just got back from our morning walk."

"You have Joy's photos at home?" she asked pointedly.

He paused, as fear seized him. What if he had been mistaken in his original investigation? What if he had missed something that had seemed insignificant? He jerked to attention in his chair, the hair rising on his forearms, as his brain jolted into clarity. His chest tightened again. He reached into his desk drawer and pulled out a magnifying glass to have a closer look at the photos. Thoughts of a social call ended. "Perhaps I should come to Seattle and look more closely at that pin. Will you be around on Tuesday?"

"I'll make a point of it." She too sounded businesslike, but that was fine.

"I have to go. I'll call you."

He hung up and began looking through the pictures again with the magnifying glass. This was why it didn't pay to let personal feelings get involved in a case. It could mean making mistakes. Big mistakes.

****

After she hung up with Weldon, Connie paced around her loft in growing agitation. It had taken a couple of minutes for what he was saying to sink in.

At first she had been surprised he had such quick access to the photos. When he told her he was at home, it hit her fully—why did Weldon have a copy of Joy's photos at his house? Why did he want a closer look at the pin? To make matters worse, she felt guilty when he said the pin was visible in the pictures. If she had been able to view the pictures of Joy she could have checked for herself. Her failure at the police station still rankled.

Maybe she should try to find out more about what Weldon had been doing the past couple of days. Perhaps there was a story in the newspaper about his trip to Blackhawk. A few quick clicks brought up the website for the *Vancouver Sun*. Nothing. In fact, the last story about the Slasher was the day after her trip to Vancouver.

"New BC Slasher Victim," the headline screamed in bold type. The picture showed police carrying out a body bag. This was the same picture she had seen in a Seattle paper. She'd been surprised to learn that the afternoon she spent at his house, he'd been dealing with the latest killing.

And then he had come home and acted like the day had been routine. He might have spent the afternoon filing reports instead of poking around a murder scene. Connie shook her head. She was getting sidetracked. She went back to the paper.

The *Sun* story was much more detailed than the account she had previously read. She paid special attention to quotes from Weldon. Near the bottom was a paragraph that took her break away.

> *Unnamed sources say the body may have been dumped as early as two weeks ago, perhaps the same day as a woman's mutilated body was also found in the park. Police say the two cases are not related, but sources say it is possible that 38-year-old Joy Perkins may have surprised the killer as he*

prepared to deposit his latest victim. Police say that her death was different than the other BC Slasher victims, but they won't rule out the possibility that she might have fallen prey to the same killer.

"Damn you, Weldon!" Connie pounded her fist on her desk. He had purposely not told her about that theory. Maybe the newspaper was simply surmising that, but he thought it serious enough that he had retrieved a copy of Joy's file. She didn't think for a minute he had been holding onto the file all this time. He had a reason for suddenly having it in front of him, and he had a reason for wanting to come to Seattle to look at the pin. He had been uninterested in it until she adamantly stated Joy had not been wearing it while they were running. Could her killer have put it on her? Could the Slasher put something similar on his victims?

The thought of Joy falling prey to the BC Slasher sent a cold shiver of dread through her, but it made sense. The newspaper said her death was different from the others, but if the man had been in a rush and simply needed to kill her because she was in the way, it would be different.

Connie began searching other newspapers with Slasher stories. They all said he mutilated his victims, cutting off certain body parts, though they didn't say which. Was that why Weldon had been convinced Joy was not part of the case? Joy had been cut, but her body had been whole. Connie had asked police about that.

She was furious by the time she finished reading the stories so she called Weldon back. Before, she had toyed with him flirtatiously, but this time she harbored no romantic thoughts. He had not lied to her, but he had misled her. The call went straight to voice mail. She called his office and asked to have him paged.

Anger enveloped her, and Connie stalked around the loft. Why the hell couldn't he have been honest? And why did she feel so disappointed that he had withheld information from her? She thought they had become friends. Hell, at times, she wanted the relationship to go farther. So he was cool and rigid. So she preferred men who lived life as a mission of improvisation. She was interested in him, and that was precisely why she felt so betrayed.

Feeling frustrated and needing something to work out her energy, Connie picked up the sheaf of papers from Joy's shoe boxes. The conversations held little interest, but they would keep her occupied until she reached Weldon. She unfolded one of the sheets and began reading.

SexyLady: Where is everyone tonight?

Mike7445: Who cares? We don't need the others, sweetie, not me and my Sexy Lady.

SexyLady: I missed talking to you.

Mike7445: I've missed you too. I was worried when you disappeared.

SexyLady: Why?

Mike7445: It was like Little Bird. She just disappeared.

SexyLady: That won't happen to me, I'm addicted to you people.

Mike7445: I thought she was too. I sent her an email and her brother told me to get lost.

Who was Mike7445? She had never seen him or Little Bird in the chat room. A sentence in the conversation grabbed Connie's attention.

Mike7445: When can I meet you?

SexyLady: Isn't that against the rules?

Mike7445: Let's make our own rules. Give me your phone number and I'll call.

SexyLady: That's not a good idea. Maybe I can call you.

Mike7445: We don't live that far apart.

SexyLady: How do you know?

Mike7445: I know a lot more about you than you realize, Joy.

The page ended, and Connie fought a tremble of apprehension. Had this guy once been part of The Lair? Where was he now? Did Joy meet him? Was he the source of her marital woes?

A sudden knocking made her yelp. She'd been concentrating so hard on her questions, she'd been in another world. Connie hopped to her feet and went to the door, peering through the peephole. Sandy waited outside, two large brown bags in her hands.

Damn, she'd forgotten Sandy was coming over. While Connie was in no mood for Sandy's perkiness, her friend's presence might erase thoughts of Weldon's disloyalty.

"I'm not sure how good company I'll be this morning," she said as she opened the door. "I've got a lot on my mind."

Sandy's blue eyes grew wide and questioning. "Like what?"

"I'll tell you later," she said with a wave of dismissal.

"This will improve your spirits." Sandy crossed to the kitchen and began pulling items out of the bag. "I have fruit for a salad, fresh juice, bagels, smoked salmon, three kinds of cream cheese, all our favorites."

"Anything is fine." Normally that would have sounded good, but she was in no mood to worry about food. Any appetite she'd had vanished as she read the newspaper articles about the BC Slasher. The phone rang, and she threw herself across the sofa to answer it.

Weldon!

To her dismay, Lisa's voice came on at her quick hello. "I've been looking at those books you gave me about angels and mysticism. Did you know that the

Assembly for Truth and Spiritual Re-awakening preaches that angels exist all around us?"

Connie stifled the urge to tell Lisa she didn't have time to talk. Her sister sounded enthusiastic about the research she'd been conducting while Connie was out of town.

"That's great, Lisa," she said, glancing at Sandy who was chopping fruit in the kitchen.

"Invite her over," Sandy called. "There's plenty for three. I didn't even tell you what I got for dessert. Cheesecake."

Even the thought of cheesecake was unappealing and Connie started to decline, but Lisa was talking again.

"Con, I want to see that pin. I don't think it was a bird. I think it may be based on one of the angels in this book. The Assembly women are given them when they join. Kind of a guardian angel here on earth to watch over them."

"Joy's was obviously missing," Connie said sarcastically and then stopped. She was letting her frustration over Weldon turn her on the others. "I'm sorry. I'm in a foul mood."

"Come over and eat with us." Sandy had picked up the kitchen extension and her voice burst across the line. "If she's going to be grumpy, I need company."

"I'll be there in half an hour."

Connie hung up and turned away from Sandy to hide her disappointment. Instead of resuming her investigation she was in for a social day.

"Why the bad mood? No calls from the inspector?" Sandy asked, shoving a wayward curl back from her face.

"How did...who..." She stopped, realizing that Sandy had no way of knowing that her mood had switched because of Weldon. The other woman giggled at her for growing flustered.

At the same time, the phone rang and this time Weldon's voice came on the line.

"Did you have me paged?" His voice dropped to an intimate level that was growing more familiar. "This is becoming a nice habit."

Connie was in no mood for joking. "You're an SOB, Weldon," she shouted into the phone, oblivious to his attempt at goodwill. "Why the hell didn't you tell me that you were again looking at the possibility that Joy could have been a victim of the Slasher? That's why you have that file, isn't it?"

His intake of breath was sharp and all traces of good humor vanished. "I gather you read the *Sun*."

"Damn right, I did. You don't need to worry about coming to see the pin. I may come back to Vancouver. I want to see Joy's file again and that picture of the pin on her lapel. I'm going to visit those other dumping sites in Stanley Park too. I want to see if they're like where Joy was found. They were, weren't they?"

"I don't want you returning," he replied curtly. "Do you realize how foolish that is?"

"I don't give a damn what you think," Connie cried indignantly. "You lied to me."

"I did not lie. I simply did not give you all the facts. I won't apologize for trying to keep that information confidential. The newspaper had no right to publish what it did. It was pure speculation and rather dangerous."

"Dangerous?" she asked, her breath catching. "To whom?"

"You for one. Have you stopped to think that the man you saw at the site of Joy's death the other day could have been the suspect? If he had chosen that as a dumping site and Joy discovered him, who's to say that he didn't go back to see if it was so disturbed that he could never use it again?"

Connie nearly choked. "Is that what you think?"

"I won't tell you what I think. If our suspect was the person who saw you and he becomes worried you saw him, you could be in danger. Do you understand that?"

"Would he come after me?" Fear crept up her spine and she shuddered.

"He has no way of knowing who you are, but he spends a lot of time in the park, so he may have spotted you. As long as you don't go there, you'll be fine."

The inspector was right, but she doubted the man had seen her any more than she had glimpsed him. Still, the thought of being in his evil presence sent a further chill through her. Another thought flashed across her brain. She recalled the burgundy van that barreled by Weldon's house later in the day. She didn't want to think about the possibility the man might have followed her.

"I'll stay away from the park."

"You should stay away from Vancouver. I have to come to Seattle anyway so I can bring the photos. The photo of the pin is...well...less graphic than the others."

"Gee, Inspector, in another minute I'll think you're worried about me."

His sudden chuckle was a nice surprise that sent ripples of awareness through her body. "That sounds more like the Connie I know, eh?"

"I'm still peeved with you, eh?" she added sarcastically, but some of the tension that had gripped her earlier was lessening.

"I'll select a special bottle of wine to make up for my lapse in honesty."

"You do that, Inspector."

Connie hung up with a smile. Her chills were all gone. Instead she felt incredibly warm. Despite the arguing, the conversation had improved her mood.

Across the room Sandy began to laugh. "Your

face is about three shades of red, Con. Don't you ever try to tell me that man is not under your skin."

Her shoulders lifted in a shrug, and she tried to erase her smile, but she couldn't. "He has his strong points."

Sandy laughed louder. "No kidding."

"I still don't think it would work. I'm not ready to settle down, and with his job, who knows what kind of baggage he's carrying around? Not to mention, he's a neat freak. Just wait until he gets a load of this place."

"He's coming here?" Sandy asked.

"We're talking about it, but look at this mess." She waved a hand at her office area, regarding its clutter with a critical eye. Research books crowded the shelves along with folders of old scripts and information. Tapes, CDs, and DVDs of old stories were heaped on cabinets.

"But you know where to find everything," Sandy said, repeating Connie's favorite phrase when someone mentioned the chaotic nature of her work space.

Dismay spreading through her, Connie stood in the middle of her office space, hands on her hips, shaking her head. What would Weldon think of her if he could see this mess, even if she could find everything? "His desk had everything neatly put away. I've got stuff everywhere."

Unable to consider the mess any longer, she walked to the window. The sun sparkled down on the deep blue waters of the Sound in the distance. She turned to Sandy. "I'm feeling claustrophobic. Let's meet Lisa at the waterfront. We can eat later."

Sandy wiped her hands on a paper towel. "Great idea. I'll call her while you change."

Connie was still grinning as she swapped her flannel shirt and sweat pants for jeans and a turtleneck. Her mood had brightened like the day after talking with Weldon. Between his admonishments, he admitted he was worried about her safety and he wanted to see her on a social basis. Imagine that! Weldon, the dour inspector, might be interested in her. The idea sent a thrill of delight running through her.

****

The crisp morning air proved to be as therapeutic for Connie as the call from Weldon. Despite the sun, the air was cold, the breeze brisk, but it brought her skin alive. The three walked along the boardwalk of the waterfront, their footsteps thumping on the wooden beams.

For a time they meandered along the walkway, pointing out landmarks across the water and feeding the pigeons that danced along the pier and the seagulls that swooped from the sky to land on the railings. But they couldn't ignore the search for Joy's killer.

As they neared the end of the pier, Connie told them about the articles she had read that indicated Joy might have surprised the Slasher and become an unintended victim.

"No!" Lisa's face became pale, her brown eyes growing shadowed and thoughtful.

"Is that why you're talking about going back to Vancouver?" Sandy asked.

"Weldon doesn't think it's a good idea."

"I don't think it's a wise idea either," Lisa said, catching Connie's arm, her voice filled with concern. "There's work you can do here. When we get back to the apartment, I'll show you the books I've been reading about the Assembly religion. Their leader, R. L. Lincoln, may be giving a speech in Seattle in two weeks. Did you know he spoke in Bellingham last month? Joy and women in her office went to hear him. Maybe that was when Joy got her pin."

The information surprised Connie. "How do you

165

know?"

"There was a newspaper clipping folded up inside the angel book," Lisa said. "Along with a picture of the man. Have you ever seen him?"

"There was a picture of him in the diary," Connie said. "He's scary looking."

"Mesmerizing," Sandy said suddenly. "After you told me about that group, I looked them up. He grew up on a farm, a commune. You know why he is named R. L.? His real name is Righteous Love. I mean, who names their kid Righteous?"

"I want to go to the lecture," Lisa said.

"I'll go with you," Sandy volunteered, waving her hand like an elementary student.

"Me too." Connie raised her hand as well and glanced at Sandy. "I thought you were too busy talking to the people in The Lair."

"The Assembly has a chat room too," Sandy said. "Did you know that? Its names are Sister Love, or Graceful Ways, and those people are sweet compared to NiteMan and SkyGirl." She stopped and flopped onto a wooden bench. "My feet are killing me. I have to sit down."

Lisa sank down next to her and lifted her head to the sun. "Who is NiteMan?"

"From The Lair. You have to wonder about those people. They are in that chat room every night. They say they help each other, but they argue as much as they offer support."

Connie wasn't convinced they were going to find their answer in the chat rooms, but she didn't say anything. In the distance, clouds formed, and a crisp breeze tugged at her hair. Their pleasant day was not going to continue for long.

"It looks like Joy did talk to others besides the people in that room. There's a Mike something. She saved a bunch of conversations with him. Have you seen him in the room?"

Sandy scrunched up her face in thought. "No, but he might be one of the people they threw out. They do that if you break the rules."

Lisa looked over at her in shock. "Throw you out? How can they do that?"

"I guess they change the name of the room and don't tell you what it is or block you somehow. They've blocked this kid Melvin to try to keep him out, but I guess he's such a computer nerd, he keeps finding a way back in."

"What are the rules?" Lisa asked.

"You can't meet each other, or try to find out personal information. I've talked to a couple of them in instant messages and while the guys are curious about what I look like, most of them say they wouldn't meet me in person if they had the chance. They don't even want to see a picture of me."

"Maybe I should try talking to the people in the Assembly chat room," Lisa said.

"You need an invitation there too," Sandy said. "That is one thing they have in common with The Lair. They're just as secretive. You could be JoyfulP. That was Joy's name when she spoke to them."

"JoyfulP?" Connie repeated. Had she seen that name on Joy's computer?

Sandy nodded with an eager smile. "That other name I told you about." She turned to Lisa. "I'll email the info to you when I get home about how to get into the group and you can take over chatting as Joyful. The Lair is more fun. The Assembly men don't flirt—at least not in front of the women. But in both groups, men have sent me instant messages. I'm thinking of meeting one of the people in person, just to see what they're like."

"No," both Lisa and Connie said in unison.

"Why not?" Sandy asked, looking from one to the other. "I've found one guy who admits he lives in Portland and another who lives here in Seattle."

"I'm starting to think this is all superfluous," Connie said with a shake of her head, tiring of the discussion. "The more I think about it, the more I wonder if Joy didn't simply stumble into the Slasher as he was getting ready to dump a woman's body, or maybe she saw him carrying the body into the bushes. You know Joy, she would be curious about something like that. She was the type who might go over and chastise him for throwing things in the park."

"If that's the case, then let police do their job and find the lunatic," Lisa argued.

Sandy hopped to her feet as clouds covered the sun. "Let's go eat. I'm getting hungry."

The pier had become crowded. Sunday tourists and families looking for a close getaway to escape the house thronged around the shops and seafood kiosks.

"Hurry, the light's going to change," Sandy shouted as they neared the street. She darted forward to join the crowd that was already making its way across the wide street. Lisa hung back as the green Walk sign changed to an orange Don't Walk, and Connie hesitated for an instant before she stepped forward off the curb and onto the street. Immediately, she could see she was never going to make it across the southbound traffic, let alone the northbound lanes. She hurried back toward the sidewalk before the light became green.

The burgundy van seemed to come out of nowhere, tires screeching as she stepped toward the curb. For an instant Connie froze in fear and then she tripped backward over the curb and tumbled behind a lamp pole as the van came so close she felt the whoosh of air from its high rate of speed. It slowed momentarily and then sped away.

Chapter Ten

"Are you all right?" Lisa rushed over to Connie and reached down to help her up. "What a jerk! I wish I'd gotten his license number."

With Lisa's assistance, Connie stood. She brushed dust from her jacket with unsteady hands. Her calf ached and when she looked down, she saw a trickle of blood on her lower leg between the cuff of her jeans and her white sock.

"I'm okay. I just scraped my leg," she said shakily. It was the second time in two weeks she'd almost been run over. Her knees wobbled, and Connie clung to the light post that had probably saved her life. She looked in the direction where the van had disappeared. Could it have been the same van she saw in Vancouver?

"Did you see the license tags at all?" she asked Lisa.

"No, but why did the idiot pull out so fast just as the light changed? It was like he wanted to hit someone."

Connie didn't want to think about that. With all her close calls the past couple of weeks, she wasn't certain what to think anymore. Certainly all these strange events could not be coincidences. With Lisa partially supporting her, they made their way across the street when the light changed. Connie tried to tell herself she stayed in the middle of the crowd because it was easier, not that she feared someone might still be after her.

Sandy rushed over as they stepped on the opposite curb.

"That guy pulled away from the corner, like he was aiming for you."

She had to face it; the van had been aimed at her. It was not an accident like the night Ralph had nearly hit her.

"Did you see the license plate?" Connie asked.

Sandy made a face. "I was watching you." She took Connie's hand on the other side. "Are you all right?"

"I will be. It takes more than a crazy driver to bring me down." She fought off her inner shakiness, forcing her voice to be calm and sure. An inner terror lurked, threatening to take possession of her emotions, but Connie refused to give in. She would not let this man—whoever he was—get her down.

All three grew quiet as they walked to the car. Connie didn't want them to know the incident frightened her. It had nothing to do with the close call. It was the fact that a burgundy van kept turning up.

****

"I'm absolutely famished," Lisa said as the three entered Connie's apartment.

Connie felt like her emotions were as volatile and changing as the storm clouds brewing outside her huge apartment windows. Between the argument with Weldon and the brush with the van, her nerves were on edge.

While Sandy finished brunch preparations, Lisa and Connie huddled at the desk to study the gold pin. Connie had no idea if it had any bearing on Joy's death, though it did strike her as odd that her sister was not wearing it when they left the hotel but had it on when her body was found.

Lisa pulled out two thick books from her tote bag. Colorful sticky labels protruded from both of them.

"Wait until you see these," Lisa began, opening

one to a sticky label. "I thought that pin resembled the angels in this book, but after seeing it again, I'm more confused."

She dropped it on Connie's desk and flipped through pages of pictures that depicted what an angel was supposed to look like. None of them resembled the pin.

"I'm not sure of the significance of the pin," Sandy called from the kitchen. "Lots of people are wearing angel pins these days."

"A couple of people at her office were wearing them when I was there," Lisa acknowledged. "That is what is so odd."

"You visited her office?" Connie jerked toward her sister in surprise. "You didn't tell me that. You said you talked to people, but I didn't know you'd gone there. I keep meaning to pay a visit. After what Weldon said about co-workers thinking she had marital problems, I figure maybe some of them could give me some answers. Did they say anything to you?"

"I didn't ask about marital problems," Lisa said, her face contorting in distaste. "I wouldn't ask about that even if I thought it was true. It seems too invasive."

"That's why I've been putting it off. Tell me about the pins."

Lisa flapped her hands like a chicken fluffing its feathers. "I told you a couple of women went with her to the Lincoln speech. They were wearing angel pins they bought at the speech. Beth Harden, one of her friends, said Joy bought one too. She also said Joy stopped wearing hers because she was moving into another realm. There are supposedly certain degrees or levels in the Assembly church and each is assigned a certain angel. Joy could have moved up to another level and started wearing a different pin. But the one we have doesn't look anything like theirs or the angels in this book."

"I think it looks more like a bird," Sandy called from the kitchen.

"Maybe," Lisa agreed. "Judging from these books, I wonder if she was getting into mystic spirits. Goddesses of the forest, or rulers of the earth—like that. I found some pages folded up inside one of the books that seemed to indicate she was fascinated with the idea of those mystic gods, Earth Mother and how animals took on heavenly spirits or could shift shapes."

"She didn't really believe that," Connie couldn't keep a skeptical note out of her tone.

"I have no idea. I just saw notes about the raven being a trickster and changing forms."

"Raven?" Connie's heart skipped. "There's a Raven in her online group."

"They call him voodoo man when he's not around," Sandy said. She walked around the corner, wiping her hands on a dish cloth. "No one seems to like him, but when I asked why they don't vote him out, no one would say anything. It's like they're afraid of him, like he really can change forms and turn up. As they were saying that, he made a comment, and no one had seen him come into the room." She shuddered and shook her head. "Spooky. It was damn eerie the way he made a comment and then his name popped up as though he could reveal it whenever he felt like it, but he'd been there all along."

Connie listened to Sandy's rambling with only half a mind. Angels, mystics, and Internet chat rooms. Did it any of it figure into Joy's death? Her logic told her it was more likely that Joy had surprised the Slasher. She forced herself back to the conversation and what Lisa was saying.

"Internet chat rooms are a joke. One woman in my office makes a practice of playing games with people. She'll pretend to be from the same home town as guys and then look up locations on MapQuest and send the poor guys driving all over to meet her."

"That's mean." Sandy tapped Connie on the shoulder. "Hey, we should suggest to Jim that we do something on that for a series. 'Games People Play Online,' we could call it. Or 'The Darker Side of the Internet.' That has to be better than Internet bargain hunting. And I've already done lots of research."

"Sounds like a good idea to me." Connie started to close the book, but it fell open and she froze. The book had a sticker at the top of the second page. Property of William Lonetree." Her gasp of surprise was so loud Lisa and Sandy stopped talking.

"What?" Lisa asked.

She pointed at the name, her throat tightening.

"Do you know who that is?" Lisa asked. "Most of those books belong to him."

"He's the stranger from the memorial," Connie explained in a strangled voice. "Weldon said the man told him he had an appointment to meet with Joy after she got back from Vancouver."

Lisa's eyes grew large and focused on Connie. "Have you talked to him?"

"I tried to see him when I was up there, but he wasn't around. I don't want to talk to him on the phone. I need to see him personally."

Will Lonetree no longer seemed critical but seeing him would give her an excuse for another trip to Vancouver. The more she thought about it and the van coming after her, the more convinced Connie was that she needed to return. If the killer had followed her to Seattle, what difference would a trip up north make?

****

Rain and wind rattled the windows, but Connie

had lit a fire in the fireplace that dominated the end of her living room. Sandy was on the computer, conversing with the group from The Lair, while Connie and Lisa read over the computer conversations in Joy's shoe boxes.

"This is the end of that pile," Lisa announced, putting down a sheaf of papers and rubbing her eyes. "She was making plans to meet this Mike guy."

Connie brushed hair from her face. It seemed like they had been at this for hours. "I wonder if she did."

Lisa's eyes grew watery and she sighed heavily. "It's sad, reading these. At times she sounded flirtatious. I wish I could ask her why she felt like she had to look for something else in her life. Was Ralph not giving her something she needed? I feel like there was a part of her we didn't know anymore. Had she changed this much? The woman in these conversations is a stranger to me. Reading these you would never think of her as having a husband and kids." She wiped a finger across her cheek.

"Did she mention in any of those conversations that she thought her husband was seeing a woman?" Connie asked.

"She acted as though he didn't matter, and this Mike was very flattering. She'd tell him about closing a house deal and he'd give her lots of encouragement. Maybe Ralph wasn't doing that. In some ways he does seem resentful of her job."

The thought of Joy living vicariously through the computer saddened Connie. Still, the information was there in black and white. "Do you suppose she was losing weight to meet this guy or did losing weight give her the urge to buy those clothes and look for someone new?"

Again Lisa sighed and shook her head. "That's the saddest part. We'll never know."

Connie opened the final shoe box and pulled out

another sheaf of papers. She wasn't certain she could bear to read many more of the coy conversations between Joy and Mike. A booklet tumbled from between the pages.

"Hey, a checkbook," Lisa said, picking it up. "I wonder why it's in here."

Connie barely glanced up. She resumed scanning the conversations, while Lisa thumbed through the checkbook.

"Hmm... I don't think this is her main account with Ralph."

"How do you know?" Connie peered at her over the edge of the papers.

"She's given me checks before. This has a PO Box on the address, not her home address." She held it out toward Connie. "See? Not only that, it had more than fifty-thousand dollars in it as of last summer. Remember when they were having money troubles and Ralph said he might have to take out a loan? Why would he do that if she had all this money?"

The points were valid, but Connie had no more answers for that any more than she had for Joy's computer conversations. Weldon said they might be having money problems. This checking account could have solved them.

"Oh, geez, look at this," Lisa's voice rose in anguish and she jabbed a finger at an entry and then flipped to another.

Feeling her sister stiffen beside her, Connie leaned over to study the book. The carbon pages contained withdrawals. One for a thousand dollars, another for two thousand and both were made out to Cash. Why would Joy need to withdraw such huge amounts?

"Here's another for cash," Lisa went on. "It's for almost three thousand. They're all around two weeks apart. Why was she doing that?"

175

"Perhaps to pay the mortgage, help with expenses?" Connie offered.

"Maybe, but why not make out a check to the exact place? Why cash? That's the thing. There are no withdrawals in here except for cash. She wasn't using this account to pay the grocery store or for ordinary shopping expeditions. She was taking out cash. I wonder why."

"Maybe to buy those clothes? Perhaps she didn't want Ralph to know she was spending so much money on herself."

"I suppose."

Another disturbing thought struck Connie. "Could she have given it to the Assembly? In her diary, Naomi said that was one of the first ways she got sucked into the church. They asked for money. Before long, she had sold all her possessions and that was one of the reasons she was so willing to move to the farm."

Lisa shook her head, eyes filled with disbelief. "I can't imagine Joy leaving Mindy or Jeremy. Do you really think she would consider moving them to a farm in the wilderness? Away from us? From Mom and Dad?"

Connie shoved aside the boxes and began putting on the lids. She'd had enough. Digging through Joy's belongings depressed her. It only pointed out how little she knew about her sister. First the marriage woes, then computer people, the religious books, now this. She and Lisa had never had the slightest indication of trouble. The thought that Joy hadn't trusted them enough to confide in her sisters bothered her.

"We should give this checkbook to Ralph," Lisa said with a sad sigh. "I wonder if he even knows about it."

They exchanged a quick glance. What would Ralph think if they'd discovered a hidden account?

Even if he needed the money, it might hurt to know Joy was hiding money. Yet they could not keep it secret. The family could use the cash, if not now, then as the children grew up and went to college.

"I can take it to him when I go to Vancouver," Connie volunteered.

"We'll both take it," Lisa announced. "I'm going with you."

"Lisa, that's not necessary. I can take care of myself."

"Oh, really?" Lisa's brows rose skeptically and she cocked her head toward Connie. "I have my doubts. It's like you suddenly turned clumsy or accident-prone. You almost got hit by a car today. Have you forgotten that bonk on the head the day after Joy died?"

There it was. She'd been trying not to think about it, but apparently she was not the only one who was concerned about all these things that kept occurring. She suspected from the first that the attack in their Vancouver hotel was not coincidence. But what didn't make sense was all these close calls. If someone was after her, was he inept? Was she lucky? One thing was for certain. Someone was watching her. Was he trying to hurt her? Or scare her? That was the question. Was it the killer?

Connie waved her hand in a dramatic gesture as though that might wipe away her horrifying thoughts. At the same time she summoned her brightest smile, hoping to dissuade her sister. If someone was after her, she could not place Lisa into the same sort of danger. She put her hand on Lisa's shoulder. "I'll be fine."

Lisa shook her head, dark hair dancing around her shoulders. "We'll both be fine because we're both going. It's about time you stopped doing all the work. If you insist on going alone, I'll simply follow you. And you know I need someone to watch out for me. I have no clue about what to do in this kind of situation."

****

Mitch stared hard at the bulletin board above his desk, a grisly tribute to multiple murders. His gaze searched for anything he might have missed during the dozens of times he had studied the board before. A map of Stanley Park dotted with pins denoted where women's bodies had been found. Pictures of the women lined the edge of the map.

On his desk he had spread out the sheets with simple bios of the women and where they were from. He studied names, hometowns, ages, jobs. What had brought them in touch with a mass murderer?

The phone rang and he grabbed it and hit the speak button. "Yes?"

"Hello, Weldon?"

Despite their earlier argument, pleasure surged through Weldon as Connie's voice came across the line. His muscles relaxed slightly. He held his pencil poised over his notepad, a normal reaction when he answered the phone, but now he simply tapped it on the pad.

"Good morning," he said, a smile stealing across his face. Hopefully no one around his desk noticed. Luckily the squad room was nearly empty and his partner, Bernie, was over in the corner fighting with the recalcitrant coffeemaker. He doodled on his notepad, outlining a face with a big grin.

"I'm sorry if I was out of line yesterday," Connie began in a low, apologetic voice. "I was furious over that newspaper article."

"I understand. Have you decided what you're cooking me for dinner?"

She paused, and a twinge of apprehension jerked him straighter in his chair. He scribbled through the smiling face.

"Well, about that..."

178

"Yes?" he questioned, his voice growing sharper as anxiety gave way to irritation. He sat forward, pencil poised above the pad.

"I need to go to Vancouver tomorrow."

"I thought we had decided I was coming there." He tossed the pencil down on the pad. Strangely enough he was looking forward to the trip. He was curious about where she lived and her life. It had been a long time since he had been this intrigued by a woman, and while part of him didn't want to take the time to get to know her, and he kept reminding himself she was merely an external part of a case, another part of him kept thinking of her. Visions of Connie bombarded him at the strangest moments. He kept seeing her at his house, playing with Bruno or the way her eyes lit up when she teased him. Even digging in his garden had him regarding the flowers with her in mind. Which would she like best for vases in the house? What was her favorite flower? What would it feel like to do more than simply kiss her?

"I know you said you might come..." she said tentatively.

"I am coming. So stay put," he ordered.

"You think I'm tempting your killer?"

He drew a deep breath. He should never have admitted his fear to her. This was the problem with becoming personally involved with someone, even on the fringes of a case. He prided himself on staying removed from personal issues, but in this instance he had let down his guard and allowed his uneasiness to show. The serial murder case had him baffled, and there was still no way of tying Joy Perkins to his string of killings unless she had suffered the misfortune of stumbling across the Blade.

The Blade. The name filled the outer corners of his notepad and sketches of various straight razors filled several pages. The papers called the madman the BC Slasher, but Weldon and Bernie knew him as the Blade. The Coroner's office had ascertained that the man killed his victims with a thin razor-like blade, the type used in barber shops. After the initial death, he unleashed a hell-like fury on the women's bodies, unlike anything Weldon had ever seen. That was what had been missing with Joy. She had been slashed, but her injuries were from a regular hunting knife.

"Weldon?" Connie asked when he didn't answer.

"I'm here," he said, as disappointment deflated him. "I don't know about tempting him. I'm not convinced that the man you saw is the killer. I simply was trying to keep you from doing anything foolish."

"Well, gee, thanks for the concern," she cooed, her voice lightening. "But Lisa and I want to talk to Will Lonetree about Joy's desire to change religions."

Weldon nodded, as his smile returned. Lonetree posed no threat, and that direction was a safe course for Connie and her sister to pursue. "If you insist on coming, I hope you stay away from the park."

"Lisa doesn't think she can ever go there again."

"I want your promise that you won't go either," he warned, noting her evasiveness.

Weldon could almost see her set face as she considered the request.

"I don't like orders."

"Which is why I am merely making a request." No sense turning hard-nosed about it. He was learning it was easier to get her to do what he wanted if he suggested.

Her sudden laugh sent a ripple of awareness through him. "You are a lot more clever about dealing with women than you pretend, Weldon, you sly dog."

"I like to think I'm a good judge of character."

"I'll make that promise for now. When can we come see you and show you the pin?"

The confusion over the pin disturbed him, though he was no longer certain it meant anything. He glanced at the board where mutilated bodies of the women were pinned alongside their facial photographs. The madman had left tokens on each, something different each time. None of them resembled the pin on Joy Perkins photograph, but he wanted to see it to be sure. While the murder weapon had been different in Joy's case, the presence of a token left by her killer could prove a connection.

"How about if you come by before noon? I can buy lunch for you and your sister."

"Great!" she said enthusiastically. "We're seeing Lonetree at 10:30."

Weldon hung up, and realized his cheeks actually hurt from his wide grin. He forced the smile from his face. He had to stop letting this crazy attraction distract him. He turned his attention to the worn files on his desk.

Someone had to stop the Blade. That must remain his main focus.

****

A fine mist dampened Connie's hair the instant she stepped out of the car, muttering a curse. Lisa appeared from the other side.

"It's a good thing I came with you," she proclaimed as they met in back of the car.

"I can change a tire myself," Connie said, popping open the trunk. "I've done it before." She leaned inside and shoved aside the box of books that seemed to have taken up permanent residence in her car. Lisa had brought them back again after finishing her research. Lifting the bottom mat, she pushed it up until she could unfasten and pull out the jack.

A semi-truck roared by, showering them with a fine spray of grime.

"Yuck!" Lisa cried. "I hate changing tires by the side of the road. Maybe we should risk the tire and try to get to the next exit."

"We're okay." Connie lifted out the spare and leaned it beside the car, casting a wary glance at the freeway. A car flew by at a high rate of speed. The freeway wasn't crowded in this lesser traveled area between Bellingham and the Canadian border and since the road was fairly straight, drivers used it to make up for lost time.

Luckily the flat was on the right side, away from traffic. Lisa felt the thumping first, and they both realized what the problem was. For an instant Connie feared someone cut the tire on purpose, but they would have felt it before leaving Bellingham. No, it was simply a flat.

Now she just needed to get the tire changed. Thick gray clouds loomed overhead, threatening rain. Hopefully it held off until they finished. Changing a flat in the driving rain would be a mess, but she hurried for another reason beyond rain. She'd been keeping a close watch on the rearview mirror all the way from Seattle. She'd seen no sign of a burgundy van, but she feared it might roar by at any minute.

Together they carried the jack and tire iron to the front of the car. Connie pried off the hubcap and began loosening the lug nuts on the tire.

Lisa stood back, eyes on the threatening clouds. "We could call Ralph. We're only ten miles from Bellingham."

Connie raised her eyes to her sister. "After what we just did, you expect him to help us?"

"What are you talking about? We helped him and the kids," Lisa yelped in protest. "That was thirty thousand dollars he didn't know they had.

Would you rather it just sit in the bank?"

"Did you see the look on his face? He was devastated." She quivered slightly and it had nothing to do with the cold mist that dampened her hair and exposed skin.

It would be a long time before she forgot the shocked look on Ralph's face when they presented him with the checkbook. His long, jowly face had gone pale before turning a dark pink. For a minute, Connie feared he would burst into tears. The worst part was that he was trying hard to hide his shock. He'd been unable to do more than sputter at first. It was obvious he didn't want the sisters to know that he'd had no idea the account existed. Finally he turned and lumbered from the kitchen. When he returned his blue eyes were red-rimmed. He thanked them, and Connie hurried Lisa out of the kitchen.

It wasn't until they were in the car and headed down the drive that both remembered they forgot to ask him about why he lied about going to the Muddy Hen.

Connie threw her weight into lifting the car. The jack groaned in progress but slowly the car rose until the wheel was off the ground. She was pleased that her weekly workouts gave her the strength for the work. As she removed the lug nuts she had previously loosened, she was surprised to see Lisa rolling the spare toward her.

"Teamwork," Lisa announced as Connie pulled off the flat tire and they made an exchange.

"Put that by the trunk. We'll leave it at a station once we get to Vancouver and get it fixed before we drive back. These spares aren't made for much wear."

Connie worked quickly to put on the spare, aware of how vulnerable she was. Too low to see over the top, she knew that someone could come up beside them in a hurry and surprise them. Should someone hit the car, it might topple off the jack and onto her. Feeling a quick rush of relief as she finished, Connie lowered the car and finished tightening the lug nuts. She carried the jack back to the trunk. Together she and Lisa replaced the jack and put the damaged tire into the trunk.

She wiped her grimy hands together and smiled proudly at Lisa, pleased the ordeal was over. "See? I told you I could do it. Do you have one of those hand wipey things to clean my hands?"

"You're pretty resourceful," Lisa said with an approving nod, pulling a small foil pouch from her pocket. "I didn't realize that."

"I keep telling you I can take care of myself. You have your little foil pouches, but see?" She pointed at a canvas bag in the trunk. "I always carry extra clothes and a first aid kit with me. Bonks on the head and close calls with nutty drivers won't stop me." Connie's gaze traveled to the freeway. No sign of any burgundy van today. If someone was following them, they were doing a good job of remaining hidden.

Lisa reached out and started to pull a yellow tag that hung from the top of the trunk. "What is this?"

"It's the emergency escape latch," Connie said, showing her the tag. "In case you fall into the trunk and it closes while you're changing the tire I guess. Not that I've ever done that."

Lisa giggled. "You do know your way around. Does the good inspector know this?"

The thought of Weldon turned her insides mushy. Connie wanted to say she wasn't excited about seeing him today, but she was. She only hoped he wasn't too angry with her for insisting on coming. He had offered to buy lunch, right? That had to be a good sign. As for her promise to stay out of the park, she'd crossed her fingers as she made the vow. Lisa didn't want to visit the park, but she also threatened not to let Connie out of her sight. As long as Lisa was with her, they would both be safe.

****

The University of British Columbia sat high on a bluff on the western edge of Vancouver. Professor William Lonetree's office was in a glass office building on the north campus. A petite, dark woman with short black hair met them in the lobby. She introduced herself as his assistant and led them to his door and knocked. Connie had not talked directly to the man. She made the appointment through the assistant.

Lonetree greeted them with a curt nod, as he came around his desk toward them. Up close, his height was overpowering, and Connie had to stop herself from stepping back. Broad shouldered, his dynamic presence filled the small room. His dark face was proud and handsome with chiseled features reminiscent of a warrior of past days. Dressed in a tweed blazer, polo shirt, and jeans, he might have been any other professor, except when he reached forward to shake hands, his head shifted and his long black hair, held by a beaded tie, fell forward. His dark eyes were stony, like black coal.

"How may I help you?" he asked, looking from Connie to Lisa once the introductions were finished. His voice was deep and his speech carried traces of a British accent.

Lisa shifted and cleared her throat, but she said nothing.

"We're here about our sister, Joy," Connie began.

"Of course. Please sit down." He gestured at two plastic chairs beside his metal desk. Connie perched on the edge of chair and scanned the office with curious eyes. Shelves were packed with books, some of them old. Most of the free wall space was hung with masks that resembled totem poles. A computer monitor occupied one corner of a desk cluttered with papers and more books. His field was First Nation Studies, and the books reflected that.

"Did you ever meet Joy?" Lisa asked, sitting forward.

He sat very straight in his chair behind his large desk, hands clasped on top of his desk. Big, powerful hands, Connie noted.

His intense gaze swung to Lisa. "I was supposed to, but no. She scheduled an appointment with me for the week after she died. When she didn't show up, I called her office and discovered what had happened."

"You were at the memorial service." Connie fought to keep her voice from sounding accusing.

His nod was curt. "Yes, I spoke to your parents. They were very...nice."

"Why did she want to see you?" Lisa pressed.

Her sister's forceful tone surprised Connie.

He looked away, avoiding their eyes. "That was a private matter."

"Mr. Lonetree, our sister is dead," Connie said. "We're trying to find out who killed her."

His head jerked toward Connie. His eyes were black daggers piercing through the air. "I do understand your sorrow and concern, but that isn't a wise idea. That is work for the authorities. What makes you think I can help you?"

Lisa removed two books from her bag and slid them across the desk. "These are yours, right?"

He blinked and put a big palm over them and pulled them toward him as if to claim ownership. "Yes. Thank you for returning them. "

"I have several more in the car," Connie said. "They were too heavy to bring in."

"I'll send my assistant to pick them up," he replied with an abrupt nod.

"Why was Joy reading those books?" Lisa

persisted. "Did she want to change religions?"

He turned sideways in his chair and his lips drew down into a fierce frown. "You should have approached her with these questions."

"She's not here," Lisa said, emotion cracking her voice.

Connie patted Lisa's arm, turning to Lonetree. "We're discovering how little we knew about our sister's present life and we realize we should have made attempts to get to know her better. We're doing that now, but we want to be certain that there was nothing that was...well...cultish, or that might have led to her death."

His brow wrinkled in a puzzled furrow. "Cultish?"

"Her husband told us she spent a lot of time on religious reading, maybe even thinking of leaving their church."

He lifted his big shoulders in a shrug. "She was simply seeking spiritual answers. There was nothing cult-like about it. She was fascinated by the idea of Mother Earth, the thought of the alignment of personality with the soul, taking control of one's destiny."

"You're saying that's not cult-like?" Lisa asked.

"In case you think some crazy cult person killed her, then know that when you're speaking of Mother Earth, the fundamental principle is the sacredness of life. Mother Earth believes in life, not death."

Lisa drew a deep breath and turned away, tears forming at the edges of her eyes. Connie understood her grief. Joy had been looking for spiritual answers toward the end of her life, as well as possibly suffering from marital problems. She had taken her questions to the online chat groups and to this strange man instead of to her sisters.

"If you never met her, how did she get the books?" Connie asked.

"I mailed them to her. She gave me a post office box number in Bellingham."

"Do you remember it?" Lisa asked.

He leaned forward and flipped through a Rolodex on his desk. "Box 790."

Lisa turned to Connie, brown eyes wide. "That was the box number listed on those checks." She faced him again, her face tense. "Did she send you money?"

The question appeared to take Lonetree by surprise. He blinked several times before shaking his head. "As I said, she simply asked about Mother Earth and how she might uncover the spirituality within herself. She was curious. Money never came up."

"Why did she want to see you?" Lisa asked.

"Returning the books, I suppose." He turned his wrist toward him, glancing at his watch. "Is there anything else?"

Connie fished in her pocket and brought out the small gold pin. She had put it into a plastic see-through bag. "Have you ever seen this?"

He took the bag and examined the contents. The furrow on his brow deepened. "Nope. Can't say I have."

"It looks like an angel," Lisa offered.

"Possible," he said with a shrug. "A lot of people wear them. It's not something that would be part of a belief in Mother Earth."

"What about a bird?" Connie added.

His dark gaze shot to her, and the stoniness she saw there surprised her.

"What about some sort of Indian god?" Lisa continued and he swung in her direction. "Or could it be used in some sort of sacred ritual?"

"Sacred ritual?" A black brow quirked up. "What kind of sacred ritual do you mean?"

"We don't know!" Lisa wailed. "That's what's so

frustrating. We have no idea of what we're looking for."

The dark eyes softened. "According to some beliefs, sacred rituals can be as mundane as a daily habit. Walking the dog can be a sacred ritual if you attribute it that way." His smile was placid, but Connie wondered if he was making fun of them.

"We don't want to take up any more of your time," she said, rising, fearing this had been a waste of time. "It doesn't sound like there was anything to her search for spirituality."

His sudden frown was fierce, black eyes becoming glacial as they challenged hers. "The search for understanding spirituality is far from trivial."

Connie's insides turned cold from the frosty glare. "Not that it wasn't important to her," she said apologetically. "I'm sure it was, but I don't think it had anything to do with her death."

"Of course not," he said with a grunt. He stood behind the desk, signaling an end to the interview.

Connie couldn't think of anything else to ask and Lisa had grown silent. Both women rose at the same time and he walked them to the door and opened it. His assistant was no longer at the outside desk. He took a quick look at his watch, impatience crossing his dark face. "I'll walk down with you and get the books."

They were nearly to the front door when Connie remembered the gold pin. She'd given it to him and not retrieved it. He had put it on his desk and must not have noticed it amid the clutter. Unless he intended keeping it? She caught Lisa's arm. "We forgot the pin."

"I'll get it," he offered.

"I can get it. Lisa, will you give him the books?"

She handed her keys to Lisa and hurried back to his office, footsteps tapping a rapid echo in the empty hall. His assistant was still gone and she crossed to his desk. The pin rested on a pile of papers, and Connie reached for it, tripping on the wheels of his chair. As she pitched forward, she started to laugh. Perhaps her sister was right about her clumsiness. Trying to catch herself, Connie threw out her hands, stopping her fall on the desk top. The corner of her fingers hit the computer mouse. His screen flickered and flew to life.

Connie started to back away and then froze. Her laugh caught in her throat. The screen displayed his sign-on page. The name on the front screen was Raven40.

Chapter Eleven

Connie's fingers shook as she started the car and pulled out of visitor parking. Her thoughts blasted at her like a shotgun. Raven! Will Lonetree was the mysterious Raven.

"What's wrong?" Lisa asked, concern in her voice as though she sensed Connie's fear. "You're white as a ghost. That guy was strange, but..."

"He's Raven," Connie croaked.

"Who?"

"Raven from the chat room."

Lisa gulped. "I thought the people in that chat room weren't supposed to know each other's real name, much less meet."

"That's the point. We didn't ask him how he met Joy." She pounded her hand on the steering wheel in frustration. "Why the hell didn't we ask him? He met her through the damn chat room. Damn, are we horrible detectives. We forgot to ask Ralph about the Muddy Hen and now this!"

"Which is why you should leave the investigating to the police. Say, you don't suppose..." Lisa began and then stopped. Anxious fingers gripped Connie's shoulder. "Maybe if she was willing to meet Raven in person, she met others, like that Mike."

Connie nodded, but she was still focused on the discovery that Lonetree was Raven40. "He keeps emphasizing they shouldn't try to find out who the others are, but he was meeting Joy? What a hypocrite! I wonder if he does that with others. He obviously talks to them outside the room."

Lisa twisted around to look back at the campus as they left the grounds. "Do you want to go back and ask him about it?"

"No." Connie glanced at the rearview mirror. The wide expanse of wet road was empty. No burgundy vans around today, but she intended to keep checking. "There is something strange about that guy. We've seen it online, and now we know who he is."

"We ought to find out who everyone else is," Lisa said. "I've been focused on the mystic stuff, but do you want me to do that once we get back?"

Connie glanced over at her sister. "Can you?"

Lisa winked at Connie, giving her a sly smile. "I can do just about anything on the computer if I set my mind to it."

A chirping emitted from Connie's purse. Lisa lifted it, pulled out her cell phone and held it open. Connie expected to hear Weldon's crisp Canadian tones, but instead Sandy's cheerful voice came across the line.

"How's Vancouver?"

"Damp," Connie said, flicking on the windshield wipers as the rain switched from a fine mist to droplets. "How's work?"

"Boring. I found a couple of story ideas, courtesy of our Ghost friend from the chat room. I was actually talking to him from work this morning."

"Is that a good idea? You know how Jim feels about people playing around on the Internet at work." Jim York had threatened to log online time if staff members used it for anything but necessary research.

"I'll tell him I'm getting ideas for a series on the Internet. NiteMan had a couple of suggestions too. These guys are online addicts so they know what they're talking about. They're my secret sources. Did you and Lisa find out anything about that pin?"

"No, but I did find out who Raven is."

"Raven? Dr. Voodoo? Do you think he killed Joy?" Sandy asked, voice lowering to a conspiratorial level.

Connie shivered despite the heat that poured from the vents beside her. The thought frightened her. In some ways it was easier to think Joy's killer was the Slasher, an unknown maniac. Had they just met the killer?

"I don't know," Connie said. "But it's reason enough for you to stop your research for the moment, Searcher."

"Well, who is it?"

Perhaps knowing would dissuade her from spending so much time in the chat room. "Will Lonetree."

"The professor who owned the mystic books? The guy you went to see?" Sandy squealed.

"I saw the name on his computer. Raven40, clear as day."

"Or dark as night," Sandy said, voice growing solemn.

A fearful image presented itself—a hulking, dark shadow standing over Joy. Beside her, Lisa was chewing on a thumbnail, her brow furrowed in thought. She had something on her mind.

"What did he say?" Sandy asked.

"Nothing. He doesn't know I found out and I'm not certain I should tell him."

"He was online this morning. I wish I'd known."

"Do me a favor," Connie said, sudden concern gripping her. "Stay off there until I get back. I don't want him to realize we're on to him. I'm not certain if this is useful, but until we figure out if it is, I want to keep our knowledge a secret."

"Got it, boss!" Sandy said cheerfully. "I'll go back to the Assembly room. Where are you now? On your way to meet the inspector?"

"Yes."

"Got your war paint on?" she asked with a giggle.

Connie rolled her eyes. "I'm wearing makeup if that's what you want to know."

"I hope you used that new foundation I got you. It makes your face positively glow."

"Thank you, Elizabeth Arden. I'll call you later."

Handing the phone back to Lisa, Connie shook her head as though it might erase Sandy's comments. She had taken special care getting dressed today. She'd spent extra minutes making certain her brown eye shadow complimented her hazel eyes, and she used just enough eyeliner to make her eyes look bigger. A smattering of rouge tinted her cheeks, and her hair was pulled away from her face and held in place by a blue and white silk scarf.

Her new knit blue pants suit could be explained because she and Lisa would be in the car most of the day. So what if the suit emphasized the round lines of her buttocks below a tailored short jacket which nicely displayed her breasts? Connie found herself wondering if Weldon would notice.

Part of her kept thinking about seeing Weldon— the part of her that buzzed every time his name popped into her head. Now the buzzing was an outright assault of eager anticipation as she guided the car through traffic toward Weldon's building. Her heart rate was accelerating the closer they got to his office, but while thoughts of him made her pulse race, did she want more? Like what? A night in bed? A relationship? No, she was too busy with work for romance, and he probably was too.

Her looks today might enhance his appraisal of her, but how far did she want this crazy infatuation to go? She wrinkled her nose. These thoughts were silly. She had to forget the personal elements and think about what was important: finding Joy's killer. She glanced at Lisa, who was gazing out the side window.

"What are you thinking?"

"I don't think it's Lonetree," Lisa said, biting a nail. "He might frighten those people in the chat room, but I don't think he hacks up women. The man is a professor."

"Look at Ted Bundy. Everyone who knew him in real life thought he was normal. He picked up victims pretending to be the boy next door."

"The boy next door," Lisa repeated, frowning. "Maybe."

****

"I think Sergeant Case needs to look closer at Will Lonetree," Connie began without preamble as Weldon ushered them to seats in front of his desk. In a way he was pleased at her quick reference to the case. Anything was preferable to dealing with the quick thrill that ran through him when he saw her coming toward his desk with a slight smile. Was that bright light in her eyes for him? Or was it her zeal over the case?

He took a deep breath, noting her colorful scarf that held back her dark hair. It made a striking appearance. He glanced down, feeling silly. He didn't usually notice what a woman wore. Wanda had always made that complaint, but he seemed to notice everything about Connie with more than an investigative eye. Things like how her clothes nicely clung to her body.

He was thinking of his own appearance too. He wore a long-sleeved, beige dress shirt that he'd bought recently because his shirts were getting threadbare, and he had taken an extra minute to study how it looked with his new brown tie. He'd even gotten a haircut the previous night, a couple of days early.

Now that he was faced with her, he felt ridiculous because she was obviously here only for the case. He held the chair for her and caught the scent of her perfume that sent a quick shudder of awareness through him.

"That man needs to be considered a suspect," she added, looking up at him, her face a serious mask.

Weldon moved behind his desk. Putting that barrier between them returned both to their official places. His voice was cool, questioning when he spoke, but inside he still felt a little warm. "The professor? Why?"

Connie's lips pressed together. "He's part of a group that Joy was talking to on the computer, but he didn't tell us that."

The computer group again. Lonetree had not mentioned it, but why should he? She gasped suddenly and turned to Lisa with wide eyes that drew his attention.

"No wonder he knew I was lying..." she said in a strangled voice.

"What?" Weldon asked, looking from one to the other. "Lying about what?"

Connie blinked rapidly and her hand flew to her chest. She turned toward him, her face losing some of its color. "I told you I got online using Joy's account and talked to those people. From the beginning he kept making strange comments, like, some people are pretending to be someone else. He has known all along I wasn't Joy."

He stared at her in disbelief. What was it going to take to get through to her what a mistake it was to conduct her own investigation or to go "undercover"? He rapped his desk with his knuckles and she jumped. "I thought I told you that pretending to be your sister online was not a good idea."

Clouds of concern floated through her clear eyes and she lowered her gaze. "It flushed him out. These people aren't supposed to know each other, but he knew her and he has known all along she is dead."

He digested the comments and then shook his head. "He didn't meet her. She never kept the appointment."

"Just knowing who she was and her knowing his name is a violation of what that room is about. They aren't supposed to try to find out the real names," she insisted.

"I'll find them out." Lisa spoke for the first time, sounding as determined as her sister.

Now that was wonderful. He had enough trouble with Connie and here was the other sister getting involved. He picked up a pencil to keep from revealing his inner frustration. These two women were headed for trouble. He tapped it on a thick notepad, hoping to work through his growing impatience. "Tell me about the pin."

Connie fished it out of her purse and handed it to him. Weldon held it up to the light, then reached into his drawer, took out a long tweezer and used it to carefully lift the pin out of the plastic envelope. He studied it without saying a word. She had been right that it looked expensive, fourteen-carat gold. He took a magnifying glass from his desk drawer and studied its design. He'd never seen anything like it. With a tiny head and spread wings it could be a bird or an angel.

"Did you ask her husband about this?"

Annoyance crossed her face. "We showed it to Will Lonetree. He'd never seen anything like it. At least he said he hadn't."

Without taking his eyes off the pin, Weldon put it back into the plastic bag. "Neither have I. I'm not certain it means anything, but since you don't remember seeing it on her before she left the hotel, and it was in the pictures, we should take a closer look at it. May I keep this?"

Connie and Lisa exchanged glances, but neither spoke. He knew Connie was worried about its significance and if she could possibly find out more if she held onto it. All the more reason for him to keep it. "We will return it," he added.

"Okay," Connie said and Lisa nodded in agreement.

"Will you show it to Sergeant Case?" Lisa asked.

"Of course."

Lisa leaned forward on her chair, biting at a nail. Connie had been doing all the talking, but he was good at reading people. He'd noticed from the minute they entered that Lisa appeared troubled. Had she seen something suspicious at Lonetree's office? He turned to her.

"Something on your mind, Miss Romero?"

Keeping her gaze focused on him, almost as though she was afraid to glance at Connie, she nodded. "A couple of other strange things have happened."

He drew his notepad toward him and picked up a pen. He sensed something important about to happen and leaned toward Lisa. "Have you told Sergeant Case?"

"I've thought about it." Lisa threw her sister a beseeching look, and Connie shook her head.

"Why don't you tell me and I'll let you know if he might find it interesting." He lowered his voice to the soothing tone he used on grieving relatives or questioning recalcitrant witnesses. Normally he wouldn't have pursued information for Case, but he sensed Connie's interest. He had a feeling if he let the two of them out of this office she would squelch whatever her sister wanted to say. It would be better to get it into the open before Connie stopped her.

"We've learned Joy had a separate bank account

that Ralph knew nothing about."

Connie gasped and reached out for Lisa's arm, but her sister drew away, keeping her wide troubled eyes focused on him.

"Go on," he urged.

"I know that may not mean much, but he also lied to us. When we went over to clean out Joy's closets, he told us he spent the afternoon at a bar but we found out it was a lie. Why didn't he tell us where he really went unless, well, he's hiding something? Joy told those computer people he had a girlfriend."

"Lisa!" Connie cried, interrupting her sister. "How can you say this stuff? We both know Ralph didn't do it."

She turned to Connie sadly, and doubt was clearly written alongside sadness in her brown eyes. "Why did he lie?" she asked in a shaky voice. "Why did she have that bank account if she wasn't thinking of leaving him? Connie, there's something strange going on. I've been thinking about it a lot. You thought he was devastated when he found out about that account, but you didn't see the look in his eyes at first. He was angry. It was like a flash in his eyes and when he got up and left I thought it was because he was about to explode."

Connie's hazel eyes grew wide with surprise, but she stopped protesting.

Mitch knew better than to interrupt. It was easier to learn information by letting the scene play out.

"You're so focused on this slasher business, you forget that Ralph might not be so innocent after all," Lisa continued. "Sooner or later you need to look at the practical side."

"That's practical?" Connie demanded.

Lisa's eyes lowered so that her gaze was level with his desk. "He had a five-hundred thousand dollar life insurance policy on her. They took it out last summer."

Again Connie gasped. She swiveled around to Weldon. "You knew that, didn't you?" she asked accusingly.

He nodded, not bothering to apologize and kept his eyes fixed on Lisa. It was one of the first things Case had learned and one of the initial reasons they focused on Perkins. The man had a policy on himself but took out one for his wife twice as large. "Is there anything else? This is information you need to tell to Case."

She blew out a sharp breath as though she might be a deflating balloon. "I know that's circumstantial but I don't want anything overlooked."

Lisa's brown eyes were troubled and misty with tears, but Connie clenched her fists. "Lisa, Ralph did not hit me over the head, or run from me in the park or nearly hit me with that van on Sunday."

His head whipped to Connie, as a feeling of dread ran pierced him. "What's this?"

"Someone nearly ran her over on Sunday," Lisa said.

"Why haven't you told me?" he demanded.

"It wasn't Ralph," Connie said, avoiding his eyes. "It was a coincidence, not like in the hotel or in the park last time."

Beside her Lisa had shifted, getting to her feet. Horror shined in her brown eyes as she faced Connie. "Do you think someone is chasing you? How could you come here knowing that? How could you deliberately put yourself in that sort of danger?"

"Exactly," Weldon concluded. At least one of them was showing a little sense. He looked down at the petite woman with her small, intense face and the neatly trimmed hair that swung around her face. Now, why couldn't he get interested in someone like that? Not this nervous ball of energy who had him all wound up inside?

But before he could even consider the thought further, a sudden movement came from the front of the room and Bernie thrust himself forward waving his long, thin arms wildly. His thin face was red, and his gray eyes were bright.

"Mitch, we just got a call from a woman who may have been an intended victim. VPD is with her."

His heart hopped to his throat as he lunged to his feet and grabbed his jacked from the back of his chair. "Sorry about our lunch plans," he said, glancing toward Connie.

Was that regret he saw in her eyes? She nodded in understanding, but he had no time for anything else. He walked rapidly behind Bernie, nerves on edge, all senses alert. This could be it. Had someone finally seen the Blade? This could be the break they had been waiting for, a mistake by the madman, which broke the case.

****

"Wait until you see what I've got," Sandy said, bursting into Connie's apartment like an exploding shell. "I've been saving and printing all the conversations I'm having with people from the chat room."

Connie stood by the window watching a late afternoon rain pelt commuters on their way home. Umbrellas lined the sidewalk. Her spirits matched the glum exterior. Instead of a pleasant lunch with Weldon she had driven home through constant rain with Lisa staring out the window in silence.

She had wanted to strangle her sister ever since she began talking in Weldon's office. Worse than Lisa's accusations was anger that her sister had not mentioned her doubts. She had seemed worried about Lonetree. Why had she turned it back on Ralph? Connie started to question her and then decided they would only argue about it. Better to just let it go for the moment.

Connie turned toward her friend. "I'm glad you're accomplishing something. That trip to Vancouver was a bust. Lisa suspects Ralph, and Weldon got called on a Slasher case."

"Did they get him?" Sandy's voice filled with excitement.

"No. I checked the news, and he attacked some woman who got away. They might have a description though. I'm going to Jim and propose that we do the story. Vancouver's only 120 miles away. What if he drives here to escape? Besides, aren't we the Northwest's cable news station? Now show me what you've got." Connie walked over to her desk.

Sandy waved at folders stuffed with pages. "I spent all afternoon online talking to those Assembly people. Check this." She set several sheets on the desk.

Connie read them over. They were similar to The Lair, short quick sentences, but the tenor was very different.

Gracious One: You will only find peace if you join us, sister.

JoyfulP: I can't leave my family.

Gracious One: We will become your family. We are all children of the Shepherd.

Angel 365: The Shepherd will welcome you.

Simon F: We can help show you the way.

Gracious One: You must leave your sinful life. Give up your material goods.

Angel 365: Share them with the church. Help us help others.

JoyfulP: You want money.

Angel 365: Money will not save you, but it can save your children.

Connie shook her head. "These people are as strange as the guys in The Lair except for the money."

"Exactly. The Good Shepherd is R.L. Lincoln, by the way. I haven't encountered him in a chat room, but I hear he takes it over. Sort of like Raven."

Connie shuddered, thinking of the big man with the piercing black eyes. He had given them little new information and acted evasive. Had he known anything about the gold pin and simply pretended not to? The guy was suspicious. So was R.L. Lincoln. She looked back at the pages. "Maybe I should go into that chat room."

"I can handle both groups. They know me, and this group is more suspicious. I think they realize I'm not Joy, but they're welcoming me back, as long as I hint I may donate. For giving up material goods, they all have computers. Get this, Joy asked to meet Shepherd."

"What?" Connie jerked her attention from the pages.

"They told her she can't until she's been purged of her other life, but I think that's another way to appeal for money. Maybe she was paying money to this group."

Connie picked up the sheets again. She thought of Naomi's diary and how the woman had been sucked in before she realized what was happening, and how she had to fight to get away. Had Joy been thinking of joining? Was that where the cash from that secret account was going? Had she joined and changed her mind?

"Tell me about Lonetree," Sandy said. "Now that I know he's Raven, I'm curious."

"He's...well, like a raven. Big, dark, mysterious." Connie thought of his dark eyes and how they seemed to pierce her, to try to figure out exactly what was inside her. Had Joy meant to meet him too? Connie had not asked if there might be something personal between Joy and Lonetree. What would he have said if she had asked? Weldon said Joy knew her killer because he lured her into the woods. What if Lonetree tailed them, approached Joy and said he was Raven. Would Joy have gone into the woods with him?

"Why didn't you like him?" Sandy asked. "That sounds appealing."

"Uh, uh. You should see this guy. Six foot three, built like a wrestler. You don't want to get caught on the wrong side of an argument with him in a dark alley. Dark, piercing eyes that practically shot daggers at me."

"It shows you can't tell a person from how they are online. I'd have pegged him as a skinny, very white Goth type. Now that we know who he is, there are couple of others in The Lair I wouldn't mind meeting." Her blue eyes shined with mischievous glee. "LastDance is bland, but DarkGhost has a great sense of humor, and NiteMan is very sweet. What do you think?"

"I'd say 'no way, Jose.' You don't know who these guys are."

Sandy looked down at the pages of her conversations. "Raven is right about one thing. He keeps telling us you can get to know a person online better than in person. On there all you have are the words you share. You don't have to be hung up on looks or superficial gestures. I understand why Joy got so caught up in this. That world can be every bit as real as this one."

"As long as you don't try to bring that world and this one together, I guess you're okay," Connie said, closing the folder. The thought that Joy had started living through the online groups bothered her. Why hadn't she emailed or chatted with family or friends?

"For all their talk about anonymity, at least four of those guys said they wanted to meet me in person. On the quiet, of course."

"Sandy, you're not going to do that. Raven may be right that all you have are the words online, but you really don't know what's at the other end. A very good liar could concoct a whole different personality."

She giggled and hopped to her feet. "You're right. I was wrong about Raven. I'm probably totally wrong about the others. I better get going. Keep those conversations, and we can talk later. Check out the ones I had with Raven."

With Sandy gone, Connie felt restless. She thought of calling Weldon, but instead she sat at her computer and called up The Lair.

Instead of a page for the chat room opening, a message opened on the screen.

"Admission denied."

What was this? She tapped on the keys to try again and received the same message.

Had Lonetree figured her out after their visit and barred her?

Chapter Twelve

Connie kept an anxious eye cocked in the direction of Jim York's office from the moment she arrived at work, even though she was nearly an hour early. Few cubicles were occupied, and even the staff from the overnight shift was in a lull period.

Shaking rain from her umbrella, she dropped it beside her desk and peeled off her raincoat. She picked up her yellow coffee mug and headed for the coffee room. The hot liquid did little to improve her disposition. Connie's email held nothing interesting except the preliminary information on Internet bargains that Sandy had sent the previous day.

Despite taking time out to chat in The Lair and with the Assembly group, Sandy had managed to amass a good deal of information. Writing a script and getting the story on the air would be fairly easy.

A glance toward Jim's office proved unproductive. His glassed-in office remained dark. Sandy wasn't in yet either, which annoyed Connie. Hopefully she wasn't playing on the computer to the point where she'd lost track of time. She was ten minutes late and there were enough people around who would notice her tardiness when she eventually showed up. Keeping track of everyone else's work schedule was a bad habit in the newsroom.

Connie focused on her own work, outlining the Internet story and typing out the beginning shell of a script. By the time she finished, her coffee was cold, and the big room around her buzzed with noise. She was surprised to discover nearly an hour had gone by.

Across the room, Jim carried a large black mug toward his office already looking haggard and disheveled even though it was only nine in the morning. His brown hair hung limply over his wide forehead, and a portion of his shirttail hung from below a nappy blue sweater. He picked up mail from his secretary's desk and flipped through it as he sipped from the mug.

Connie hopped to her feet and followed as he went to his office. She knocked on the open door as he sat down. "Hey, Jim, got a second?"

He tossed the mail on his cluttered wooden desk and took another sip of coffee, never looking up. "Sure, come on in."

"I wanted to let you know we're ready to write up the script on the computer bargains," she began, taking the seat beside his desk.

"Good. I want it to air today." He leaned his elbows on his desk and began opening envelopes with his thumb.

She leaned toward him, keeping her voice low, hoping the urgency would pull him away from his mail. "I wonder if maybe we can work on a more serious story."

He slowed his letter opening, and his blue eyes regarded her coolly over the top of tortoiseshell glasses. "Yeah?"

"This consumer bargain stuff is fine, and if you want Sandy to compile things, I can help her write them, but I'd like to go back to crime pieces. It seems so much more valuable."

His hand flew up like a school guard holding a stop sign. "The audience loves bargain stuff. That is news they can use. Unless you come up with something amazing, crime is routine. Blood and guts. The search for old killers, gang violence, drug abuse, it has all been done."

She was not to be so easily dissuaded. "We

haven't done anything on the BC Slasher."

He dropped an envelope on the desk. She had figured this might get his attention. "BC Slasher?"

Connie stifled a smile, licking her lips. Now she had his interest. She plunged on. "There's a man in Vancouver who's killed at least eight people. Hookers, mostly, but he's slicing them up and dumping their bodies in Stanley Park. It's the sort of thing we used to investigate when we were doing our crime reports. We're talking about a serial killer here."

"When was the last body found?"

"Last week."

A long finger tapped his chin, and his eyes grew thoughtful. Then to her dismay, he gave a big shake of his head, lanky hair tossing. "This isn't a case for the investigative team. Sounds like an ongoing case to me. We'll put a regular reporter on it."

Before Connie could protest, he pushed a couple of buttons on his phone.

"Yeah, boss?" The speaker phone crackled to life. Lem Turner's voice was deep, cultured, a throwback to days spent as a radio announcer. As Assignment Manager at the cable operation, his knowledge of the area was invaluable.

Skillfully avoiding Connie's glower, Jim leaned forward and spoke loudly. "You know anything about a serial killer up north? Some guy cutting up hookers?"

Lem hesitated before replying. "A couple of local stations had something on their late news last night. Police released a composite sketch. Do you want us to get it?"

"I want a reporter assigned and I want that story on tonight. Get the composite and start promoting that we'll have a full live report. Get it? A live report."

"But...it's in British Columbia," a sputtering

voice protested.

"I don't give a damn if it's in Montana. Live tonight," Jim barked. He snapped off the speaker phone and looked up, blinking, as though surprised to see Connie sitting beside his desk.

"What else?"

She drew a deep breath. Jim was great at making decisions and issuing orders. He didn't like being questioned or contradicted. "Should I go along as a field producer?"

"You've got your bargain story. I told you I want that on the air tonight."

"I know more about this case than whoever you put on it," she argued. "I've been following the story...because of my sister's murder. I've been reading the papers, talking to police and the special task force investigating it."

"Which is precisely why I'm not putting you on it."

Frustration spread through Connie like flood waters gone berserk. "Sandy can write the bargain story. She's done most of the work."

His head jerked up. "Did you hear what I said? I'm not letting you do it. You're too close to this. You're still grieving over your sister. You need to work, but at something light and fluffy. We might make Internet bargains a regular weekly feature. Did Sandy tell you that?"

"No." Her enthusiasm deflated like a party balloon still floating around the next day. She had gone in to him with her great idea and been shot down. Connie's shoulders slumped as she walked back to her desk. Damn! She'd wanted to do the Slasher story. Poking her head into Sandy's cubicle, Connie looked around for her assistant, but she still wasn't in.

Gloria Tremaine, who shared the cubicle, looked up from her computer. "Looking for Sandy? She called in sick."

Great! Just what she needed to make the day perfect. She would have to write the story herself and make certain all the graphics got ordered correctly and the video was in place. The minute she arrived at her desk, Connie hit speed dial for Sandy's home.

"Are you okay?" she asked, trying to sound concerned instead of annoyed. "They told me you were sick."

"Sort of." Sandy sounded more cheerful than sick.

"Sort of?" Connie asked, fighting down a wave of irritation.

"I'll tell you about it later." The distinctive sound of a computer beep sang out across the line.

"That's an instant message," Connie charged.

A lighthearted laugh floated back to her. "I'll call you later, babe." She hung up before Connie could ask if whatever she was doing was pertinent to work.

The day didn't improve. As Connie swung back to her computer, the cheerful face of Lynda Dillinger popped over the top of her cubicle. "Got a sec? I have a couple of questions."

A moment of dread hit Connie. Had Jim assigned Lynda as the reporter on the bargain story? That would seal Connie's fate as having to do all the work. As the statuesque reporter entered the cubicle, Connie saw she held a clipping. "The Slasher Unmasked," read the headline.

"Jim says you might have some background on this story," she said, waving the clipping. "What can you tell me?"

Keeping her annoyance buried, Connie briefed Lynda, resenting Jim for putting her in this position. It was like rubbing salt into a wound. He'd given her story to someone else and was using Connie to gather information. As a producer, Connie normally did that work, but to have to do it for Lynda, one of the laziest reporters on staff, who made her mark with her platinum hair and long legs, filled Connie with indignation.

She gave her Weldon's name and number and fought off a quick wave of envy. What would he think of Lynda when he met her? Lynda's perfect white teeth gleamed as she smiled and tossed her blonde hair. He had to be made of cast iron not to notice the woman. Would the leggy blonde appeal to him? What kind of woman did he like anyway?

"I can call him for you," Connie offered. "We've had dealings in the past."

"I need to interview him personally if he's been investigating the killings."

Naturally.

"Tell him I sent my best," Connie said in a disheartened tone, though she doubted he would think twice about her once he met the leggy reporter.

Once she was alone, Connie tried his number to let him know they would be sending a crew to do a story, but she got no answer. Frustration seized her, but she had no reprieve. Lynda was off to do the Slasher story and she was stuck in her cubicle, writing a report on Internet bargains. Sometimes life just wasn't fair.

****

"Sergeant Case."

Connie breathed a quick sigh of relief as the voice sounded on the line. She had been trying to reach Weldon most of the day, but he hadn't answered. Now she had turned to the sergeant and she was relieved to hear his voice. "I wanted to see if Inspector Weldon gave you the pin, or if you've been able to find out anything about it."

"It's similar to pins I've seen in stores. It's

211

unusual that you didn't see it on her before she went running, but I've examined the pictures. She was wearing it when she was killed."

"Do you suppose the killer put it on her?" she asked.

"It's more likely she set out to run, realized it was in her pocket and pinned it on so it didn't fall out."

That made sense, and Connie grimaced. Case had always impressed her as a capable, logical man. He wasn't quite as intense as Weldon, but she believed in his intuitive abilities. She thought he was looking in the wrong direction for Joy's killer, but she didn't think he would overlook any important piece of evidence.

"Did Weldon tell you about Will Lonetree?"

"What about him?"

Connie explained about the online group and their choice not to find out who the others were. Case listened without interruption, so she didn't know if he was bored or taking notes.

"I appreciate your efforts, Miss Romero. Please don't get me wrong, but I don't think he has anything to do with your sister's death. I've checked him out. He said he never met Mrs. Perkins, and we haven't uncovered any evidence to dispute that."

"You still think Ralph did it," she said with a sigh.

"We're continuing to pursue that, yes. Your sister has her own doubts, and now with this discovery of a hidden bank account, I'm confident we're headed in the right direction."

"Did Weldon tell you about that?"

"Your sister called this morning."

Frustration gnawed at her insides. No wonder Lisa had been so quiet on the drive from Vancouver. Connie wanted to ask why she'd changed her mind about Ralph, but feared an open argument. Over the years their divergent natures had led the sisters to disagree over a lot of things. Their natural practice had become to drop the matter, rather than argue, so she had not asked questions. Naturally Lisa's practical side would focus on the known, and with his strange actions, Ralph was an easy target.

"I'm sorry I didn't get to talk to you and your sister yesterday. If I had known you were coming, I'd have made time," Case said in a slightly accusing tone.

They hung up a few minutes later, and Connie felt like she had learned more about her younger sister than her older one. A picture of her and her sisters taken a couple of years earlier caught her eye. It was tacked to the cubicle wall. She touched Joy's face, wanting to ask for forgiveness for not being successful in finding her killer. Could Lisa and Sergeant Case be right? Perhaps she was being overzealous trying to blame the BC Slasher or Lonetree. In some ways, the other prospect was more ominous. Had they befriended a killer all these years?

She started to call Lisa, but the phone rang first. Sandy's cheerful voice was a surprise.

"I'm feeling guilty that I left you in the lurch, but you'll be happy about it later."

"Why?" Connie's heart skipped. "What are you up to?"

Sandy giggled. "I wanted to tell you I'm probably going to call in sick tomorrow too, but I'll call you tonight. I've been in that Assembly chat room all night and I've figured some things out. I'm saving it all and I'll email it to you."

Connie's heart began to pound. "Like what? I tried to get into The Lair and got barred."

"Don't worry about it. I'll explain it later. Eeks, I'm getting a call. Gotta go."

Connie put down her phone feeling frustrated.

What had Sandy learned? Figured out? The words rang in her ears.

"Connie, is that story written yet?" Jim's face appeared at the edge of her cubicle. "We need to get it to an editor."

Frustration rippled through Connie, but she forced herself to push aside thoughts about Sandy as she went to meet the reporter.

****

"Good work," Jim said, leaning into her cubicle minutes after the bargain story aired.

Connie smiled at her boss. It had turned out well. "Most of it was Sandy's research," she acknowledged.

"Another job well done by the consumer team," he replied.

Calling them the "consumer team" was not a good thing. That meant he was already ruling out the investigative element of their work.

"I'll let her know you liked it. I was just about to call her." She'd been trying to reach Sandy for the past hour. She had a question about the story, and when Sandy didn't answer, she began calling more often. Now Connie was growing worried. Where was her friend? She reached for the phone and realized Jim still stood by the doorway.

He held out a printed page. "Take a look at this. I may send you up north tomorrow. There's a fight going on over gas prices at the border, according to Lynda. Lines like we haven't seen in years. You could check it out and we can send someone on Friday to do a live report."

Jim loved his "live" reports. "Why don't you have Lynda do it?" Connie suggested, trying to keep from sounding sarcastic. "I understand her Slasher story didn't work out."

"Truck broke down," he said, but that wasn't what Connie had heard. Lynda had gotten the crew lost and been unable to reach Weldon. She'd had to make do with the composite and old video salvaged from a Canadian station.

Connie might have been gleeful at the turn of events if she hadn't been trying to get hold of Weldon herself. Like Sandy, he had not answered his phone all afternoon. Where the hell was everybody?

Jim handed her the sheet of paper. "We'll decide in the morning."

Connie turned up the television monitor across the cubicle as a graphic that read "The Slasher" popped up behind the anchor's head.

She noted her watch. Not only had Lynda not done a live report, but this story had been slated to air half an hour ago. Even Connie's feature had run earlier than intended because Lynda's story must not have been finished in time. The story mesmerized Connie, despite its lack of anything new and its lateness.

"This is where victim number eight was found, only a few days ago," Lynda said, trying to sound properly dramatic. "Her name was Queenie Ambrose, a known prostitute who was unlucky enough to have the BC Slasher as her final customer. Authorities would not comment on the case today, but here's what they told the Canadian press."

The sound was with Weldon, labeled three days earlier and in it he spoke about the discovery of Queenie Ambrose's body as well as the other seven victims. The video showed the various locations around the park and Connie noted how much the wooded locations were like the same place where Joy had been killed. He finished by talking about a woman who had managed to escape the killer and provide their first break—a description of the Slasher.

A composite sketch flashed onto the screen. "This is the man," Lynda's dramatic voice intoned. "He's described as five-foot-eight, thin and wiry with blue eyes and thinning reddish hair."

Connie studied the picture carefully, wondering if she'd ever seen him. The man was thin-faced, eyes narrow and close together. His hair was combed forward in a wispy point over a wide forehead, while his ears stuck out like jug handles from the side of his long face.

She was relieved there was no resemblance to Will Lonetree, though she had not labeled the big man as the serial killer. Joy was probably his only victim. Thoughts of him brought a chill to her. That man was hiding something.

She turned her attention back to the screen and a picture of a white SUV. "The man is said to be driving a black vehicle, similar to this model."

Connie let out her breath in a huge explosion as Lynda concluded her report. She felt like she'd been tense the whole time she was watching the story and now her muscles relaxed. That day in Stanley Park she'd felt like the man who ran away was bigger than the man described by Lynda. More like Will Lonetree. Besides, the Slasher's car was black, not burgundy.

Feeling relieved, Connie packed up her bag and turned off her computer. Jim had mentioned going north the next day and the more she thought about it, the better she liked the idea. She wanted to go to Bellingham to further investigate Joy's death. This could work for both her and the network. She could research the gas story and do some poking around in her free time. Perhaps she could check more on Dick Farley's money problems or talk to the women at Joy's work place.

The sky was an inky shade, and streetlights were twinkling on as she stepped onto the sidewalk.

A fine mist dampened her hair and raincoat. Connie walked the few blocks to her apartment thinking of Sandy and her odd behavior. She was tempted to go see her, but she lived nearly ten miles away, and in the distance, the brake lights on the freeway heading north formed a continuous stream like a string of red Christmas lights. Maybe later.

Connie started to cross the street to her building before noticing the burgundy van parked halfway down the block. Shadows prevented her from seeing if a driver sat at the wheel. She paused on the sidewalk, waiting. She would have to cross directly in front of it. Was she seeing things? There had to be plenty of burgundy vans in the city. She stepped off the curb and crossed the street, watching for movement. The van didn't budge.

Stepping into her loft, Connie felt her muscles relax. "You're being paranoid," she whispered. She shed her rain coat and turned on the switch that controlled lighting in the entire apartment. Low light bathed the cavernous room. She crossed to her bedroom area, switching on the computer as she passed it. As soon as she donned a warm sweat suit, she signed onto the computer, waiting for her call from Sandy. Emails from Lisa and Sandy greeted her.

Lisa's was a quick note of apology and a promise to call later. Sandy's was equally terse, but it sent an electric shock through her.

"I've got the goods," it read.

Connie grabbed the phone so quickly she fumbled it. Had Sandy figured it out? Who could it be? She'd been looking at the Lair group and researching the Assembly. She called Sandy's apartment, but the phone simply rang without going to voice mail. Sandy had call-waiting so perhaps she was using her other line on an important call.

As she put down the receiver, the phone rang

and she grabbed it, hoping Sandy was calling back. Weldon's measured tones were a relief as much as they were disappointment.

"I've been trying to call you," she said, feeling a smile overtake her face. She'd been on pins and needles most of the day, waiting for his call. At times she felt like a teenager waiting to hear about a Saturday night date.

"Sorry. I've discovered my cell phone doesn't work in Seattle."

"You're here?" she asked, shock waves of pleasure running through her.

"Yes, and I'd invite you to dinner or invite myself over except we're on a stakeout."

"A stakeout? Here? The Slasher?" she said breathlessly.

"I can't tell you. Nor can I reveal where I am. I just wanted to get back to you since you left several messages. Will you be around tomorrow? I may stay over tonight."

"I...well..." She wrinkled her nose, knowing she would probably be on her way to Bellingham as soon as she got to work. "I...don't know. I may have to go on assignment."

Again he chuckled, a low rumbling sound that sent her pulse soaring. "I'll call you early. Maybe I can buy you breakfast."

Excitement sprouted goose bumps on her arms. "Sure," she cooed with a smile.

"And, uh...Connie?" he began.

He hadn't said her name quite like that before, almost a low intimate sound that was slightly breathless, and fresh waves of delight rippled through her.

"Perhaps we can talk about something other than the case this time."

"Yes!" she replied breathlessly. Hanging up, Connie caught sight of her face reflected in the oval mirror over her dresser. A wide smile split her face.

She didn't know the last time she had smiled quite that big. Her face glowed, even without makeup.

Chapter Thirteen

The morning sun warmed Connie's face as she walked along the sidewalk in downtown Bellingham. The storms of the past few days had swept through and left a day so crisp and clear that the white crest of Mt. Baker was visible to the north. Every so often the volcano spurted steam, but today only snow blew from the white summit. The Olympics raised like magnificent towers to the west while the blue-green waters of the Puget Sound shimmered jewel-like in the morning sun. The only thing that would have made the day better was if she had been able to start it off by seeing Weldon. Very mysteriously he called to cancel breakfast while she was dressing. She was disappointed, but she used the time to get an early start for Bellingham.

At the corner of the block, she spied the banner for Moreland Realty, where Joy had worked for the past two years. She turned and walked into the door of the three story brick building. The outer reception area greeted customers with a quiet elegance of gray carpet and dark cherry wood furniture. A front desk that resembled a judge's bench was poised in front of a hall. A young receptionist slouched at the desk, studying red fingernails in boredom. One side of the room was filled with bulletin boards displaying homes in Bellingham, mountain retreats, and cabins in the nearby San Juan Islands. The other side held two pictures on metal easels—a large poster-sized photo of Dick Farley, with the title "Realtor of the Month" and a few feet away, a smaller framed picture of Joy. It was wreathed in flowers with the statement "In Memoriam."

Connie approached the desk. "I'm looking for Mary Sue Baker."

"Do you have an appointment?" the girl asked, running her finger over an open book of times and scribbled names.

"I just wanted to see her for a few minutes." She had not called ahead. If the woman wasn't in, there were others she could see instead. Connie didn't know many of Joy's co-workers, but she had met a few, like Mary Sue, at holiday parties.

The girl pushed down a phone key and spoke in a low voice into the mouthpiece as Dick Farley stepped into the reception area. He stopped when he saw Connie. He stood absolutely still for a moment and then moved forward, ever the salesman in gray suit, blue tie, and white shirt. His neatly cut brown hair was slicked back and his handsome if slightly pudgy face adopted a wide smile probably meant to be compassionate.

"Aren't you Joy Perkins' sister?"

"Yes." She summoned her own fake smile.

He took her fingers and shook them with a limp grip, murmuring condolences. His words didn't register in his blue eyes which were cold, brittle pieces of ice. He was gone quickly, as though he could tell she had nothing to offer him.

Behind her she heard the click of heels on the tile floor, and Mary Sue Baker appeared in the hall. A short, chunky woman with straw blonde hair and a too-wide smile, she marched forward and greeted Connie as though they were long lost friends, hugging her.

"Is there some way I can help you? I thought your sister picked up Joy's things last week."

Connie smiled in acknowledgement. "I had a couple of questions I wanted to ask."

"Certainly." The woman led her down the hall to

a well lit room that contained an empty desk and several chairs. Mary Sue pointed to a padded chair in front of the desk, wrist jingling with a row of small gold bangle bracelets.

"May I offer you coffee, water?" Her smile was pleasant, but like Farley, it didn't extend beyond her thin lips. Her blue eyes were wary and curious.

Connie was thirsty, but she didn't ask for anything. She cleared her throat and sat gingerly on the chair. "Joy always said good things about you."

"That's nice to know." Mary Sue sat very straight behind the large, empty desk, as though that might make her taller. She looked more like a prosperous housewife on the town than a successful businesswoman. Her round face carried too much makeup, especially eye shadow in a glistening blue color that framed eyes hidden between black rings of eyeliner and mascara. Her cotton sweater stretched across enormous breasts, while her khaki slacks pulled across an ample middle. A gigantic diamond ring sparkled on one pudgy hand.

"I don't know how much you know about Joy's death..." Connie began.

"Some madman without regard for human life killed her. I saw a story on the news last night about a killer in Vancouver. Could he be the culprit?" Her plump, pasty face showed little emotion as she spoke.

"It's a possibility, though the police won't admit it. I've been doing a little investigating myself. See, the police suspect Ralph..."

"Ralph?" Mary Beth laughed, a brittle, hollow sound. She waved her arm in a gesture of dismissal, sending the bracelets jingling. "You can't be serious."

"Did you or did anyone in the office tell Vancouver authorities they were having marital problems?"

The woman blinked, drawing back, clearly

surprised. She put a hand to her short blonde hair which glistened with spray. Connie doubted it would move even if a hurricane struck.

"I'd never discuss one's personal affairs," she said huffily. "I hope you don't think I did it. Even if I'd witnessed something, I'd never spread rumors."

"I'm not accusing you. I'm just trying to find out..."

"Have you asked Dick Farley?" she asked, rubbing well-manicured hands together. "His desk was next to hers. He might have overheard arguments, but I'm not certain that's something he'd discuss either. We pride ourselves on sales, not gossip."

Connie ignored the supercilious tone. "What about Farley? They were competitors, weren't they? What kind of man is he?"

"You don't suspect Dick?" Brown pencil-drawn eyebrows lifted, and her eyes narrowed. The look of curiosity was disappearing, replaced by irritation.

"How much do you know about him?"

All traces of goodwill disappeared as Mary Sue Baker's red lips grew taut into a thin straight red line. "Do the police know you're asking questions like this?"

"Yes," Connie replied, feeling defensive.

"You're asking about Dick? Throwing suspicion on him?"

"Not suspicion. I'm simply curious."

"You're speculating about Ralph?" Her head shook so vigorously a strand of hair actually moved. She patted it back into place immediately. "I don't think Joy would have liked that."

"I want to see that justice is done."

The plea did not calm Mary Sue. She stood, clearly indignant. "I'm not going to answer personal questions."

"I didn't mean to offend you," Connie attempted

but Mary Baker turned and stomped to the door.

Wonderful! Who had given that information about marital problems to Sergeant Case? Maybe she should go back to Vancouver and look over the investigation transcripts. Connie was walking toward the front door when a young redhead came through the glass doors. She did a double take when she saw Connie.

"Aren't you Joy's sister?"

"Yes," she said with an eager smile. She'd be different this time around, if the woman would speak to her. Connie recognized her face from one of Joy's parties, but she didn't know the name. Tall and elegant with pleasant brown eyes, the woman appeared to be the exact opposite of Mary Sue Baker. She wore a navy blazer over wool slacks and very little makeup.

"Is there something I can do for you?" the woman asked.

"I was just checking..." Connie feigned a show of grief-stricken emotion, summoning tears and wiping her hand across her cheek as though fearing she might cry. "I've been thinking about my sister a lot, and I figured the people who worked with her probably knew her best."

The woman nodded. "Of course. I have a few minutes."

Bingo! Connie hid a smile beneath pursed lips, and the woman led her to the conference room again. Her name was Gayle Starling.

"Joy and I grew close the last few months," she confided with a sad smile. "We'd go to lunch or to Seattle to shop."

"Was she happy?" Connie asked, and she could sense the woman's sudden confusion. She reached out her hand. "I feel sad I didn't get to spend time with her. I guess I just want closure."

The woman grasped her fingers in a warm grip.

"I know what you mean."

"Someone said she and Ralph were having problems with their marriage. I don't believe it, or maybe I don't want to believe it."

The woman hesitated, and her eyes shifted from right to left. She seemed to consider what to say. "That doesn't matter now," she said finally.

"I guess not. As long as she was happy."

The woman took a deep breath and managed a smile. "Oh, she was happy. Blissfully happy."

Feigning confusion, Connie smiled, as though the woman was delivering welcome news. "Then whoever was saying that about the marital problems was wrong."

As open and friendly as the woman had been at first, she closed up like a book slamming shut. Skillfully avoiding Connie's eyes, Gayle looked around the room as though it was bugged. "I said she was happy. I didn't say it involved Ralph."

Connie gasped, a sound that rang so loudly around the sterile room that she put her fingers over her lips. "Are you saying she was seeing someone else?"

"I'm not saying anything." Again, the change. The figurative book shut and her gaze slid around the room, looking everywhere but at Connie. "I'm saying she was acting like a kid in love. New clothes, new look. Do you know how many times I tried to get her to dye her hair and she wouldn't do it. Until last month. She did a whole makeover. She never used to want to go to Seattle with me, and then a few months ago she begged me to take her. Maybe it was to get more life back into her marriage. What with Ralph..." She stopped.

"What?" Connie prodded.

"I don't want to be accused of telling tales out of school." Her smile was genuine.

"Like I said, she was happy. When I'd ask why,

she'd give me a secret little smile."

Connie thought of the new shoes in Joy's closet and the clothes that she and Lisa could not explain. What had changed her into this sudden fashion maven? "What about her relationship with the people here? I know she was friends with you and Beth and Mary Sue."

"Beth, maybe, but Mary Sue..." Gayle waved at the closed door as though Mary might be outside. "She's a big gossip, but if you ask her anything, she pretends like she doesn't know and gets offended that you ask. Joy and I never trusted her, and it turns out we were right."

"Why?"

Something shuttered in her brown eyes, and she drew back and shook her head. "Nothing."

"What about Dick Farley? How did she get along with him?"

She blinked rapidly. "Why are you asking about him?"

Connie pretended confusion. "I was curious. I mean she mentioned him from time to time. I guess as competitors."

"Oh, definitely. He was never so happy as when he'd get a listing on a big property that she wanted to go after. Since she's been gone, he's picked up a couple of big listings she'd been working on."

"So he's benefited from her death," Connie suggested.

She shook her head. "The boss split her listings among all of us."

"The sign says he is salesman of the month. That's worth money, isn't it?"

Gayle lifted her slim shoulders. "I suppose. A couple of thousand dollars, but he and Joy enjoyed the competition more than money."

Connie could feel her Farley theory disintegrating. The information held no motive for murder. A couple of thousand dollars? Ralph with his large insurance policy had a bigger motive. The woman's next words sealed the discussion.

"Poor Dick. I don't think he'll earn nearly as much money this month without Joy being around to spur him on."

"What about..." She wasn't certain how to start, but she plunged right in. "Did you go with her to see R.L. Lincoln?"

The woman drew back and sniffled. "Heavens no! What a sham! I can't believe those women got so intrigued by that fraud, buying pins and books, emailing back and forth. I told them that all those people wanted was money. Joy was lucky to get clear of them."

"Did she get clear?"

"I think so. They wanted her to get rid of all her possessions, leave her family. She wouldn't do that. After meeting the good reverend, Joy seemed to snap out of it."

Connie nodded. This was good news. Besides, if they wanted Joy to give up material goods, why was she buying them? "Perhaps I should talk to Beth."

The woman blinked and jerked upright, her eyes filled with surprise. "Beth?"

"Do you know if she's here?" Connie asked, glancing around. This woman hadn't been much help. Maybe Beth would be better.

Gayle looked pained, staring down at her nails before looking up at Connie with sad eyes. "Beth quit last week. She and one of her friends went to British Columbia to join that damn commune. We don't know if she went or they forced her to go. At least it made everyone else in the office realize they better stop fooling with that bunch. No one's wearing those stupid angel pins anymore."

Connie digested her words, considering what this discovery meant. Could Joy have been involved with the group and then refused to leave her children or her new material goods? Could one of the group have followed her to Vancouver and tried to kidnap her? This was a situation that deserved another look.

The office had provided one answer. Joy's death would not have helped Farley or provided the money he needed to pay his taxes. Without Joy around he no longer would be as driven to competition. That crossed him off her suspect list.

Maybe she should go see Ralph. She could take him to lunch at one of Joy's favorite restaurants—one with a view of the harbor where they could look at the snowcapped Olympics and talk about her sister. Perhaps she could get him to confide in her about their marital troubles. Maybe she could ask him why he lied to her and Lisa about spending Saturday afternoon at the Muddy Hen. Maybe he might have noticed if she was thinking of leaving with Beth and her friend.

She checked her watch. If Weldon called and said he was free, she would rush to go home, but she saw no reason to head back to Seattle yet. She'd already checked the gas story, doing preliminary interviews and looking for gas lines. They did exist, but the station attendants said it happened more on weekends when Canadians came across the border looking for bargains. High taxes and high prices in British Columbia coupled with a low exchange rate on the American dollar were causing the lines.

Connie turned down the street toward Ralph's office. She was steps from the front door when he emerged. She started to call him but stopped. Ralph looked very different than the last time she'd seen him. Gone were the rumpled clothes and haggard appearance. His portly figure appeared more slender, though she could understand his losing a few pounds. He wore a neat blue suit that appeared expensive, even from a block away. Suddenly his name rang out. She stopped. Near the corner, a short, pudgy woman waved at him. Even from her location Connie recognized Mary Sue Baker.

This didn't mean anything, did it? She could be meeting him as a friend. Except as a friend, she was probably going to tell him about Connie's questions. She turned and walked back toward the lot where she'd parked her car before they saw her.

****

Connie called the station on her way back to Seattle. She hoped for a message from Weldon, but there was nothing on her voice mail and her cell had been working all day. She transferred to the assignment desk just in case he had called there.

Lem, the assignment editor, had no messages, but his voice was filled with concern. "Have you talked to Sandy?"

"I've tried her several times, but she didn't answer. I figured she went to work." Sandy was her next stop on her way home. She wanted to find out what she had learned.

"She hasn't come in and no one's taken a call from her that I know of."

Connie's breath caught. "That's not like Sandy."

"I know. We're a little worried here. Even Jim," Lem said in a quiet voice.

She fought back a sudden feeling of concern. "I'm on my way back and Sandy lives on the north side. I'll keep calling and if I haven't reached her by the time I get there, I'll stop by her apartment and check."

Dread settled over Connie, much like the day when she rushed to get back to the hotel to make certain Lisa was okay. Now she stretched the bounds of the speed limit trying to get to Sandy's apartment.

Fear seized her fully when she saw a line of police cars and other vehicles clogging the street.

229

She recognized the unmarked cars as police vehicles. With a pounding heart, Connie race-walked into the building. A meaty hand halted Connie in her tracks the instant she stepped through the unlocked security door.

"Sandy?" she asked, trying to see around the uniformed cop's bulky figure.

He stood like a tree, blocking her entrance. "Do you know a Sandy Sinclair?" he asked, crossing his arms, but not moving an inch to let her in or see behind him.

"Yes? Where is she?" A quiver of alarm spread through her like a cold chill.

"She's been found dead in her apartment."

"No!" Her cry was loud, or perhaps that was someone else yelling. "No!" Connie ducked around the officer as he shouted at her to stop. Her footsteps clicked on the tile as she hopped up the stairs to the second floor with him huffing after her.

The hallway outside the small apartment was stifling, filled with strange people scurrying around. The area was a maze of color, blue uniforms, white lab coats, and yellow crime scene tape that stretched across the apartment's doorway. The coppery scent of blood filled the air. Connie approached the door and started to step under the tape, but a young, uniformed police officer appeared in front of her, while the other officer from downstairs came up behind her.

"You can't go in there," he panted.

"You're sure it's Sandy?" She stood on her toes and strained forward to see into the room. First Joy, now Sandy. This couldn't be happening.

"The landlord identified her," the young officer in front said, holding out his hands to bar the door as though he knew she would slip around him or the tape at the first opportunity.

One of the men in a suit glanced in their

direction. Her heart dropped as Connie recognized him as Mitchell Ryan, the head of Seattle's homicide squad. She waved a frantic hand at him.

"Lt. Ryan, remember me? Connie Romero?"

"No press," he said, holding up large hands.

"I'm a friend of Sandy's," Connie called. "She worked with me. What happened to her?"

Ryan broke off from a conversation and lumbered toward the door. Short and portly, he wore an ill-fitting, sagging blue suit. His gray athletic shoes didn't fit the suit and his tie hung at a haphazard angle. Although opposite of Case and Weldon in appearance, his unkempt demeanor cloaked a razor sharp mind. He'd amazed her in the past with his thorough procedures and overall knowledge of murder cases. His presence there could only mean one thing. Sandy had been killed.

Murder. It sank in slowly, like water on an already soggy plant.

"Was she...killed?" she asked.

"Looks like it," he said bluntly. "When was the last time you saw her?"

"Two days ago, but I talked to her yesterday."

He gave a sharp nod of his head and asked for her phone number. "We'll need to talk to you later," he said before turning and waddling away.

The large-shouldered cop who had huffed up the stairs after her took a position in front of the door, as though concerned she might still try to enter. Connie poked her head around the big officer. She caught a partial view of the sparsely furnished main room with its polished hardwood floors. Small knots of people moved efficiently, each concentrating on a specific job, though she had no idea what they were doing. The corner occupied by the pull-down bed when it came out of the wall was empty, but several technicians worked near the sofa. A thin-faced man in a black suit snapped pictures.

She leaned around the door to peer farther inside. Papers littered the floor near Sandy's makeshift desk which consisted of a white tabletop astride two white laminate file cabinets. Several men wearing plastic gloves were going through papers on the desk. She leaned in the other direction and her breath caught as her gaze rested on a yellow blanket that covered something lumpy. The body. A small pool of blood smeared the floor around it and one bare foot stuck out of one end.

Connie recognized the purple color on the toenail. Sandy. Covering her mouth in horror with her hand, she gulped back the bile that rose in her throat. As she turned away she smacked right into Weldon. He caught her as she stumbled slightly, and she gripped his hard arm in a tight vise and leaned against him, oblivious to the crowd around them.

"It's Sandy," she cried, nearly choking again. "My friend. I can't believe it." Connie was so stunned even tears did not come. Joy and now Sandy. It was incomprehensible.

He pulled her away from the door and back out of the building, keeping his arm around her. Only when he had her seated on a cement block at the edge of the entrance did he let her go.

"Are you all right? Do you want me to get you something? Coffee? Water?"

Only then did it register that Weldon's presence was abnormal. Why was he at Sandy's apartment? "What are you doing here?"

He stood back, hands on his hips, his face grim. "Our surveillance didn't come to anything, so when I heard the call for this, I came over."

"You didn't think it was me, did you?" she asked fearfully.

His clear green eyes settled on her, and while he didn't answer, she could read the look of concern. He tilted his head up as someone upstairs threw open a window. He reached over and touched her arm with a gentle hand. "I want to go in and have a look, eh? I don't think it has anything to do with me, but there were reports the Blade was headed south. I want to get a look myself while I'm here. Can you wait? "

His hand brushed hers, caught it and squeezed. Normally the touch might have made her heart jump. Now she was too numb. She nodded. "I told Lt. Ryan I'd answer some questions for him."

Connie wrapped her arms around herself, as a chill ran through her. The January sun provided little warmth and was starting to sink behind the mountains to the west. The shadows grew longer on the street and a slight breeze ruffled her hair. Connie had been to crime scenes before, but like with Joy, shock held her captive in a near stupor. People moved around her, but everything was a swirling mass of colors and disembodied voices.

Lt. Ryan came out and stood over her, notebook held in front. "She was a friend, huh?"

Connie drew a deep breath, testing her voice. She almost expected it to come out as a squeak from her tight throat. "Friend, co-worker. She didn't show up for work today. I came by to check on her."

"When was the last time you talked to her? You said it was yesterday?"

"In the afternoon. How did you know to come over here?"

"The neighbors called in a disturbance late yesterday, but the officers who came by found nothing. No one answered the door. Today we got a call from her work that no one had seen her for two days or knew where she was. When the officer went in, that was what he found. Looks like the place has been totally trashed. TV smashed, computer busted up."

The damage to her apartment didn't bother her as much as his first words. "Her work? They told me to come by and check on her."

Weldon burst from the building, a scowl on his face. "Connie, I don't want to trouble you, but...you know that pin, eh?"

"Pin? The gold pin?" Her heart began to thud in fear.

His nod was quick. "The one your sister was wearing. Did your friend have one?"

"Not unless she bought one in the past couple of days, but I don't think she would. We were still confused about what it meant."

"Did she ever see it?"

"I showed it to her, but if she found another like it she would have told me. She was supposed to call me last night. Do you suppose..." She stopped, unable to continue. Sandy had not called because she couldn't.

She looked up at Ryan and he shrugged his big shoulders. "The coroner will figure out the exact time of death."

Weldon nodded abruptly. "I'm going to call Sergeant Frank Case to come down." He turned to Ryan. "Can you wait to move the body until he gets here?"

"Why?" Ryan asked.

"I have a similar case, or I should say, Frank does. It may be the same man."

Connie gasped, and as she glanced at Ryan, he appeared just as shocked.

"The same man who killed Joy?" she asked in a breathless voice.

"Possibly," Weldon said. He turned to face Ryan. "Can you come in here for a minute?"

Connie struggled to her feet, fighting off the shakiness in her knees that threatened to drop her to the ground like a melting puddle of Jell-O.

"She has a pin, doesn't she? She's wearing a pin," she rasped in a voice she didn't recognize.

Chapter Fourteen

Burning logs crackled in the fireplace, flames leaping high, but Connie shivered in the floral comforter wrapped around her shoulders. Her stoic demeanor reminded Weldon of the rainy day at her sister's death site. He wished he had not told her about the strange gold pin. The sight of her dead friend on the floor had been bad enough. It would be a long time before he forgot the sight, and he'd been present at murder scenes for years.

He couldn't imagine what a novice like Connie was thinking and feeling. A haunted look still filled her normally alive eyes, and her face was stony, like beautiful carved granite. She was beautiful. The more he saw of her, the more he was convinced of that.

He'd been wanting to see her for days, but not like this. She sat on a low chair, huddled inside the comforter. She'd done much the same outside Sandy's apartment that afternoon. She'd remained sitting on the stoop wrapped inside a jacket, arms wrapped around herself for hours, refusing help or comfort, simply sitting.

Weldon found her liquor supply on his own after bringing her home. He poured sherry into a juice glass and carried it to her. Connie blinked, as though surprised by his presence, but she accepted it, and thanked him in a low voice. She took a gulp and coughed slightly, her face wrinkling in distaste.

"I'm sorry," he said. He should have put her in a taxi and sent her home earlier. She insisted on staying while police completed their investigation and until the body was carried out, but he should have found a way to send her home.

People from the cable network had come by and while he didn't hear what she said to them, he saw the way she reacted. They cried, and she comforted them. As long as others were present she presented a strong front, but through it all, she had a dazed look.

"Thank you for bringing me home," she said quietly. A co-worker brought her car home while Weldon drove her.

"You should eat something," he urged. "I looked through your refrigerator, and you don't have much, but I can make a mean grilled cheese sandwich. Or I could order pizza, eh?"

"Thank you, but I don't think I could eat anything." She cradled the glass between her hands and sipped at the sherry, her haunted eyes still on the fire.

Weldon took hold of a hassock and dragged it over to sit beside her. He wanted to reach out and touch her, comfort her. No longer did he worry about whether or not that was personal contact. She was hurting, and he wanted to share her pain if that would remove some of it. Whether he liked it or not, she was no longer just another murder victim's relative. She had become something else to him in the past couple of weeks.

"I know how you're feeling," he said, starting to reach out to her and then stopping. He clasped his hands together instead.

"You said that last time." Her voice was dead, filled with emptiness.

He shifted closer to her, and reached out a tentative hand to touch her shoulder with gentle fingers. "I meant it."

She looked at him sadly, her pink tongue flicking out to lick her lips. "How could you begin to know? My sister? My friend?" Her eyes grew misty, and he thought she might cry, but she didn't. She inhaled a shaky breath instead.

He squeezed her shoulder. "I've been in this business for a long time."

"And seen strangers die," she intoned accusingly.

He lowered his hand from her shoulder. "That wasn't why I said that." He drew a deep breath, a mental debate erupting in his head. How well did he know her? Did he want to share with her what to him were two of the hardest events he'd ever survived? Could she understand? Would she even try and was this the right time to discuss his grief? He had no easy answers. Weldon rose. Maybe he needed a drink himself.

Connie lifted her empty glass to him. "May I have another?"

He took her glass and poured one for himself as well, still debating what he should tell her. After handing her the second drink, he pushed his hassock closer to her.

She touched his bare forearm, sending an electric shock through him. He had loosened his tie and rolled up his sleeves after they arrived at her house. She had taken a hot shower and wrapped up in the blanket. He could understand her desire to bathe after leaving the murder scene. He'd had to make do with washing his face and hands and he had spent hours in that bloody death tomb.

"You look like a regular guy," she said, attempting one of her teasing smiles.

He tried to smile back. "Don't be too sure, eh?"

"How's Bruno?"

"Probably unhappy. I had to leave him in a kennel because I didn't know when I'd get back."

"You were looking for the Slasher?"

"I don't want to discuss that case."

The Blade was on the run and out of control, that was obvious. Up until now, he had been so cautious, one step ahead of the police. He'd attacked his last victim in broad daylight, throwing her into his van and tying her up. Only haste had proven his undoing. She had seen the razor. While they talked about the women being slashed, they had never given an indication of the type of blade. She had described it as a gold blade that opened. The Blade cut off one of her fingers, taking his memento as he always did, marking his victims before killing them.

Knowing she was facing death, the victim managed to get free of her bonds. When he stopped, she escaped the van and ran down the street, bloody and naked. The Blade had run too. They closed all the roads out of Vancouver, setting up roadblocks, checking each departing ferry, expecting him to go north. When his stolen van was discovered in Tacoma, Weldon had come south. The van was a bloody mess and might still prove to be a treasure trove of evidence, and it had given him some new leads to pursue, but he still had no idea who or where the Blade was.

Connie touched his arm again, as though realizing her comments had sent him off into another world. "I'm sorry. I shouldn't have brought that up."

"It's been a rough couple of weeks," he acknowledged, taking a gulp of sherry and relishing the burning trail that snaked down his insides.

"I can't believe it," she said in a cracking voice filled with pain. "Joy and Sandy murdered. By the same person? Do you really think that?"

"You saw the pin." He'd had a digital photo taken of that small portion of her friend's body so she could view it, but they both recognized it as similar to the one her sister had worn.

Her lips twisted into a frown. "This proves

Ralph didn't do it, right? He was in Bellingham this morning. I saw him."

"Your friend might have been killed last night. We can't rule him out. What if she discovered evidence that tied him to your sister's death?"

She shook her head. "Sandy was investigating the Internet information."

He pressed his lips together to keep from questioning her comment or lashing out at her for involving her friend. He had a feeling she was already carrying that load of guilt.

"What if one of them had detailed information about the marital problems?" he asked. He still didn't trust Perkins, despite her support. Case felt he was close to breaking the case and getting the final evidence that Perkins had committed the crime or hired someone to do it. The latter was more probable. Where did Sandy Sinclair fit in? He didn't want to think about it, especially given what Connie had said moments earlier.

"I'm going to find out who did it," she said.

This time Weldon couldn't stop himself. Her words raised a spark of irritation. "Please don't say that. Tell me what you meant about your friend helping you in your investigation."

A tear edged out of her eye, and she wiped it away. "That's the worst part. She told me yesterday she had information for me. That she'd figured it out. I thought she meant the Internet connection, but now I wonder if she didn't mean she knew who did it."

"Let this go, Connie," he urged. "Before anyone else gets hurt. Or you do."

Her sad eyes turned up to him, misty and forlorn. "You don't know how it feels, knowing my sister is gone, and now Sandy."

"But I do." He drew a deep breath, finished the sherry and put the glass on the floor. Reaching out, he took her hand. It was surprisingly cold. He clutched it and held it, as though the physical connection was necessary before he could continue.

"I've never told you about my father," he began. "He was an inspector in the mounted forces. My brother Eric wanted nothing more than a career in law enforcement, like my dad and uncle. But I couldn't do that. I spent too many nights sitting up with my mother, my stomach in knots while we waited for my dad to come home. I went to college to study business. I wanted nothing to do with law enforcement. I'd seen how it consumed his life. When I was a freshman, away in Ottawa, he was killed, gunned down in a battle with drug lords in Vancouver. I remember I wanted to go after the man. To make him pay for what he'd done to my father, and the devastation the death caused my mother."

She squeezed his hand, putting down her glass and grasping their joined hands with her other hand. A trace of a smile touched her lips. "So you followed in his footsteps."

"Not right away. I dropped out and came home. I was going to conduct my own search for the man. I didn't know the first thing about investigative techniques. I went undercover, walking the streets, pretending to be a drug addict."

"You? Outside a suit?" she asked, attempting to laugh.

He smiled. Some of the color was coming back to her soft cheeks. "I wasn't very good at what I was doing. I ended up putting real undercover officers in danger and nearly getting one killed. That was when I realized the importance of my father's job and Eric's desire. That was when I changed careers. I've never regretted it. Every time I hear someone say they want to get the person who hurt their family, I've understood. But I also know it's best to let the experts do the job."

Her head turned toward the fire and then back to him. A look of surprise and desire glowed in the depths of her hazel eyes, or maybe it was the reflection from the fire. Her soft fingers lifted to brush his chest, her fingertips pressing against his shirt. Weldon inhaled sharply as a rush of excitement coursed through him. Her breath was coming faster, but so was his.

The flames in her eyes grew, and he could see her need and her questions as she moved toward him. Wrapping her arms around his neck, she pulled him to her, and they tumbled the short distance to the rug. He started to jerk away. This was wrong. Still, she was warm and smelled like violets, and the touch of her curvy body coming against him was having a profound effect on him.

"Please hold me," she said in a low pleading tone.

"Of course," he agreed. She felt good in his arms. Right. He closed his eyes, letting her scent, the touch of her hands and the feel of her soft body envelope him. The fire crackled beside them, and for a wild instant, he let himself think how wonderful it would be to take her to bed.

Her hands stroked his chest, slipping inside his shirt to explore his bare skin. The touch was electric, and sent wild waves of want through his system. His body grew rigid, and loss of control was seconds away.

"Please... " she said, but her voice caught. Still, as her hands moved along his body, he knew what she wanted.

"This can't go any farther," he said gently, fighting back the urge to do more than hold her. "I don't want to use you."

"I need you," she said quietly, insistently.

He smoothed her hair back from her face,

fingers stroking the black hair, enjoying the silken touch. He could see the need in her eyes, but it wasn't physical desire. She wanted to forget, to do something to remember they were both alive. It wouldn't work, not tonight. He'd never forgive himself if he followed through on what his body desired. "I know. I want you. But we can't. Not like this."

Connie leaned toward him, and touched her lips softly to his. He returned the touch without thinking. She tested his mouth again, teasing, enticing touches and he found the will to stop growing weak as his resistance faded.

He kissed her fully, opening her mouth with the tip of his tongue. Her lips were soft, every bit as intoxicating as the last time. She tasted vaguely of sherry and for an instant he wanted to lose himself her arms. Then duty called, and he pulled away.

"I told you, we can't do this. Not tonight," he said, regret filling him. "Connie, I hope you understand."

"Damn you, Weldon, I do," she said in a strangled voice, lowering her head to his chest. That was when Connie began to sob.

****

Connie woke slowly to the smell of coffee. Her first thought was of Sandy. Her friend was dead. The thought was like picking at a scabbed-over wound. It ached and reopened, becoming bloody and raw. She gulped back a tear.

The coffee scent woke her sense more fully, and Connie blinked. Someone had made coffee? Who was in her apartment? Then she remembered. Mitch had stayed. She was half pleased, half embarrassed. The thought of him spending the night at her place, even if he had slept on the sofa, brought a flutter to her insides. If only he had stayed for some reason other than her tearful outburst. He had been very good about it, holding Connie and whispering soothing words until she quit crying. After she blew her nose and washed her face, he fed her a big cup of tomato soup, poured more brandy, and ordered her to bed.

Mitch! Somewhere in the midst of that crying spell, he had gone from being Weldon the coldhearted cop, to Mitch, compassionate friend.

She flinched as she recalled how completely her composure had fractured. What would he think of her total break down? Poking her head out of her comforter, Connie peered around the room, seeking his presence. The sofa was empty, and sheets, a comforter, and pillows were neatly stacked on the arm.

A further glance found him at the kitchen table, a mug of coffee in front of him as he read the newspaper. He looked very different from the together man she had come to know. His sandy hair was mussed, and he still wore the beige shirt he'd had on the day before. It was open at the collar and the sleeves were rolled up. The front was wrinkled. Connie smiled; she didn't know he could wrinkle a shirt. A small black stain across the middle erased her smile—the remnants of her mascara.

He seemed to sense her waking and as his gaze swung toward her, he rewarded her with a warm smile. "Good morning."

She wanted to dive back under the covers as his green eyes came to her. A wave of self-consciousness swept through her. Like him, she still wore her clothes from the evening before. The sweater might not show wrinkles, but the denim skirt did. She'd fallen asleep in her clothes, wrapped in her comforter after he fed her. Memories of his tender care elicited a quick round of jumpiness in her stomach.

"Morning," she mumbled and rolled out of bed. Catching a glimpse of herself in the dresser mirror,

Connie winced. Big black circles rimmed her eyes and her hair stuck out in all directions. She tugged at her wayward hair, but only a good brushing would remove the tangles.

"Would you like breakfast?" he asked from across the room.

"I can cook," she offered, attempting to smooth down her hair. "All I need is a quick shower."

"You take your shower. I'll do it." He got to his feet and padded toward the kitchen. Mitch Weldon in stockinged feet? The picture brought a smile to her face, and she stifled a giggle.

She showered and when she emerged she felt much better. Her face was pale so she put on a touch of light makeup and then pulled her wet hair into a ponytail. Wrapped in her a terry robe, she shut herself in her dressing area, trying to decide what to wear. She wanted to look good, but not provocative. Finally, she settled for her best burgundy silk jogging suit. She put on a hint of makeup, not wanting to appear too forward.

When she emerged, he had fixed them a cheese omelet with orange juice and toast. They ate in near silence. Connie tried to apologize for the evening before, but he shook his head.

"It was to be expected."

Unlike the way she felt about herself, Connie found Mitch in the morning an appealing sight. He hadn't shaved and a light stubble shadowed his cheeks and chin. It made him seem less untouchable. Not that she'd been so reticent about touching him the night before. That thought turned her cheeks warm.

The sight of him sitting in her apartment having breakfast sent a buzz humming through her brain. This was something she could never have imagined, and yet there he was. It was intimate, appealing, and very distracting.

"Why aren't you married?" she asked, trying not to sound too curious.

Leaning back, he tapped his napkin against his lips, having finished his eggs. "Just lucky, I guess." He attempted a smile, but it didn't cross his lips, and his eyes remained grave. He cleared his throat, looking away toward the windows which were streaked with an early morning rain. "Actually I was married for five years."

That surprised her and she blinked, trying to drink it in. "No kids?"

"One," he said. "A son."

Connie tried to stifle her curiosity, but that was like trying to derail a locomotive coming down a hill.

"Do you see him very often?" Why had there been no pictures of the boy at his house or on his desk? She guessed the two men in uniforms were his brother and father. What about his son?

"He lives with his mother and stepfather in Ontario. I wanted him to have a real home, and a father who could always be there for him." His eyes met hers, and for once he was not a police officer. He was a man who had known his share of pain. The depths of his emotion shook her as much as his kisses had, and she realized the importance of what he was sharing.

"I never wanted him to have to go through what I did," he continued. "Those terrible nights I'd sit with my mother waiting, not to mention the times my dad was wounded or hurt. I hated worrying that some night someone would appear at the door, letting us know he was dead."

The thought of a young Mitch consoling his mother tugged at her emotions. "Is that why you never remarried?"

He put down his napkin on the table and got to his feet. "I don't know." He turned away, obviously uncomfortable with that subject or perhaps he was having second thoughts about what he had shared with her. "I'm going to get my bag. I'd like to clean up."

After he walked out the door she hit her hand against her thigh. "Dummy!" she muttered. "How can you be so damn insensitive? He gave up his son, what does that tell you?"

The discovery that he might be so sensitive surprised her. He'd always seemed so logical and cool. She'd never given him credit for having emotions or feeling pain. He'd sacrificed their relationship so his son didn't have to worry about his father getting killed. That probably was why he hadn't remarried. He didn't want another woman to go through that.

The phone rang, and she grabbed it.

"Oh, Connie," came Lisa's horrified voice. "I just heard on the news about Sandy. Why didn't you call me?"

The previous evening had dissolved into a bad dream, thanks to Weldon. She had sat outside the apartment, like a lost dog waiting for his master to return. Connie couldn't recall specifics. People milled about, talking in low voices. Police, neighbors, curiosity seekers? Probably all of them. Jim arrived along with several co-workers. He offered Connie the next couple of days off, and she agreed.

She had totally forgotten to call Lisa. There was more she needed to tell her sister, something the police had kept hidden. She had not told Jim, fearing he would insist on getting it into that night's story.

"Lisa...the thing is...Sandy's death might be tied to Joy's."

"What?" Lisa nearly shrieked across the line.

"She had on a gold pin. Like Joy's."

"Oh, my gosh. You better curb your Internet activities for awhile. This could be dangerous."

The thought of the Internet no longer appealed

to Connie. If someone from the chat room was to blame, she was just as responsible. She started Sandy talking to them. Even if they weren't to blame, Sandy's death was her fault. It had to be someone who turned on Sandy for trying to find Joy's killer. If her assistant hadn't tried to help Connie's headstrong search, Sandy would be alive, sitting at her desk at work today.

"Connie?" Lisa said when she didn't answer. "Did you hear what I said?"

"Yes, but I don't know about one of them being the killer. They weren't supposed to know where each other lived."

"She was thinking of trying to meet one of them."

"I don't think she did. She stayed home from work, and police think she was killed that night. She told me she was talking to people online, both that Lair group and the Assembly."

"You think it could be that church group?"

She told Lisa about what Gayle had told her about Beth.

"Now that I think about it, Beth was acting strange when I was there," Lisa said. "She was wearing drab clothes, no makeup, and her only jewelry was that pin."

"Maybe she wanted Joy to go with her." Discouragement gripped Connie. So many questions. "I wish I knew who Sandy talked to. She was supposed to email me, but she never got around to it."

"Maybe we should check her computer," Lisa suggested.

"It was broken, like the person wanted to make certain there wasn't anything there." A feeling of apprehension jerked at Connie. She hated thinking about this. "At least this clears Ralph. I saw him in Bellingham yesterday."

"He was here the previous evening," Lisa said.

"In Seattle?" Connie asked in surprise.

"Yes. I guess something got left in one of Joy's pockets, so he came by and picked up a couple of jackets. You know, Sandy called me about him right after we got back from Vancouver. I guess you told her that I suspected him? She wanted to know why, so I explained about the Muddy Hen and that bank account and the insurance."

Both left it unsaid, but Connie knew what her sister was probably thinking. What if Sandy looked into the possibility of his guilt? What if he, no, she didn't want to think about that.

"Sandy told me the people on the Internet were pretty sure he was messing around," Lisa said when Connie didn't reply.

"I asked around at her work. Mary Sue actually got huffy about it. Anyway, if you think Ralph did it, what's the big deal with the Internet?"

"You should still be careful. If you want that list of names, though, I'll get it, and we can give it to the police and let them check it."

"Good idea." Despite her comments to Mitch, Connie wasn't certain she wanted to continue her role of amateur sleuth. His comments about his father's death had touched her and the more Sandy's death sank in, the more Connie knew it was her fault. Still, the killer's name might be on that list. They could feed the list to Case or give it to Mitch.

The outer door opened and Mitch entered carrying a small black bag. Her heart skipped. She hadn't had a male visitor in a long time, and she was pleased it was Mitch. Seeing her on the phone he waved toward the shower and went through to the bathroom.

"Are you going to work?" Lisa asked.

"Actually, Mitch is here," she said in a near whisper. "He was in town yesterday and he stayed over."

"The good inspector?" Lisa's voice lightened. "The two of you, huh?"

"It's not like that."

"Connie, I saw you making eyes at him, and the other day when we went to his office he never took his eyes off you. No matter who was talking, he was watching you, and it wasn't in a professional capacity."

Connie rolled her eyes. She could tell what was on her sister's mind. "Don't start thinking 'happily ever after.' You know that's not me."

"Your problem is you're so damn frightened of commitment," Lisa said. "You think it will tie you down."

"I won't be tied down," Connie announced in as firm a tone as she could muster.

"Exactly! That's why you turn aside men who interest you," Lisa continued in her most serious voice. "You've always equated getting involved with settling down—like it would be turning into Joy."

"I hardly think so." Connie glanced at the closed bathroom door as the shower turned on. The thought of Mitch behind it, naked, made her tremble in a good way, but that wasn't what Lisa had in mind. "I wouldn't turn my back on a sexy man," she said, trying to turn Lisa's lecture into something less severe.

Lisa's quick laugh flew across the line. "I'll let you go and call you later to see how you're doing. I'm working from home, so if you need anything, don't be afraid to call."

Connie hung up, thinking about Lisa's comments about Mitch. Had he been watching her when they were in Vancouver? She touched her fingers to her lips, thinking again of his kiss. Had he wanted her last night? He'd said so, but then why had he been so careful about stopping? Why so adamant that they go no further?

Would she have burst into tears and lost control so badly if he had gone forward with their lovemaking? Probably not. She was looking for an outlet, a release. Connie wrinkled her nose. No wonder he had stopped. With his vast experience dealing with grieving relatives, he probably knew that. By now she knew him well enough to know he would never take advantage of a situation like that. The man was too much of a gentleman.

"Damn gentleman," she muttered. Connie smiled to herself, picturing him naked in her shower, lathering his body with soap. She had touched his bare chest the night before. She now knew how hard and muscular it was below a thin mat of hair. The image of him washing his body brought shudders of excitement to her. What would he do if Connie suddenly walked into the shower right now and presented her naked body to him?

It couldn't happen, of course. Even if she had the nerve to do it—which she didn't—a man like him would want to make the first move. She'd been plenty aggressive that first time—she needed to let him make the next move. What would happen if they found themselves in that sort of situation, but without the emotional baggage? Would he pull back again?

Shaking aside thoughts of Mitch, she forced herself to focus her attention in another direction. She needed to concentrate on work. She signed on to her computer and found the gasoline price notes she had taken in Bellingham. She began filling out orders for graphics and began writing a script. For once the idea of writing a simple consumer story was preferable to writing about death and drug lords.

The shower stopped and moments later, Mitch emerged, carrying his black duffle bag. His quick boyish smile sent her pulse racing. Damn, he looked appealing this morning. The familiar sandalwood scent of his aftershave wafted across the room to her, setting butterflies to fluttering inside her stomach. He was dressed in his normal work uniform—pale blue dress shirt, rather boring beige tie, and nicely pressed brown wool slacks.

"I'm going to meet with the local police this morning and then go back to Vancouver," he said. "I'd propose lunch, but I don't think I'll be here that long."

He seemed afraid to come too close to Connie, moving along the edge of the living area, transferring his bag from hand to hand as though it might be a shield. Would he throw it up in front of him if she came too close?

"That's okay. I'm doing some work." She gestured at her computer.

"Not Internet surfing like your friend," he said in a hard, warning tone.

"I'm finishing the story I was working on yesterday. I promised Jim I'd email him the script. See, you can read it if you want."

He walked toward her, and she was disappointed that he didn't believe her. He read the script and nodded abruptly. "Not bad."

"Well, it's a beginning," she said with a shrug. "It won't be as good as our bargain piece that ran the other night, but it's okay."

He tapped his fingers on the desk, his head nodding. "I have to go, but if you hear anything, let me know, eh?"

"This case doesn't involve you and the Slasher investigation, does it?" she asked.

A shutter passed over his green eyes, as though closing the issue. "No. I went over to the location to be certain, and while this might be related to your sister's death, that's Case's jurisdiction. I'll be going back to Vancouver."

"Might be related?" she asked in surprise. "Weldon, what does your gut tell you?"

"My gut?" He turned over the words as though they were foreign to him. "Well, I know what my instincts say."

"Don't play games," she replied bluntly. "My gut, and it isn't even a cop gut, tells me they're related."

"I hope you weren't serious last night when you said you were going to try to solve this." Concern filled his eyes, and she looked away.

Unspoken was the accusation that she felt herself—that she had caused Sandy's death with her haphazard investigation of Joy's death. "No," she said softly, twisting her lips into a frown. "I learned my lesson."

"Good."

They stood a few feet apart, an uncomfortable silence mushrooming between them. His green eyes watched her closely, but she could not read what was there. She wanted to reach out and touch him, but she'd been forward enough the last time they parted like this. Instead, she simply smiled.

"The sofa is available any time you're in Seattle," she said, trying to sound flip, but it didn't come out as smoothly as she would have liked. "Take care of yourself, Weldon. Thanks for being so kind last night."

"Kind," he repeated with a grunt. "Sometimes I think you need a guardian angel."

She bristled. She was tired of everyone thinking she needed someone to take care of her. "I really can take care of myself."

His lips pulled apart in a tight smile. "Of course. Bye, Connie."

He turned and walked to the door, footsteps clicking on the wooden floors. Connie wanted to run after him and hug him, but she held back. She'd lost her composure with him too many times.

Chapter Fifteen

"I got the names and profiles for all the people in the Assembly room and the Lair," Lisa said proudly when Connie answered the unexpected knock at her door two hours later. Her sister tapped the black briefcase that was slung over her shoulder.

"Why? I thought we agreed to stop..."

Lisa shook her head as she marched in the door. "You're so damn stubborn. It's the only way to stop you from continuing."

Connie said nothing. For the past couple of hours she had busied herself playing games on her computer, but she knew it was only a matter of time before she tried to get into the Lair again or checked her email for Sandy's notes on how to get into the Assembly chat room.

Lisa unzipped her bag and took out a file folder. She pulled a sheet of paper from it and held it out for her sister's perusal.

"How did you ever find this?" Connie asked, her gaze running over the list of names and addresses. They should have done this from the start.

"It's not too hard when you're a computer geek." Lisa closed her fingers into a fist, and pretended to polish it against her shoulder.

Connie perused the list. She didn't like to think that one of these people might be responsible for Joy or Sandy's death, but at the same time, she wanted police to know everything possible.

Lisa's gaze roamed the apartment. "When did the inspector leave?"

Looking up, Connie stuck her tongue out at her

sister. "Not that it's your business, but he left early this morning, right after breakfast and he spent the night on the couch."

"Of course he did," Lisa said with a giggle. "That's what I'd figure from him. He's a gentleman, unlike most of those loose guys you hook up with."

Connie rolled her eyes. "A gentleman. Whoopee! Sometimes you want a guy who will just jump your bones."

"That's always been your problem. You prefer the 'jump your bones' guys, because they don't ask anything from you but fun."

"Don't start, Lisa," Connie said, holding up her hands in a "stop" gesture. "I've got too much on my mind right now. Besides, you're not exactly up to your neck in date offers."

"Because most guys do just want to jump your bones. Okay, you're right. Enough playing around. Let's go through that list and tell me what you think."

Connie studied the list again. "Okay, NiteMan's real name is Mike Daniels, and his occupation is listed as plumber. His address is Portland, Oregon. That's within driving distance to Seattle and Vancouver. So is DeadlyGhost, the truck driver from Montana. DarkMaster is a salesman from Kentucky and LastDance is a computer consultant from Northern California. JustMelvin comes from Texas. His occupation is listed as student. We can probably rule those last three out, unless they come up here. What about Mike7445?" She turned over the last page.

"Mike? The plumber's name is Mike," Lisa said, pointing at her sheet. "There wasn't a screen name that had Mike in it on either the list you gave me or the one Sandy provided."

Connie shuffled through the file folders piled high on a corner of her desk until she found the clipped together sheaf of papers taken from Joy's shoe boxes. She held up the sheet on top for Lisa to read.

SexyLady: Do you meet lots of people on here?

Mike7445: Not really.

SexyLady: Why not?

Mike7445: I don't know. Some strange people in here.

SexyLady: Like everyone in the chat room?

Mike7445: I know them. We're there every night, and it's usually the same crowd.

SexyLady: They don't seem to like you.

Mike7445: Just sometimes we get in fights, like any family.

SexyLady: Have you met any of the people from that chat room?

Mike7445: No.

"What do you suppose happened to Mike?" Lisa asked.

"Sometimes they throw people out of the room. Like if they try to meet some of the others, and I read in some of the conversations between Mike and Joy that he had asked her about meeting him. Maybe we should send email to Mike and find out who he is," Connie suggested.

"Maybe," Lisa said, but even as she spoke, she was shaking her head. "I'm not sure it's a good idea. What if he's the killer? That might alert him."

"Could you find out his name?" Connie asked.

"I can try." Lisa sat down on Connie's chair, positioned the computer monitor and mouse to her comfort and began tapping in quick motions on the keyboard. After a few minutes, she shook her head. "Nothing. It's like he doesn't exist anymore."

"Are you certain?"

"He's not listed anywhere I've looked."

Connie's gaze fell on the list Lisa had shown her

originally. "How do you do that? Find out those names?"

"Different ways. Sometimes a simple search works. Other times you have to dig a little. The computer has put us out there for everyone to look up. It's frightening how much you can find out about a person online."

"So even with a rule about not finding out who each other is, it's pretty easy to look up people. Any of them could have been looking up the others."

"It's not always easy, but it can be done if you're computer literate. But even that doesn't guarantee who's at the other end. Think of it. You're online pretending to be Joy. Even Sandy was lying about who she was."

"Sandy. Damn, I'm going to miss her. I keep thinking of the other day when we were all here. Remember how excited she was?"

Thoughts of the perky blonde brought silence to them both. Connie knew it would be a long time before she forgot the horrible sight or smell of her friend's apartment. Movement beside her jerked Connie from her reverie.

Lisa pulled another file folder from her bag. "I have more to show you."

"What?"

"The Assembly list. Not only that..." She handed Connie a bundle of papers that were clipped together. They looked like they had been taken from newspaper articles on the Internet. The headline of one was "Religious Leader Arrested on Fraud Charges."

R. L. Lincoln was arrested yesterday on charges of fraud and embezzlement in connection with the Assembly for Truth and Spiritual Re-awakening.

He is accused of bilking millions of dollars from hundreds in the Northwest who either joined the church or sent donations to his special foundation. The Assembly for Truth and Spiritual Re-awakening was established nearly ten years ago and proposed the birth of a new spiritual existence. Thousands have donated to his church. Although he denies that he took any money for himself, he lives in a multi-million dollar estate, while followers live in one-room huts at his religious compounds in eastern Oregon and British Columbia.

Connie lowered the article and looked at Lisa "I wonder if we can find a connection between Sandy and Joy."

Lisa rifled through the papers. She handed another page to Connie. This one showed Lincoln in handcuffs being led away by police. On his suit lapel was a small circular gold pin.

Connie's breath caught and her finger jabbed at the page. "Is that…the pin?"

"Looks like it," Lisa agreed with a nervous laugh. "I wonder if that was where Joy was sending that money from her secret account."

"Maybe. I had started to think it was another man." She told Lisa about Gayle's comments that her sister had dyed her hair and made the shopping trip to Seattle.

"That doesn't rule out Lincoln or the Assembly," Lisa said in a quiet voice when she was finished. "He was said to have several wives, and while the others are living in those communes in poverty, did you see the woman in the picture next to him? That's one of his wives."

Connie studied the picture of a woman in a fashionable suit with large earrings and strands of pearls. Could Joy have become involved with this man? More and more she was discovering that they had not known what was in Joy's head the last couple of months of her life.

"Not only that," Lisa said, "but when I went to find the names of the people in the Assembly chat room, it appears they're all from the same account, owned by Jenny Lincoln—R.L. Lincoln's daughter. Not only that, they're all coming from the same hub."

"I don't understand."

"I was able to trace the origins or external IP address of the computers originating the messages. It's all the same. That tells me they're all either in the same room or the same house. Look at those conversations. The group is working on two people. Person number one suddenly gives in and finds the light, putting the pressure on person number two. The whole thing is a scam to get that other person to join or send money. Read these conversations. I was able to hack into their computer as an invisible guest."

Protector: I can sense your questions. You are losing your way.

Genesis: Not losing it, but I'm not sure what you want.

Morninglight: We only want what you want. The choices are yours.

Sweetprayers: You must give up this world. Only then can you enter the next.

Genesis: I can't leave my family.

Protector: For a short time you must study alone. Then you may bring them into the fold.

"This resembles what Sandy showed me," Connie said. "She talked to this group as Joy."

"The question is why would someone kill her?" Lisa asked.

"According to that book I read, they won't let you get out once you're in." Connie began to pace, ideas coming to her. "What if Joy threatened to stop sending money? Or expose them? Lincoln was arrested last week, but I'll bet they've been investigating him for months. What if she said she'd go to the authorities or testify against him?"

Lisa's eyes grew wide. "But murder? You think Lincoln or his followers would do that?"

"Absolutely. You're talking about millions of dollars. What if they found out Sandy was looking into their dealings? She was with a news network. She'd be more of a threat than Joy. I wonder if we should go to that compound..." She walked to the computer and signed on.

Lisa grabbed her arm. "Connie, what are you doing?"

"I'm going to check their exact location. We might be able to get onto the grounds by pretending we're interested in joining. Oh, wait! Beth! That friend of Joy's joined. Maybe we can get in touch with her family and find out where she is. She could get us—"

"No!" Lisa stopped her hand on the mouse as Connie prepared to click. Her brown eyes grew anxious, fearful. "Don't involve yourself. You're going to get into trouble. Think about Sandy and be practical for once. Let's turn this information over to the police."

Connie sighed and lifted her hand. She wasn't going to get into a wrestling match over the mouse. "I wonder if there's some way to pursue this without going there."

Lisa relaxed. "What about her Internet friends? They seemed to be the only people she was talking to there toward the end. I wonder if they knew anything."

Despite her earlier abhorrence of the chat room, Connie knew it was a possibility. "She talked to Raven about spirituality. Perhaps it was a group discussion. We can check that."

Lisa's frown deepened, and she tapped a finger against her chin in thought. Connie reached for the mouse, glancing at Lisa to see if she would continue to protest.

"Let's both do it," Lisa agreed with an affirmative nod. "We can use the laptop."

"Good idea. I'll get on as SexyLady on the laptop and you get on as Searcher. Sandy gave me her password, in case I needed it."

Lisa gulped, wavering. "Searcher? Is that a good idea?"

"These people shouldn't know she's dead. Only the killer knows. If he's out there, maybe he'll tip his hand. No one has ever indicated they know Joy is gone. Maybe this will clear all of them from Sandy's death too. Oh, hell, I just remembered. Last time I tried to get on, I couldn't. I was barred from the room."

Lisa drew up her small shoulders, her hesitation disappearing. "I'll get you in," she said with a wink.

To Connie's surprise, once they were set up, she was immediately taken to the room, even before Lisa had to work her computer magic. Not many people were in the chat room.

"Let's not get into questions about the cult too quickly." Connie didn't want to rush her questioning and end up as she had with Mary Sue Baker.

SkyGirl: So, Sexy, you just turn up again.

SexyLady: I've been working pretty hard.

DreamBaby: Don't let her get you down. I've been working too.

SexyLady: What do you do, Girl?

SkyGirl: None of your business. That question is off limits, remember?

Searcher: Don't be so touchy, SkyGirl.

SkyGirl: You're her friend. I don't expect you to criticize her. You better be careful or we'll vote you both out.

"Wonderful," Connie said, making a face at the monitor. "I'm making them angry."

"I don't understand why Sandy and Joy were so involved with these people. They're rude."

"Is one of them a killer? Maybe..." She waved at Lisa as another thought occurred. "Watch this."

SexyLady: Like you did Mike?

SkyGirl: Mike? Why bring him up? That was ages ago.

DreamBaby: Even you agreed he deserved it.

Lisa laughed, catching Connie's intent. "Okay, my turn."

Searcher: Who is Mike, and why did you vote him off?

SkyGirl: Ask your friend.

"Damn!" Connie pounded a balled up fist on the desk.

Judy1975: I'm not sorry we voted him out. I was tired of his hitting on us.

DreamBaby: Tell me about it!

SkyGirl: Don't try to say that he didn't hit on you, Sexy.

Judy1975: He wanted to meet me in person.

DreamBaby: Really off limits.

SkyGirl: He was funny sometimes.

DreamBaby: Funny didn't mean he could break the rules.

"This is slow going," Connie complained with a sigh. She had made one discovery about the mysterious Mike, though. He had been trying to meet the women in person and that was why he was tossed out of the group.

SkyGirl: I think that's what happened to *Little Bird*. Mike drove her away or she quit because she decided to meet him.

They had mentioned Little Bird before. Another thought popped into her head, but before she could type, Lisa's fingers were flying across the keyboard.

Searcher: Was he funnier than Raven?
SkyGirl: Nothing funny about Raven.
DreamBaby: He's too busy with his voodoo and mystical crap.

Connie met Lisa's glance across the desk, and she hooted. "Okay, Lisa! There we go."

SexyLady: Yes, but he's become our spiritual father.
DreamBaby: Says who?
Judy1975: I thought we decided religion was off limits. Don't try that crap again, Sexy.
DreamBaby: Yeah, you talk religion and then you flirt with the guys.
SkyGirl: No religious discussions. We agreed.

Connie frowned at the screen. "Well, that takes care of any connection between the Assembly and the Lair." But Lonetree knew about Joy's search for a new spiritual life. Had he, despite that talk about Mother Earth, turned her on to the Assembly? Gotten her financially involved? Killed her when she decided to quit? "I wonder if he knows Lincoln. Maybe he works for him. I really don't trust that guy."

His evasive behavior when they went to see him bothered her. An image of the large man with the deep, inscrutable eyes flew into her mind. Mitch said the professor had an alibi for the day Joy was killed. Did he have one for the day of Sandy's death too?

Lisa tapped out a message, eyes never leaving the screen. "Do you really think it could be Lonetree? He's a college professor."

"Who specializes in religion," Connie countered.

"Native American culture. That's hardly theocracy." Lisa glared at her across the top of her computer. "Did you see his office? He's into Mother Earth."

"He's into spirits. He had masks all over his

walls. Why are you defending him?"

"I'm not. Just questioning. Maybe these people can tell us more about him." Lisa typed out another response.

"We know more about him than they do," Connie said. "We know his name."

"It doesn't hurt to try."

Prettyone: I'm very happy! Met the man of my dreams last night.

SkyGirl: Another computer guy?

PrettyOne: Not this time. He lives downstairs.

SkyGirl: About time you wised up.

Searcher: You don't think you can meet people online and fall in love, Skygirl?

SkyGirl: Where have you been, Searcher? Don't you know that?

DreamBaby: Maybe that's what she has been searching for all along.

Searcher: Maybe.

SkyGirl: Don't be silly, Searcher!

Searcher: You think it's silly to find someone on here?

"Lisa, what are you doing?" Connie was trying to think of ways to bring up Raven's name, and her sister was getting caught up in conversation.

"These women are so preachy, inflicting their rules on everyone else."

SkyGirl: You can't find love online.

PrettyOne: It's better to find someone to be with physically.

Searcher: You could find someone online, and meet in person.

Raven40: Personal meetings are not part of our agreement

Lisa shrieked and Connie jumped, jerking up in her chair, the hair rising on the back of her neck. Once again, the mystifying Raven had made a

263

comment before his name popped onto the list of people in the room.

"Oh, hell!" Lisa's chest heaved, her breathing audible.

"This might be just what we need." Connie began to type. For once she was going to keep up with the conversation, even though her hands shook.

SexyLady: You don't think people in this circle have ever met?

Raven40: No. We all agreed.

SexyLady: I know some people have!

"Stop," Lisa pleaded in a high voice. "We weren't going to get involved like this. Let's turn over what we know to Sergeant Case."

Connie's decision to stop investigating disintegrated, given Raven's presence. "This guy knows that SexyLady is not Joy anymore. He knew her screen name. That means he should also realize that Searcher is suspect, since we introduced Searcher as SexyLady's friend. What if Sandy talked to him and he convinced her to meet him? He would have known she was a plant."

"Didn't you tell her about what we discovered in Vancouver?"

A horrifying thought crossed Connie's mind. "Yes, but you know Sandy. What if she tried to take matters into her own hands? What if he did meet her? She said she had it figured out. She left me a message to that effect."

Their eyes met across the desk, and the terror in Lisa's large brown eyes mirrored what Connie felt.

"Let's get off," Lisa urged again.

Connie waved her hand up and down to calm her jittery sister. "Just a minute," she said, as she studied the screen. "He can't hurt us. He's in Vancouver, and he has no idea where we are. Let's just see what he says."

Lisa whimpered in concern as Connie read

Raven's response.

    Raven40: Do you know something?

    SexyLady: What's wrong, Raven? Are you afraid not everyone is living by your rules?

    DreamBaby: You better. Or we'll vote you out, right?

    Raven40: I don't think you're one of us anyway.

    SkyGirl: Let's vote her out.

    Raven40: Tell me, Lady. What do you know about us? We've been together for months and should know each other. Do you know if we are who we say we are?

More mewling noises of fear and worry erupted from Lisa. She was growing frantic, waving her hands at the computer and twisting in her chair frantically. "Connie, stop! Let's call the police."

Connie was determined to press forward.

    SexyLady: I know who you are.

Connie regretted her words as soon as she typed them. She should not have said that, but she was still rocking over the realization that Sandy might have tried to tackle the truth about the frightening man by herself. Naturally her headstrong researcher would not back off. Connie should have realized what Sandy was up to the day she called in sick. If Connie had gone to the girl's house, perhaps she could have saved her life. Connie clenched her hands, trying to stop shaking as she and Lisa watched the monitor, waiting for his reply.

    Raven40: And I know you.

As Connie read the words, another screen appeared. Lisa cried out again, and Connie nearly bolted out of her chair. On the computer screen was an invitation to a new chat room—The Truth Room—and it invited her and Searcher to join him.

"Are you going?" Lisa asked in a hushed tone.

"Of course," Connie replied, trying to keep her

voice steady. She clicked to accept the invitation and her name appeared in a new chat room along with Raven 40. Searcher's name blinked in seconds later.

Raven40: Hello, am I right in assuming I'm addressing the Romero sisters?

Chapter Sixteen

"He knows us!" Lisa's frightened cry echoed around the loft.

Connie's heart thumped and she could barely type. Her hands trembled, but she managed a reply, even if she misspelled his name.

SexyLady: Yes, Mr. Lontree.

Raven40: You knew when you came to see me?

SexyLady: I saw it on your computer when I went back for the pin. But you knew who I was. You've always known.

Lisa rocked in her chair, her voice breathless as she chanted. "Oh, damn, oh, damn, oh, damn."

"Will you stop that?" Connie was growing impatient.

"The other people from the chat room are sending me messages," Lisa explained. "DreamBaby wants to know if we've been taken to the woodshed. What shall I tell her?"

"Tell her yes. Let them think what they want." Connie ignored an instant message that popped up on her screen. She didn't care about the others. She needed to focus her attention on Raven.

Raven40: I knew you weren't Joy. Not sure until I met you and your sister about who you really were, Lisa.

SexyLady: You got it wrong.

Raven40: You're Connie and Searcher is Lisa.

Connie didn't bother to correct him. If he killed her friend, he knew that Lisa had taken over the name. As long as they were together, they were safe. Her gaze slid around her apartment, gauging security. There was only one door, and she'd put the dead bolt on when Lisa arrived. Unless someone had a tall ladder they could not reach the windows.

Raven40: Why so quiet, Searcher?

SexyLady: She's being questioned by the others. They noticed we disappeared.

Raven40: Tell them you're being taken to task for breaking the rules.

Searcher: I did.

Raven40: Ah, the silent Lisa. May I ask what the two of you think you're doing?

SexyLady: We told you. We want to find out the truth about Joy's death.

Raven40: You think you'll find it in The Lair?

Connie hesitated. She needed a way to draw him out.

SexyLady: Maybe.

Raven40: You realize that what you're doing is stupid and dangerous.

SexyLady: Why?

Raven40: If one of those people is the killer, they will know like I do that you're lying.

Her breath caught and she wadded her hands into fists, willing them to stop shaking. She rubbed them together trying to warm them.

SexyLady: You're the only one who knows who we are and about looking into Joy's murder. Where were you on Tuesday?

Raven40: In class.

Searcher: All day?

Raven40: It was an all day lab.

Searcher: But you were online.

Raven40: Why are you asking? I was on the computer talking to you while I supervised the class.

Lisa met her anxious glance across the desk.

"He's playing games," Connie said.

The sudden ringing of her cell phone burst across the room like an explosion, making them both jump.

"Keep him talking," Connie said, reaching for the phone. She crossed her fingers, hoping to hear Mitch's quiet, cultured tones.

The deep voice at the other end of the line was unfamiliar. "Miss Romero?"

"Yes?"

"William Lonetree here."

Like before when they cried out at his sudden appearance Connie almost screamed. As it was she must have worn a look of horror, because Lisa seemed to grasp her feelings. Her brown eyes widened and fear flashed in them.

"Yes…" Connie croaked.

"You sound frightened."

"No." She tried to bring her quick breathing to a normal level, and turned away from the phone to clear her throat so she could force her voice to sound as natural as possible. No need to let him know that his call made her heart pound like jackhammer.

"You should be, Miss Romero. You have no idea who I am."

Connie licked her lips which had gone dry. She would not let him hear how terrified she was. She spoke slowly and evenly into the phone. "You said you're William Lonetree, and I recognize your voice. I gave you my card with my cell phone number the other day."

"I'm sorry if I startled you, but you knew my screen name."

"Does anyone else know it?" she asked.

"From the chat room? No."

"How did you connect with Joy?"

He cleared his throat, and she sensed hesitation.

"Why didn't you ask this the other day?"

"I didn't see your computer till we were leaving."

His voice grew accusing. "Is that why your sister came online the next day and tried to nail me down?"

Connie's glance flew to Lisa who was watching closely, chewing on a nail. "That wasn't Lisa. She didn't take that name until today. It was my assistant, Sandy."

Again the hesitation before he replied. "Then she should be able to tell you that we chatted until the lab ended at three in the afternoon."

"I could ask her. Except... she's dead."

"Dead?" He sounded surprised. He was either a consummate actor, or he had not known about Sandy.

"As in murdered, Mr. Lonetree. Just like Joy." She fought to keep accusation out of her voice.

He didn't answer for a few seconds. "What do you mean, like Joy?"

"Stabbed. Mutilated. Little pin on her body."

He drew a deep breath. "We need to talk, Miss Romero. In person."

Goose bumps broke out on her arms. Was this how he lured Sandy to her death? "Do you want me to come up there? Or will you come here?"

"What are you doing?" Lisa whispered in a frantic tone. "Hang up! Let's call the cops."

Connie lowered her head and cupped her hand over her ear to hear Lonetree better.

"It's difficult for me to get away. I have a weekend lab tomorrow morning."

"I can be there tomorrow afternoon."

At Connie's words, Lisa gestured frantically, shaking her head.

"Call me when you arrive," Lonetree said. "Now I'm returning to the chat room. I'd appreciate it if you stayed away. There's nothing for you there."

The chat room had never been appealing, so the directive meant nothing to her. "Don't worry, Mr. Lonetree. Your sacred chat room is safe from us."

She wasn't as certain they were safe from it. Clicking off her phone, Connie dropped it to the desk as though it was hot. Fear skittered up her spine. "I hate that man."

"You're not going to see him alone. I'm going with you," Lisa asserted.

"I don't want you in danger."

Lisa's tension dissolved into a sudden smile. "You nut. You could be in danger if you go without me."

Connie did not protest. If Lonetree was the killer, he could not attack them both. "I don't trust that SOB worth a damn. I think he's lying. Mitch thinks he's so innocent. Maybe I'll have him meet us and stand outside and listen, or we could wear a wire or something."

Lisa shook gave her a weary look. "Stop. We're not going to become decoys or play games."

The thought of putting herself in danger held no appeal, but she wanted to make certain Lonetree got caught if he was guilty. She would not let him get away with killing her sister and her friend.

"Damn," Lisa cried, her attention swinging back to the computer monitor. "I've got all these messages."

Connie had forgotten they were still online. She had a series of instant messages lined up on her screen. She clicked them off without answering.

"Here's a message from NiteMan, asking if we got tossed out."

"Yeah, well, Raven, the jerk, told me we should stay away from the chat room."

"Are you going to do what he asks?" Lisa asked.

"For now. What are you going to tell Niteman?" Connie asked.

"Might as well tell him yes. I don't intend going back either and it will explain what happened to us."

"I guess. I wonder about Little Bird. Maybe we should email her. Since they tossed her out, maybe she would tell us what she knows about Raven."

Lisa wrinkled her nose in distaste. "I think we should turn this over to your inspector or Sergeant Case."

"He's not my inspector!" Connie said, but the thought of Mitch made her smile for the first time in hours. Now she had a reason to call him when they went to Vancouver.

"Here's LastDance. He feels bad and wants to keep in touch. What should I say?"

"Tell him sure. Maybe we can get someone to talk one on one now that we've been told officially to go to hell by Papa Raven."

"Okay," Lisa agreed. She tapped rapidly on the keyboard.

Connie rounded the desk and stood behind her sister to check what both were saying.

Searcher: I'll keep in touch.

LastDance: Good. I like you. You've been a breath of fresh air.

Searcher: Well, darn, you'll turn my pretty head.

LastDance: I'd love to do that.

Searcher: You're a flirt.

LastDance: I hope you are too.

Lisa looked at Connie, eyes filled with bewilderment and yet a trace of a sparkle too. "What should I say?"

Connie patted her shoulder. "You're doing fine. 'You'll turn my pretty head?' Have you ever said that to a guy in person?"

Lisa's cheeks turned bright pink and she giggled. "Actually no. That's the thing about this damn computer. I find myself writing emails to people saying things I wouldn't dare say in person. Now I'm flirting with these bozos."

"Just don't get carried away," Connie warned, thinking of Sandy. Had Joy done that too? The thought made her quaver with trepidation. "I'm going to send a note to Little Bird and see if she'll talk to me." Connie typed a note, re-typed it and finally sent it:

I have joined the ranks of the undesired.
I just got tossed from the Lair for breaking Raven's rules.
> *Care to commiserate?*
> *Sexy Lady*

A sudden laugh erupted from across the desk as Connie sent the email. Her sister was laughing? Maybe the computer would be good for her. Computers were her life after all. Maybe she might even find romance. While Connie was too busy with work for romance, sometimes Lisa seemed afraid of the idea.

With her sister occupied, and the email sent, Connie looked around the room, seeking something to do. She didn't feel like cleaning up. The continued presence of the sheets and comforter on the sofa arm indicated Mitch had visited and might be back.

Mitch! She looked at her cell phone, tempted again to call him. She reached for it and stopped. No, it was best to let things simmer for a while.

****

The scent of Connie's lavender soap remained in Mitch's nostrils all morning. Not very masculine, but a very pleasant reminder. Every time he moved, he felt her presence or his mind floated back to the way she had looked as he said goodbye. It was a good thing that the most strenuous brainwork he had to do was keep the car between the lines as he drove to Vancouver.

Luckily, in the middle of the week in February,

traffic was sparse along the interstate. Heavy clouds threatened rain as he passed through the Skagit Valley with its farms and sprinkling of small towns.

He forced his thoughts back to work. He needed to concentrate on the Blade. The man was due to make a mistake. He'd been sloppy on his last attempt. Hopefully he'd make a bigger error the next time and they could catch him before anyone else died.

His cell phone chirped and he tapped the "talk" button and lifted an earpiece to his head. He smiled, hoping to hear Connie's voice. Instead, Case came on the line. That was a surprise since they'd parted less than two hours ago at the Seattle Police Department.

"Hey, Mitch, sorry to trouble you. Where are you?"

"Just north of Mt. Vernon." He hadn't told Connie but he had stopped to talk with Ryan and Case before leaving Seattle.

"I'm leaving Seattle, but I need a favor. Can you stop in Bellingham for some surveillance work on Perkins?"

Mitch straightened up in his seat. "What's up?"

"We're working on the victim's damaged computer. One of the techies here thinks he can get information, even though it was busted up pretty good. He managed to get into her email and found some of her last transmissions."

"About Perkins?"

While they knew the cases were related he couldn't see how they would tie Ralph Perkins to the young woman's death unless fingerprints were discovered or witnesses came forward saying they had seen him near her apartment.

"The girl sent him email the day she was killed, threatening to expose him," Case said.

"Expose him?" Weldon stiffened. There it was!

The connection.

"Perkins apparently was having an affair with a woman from his wife's office. The girl uncovered it."

"Well, now things begin to make sense, eh?"

"There's more. He emailed her back asking her not to say anything until he could talk to her in person. He said he would be in Seattle that afternoon and wanted to meet her. Her reply is damaged, but I have a feeling that she agreed. The M.E. places time of death between three and seven. It seems to me Mr. Perkins needs to give us some answers. I've called his office and learned he was out of the office that afternoon."

"Do you want me to find him? Talk to him?"

"He's at work, but I'd like you to keep an eye on him until I arrive. I'd call Bellingham police, but I prefer someone I know. I don't want to alert him. Ryan's heading up there too."

"You owe me a large cup of coffee for this," Mitch said, "but it's no problem. I should be there in less than half an hour."

"Ryan is calling Bellingham and asking for a search warrant on his house. I think we have our man."

Connie quickly filtered through Weldon's thoughts as he hung up, but there was no way he could let her know what was happening. That was a clear violation of ethics. If she even had a hint they were going after Ralph, she might call her brother-in-law and spook him. Mitch stepped harder on the gas. The sooner they got this straightened out, the sooner Connie was no longer in danger and the sooner he could think about her in terms of things other than murder.

Like thinking about the scent of lavender.

****

Connie paced her apartment, her stockinged feet thudding on the hardwood floors. Lisa remained on

275

the computer. Every time she tried to talk to her, Lisa waved her off. Now, a sudden burst of laughter erupted from Lisa.

"What's so funny?" Connie asked.

"This guy. His name is Tom and he says he's glad I got tossed out. He says now we can talk like normal people and that's what we're doing. He likes romantic movies, just like me. Loves the Rolling Stones and Janis Joplin. He even likes hiking."

"Wonderful," Connie said in a sarcastic tone. Sandy and Joy had both been captivated by their online chatter and both were dead.

"Well, you have your cop," Lisa teased. Then her cheeks grew pink. "What am I saying? This isn't going anywhere. According to my list he lives in Northern California."

Leaving Lisa to chat, Connie sat down to work. She needed to remove the material she'd put into Joy's laptop and transfer it to her home computer. Joy's laptop had gone to the screensaver and she tapped the keyboard. It froze. Another quick tap didn't help. She pressed her fingers on the touchpad, but still could not unfreeze the screen. "Damn thing is frozen."

"Hmmm?" Lisa seemed to realize Connie was having problems and glanced up. "Need help?"

"Can you get this working?"

Lisa leaned over and inspected the screen. She hit a couple of keys, but like with Connie, nothing happened. "I'll fix it. Flirt with Tom."

They exchanged places, and Connie read over the comments.

Searcher: I'm not trying to hide anything. That group was rude.

LastDance: They're okay, just cautious.

Searcher: They seem cold.

LastDance: We are honest. It was a pledge we made.

Searcher: How do you know if someone is lying?

So Lisa had not been simply flirting. She was pumping Tom for information. Connie's fingers hovered over the keyboard as his reply flew up on the screen.

LastDance: I can tell. You need to get to know the mind.

How did she answer that?

Searcher: Isn't that hard on a computer? It's anonymous.

LastDance: Not if you take time. I can tell what a person is like from how they chat. Friendship doesn't work if it's mechanical— or lust.

Searcher: This is true. What are you looking for?

LastDance: At this point in my life I'm different than most. I don't waste time with shallow stuff.

She could see why this guy might appeal to her practical sister, and conversing with him wasn't difficult. It was easier conducting a personal conversation than trying to keep up with four or five different people in the chat room.

Searcher: I don't either.

LastDance: We can be friends, but I don't know where you're from.

Searcher: I'd tell you, but then I'd have to kill you.

She stopped. That might normally be a joke, but under the circumstances it wasn't funny.

LastDance: Like a black widow? Would it be worth it?

Searcher: Just being funny. No, I'm from the West Coast.

LastDance: Me too. Are you from LA? San Fran?

Connie hesitated. Should she tell him? She had no intention of meeting him.

Searcher: Seattle.

LastDance: Talk about a coincidence.

Searcher: Why?

LastDance: I'm from Seattle too.

Connie's gulp was so loud that across the desk, Lisa jumped.

"What?" she asked.

"Tom's from Seattle."

Lisa shook her head, not comprehending. "So?"

"No one on the list you showed me was from Seattle." Connie fumbled on the desk for the list, but another line was coming across the screen.

LastDance: Just moved here at the end of last year.

"He just moved here," she explained and typed a reply.

Searcher: To be near me?

Lisa sat back and waved at the computer. "Did you do this? Put this MyStuff folder in the program file? It doesn't belong there. I can transfer it to the document folder, or put it in its own place if you want."

"My stuff?" Connie asked, distracted by Tom's next words.

LastDance: Maybe. Should we meet for real?

Lisa gasped suddenly "Oh, my gosh, I think it's Joy's."

"What?" Connie hopped up from her chair, sending it swinging. She came up behind Lisa who had opened the file. Several icons popped onto the screen.

One said Joy Journal, another was labeled Joy Letters, and a third was called Joy Biz. The sisters exchanged surprised looks.

"Have you ever seen that?" Lisa asked.

"I didn't know it existed. Where was it?"

"The program file. I was checking to see that everything was okay and I noticed it. I don't know of a program called M-Y-S-T-F. That's why I opened it and it says My Stuff."

Connie drew a sharp breath. From behind her came the chime of Tom replying to her last comment.

"Oh, damn," Lisa said. "We forgot about Tom." She rose and returned to the other side of the desk. "I'll tell him I'll talk to him later."

"He wants to meet," Connie warned.

"Well, maybe." Lisa punched something into the computer as Connie maneuvered the mouse over the Letter file. Could this help them? She tapped, and a new series of icons flew up on the screen. They were labeled by a line of numbers.

"It's dates," Lisa said looking over her shoulder.

"How do you know?" Connie asked in bewilderment.

"Can't you tell? December or twelve, seventeen or the date and last year."

"Oh." Feeling stupid, Connie tapped on the first one.

Leave him alone, you bitch! He has been mine from the beginning and you won't come between us. You'll die first.

279

Chapter Seventeen

The threatening letter was like a bombshell. It shattered around them, sending waves of fear crashing through the air. The aftermath left a deafening silence. Connie's throat constricted and she nearly choked as bile rose. She and Lisa turned to face each other. Lisa's face was a pale mask of horror.

"Oh, my gosh," Connie croaked, fighting down nausea. "Who do you suppose sent this? There's no signature." With trembling hands, she clicked another icon and opened another letter. While not a death threat, it was equally vitriolic.

He is toying with you. He loves me, and you are in the way. Leave him alone or I will make you pay. Get out of our lives. Do it now before I have to hurt you.

"We need to take this to the police," Lisa said, gesturing at the screen, voice high and excited. "You better call Sergeant Case and let him know. This woman threatened Joy."

Connie read over the notes. Why would someone write such angry letters? "This sounds like a triangle. What do you think?"

"Maybe."

"Let's open the other letters." Before she could react, her main computer sang out a familiar refrain.

"You've got mail," the electronic voice said.

The unexpected sound made them both jump. Lisa gave a quick cry, and they faced each other and laughed. This was ridiculous. No one could come inside without permission, unless he flew in through the second story windows or flew digitally out of the computer monitor.

"Are we jumpy or what?" Connie asked, shaking her head and laughing. She rolled her chair away from Joy's laptop to her computer to check on the mail.

Clicking the mailbox icon, she pulled it up. "It's from Little Bird. Well, that was fast."

Lining up the arrow from her mouse on the letter, she clicked.

Please leave us alone. Haven't you people hurt our family enough? My sister is gone. Please don't ever write to her again.

The note was signed Jerry Penrose.

"This is odd." Connie read it aloud. "What do you suppose happened to his sister?"

"What was that name again?" Lisa asked.

"Little Bird."

Lisa began tapping on her laptop keyboard in rapid strokes. "I'll see if I can find out anything." Seconds later she looked up proudly. "Her name is Kelly Penrose from Portland."

"Kelly Penrose? I know that name." Connie couldn't remember where she'd heard it, but sometime in the past couple of weeks she'd run across it. She shook her head. "Well, never mind. I'm not going to write back unless we find out Little Bird sent those notes. Can you figure that out?"

"Maybe." Lisa tapped her fingers on the keyboard, frowned at the response, tried again and finally her face scrunched into a grimace. "Sorry. Nothing."

Connie sighed. "Oh, hell, let's wrap this up. This computer thing never appealed to me."

Lisa agreed, but she cast a longing eye toward the screen. "I wonder if I should talk more to Tom."

"At least he sounds normal. He gave Sandy bargain ideas."

Her cell phone chirped, and Connie reached for it. At least this time they didn't jump. Her mother's frantic voice was a shock.

"Connie, they've arrested Ralph."

Dismay gripped her and she waved at Lisa as she hopped to her feet. "Ralph? Arrested? By whom, Mom?"

"That cop from Canada who was at the service. Ralph called me to come over and take care of the kids when they get home. When I got here, they were leading him away in handcuffs. He was practically crying. I called Dad, and he's gone to see if he can find a lawyer, but I thought I should let you girls know. The police are searching the house. They have a warrant."

"Okay, Mom, calm down. Lisa's with me. We'll be there in a couple of hours."

Her mother let out a big sigh of relief. "Thank you, baby. We need you both here. Ralph's at the jail, and I have no idea what to tell the kids. We can't stay at the house. The cops are running around dumping things, going through all the drawers, doing who knows what. As if that poor man needed more misery."

"Okay, just concentrate on the kids. They're going to need you." Connie forced her voice to sound calm, although her insides churned. She couldn't fathom why police would suddenly arrest Ralph. Was Weldon there? Why hadn't he called her if he knew it was about to go down?

This was no time to be sidetracked by thoughts of him. Joy's children needed help and so did her parents. Her mother handled emergencies that came her way with advice and food. This was a different circumstance.

"I'll be fine," her mother murmured, sounding stronger. "I'll pick up the kids and take them to the mall. I'll keep them busy until the cops are done."

"Good. We'll be there soon." Connie flipped the phone closed and turned to Lisa. "They've arrested Ralph. I don't know why, but it sounds like Weldon was there."

"Why now?" Lisa asked.

"I don't know, but I intend to find out." Outrage bubbled inside her like water coming to a boil. Connie punched the familiar area code and phone number into her cell with such vehemence she nearly dropped the phone. When Weldon came on the line, her furor exploded like an overflowing pot.

"Damn you, Weldon, what the hell do you think you're doing?" Too pent up to sit down, she began pacing the floor as she hollered into the phone.

"Connie, I was going to call you." His voice remained tranquil but she was not about to let it calm her down.

"Before or after you arrested Ralph, you son of a bitch?"

His intake of breath was sharp and he paused before answering. "Bad news travels fast."

"Don't play coy!" she shouted at the phone. "I hope you're pleased. You're ruining a good man."

"You should understand I couldn't call before the arrest. It would have been unethical." How could he sound so calm?

"Damn your ethics. You knew I would call him before the cops got to him."

He hesitated, but when he spoke, a hard edge had entered his tone. "I feared that."

"How could you let them do that? How could you be part of it? And before you deny it, my mother saw you."

"Did your mother tell you police went through the house?"

"She said they were searching it, but that's the silliest damn thing I've ever heard."

"Not so silly," he said, voice growing harder.

283

"For your information, they may have found the murder weapon."

"What?" She couldn't stop a loud shriek from erupting.

Even Lisa jumped from her spot at the desk. She had not moved, merely watching as Connie paced and shouted.

Despite her outburst, Weldon's tone remained calm. "They found a knife hidden in the basement with blood on it. They'll do analysis, but Frank and I agree it looks like it's the murder weapon."

"No," she said breathlessly, as her anger exploded into raw emotion, and tears rolled down her cheeks. She had to keep from choking as she spoke. "You're wrong. Ralph wouldn't do that. He adored Joy."

"Husbands have killed out of love before," he said quietly. "I appreciate your loyalty, but it all adds up. No alibi, the large insurance policy. "

Connie wiped her hand across her wet cheek. "What about Sandy? You're not going to tell me that Ralph killed her?"

"Apparently your friend sent him email the day she was killed. He convinced her not to tell anyone until he could talk to her in person."

The fight went out of her and Connie sank onto the sofa, her knees turning rubbery and unable to hold her up. Tears poured down her cheeks untouched. "I have to go, Mitch."

"Are you all right?" he asked, voice taking on a note of distress. "Do you need me to call someone for you? Maybe your sister?"

His stab at concern didn't lessen her sense of betrayal. "She's here. Don't worry about me. I can take care of myself." Connie snapped the phone shut. After taking a deep breath, she turned to Lisa. "They may have found the murder weapon. It looks like you were right all along."

Lisa's eyes were filled with tears. She sniffled. "I wish I'd been wrong."

"We need to get to Bellingham, but I guess we don't have to go to Vancouver."

"I may go anyway," Lisa said, voice hardening.

"Why?" Talking to Will Lonetree no longer seemed as critical. What could they hope to find out?

Her sister waved at the computer. "I opened Joy's Journal while you were on the phone." Her lips trembled, and she gulped back a sob.

A chill ran through Connie. She stepped over to the desk and peered over Lisa's shoulder.

Raven says to let him go. But I can't. We belong together. I love him so desperately I can't sleep at night without calling him and saying goodnight. My morning can't start until we talk. How long before we can be together? I don't care about the others. All I need is him.

Connie stared at Lisa in horror. "What the hell?"

Lisa gestured toward the screen. "It gets worse."

Connie grasped Lisa's hand, squeezing it tightly as she lowered her eyes to the screen and continued reading.

Ralph can't really blame me for what I've done, not while he continues to see Mary Sue. Even Raven agrees. I should leave. Whatever happens, I won't give him up. I've never loved anyone so desperately.

There it was—the bitter truth that existed all along. Ralph was seeing Mary Sue, and Joy had turned to another man.

Tears threatened, and her throat constricted. She was barely able to breathe and her insides churned. How could Joy and Ralph have come to this point and the two sisters never realized it? Certainly Joy had not intimated it to their mother. She would have said something.

"I almost wish I didn't know. I feel like we're invading her privacy."

Lisa grew thoughtful as she stared at the computer screen. She pulled at her lower lip. "I'm still going to Vancouver," she blurted.

"Huh? You agreed with police about Ralph," Connie pointed out.

"I want to know about this man." Lisa jabbed at the screen. "I want to look Will Lonetree in the eye and ask him if he's the man she talked about."

"What?"

"I read other letters. One of them was from the man. He told her it was over, and he didn't want to see her anymore. He said all her pleading wouldn't change things, even if she sent him money." Her eyes fixed on Connie, wide and filled with hurt. "She was giving the money to that man. He told her he didn't want her to think she could buy his love."

"You think it's Lonetree?"

Lisa thrust her finger at the first journal entry with Raven's name. She underlined it invisibly with a fingertip.

"We'll both go see him," Connie said, taking a deep breath. She knew how her sister felt. "He may not have killed her, but he's just as responsible."

"Damn right," Lisa said in a hard tone very unlike her normally placid self. "I want to look that jerk straight in the face and let him know it."

****

The stuffy motel room prevented Connie from sleeping. The bed was hard, and the carpet smelled of disinfectant. Every so often the heater kicked on or shuddered off. The windows were not made to be opened, and stale air poured from the vents. Or maybe she was just exhausted from the events of the previous forty-eight hours and too exhausted to sleep. Sandy's death, the discoveries about Joy and now Ralph's arrest—it had finally taken its toll.

Connie shifted on the hard wooden chair in front of the computer screen, which cast a dim light. She clicked her mouse to turn over another card. Hopefully the monotony of Solitaire would eventually lull her into wanting to sleep. Across the room she could hear Lisa's even breathing. Next door, her mother and father and the children had stopped moving hours ago.

The police completed their search of Ralph's house too late to get it in any sort of order to take the children home. Connie didn't think she could stand to be there anyway. She and Lisa would help clean up in the morning and then the children would leave with their grandparents for the San Juan Islands. There they would be away from newspapers, police, and the turmoil bubbling in Bellingham. Connie feared the children were going to find out soon enough about their dad being in jail.

Ralph's arrest still rankled. She found it hard to believe that he killed Joy, though the letters on Joy's computer and journal entries appeared to be one more nail in his coffin. Connie and Lisa called Case about what they found on the computer and agreed to turn over the information to him after their visit to Lonetree.

Would she see Weldon during the visit to Vancouver? Connie hadn't decided. She felt hurt by his failure to call about Ralph's impending arrest, but she knew him well enough to understand that his work ethics and sense of honor would not allow him to do anything else.

A yawn overtook her and Connie considered climbing back into the hard bed and trying to sleep, but her brain remained restless. The card game swam before her tired eyes and Connie closed the game and called up an Internet browser. She had nothing to do, but perhaps web surfing would make her sleepy and it was less intrusive than the television. She tried to go to The Lair, but the room no longer existed. Raven had changed its name.

Damn jerk! While she felt ambivalent toward Weldon, she wasn't as generous toward Raven. He'd ruined Joy's life and been responsible for Sandy's death as surely as if he'd wielded the knife. If Ralph was guilty, he had killed Joy because of Raven. The mysterious online mentor was the real culprit. He had come between Joy and Ralph.

The Lair might be out of reach, but what about the people from the room? Might they be online? Connie found that DreamBaby was on, but the woman's normally nasty disposition was not something she could handle at this hour. There was no sign of Raven, not that she would have talked to him. Other names began to pop into her head. SkyGirl? She was not online, nor was NiteMan or DeadlyGhost. What about LastDance?

When she discovered he was online, she sent a message to him.

SexyLady: Remember me?

LastDance: Of course. How is life without the group?

SexyLady: I'm furious with Raven.

LastDance: We all are. We liked you and Searcher.

SexyLady: Why don't you get out?

LastDance: We've been together a long time. Like family. You're going to miss them.

Connie had no idea how Joy had gotten involved with the group or how long she was with them so she didn't want to bring up questions.

SexyLady: I guess. Sometimes it was mysterious though. Raven especially.

LastDance: I've never been mysterious.

SexyLady: You don't like being mysterious now and then?

LastDance: I am not good at making things

up.

SexyLady: Was that aimed at me?

LastDance: I get the feeling there is more to you than meets the keyboard.

Except for her earlier chat as Searcher, she had never talked to this guy Tom alone. His perception surprised her. He seemed to know something was wrong. How was he able to figure her out? She needed to send him in a different direction, but she wasn't certain how to do it.

SexyLady: Why do you say that?

LastDance: I'm a good judge of character. I can read between the lines.

SexyLady: What do those words between the lines tell you now?

LastDance: You need help, friendship. Now you're without us, the family.

Was he serious? Strange, but they all seemed to regard the group that way—as a family. Raven was the informal leader or father figure, with his rules and decisions. Was that how Joy had considered the group? As another family? Maybe this guy held some of the answers she was seeking about Joy.

SexyLady: Family? Is that how you see that group?

LastDance: They've always been there for me. I'll always be there for them.

SexyLady: But I've been disowned.

LastDance: Maybe now we can get to know each other.

SexyLady: Maybe. I like to get to know people.

LastDance: I should help you now that you're alone.

SexyLady: Help? How?

LastDance: You tell me. I think you're hiding something.

Was she that transparent? How could

LastDance see right through her so easily? She leaned over the keys, trying to decide what to say.

SexyLady: I have my reasons.

LastDance: I'm sure you do. Maybe we should meet for real.

Her breath caught. Did that make sense? Why should she meet him? Maybe she could confide in him, tell him about Joy and Sandy and see what his thoughts about Raven might be. Did it matter anymore? Yes. Ralph's guilt was still a question mark for her.

SexyLady: How do you know we're close enough to get together?

LastDance: Your friend Searcher lives in Seattle.

SexyLady: Yes, I'm there too.

LastDance: So am I. Maybe we should meet.

SexyLady: I'm not sure.

LastDance: You don't trust me, even though we've been in the same group for months?

SexyLady: I don't know you in person. I don't trust strangers.

LastDance: I know that. Neither do I.

The screen swarm before her eyes. Enough of this. Connie yawned as her eyes closed involuntarily. The hard bed was calling. The clock on her computer read 3:52, and another big day would dawn soon. Time to sign off.

SexyLady: I will be out of town tomorrow, but maybe we can talk again. Or meet.

LastDance: If that's what m'lady wants.

Connie signed off and eyed the computer warily. LastDance seemed nice, as Lisa and Sandy both indicated. He was different from the others in the group, which remained in question. He defended it as family, and while she admired his loyalty, she would never understand the devotion to it. As for meeting him, she wasn't certain. Maybe she and

Lisa could do it together.

****

"I feel guilty about this," Lisa said as they drove toward the University of British Columbia. "Maybe we should have stayed to help with the kids."

"We cleaned the house, and Dad is dealing with the attorney. Mom is going to enjoy doting on those kids. As it is, we're running late. We should have been in Vancouver three hours ago. Now we'll be driving back in the dark." Connie peered through the windshield at gray, threatening clouds that hid the surrounding mountains. "We'll probably be driving in the rain."

"The weather report said we might get snow this afternoon," Lisa added.

"Wonderful. Another pleasant winter day."

"Poor Ralph," Lisa said. "He looked so devastated this morning. I know I blamed him, but for a minute I hoped I was wrong."

Connie said nothing. Ralph continued to protest his innocence and her parents still believed in him. Neither she nor Lisa had the heart to tell them about his affair and Joy falling in love with another man. Much as she wanted to protest his innocence, there was no way to do that if police had really found the murder weapon in his house. Added to that was his request to Sandy not to divulge his affair. Connie had not asked about the affair during their visit that morning. She confined her time to simple condolences and assurances that her father was finding the best attorney possible.

Connie turned the corner into the parking lot in front of Lonetree's building. They had called him once they hit the city limits and he directed them to come over. He met them in the lobby, unlocking the front door and leading them to his office.

He closed the door and they took the same chairs as they had during their previous visit. The big man proved as imposing as ever, wearing a black turtleneck under a long white lab coat. His long black hair was swept behind his ears.

Tall and commanding, he stood behind his desk and looked from one to the other, black eyes hard and unreadable. "How may I help you ladies today?"

Lisa and Connie exchanged glances. Now that they were here, Connie didn't know what to say.

"We had a few questions about Joy..." she began. She appealed to Lisa for help, but despite her previous bravado, her sister's eyes focused on the floor, as though afraid to look him in the eye. Wasn't that why they both wanted to come?

"Didn't I read this morning that her husband was arrested?" he asked as he seated himself across from them and leaned forward across the cluttered desk.

"Yes," Connie admitted, licking her lips and searching for the right words. Damn, this guy made her nervous.

Lisa shifted, raised her head and faced him directly. When she spoke, her voice was level, if somewhat tense. "She was seeing someone else, did you know that? Ralph killed her because of another man, and we think we know who he is."

His black eyes fastened on Lisa. "Why share that information with me?"

"Was it you?" Connie demanded.

His dark face swiveled to her and the intensity of his gaze was like being in the headlights of a big rig going eighty miles an hour.

A sudden, incredulous laugh burst from him. "Is that what you think?" His attention swung to Lisa. "You think I was having an affair with your sister?"

His amused reaction disturbed her. Could they be wrong? "I have Joy's laptop. It has email in it, plus her journal."

"And it mentions me?" he asked, not the least bit

put off by her accusation.

"It says Raven told me to give him up," Lisa said.

"To give *him* up," he said, eyes flicking from one to the other. "I have no idea why your sister confided in me. Maybe she was looking for a father figure, someone to counsel her and yet someone with whom she shared no emotional attachment. I told her to give him up. She needed to discuss this with her husband and work it out. The same with her spiritual search. The answers come from within, not a blind search."

"Did she ask you about the Assembly of Truth and Spiritual Re-awakening?"Lisa asked.

The fear about Joy being a victim of the cult had largely fallen by the wayside, but if Raven knew about the affair, perhaps he could answer that too.

"That phony church," he snapped in disgust. "I warned her about that bunch. She was excited about seeing the leader, Lincoln, wanted to meet him, but I warned her they wanted nothing but her money. We've had that group up here for years. That was part of why I sent her the books and agreed to meet her."

"They wear pins, like the one we showed you," Lisa noted. "Our friend Sandy had a pin like that when she was killed."

He fixed Lisa with his dark-eyed stare. He leaned forward across the desk and Connie had to fight to keep from drawing back. His black eyes were like obsidian, hard and unyielding and when he turned them toward her, she felt like he could drill inside her skull and examine her very brain matter.

"Why did you come? Something is bothering you, isn't it?" His voice was as unyielding as his eyes, and his frosty gaze traveled from one to the other, back and forth like a tennis match. He began tapping a pen on his desk blotter. Except for the tapping, the room was eerily silent.

Connie glanced at Lisa, but she was looking down again, picking at a spot on her brown plaid wool skirt as though it was the most interesting thing in the world. She licked her dry lips before speaking. "Well, Ralph was arrested, but I'm not convinced he killed Joy."

Lonetree dropped the pen. "Do you think someone from the room did it?" he asked. The sudden softness in his voice was more ominous than soothing.

"Do you?" Connie replied.

He sprang to his feet in such a quick fluid motion, it was like a striking rattlesnake. As her eyes met his in alarm, he fixed her with a hypnotic stare. The black eyes burned with an intense inner fire.

"To be honest, it has crossed my mind on several occasions."

Chapter Eighteen

Connie gasped as Lonetree broke his gaze as though he had said too much. He dropped onto his chair. For once, he avoided looking at either one of them, flipping through papers on his desk before resuming the tapping. His face was a chiseled mask, and a muscle twitched in his taut jaw.

"You thought one of them might be the killer?" Lisa asked in a choked voice.

Lonetree tilted his head as though listening for some specific cadence from the tapping. He appeared to weigh how to answer and finally shrugged in response. "I couldn't rule it out. What does anyone know about who those people are?"

"Then why do something like that? Foster the anonymity?" Lisa demanded.

"I didn't start that room," he said, impatience thick in his voice. He tossed his pen onto the desk. "We met in other rooms and enjoyed talking. The premise was to focus attention on our online personas and stay away from labels, like we found in other rooms. I didn't originate the rules, but I agree with them. Our off-line lives must be kept separate even if we discuss them."

Sensing he was in a talkative mood, Connie pressed forward. "Joy was one of the original members?"

"Yes. And we grew over time. If we went to other rooms and met people who fit our group, we invited them to join. Joy was good at recruiting new members. She was friendly, though sometimes she took it too far and became flirtatious. Teasing men, trying to get their attention."

"That doesn't sound like Joy. She's always been friendly, but a flirt?" Connie said.

"How can you say that? You saw those old chats she saved," Lisa blurted. She turned to Lonetree. "Did she flirt with you?"

His smile was grim. "Yes, but I sensed from the beginning that she had ulterior motives. Later I realized she wanted some way to get even with her husband. Eventually we became friends, talking about other things, like religion. I tried to help her, but she was looking for something else."

"Why didn't you tell us about her wanting to have an affair?" Connie asked.

Again, the ping-pong glance from one to the other. "You were her sisters. It wasn't my place to tell you."

"What about Sandy? You said she talked to you?" Connie asked.

His dark eyes pinned her to the chair. She felt like a bug being mounted in a collection. "I thought it was one of you. She was acting very much like Joy, focusing on the men."

"What about Mike7445?"

"What about him?" The big man looked surprised. "He hasn't been around for months."

"Is it possible that Joy met Mike in person? That he was the person she had the affair with, or wanted to meet?"

"Possible." He steepled his hands and tapped his fingers together as though considering the possibility. "He was dismissed because he constantly pursued the women online. A couple complained to me. That was when I took on the role of chat room monitor."

"Is that how you see it? Dismissed?" Connie fought to keep her voice from sounding sarcastic.

"I won't apologize for my role. If anyone breaks

the rules they are thrown out. That's the only rule except you can't bring in someone you know personally."

"You let us do that," Lisa pointed out.

He nodded slowly. "I had a good reason. I wanted to see what you were up to. I'm the only one who knows you're not Joy, but the others sense something's wrong. The cadence of your answers is different than Joy's."

"If the killer was in the room, he knew I wasn't Joy," Connie said.

"And he knows you're not Sandy," he said, turning to Lisa.

Lisa's head jerked up and she met his eyes with sudden fierce determination. "The killer isn't in that room. They arrested Ralph."

He nodded slowly. "And I for one was pleased to be wrong about the room."

Lisa rose to her feet, bristling with anger. To Connie she looked like a cornered cat with its back and fur drawn up. Tears pooled in her eyes. "He might have used the knife, but I hold you responsible. You and that stupid room. You made her think she needed those people instead of us. We were there. She should have come to us with her problems, not you."

As quickly as her anger had risen and erupted, it ebbed and tears spilled from her eyes. Her shoulders shook as she sobbed.

Connie fumbled in her purse for a tissue, but Lonetree was on his feet. He perched on the edge of his desk and after twisting to pull a tissue from a box by his computer, he held it out to Lisa. She took it with a murmured thanks. Leaning forward, he placed a large hand on her shaking shoulder.

"I'm sorry you feel that way. I tried to tell her to seek counsel from those closest to her. I even suggested that trip with the two of you after that

Christmas trip to California was such a disaster. My advice was to turn to her confidants."

Lisa had stopped sobbing and was wiping her cheeks. She looked up at him, questioning eyes still wet with tears. "That Christmas trip was a disaster?"

She sounded as stunned as Connie felt. Joy had never mentioned that; neither had Ralph.

"How did you know?" Connie asked.

His eyes flickered over to Connie momentarily, but his attention was firmly on Lisa. He drew a deep breath as thought making a decision. "She knew her husband was being unfaithful. I think she had thoughts of her own affair, but she hoped to repair the marriage on that trip. Instead the woman called or he called her and Joy discovered who she was. I think it was someone close to her, someone she knew."

Connie felt a tremor of anger. Mary Sue! One of her friends and co-workers according to the journal entry. Beside her, Lisa was calming down, or maybe it was the large hand that rested on her shoulder that was transmitting some sort of inner strength to her. Her tears were gone, and he handed her another tissue. Whatever was calming her, Connie wasn't going to let him take control of Lisa as he had Joy. She moved between them, wrapping an arm around Lisa, dislodging his grasp. "I'm sorry we bothered you."

He retreated, but stayed seated on the front of the desk as though ready to offer support if Lisa needed it. "I'm sorry too. I'm beginning to think the group is doomed."

"Why?" Connie asked.

"Your sister is not the first death," he said, folding his arms. "A woman named Kelly Penrose was killed several months ago."

"Little Bird was killed?" Lisa asked, voice shaky.

"You know the name?" Surprise filled his dark eyes.

"We emailed her," Connie explained. "Her brother told us to leave her alone."

"That doesn't surprise me. Joy and she were always arguing, exchanging threatening, nasty notes."

"Death threats?" Connie asked, thinking of the letters on the computer that they were taking to Case.

"Yes," he acknowledged. "Joy forwarded several to me."

"May we see them?" Lisa asked, leaning forward, all hint of her earlier shakiness gone.

He looked from one to the other, considering the request and then returned to his chair. His long fingers tapped on his computer keyboard with a surprisingly light touch. Without being invited, the sisters walked behind his desk as he called up a letter. Connie recognized it as one they had seen in Joy's computer, but without a signature. He opened another.

"They're the same letters," Connie acknowledged. "She also had letters the man sent her, telling her to leave him alone, that he was involved with someone else. Did she send you those?"

"No." He blinked at the screen, fingers tapping a rhythm on the desk. "She never mentioned that."

"You never knew who the guy was?" Lisa asked.

"No." He clicked off the screen as though the letters disturbed him. Lisa returned to her chair and Connie followed.

"Did you tell the police about those letters?" Lisa asked. He had obviously known about the affair when he spoke to Weldon.

"Kelly's dead. She was no threat to your sister."

"If you never knew any of the names, how did

you find out about Kelly Penrose?" Lisa demanded.

His eyelashes fluttered and he paused before speaking, as though weighing what to tell them. "When Joy and Kelly started their hate mail campaign, I took time to look them up. After Kelly died, I began investigating everyone in the room." He looked from one to the other. "I'm saying this in confidence. I don't want you telling the others."

"I looked them up too," Lisa announced, producing her list from her purse. She had totally regained her composure, and she held it out to him proudly.

They compared notes. The only person he had listed that they had not found was Mike. He had discovered him in Chicago.

"He was thinking of moving to the Northwest, so it's possible he tried to meet her or Kelly. Kelly was in Portland."

"How was she killed?" Lisa asked.

"Stabbed while she was jogging by the Columbia River."

Connie had been half listening to the conversation, but now she jerked her head up, horror racing through her. "Wait! I read about her when I was looking for cases similar to Joy's. I thought her case might be related. Maybe it is, and that proves Ralph is innocent. He wouldn't know Kelly Penrose."

"They arrested a transient in that case the other day. I checked because of Joy," he said. "I think you have to accept that her husband killed Joy."

Lisa nodded in agreement. "I've studied the others. Tom, NiteMan, even JustMelvin. I can't see them coming after Joy."

"Tom?" Lonetree questioned, his dark brow furrowing.

Lisa's cheeks glowed with a bright pink hue. "I mean, LastDance."

He said nothing, frowning at Lisa in a silent

accusation. For a minute she looked apologetic, shrugging a shoulder and when his fierce look persisted, she tilted her chin in surprising defiance.

"We're out of the group, Professor Lonetree. Why shouldn't we talk to anyone we want?"

He drew back as though she had slapped him. "Don't you realize this could put you in danger?" His big hand came down hard on his desk. "You need to stop immediately."

"I've talked to Tom several times away from the room. He's very nice and normal. I may meet him in person," she challenged.

For the first time since they'd met him, a stunned look came over Lonetree's face. He shook his head and opened his mouth to speak. Then he clamped it shut and turned away.

Connie was more shocked by her sister's latest outburst than her earlier tirade. She had known Lisa was furious with Lonetree, but her sister was surprising her.

"We better go," Connie said, because she sensed Lisa was prepared to argue further. "Goodbye, Professor. We won't bother you or your group again."

****

Stepping outside, they were greeted by a light snow. Connie held up her hand, catching the flakes. "Damn, just what we need," she said, eyeing the thick gray clouds. "I'm glad we're finished with Lonetree or Raven, or whatever his name is."

"He has a gentlemanly streak," Lisa said, as they reached the car and she climbed into the passenger side. "Maybe even a sense of romance. Did you notice the poetry books on the shelves behind his desk? I didn't pay attention last time, but he has works like Byron, Shelley, Browning, and even sonnets from Shakespeare. They look well-read."

"Sense of romance?" Connie hooted as she settled in and put the key into the ignition. "Don't tell me you think highly of him. You went after him like a badger."

Lisa giggled, putting her hand to her mouth. "I did, didn't I? I wonder if I should apologize. He is different, but there's something about him. I can't describe it. When he was holding my arm, it was, I don't know…soothing. Maybe it's because he's big. The protector."

"Sure. And the pipsqueak was laying into him like David versus Goliath. You really spoke up. I couldn't even do it like that."

"He doesn't scare me. It was like I knew he couldn't hurt me, or wouldn't. Maybe it was those poetry books. I can't believe he got so upset over my talking to Tom."

"You're upsetting his personal group." She looked over at Lisa with a teasing grin and poked her with a bent elbow. "So you've been talking to Tom regularly?"

Lisa turned away, though Connie could see her cheeks redden. "I…I may meet him."

"I talked to him too," Connie admitted.

"See? Isn't he fun?"

Connie could not understand the allure of meeting people from the Internet. "He seems okay, but if you're going to meet him, I'm going with you."

"Why?"

"It's like today. You insisted on coming with me. We're all we have now. We have to stick together."

Lisa laughed. "All right, I'll take you with me. I'm nervous about meeting him, but it's not because I'm afraid. And I only came to tell off Raven."

"I'm glad you did. Someone needed to. He'll think twice before he takes on the Romero sisters again."

Lisa's face sobered. "I kept thinking about Ralph and how unhappy Mom and Dad looked this morning. I guess it was all bottled up and I just let go on him. Can you believe Joy never told us about Ralph's affair or that man? But she told him?"

"I know. I keep thinking she meant to tell us that weekend. But now it looks like it was all his idea." Connie shook her head, and she looked across at her sister. "Let's never do that. Turn away from each other, or share our secrets with a stranger first."

Tears leaped into Lisa's eyes and she reached over and squeezed Connie's arm. "Never. Sometimes I think Joy turned away from us because she envied us our jobs and single lives. But sometimes I think I don't get involved because I've been afraid I'll end up like her—living only for her kids and husband, not herself."

"Maybe that's what she was searching for in the past year," Connie said sadly.

"Do you feel that way? Like you want to stay single because getting married means giving up your personal identity?"

Connie started to shake her head, but then stopped. What was it Sandy had told her? She was afraid a commitment would mean her own life was over? Her reply was lost as the car skidded, and both women cried out. She struggled with the wheel, seeking to bring the car back in line. The drive back to Bellingham would be an icy nightmare.

"We better call Mom and let her know we're going to be very late. I think they wanted to catch the last ferry home. Maybe they should go without us."

Lisa pulled out her cell phone and put through the call. Connie could tell immediately her mother was unhappy. Lisa put her hand over the phone. "I guess Dad is staying in Bellingham. This lawyer thing is turning into a mess so Mom's taking the kids home alone." She turned back to the phone. "Let me call right back."

"What does she want us to do?" Connie asked as Lisa closed the phone.

"She didn't say so, but I think she wants us back as soon as possible. The kids are asking questions. Poor little things, it's like they're orphans."

Connie looked out at the snow. "I hate the thought of having to make another trip back here later, but it'll take us at least an hour to get over to the police department and back here."

"I could catch a flight back," Lisa suggested. "That way I can help Mom. We could get the ferry tonight, and you can stay over and not have to drive back in the snow."

Practical Lisa had it all worked out. "I suppose."

"Weren't you going to call the inspector?" Lisa prompted.

Connie almost sent the car into another skid. She'd been having an internal debate on that issue most of the day. "I'm furious at him over Ralph."

"Be honest." Lisa said, with a roll of her eyes. "You want to see him. You just won't admit it."

"You're not afraid to leave me alone?" Connie teased.

"Ralph's in jail and Lonetree is not a threat. We're not that far from the airport. Drop me off and go see Sergeant Case. Then you can stay over and call your inspector."

Connie would have argued except her cell phone rang. The sound of Weldon's voice sent a rush of excitement through her.

"Connie? I understand you're coming to see Case. May I buy you dinner while you're here?"

"I won't be here long, Weldon," she said crisply, shooting a glance at Lisa who began gesturing wildly. "We saw Ralph this morning." Her voice was pointed, angry.

"I would like to see you. To explain."

Lisa was now yanking on her coat sleeve and

nodding vigorously.

"I've been thinking about staying over so I don't have to drive through the snow..."

"Good idea. Why don't you come for dinner? I'll cook this time. I'd appreciate the opportunity to talk with you. I don't like the idea of hard feelings."

His tone was apologetic, and she could picture his earnest, handsome face. Her stomach began its usual dance. Maybe she should let him explain.

"I have to take Lisa to the airport and see Sergeant Case. I could be there in two hours."

"Excellent. Do you remember how to get here?"

"Of course." She signed off and faced her sister who was giggling. "I can't believe I agreed to see him. I wonder if he means I can stay with him?"

Lisa's giggle became a howl. "You could end up getting snowbound."

****

Connie dropped Lisa at the airport and turned north, back toward the city. The snow fluttered down in large flakes, and it might have been beautiful if she hadn't had to maneuver her car through it. Rush hour had started early as the threat of snow moved in and cars clogged the slushy streets. By the time Connie reached the Vancouver Police Department, darkness had fallen. With no place to park on the street, she pulled into a nearby lot.

An icy wind slapped Connie as she stepped from the car and wrapped a scarf around her head and neck to ward off the snow. Wind gusts swirled snow around her, stinging her cheeks. Reaching inside, she pulled the computer from the back seat. With her head lowered against the cold, she trudged along the icy sidewalk. Without warning, someone shoved her from behind. Connie tried to keep her balance, but another push sent her toppling to the icy pavement. She never saw the man who grabbed her purse and yanked the computer bag from her shoulder. She wasn't going down without a fight. Connie gripped her purse tightly, but he yanked it from her.

"Help," she screamed as loud as she could. "Someone help me!"

He was gone instantly, running down the street with surprising agility, disappearing into the crowd of commuters waiting at a nearby bus stop.

Connie staggered to her feet, heart thudding more from exertion than fear. Luckily her keys were in her pocket. As she looked in the direction the man had run, she spied her purse on the ground, contents strewn about. He had either dropped it or taken her wallet and tossed it aside. She retrieved the bag and gathered makeup, coins and cell phone with shaky hands. Only then did she realize he had gotten away with the computer.

****

"You need to be more careful," Weldon said as he greeted Connie at his door and helped her take off her coat. She looked none the worse for the wear as she shook snow from her hair in the hallway and gave him her wide smile. In fact, she looked alive and healthy with her cheeks pink from the cold and bright, inquiring eyes.

"I'm fine," she said.

He wasn't. His nerves were on edge, had been since he'd heard about her attack downtown. It couldn't have anything to do with Perkins, could it? He was in jail. As for earlier concerns that she'd been spotted by the Blade, there was no way the Blade would let himself get that close to possible capture over something as insignificant as a laptop. Or perhaps he meant to grab her? Her wild shouts had brought immediate help and officers. Case and the other officers agreed it had been a random attack by someone seeking money or something easy to pawn. The area was known for its rough characters.

He looked her up and down. Connie wore a beige sweater and brown turtleneck over wool slacks with tears at the knees. Her hair shone in the hall light, and her face fairly glowed. Just her presence made him feel lighter, happier. Her smile sent a buzz through his system.

The visit was the welcome end of a long afternoon. He had spent the day tracking down connections between the Blade's murder victims. They might be prostitutes or missing teens, but he was beginning to see a pattern, a pattern that bothered him. He was supposed to be off, sent home by his captain because he'd been working round the clock since returning from Seattle.

He had spent the day away from the office, but not away from the case files. He would still be sitting in front of the map in his den, if Case hadn't called to tell him Connie was coming to bring him her sister's computer with threatening letters. According to Case, they might help build a circumstantial case, but they weren't hard evidence like the knife.

Mitch might have passed on calling her or trying to see her, but he did want to apologize. Besides, he required a break. His brain was growing stale, as his captain charged. He needed to wipe his brain blank and return with a fresh attitude. Connie could provide a welcome distraction, perhaps the only one that would totally take his mind off the Blade. He'd tried gardening and taking Bruno to the park. He'd found himself visiting dumping sites instead.

"I'm pleased you came," he said in a gentle tone. "So is Bruno."

The Irish Setter loped into the hall and jumped on her. Falling to one knee, Connie buried her face in the dog's soft coat. After a sloppy greeting, she finally pulled away.

"I'm glad to see him. It's been a hell of a day," she said with a sigh.

"If Perkins wasn't in jail, I'd be worried someone was still after you," he admitted. "Please sit down, and I'll get you a glass of wine."

While she settled in, he poured wine with a nervous hand. He could almost feel her eyes surveying the room. What was she thinking? He handed her a glass and sat across from her, uncertain what to say.

"I...um...can't stay too long," Connie said, as she sipped wine. "The snow's coming down pretty hard, and I haven't arranged a room yet."

He stared at his glass and the wine's soft burgundy color. He weighed her words and licked his lips slowly, feeling tongue-tied. Why could he question witnesses, cajole criminals and he couldn't speak to her? He tapped his toe on the floor as though loosening a spot of carpet. "You let me use your sofa. I have a guest room. Let me...return the favor."

A playful smile crossed her face. "Sounds like a deal, Chief. Let me help you fix dinner."

His insides went from jumpy to turbulent as cascading waves of excitement filled him. This would definitely help clear his mind.

****

They cooked together, Weldon concentrating on steaks while Connie chopped vegetables for a salad. Her senses had come alive the minute she arrived and the air crackled with electricity as they moved about the kitchen. She studied him surreptitiously, trying to decipher her feelings. Physically he excited her. Every time his hand brushed hers, her skin tingled. When they ran into each other and he steadied her, she grew weak, her very core melting like a candle.

He was so appealing in his argyle sweater vest

with the brown tie and gray slacks. His sandy hair was neatly combed and his lean face looked newly shaven. Here he was, fresh as the new snow, and she felt like a damaged piece of luggage with her torn slacks. She would have changed clothes, except the only other things in her bag were her dirty jeans from cleaning. She put those in to wash to wear the next day.

How did she feel emotionally about being with him? Connie suddenly didn't want to talk about murder or their differences concerning Ralph. She steered the conversation in a different direction as they sat down to eat. Over steaks and salad, she described her childhood in Bellingham, while he told her the trials of being a police officer's son.

What was he thinking? He never let on, though he was a perfectly pleasant host. This was good for her too. He made her feel safe, and she needed that right now. While he took out the garbage after the clean up, she went to light a fire.

Troubling thoughts struck her as she sat alone waiting for him. Why would someone attack her? For the computer? Why? She and Lisa had been through everything and the most damaging information had been the journal and letters. Besides, Lonetree had copies.

In fact, the only people who knew about the letters on the computer were Weldon, Case and Lonetree. Had he lied about having an affair with Joy? Why take the computer? The answer was simple. Universities were conservative about their professors. He wouldn't want a scandal that named him as the "other" man responsible for getting Joy killed. Perhaps there was other evidence she and Lisa had not discovered. Connie shook her head. She needed to stop thinking that way. She had been attacked by a thief looking for quick money.

Mitch entered and handed her a glass of port.

She fought to keep him from seeing her accelerated breathing. His hand touched her arm, sending shock waves through her system.

"About Perkins, I can't apologize for not calling you. You know it wouldn't have been right."

Connie made a face. "I don't like it, but I understand. Good old ethical Weldon."

"Why do you make duty sound so unpleasant?"

A quick spurt of guilt ran through her. "I don't know." She concentrated on the tawny wine she held. "I respect what you stand for, and I..."

His hand rested on her shoulder and moved up to her hair, stroking it, pulling it through his fingers.

Her breath quickened. "Did you bring me here to seduce me?"

Weldon pulled back sharply, dropping his hand, confusion etched on his face. Connie regretted her words. She stretched across him to put down her glass, aware of his sharp intake of breath as her breasts brushed his arm, but both were aware of her sudden shudder. She touched his shoulder gingerly.

"I'm sorry. I didn't mean to tease."

His face turned a pleasant pink, and she traced a finger across a chiseled cheek. He inhaled and turned his face toward her hand. He covered it gently with his fingers and pressed it to his lips and kissed it.

"I haven't thought of much besides you since I left your apartment." He leaned forward and put down his wine.

"Me either," she said in a hoarse voice. He lifted her hand and placed it on his shoulder. He moved forward and his lips touched hers gently, testing them, tasting them. She stroked his shoulders as he pulled her toward him, wrapping his arms around her.

His tongue flicked into her mouth, exploring, enticing as the kiss deepened. He broke it long enough to drop soft kisses on her cheeks and her sensitive throat. Then he claimed her mouth again in a searing kiss that sent hot lava racing through her blood. Her insides ached with growing need. Connie moaned deep in her throat and her fingers pushed inside his shirt to touch his chest.

He broke the passionate kiss, and she reached for him, but he put a large hand on her jaw and held her face from him, looking down into her eyes. They were both breathing heavily, and she could see the brilliant light of desire in his eyes. He wanted her, and the searing heat growing inside her lower body said the same.

He grasped her hands. "I don't want to rush you. I know you're vulnerable."

She was touched by his sweetness, and pulled her hand from his to stroke his cheek. "You're not rushing anything. This would have happened even if we had met some other way."

A fiery glow burned in his eyes. He leaned forward and kissed her again, and she knew this time he would not pull back. They fell back on the sofa and she could feel his hardness as he moved against her. There would be stopping this time.

His hand slid along her abdomen and slipped under her sweater, lighting fires on her bare skin. Gentle fingertips drew magic circles on her stomach, and she ached for them to find her breasts. Her chest heaved and her fingers unbuttoned his shirt.

One hand slid up to cup her breast and then inside her bra to tease an already hardening nipple. His other hand reached around her back to undo her bra. She moaned with uncontrollable desire. Had she ever wanted anyone this badly? Her blood boiled with need and her insides felt vacant, needing fulfillment. It was an eternity before hands found her bare breasts, stroking them, turning the nipples into hard pebbles.

He slid her sweater up over her head and sat back to admire her naked upper body.

"You're beautiful," he whispered and she felt like the most desirable woman in the world.

Connie brushed his cheek with her fingertips, pulling his head down and he took one breast into his mouth, lips and tongue circling the quivering nipple.

She shuddered with want, whispering into his ear. "I want you, Mitch. Make love to me."

He pulled away and for a second she feared he might stop. His eyes were drugged with desire and fiery need as he lifted his head. "Yes, honey," he said, voice husky. "Let's go to bed."

Chapter Nineteen

Weldon leaned forward to open the bedroom door, his chest brushing her shoulder and sending a jolt through her that propelled her inside. Her skin tingled, hell, her whole body tingled, feeling alive and waiting. Behind her, he closed the door and clicked a light switch. A golden glow flooded the room from a lamp near a king-sized bed. Like the rest of the house, the room was neat, Spartan.

She turned to him. His gentle fingers touched her bare shoulder as he pushed her sweater fully off. He stared at her breasts, his breath quick and ragged. Sexual need snapped like live electric wires around them.

He leaned toward her, his full lips hanging open with hunger and he kissed the top of her head, her cheek, and finally claimed her lips with his. Their lips ground together, his tongue sliding into her mouth, tasting her, exploring its soft inner depths.

She moaned, kissing him back with as much vigor. She met his tongue with her own, thrusting it into his mouth as his withdrew. Her lower body flamed with want, warm and aching, and she shuddered in his arms as they fell onto the bed.

His body covered hers and white-hot lava raced through her lower regions. Her leg rose around his back urging him forward, and his erection pressed at their clothes, teasing her with desire and need.

They were breathless as he broke the kiss, and Connie pushed off his shirt. Had she ever wanted someone this much? She looked up at him, fingers playing along his bare chest.

Her insides swelled as she realized it was more than want. She was falling in love with him. Despite their differences, this was the man she wanted.

Weldon's warm gaze roamed over her breasts, fingers dancing along her skin. "I can't get over how lovely you are."

She had heard the words before, but she liked hearing it in that husky voice from this man who was growing to mean so much to her. She raked her nails lightly over his chest, fingers circling his nipples. His hand stroked her abdomen and undid the button and zipper of her pants. She did the same to his and in seconds their clothes were gone. The sight of his long, lean body was intoxicating, and her lower body grew even more heated, like boiling lava flooding her veins. He was magnificent—all long hard lines, the muscles well defined in his thighs and arms.

Her control disintegrated into primal want. Their breath erupted in quick, ragged gasps. She leaned toward him and rubbed her cheek against his chest, then flicked her tongue out to lick it until she edged her way to one nipple. He groaned, put one arm around her waist and lifted her on top of him. She lowered her body to his, opening herself and welcoming him into her warmth.

Their joining was exquisite, unlike anything she'd ever experienced. He filled her as though she had been empty until now, a mere shell. They moved together quickly, almost as though out of frustration, and then slowed until she could feel his body rising inside her. Her body responded, quickening their movements, the thrill escalating until she was crying out and their bodies shuddered fiercely in satisfaction.

Connie collapsed against him trembling, wrapping her arms around his neck and kissing his ear. She wanted to whisper she loved him, but held back. It was enough to be with him. Enough to know that she had found love.

****

Weldon woke early the next morning, but he didn't beat Connie. The pillow next to his was empty, though her scent lingered in the hollow. He inhaled sharply, drinking in the sweet smell.

How long had it been since he enjoyed a woman like that? Since he woke feeling like a man with every inch of him vibrant? He could still feel her hands on him, the touch of her soft body under his.

He stretched and sat up, looking around for any trace of her. Their clothes lay in a crumbled pile by the bed. She'd teased him that she doubted he ever left clothes on the floor. At one point he almost got up to fold and place them on the chair. She'd smiled as though knowing what he was thinking. He resolved the issue by taking her in his arms.

Weldon rose, looked for his robe and found it missing. He smiled, hoping that she was wearing it. Doing something he normally would not consider, he picked up his pants and put them on. He wandered into the bathroom, but found no sign of her, though his robe was tossed carelessly over the counter by the sink. He hung it on a hook behind the door.

When he opened the drapes to let in the early morning sun, only gray dawn showed. It was bright enough to see the blanket of snow on the ground. He grimaced and flexed his upper body. The driveway would require shoveling. Where was Connie? As if in answer, the scent of coffee drifted into the room.

"Connie?" he called as he walked down the hall.

When he received no answer, he went looking for her, searching room after room. He discovered her outside in the snow, frolicking with Bruno. She tossed a ball to the dog and hugged him in reward when he brought it to her. She was so alive, unfettered and free. He examined what he could see of her curvy body, the parts not hidden by one of his down jackets. His thoughts went inside the jacket, mentally peeling it away to consider what was below, the gentle curves and soft skin that brought him such pleasure.

After putting on a sweater, he opened the door and walked onto the snow covered deck. A bitter wind bit his face and ears, and he shoved his frigid hands into his pockets. As though sensing his presence, she looked up and waved. Her face broke into a wide smile.

"Do you want breakfast?" he called.

She leaned down and wrapped her arms around Bruno and rubbed his coat. "What do you say, fella? Are we hungry?"

Bruno's response was a bark.

"Sure," she called back. "Make it for three."

Connie ran toward him, clumsily, because she was wearing his snow boots, hair erupting in all directions from under a knit cap. To him, no woman had ever looked more lovely. Her cheeks were flushed and her hazel eyes glowed. He dared to hope that he was responsible for that gleam.

Bruno thumped up the steps, and she came behind him, waving a pair of ski gloves. She stopped at the top of the steps, and he wondered if she meant to kiss him. Instead she dropped her eyes almost shyly. He put a hand on her shoulder, feeling slightly embarrassed himself. She took his simple touch as an invitation and leaned toward him. Awkwardly he kissed the side of her face.

Connie laughed as she wrapped her arms around him and nuzzled his neck. That developed into a warm morning kiss that sent new tingles of want running through his body. Damn, would he ever get enough of her?

"I'll fix breakfast," he offered. "And then I'll clear the walk."

"I can fix breakfast," she corrected, "while you get dressed. Bruno and I already shoveled the drive and walk."

Weldon stared at her in wonder. Pride and desire swelled inside him. Was there anything this woman couldn't do? He wasn't going to argue about fixing breakfast. The idea of her in his kitchen, fixing his breakfast was appealing. He wanted to ask her if she could stay the day, but he didn't want to rush their growing relationship.

When he emerged from the shower, scrambled eggs, bacon, and toast waited for him on the kitchen table. She managed to brighten up the table by using daisies from the greenhouse. They sat in a cup in the center.

The morning should have been happy and bright as the table setting, but it dampened his spirits and he wasn't certain why. The domestic scene should be pleasing, but it was like a wake-up call. What next? What did she expect from him? What did he want from her?

A dim shadow rose between them, as hard and palpable as a brick wall. Uncertainty turned him awkward. He wasn't prepared to discuss the future or their relationship, and he didn't think she was either. Breakfast became quiet and tense.

"You're going back today?" He touched his napkin to his lips, his tone neutral, though he wanted her to stay.

"Yes," she said with a grimace that he found strangely endearing.

He liked the way she twisted her lips up and wrinkled her nose until one eye was barely visible. She might have been making monster faces at a child. "I promised Mom and Lisa I'd...uh, help them with the kids. We're all they have now."

He dropped his gaze. Unspoken was the accusation that he was one of the people responsible for taking their father from them.

"They've gone out to the San Juans and Mom's going to keep them for a while. I'm going to take some time off, until we can figure out what we're going to do."

He nodded, unable to look up at her. "Work is going to be busy for me too in the next couple of weeks. This Slasher case..." He stopped, realizing he was using that word he hated.

"I understand," she said softly, taking a quick drink of water as though she was on the verge of choking. "And then there's Ralph. Dad's helping him get an attorney."

There it was. The reason for the wall between them.

"Mom and Dad think he's innocent," she continued, face suddenly glum.

"Do you?"

She chewed slowly on a piece of bacon and finally shook her head. "I don't know anymore. He was having an affair and she was looking for men online. Raven won't admit it, but I wonder if that was why he was meeting her too."

"Raven?" The name was familiar, though he couldn't remember why.

"Will Lonetree. I don't trust him, but you say he had an alibi, and he says he was in class the day Sandy died."

Her troubled eyes met his. Such pretty bright eyes, he thought. If only they were happier. The night before they danced with excitement as she lay below him. A quick spark of desire ignited in his blood, and he wondered if his face was turning red as he thought about their moments in bed. He lowered his hungry gaze and murmured to her. "He's okay, just a little different."

"Hmph!" was her reply.

Weldon didn't say anything else. This wasn't

what he wanted to discuss with her this morning. He wished he could stop her. Get up and tell her to let it go. She wouldn't, of course. Connie was as hardheaded as she was beautiful

"He's almost like a cult leader," she concluded. "He has all those people in that room under his thumb."

"He can do what he wants as long as he doesn't harm anyone."

"But it is harming people," she argued. "Look at Joy."

"He couldn't have known that her husband was going to snap," he said coolly.

"Snap?" She shook her head vigorously, and her dark hair danced around her shoulders like a silken curtain. "I don't think Ralph snapped."

This was dangerous territory. Even with the discovery of the knife, she was not convinced of Ralph's guilt. He didn't want to argue and drive a rift between them. The night before had been so special. Why couldn't the morning be the same? He made a point of glancing at his watch.

"I should get showered and changed so I can hit the road. I want to check in with Dad and Ralph and catch an early ferry."

Weldon did not try to stop her, though part of him wanted to. He picked up his plate and stacked hers on top. "I'll clean up while you get dressed," he mumbled.

He tidied up the kitchen, listening to her shower and move around the bedroom. It felt so right to have her in his house. Why couldn't he ask her to stay? But what would follow that? How did he really feel about her? In bed she was tremendous, but a woman like Connie deserved more, even if she didn't demand it. What did he have to offer? Love? The word was so foreign he hadn't considered it in years.

Connie was silent when she came out of the

shower. She wore a sweater that showed off the gentle curves of her breasts, a turtleneck, and jeans. Her dark hair hung loose and shiny around her shoulders. She wore only enough makeup to enhance her pink cheeks and hazel eyes. For once she seemed uncertain, unlike the woman who normally tried to embarrass him. He wanted to touch her, but held back.

"I'll call you later," he volunteered as they walked down the stairs toward the cleared driveway.

"Sure," she said, clicking her car alarm and popping the trunk. He set her small bag inside and faced her. There were so many things he wanted to say, but he had no idea where to start.

She reached up and touched his cheek. "You take care of yourself, eh? Don't let those killers get you?"

The comment stunned him, though he knew she was joking. "You're the one who needs to take care," he responded, feeling his cheeks grow hot.

"I can take care of myself, Inspector Weldon," she said with a laugh that made his heart skip. "Sometimes I think I can do a better job of it, especially around the house."

He didn't disagree. She did amaze him with her practical skills, and she hadn't mentioned the stellar job she'd done shoveling snow. He considered it a real chore, but she had done it while he slept.

"Well, you're right," he said, feeling a touch peevish. He wasn't used to having women do things, much less remind him of his inadequacies. "You can take care of yourself. Sometimes I wonder if you really need a man around."

He regretted the comment immediately, though her brows raised and lowered and she gave him a big wink. Her sudden smile sent a buzz through his lower regions.

"I think you know I do." She leaned forward and

kissed his mouth quickly.

His breath quickened and his heart kicked into overdrive. He wanted to pull her toward him and kiss her soundly, but as a car drove down the street he realized they were in the open and anyone could see. The neighbors were probably already having a field day over the fact that a strange car had stayed through the night.

He pulled back from her. "So long, Connie."

She giggled as though she knew what was on his mind. "Thanks for letting me stay."

He nodded and walked her to the driver side door, opening it for her. She gave him a final wave and slid inside.

Watching as her car drove down the street, Weldon considered calling her on her cell to see when he might see her next, but stopped. It might be better to let things stew for the moment.

****

A slight brisk breeze tugged at Connie's hair and chilled her cheeks as she darted between sunlight and shadows on her bicycle on her way to the Seattle waterfront to meet Lisa. The distant waters of Puget Sound were choppy today, licked by the breeze into small whitecaps. Winter sun provided a glare that was almost painful without sunglasses.

Connie signaled and turned right. She was traveling swiftly but with no sense of purpose, letting her fancy carry her forward. She felt that way about her life right now too. For years, she consumed herself with building her career. She knew what she wanted and she headed there. Now she was no longer certain about anything.

First there had been that horrendous memorial service for Sandy the previous day. She and Lisa clung together, and neither had been able to attend the post-service gathering. Connie had taken off from work for the rest of the week and would return to her parents' house for the weekend, but she wasn't certain about the following week. Sandy's presence would loom like a specter when she returned to the office. Perhaps she should request going back on the road as a field producer.

But that would mean leaving Mitch. The thought of falling in love with him was at once exciting and yet frightening. Did she want to stay, where he was nearby, or pursue her career in some other location? In the past, selecting the job as her number one priority was so simple. The emotional sensations running through her were new and raw, something she'd never experienced. She wasn't certain she liked them either. Hadn't Joy once loved Ralph? Look how they turned out because Joy let her feelings for him take control over her life.

To make matters worse, Connie hadn't heard from Mitch in four days. Maybe she shouldn't have given him that final kiss in public. He seemed eager to get rid of her after that. The longer they went without talking, the more uncertain she became. Connie worried she might have offended him, but normally that wouldn't matter. Now it did, and even that disturbed her. Calling him was out of the question. She didn't want to seem too eager, but what if he never called? This was like some big romantic drama, but she'd never played one to this extent. His reaction mattered, and she didn't want to take the chance of discovering he didn't want her. She'd never felt so damn vulnerable in her life and she didn't like it.

How was he feeling these days? She knew he was special, but did he feel the same? Wasn't this where they were supposed to have a talk? Didn't she hate romances where the characters stayed apart because they didn't speak? Yes, but now this romance involved her feelings, her insecurities, and that was different.

Besides, could they have a life together? Mr. Rigid and Ms. Play-it-by-Ear?

She sighed. In bed the combination was unbeatable. Her body still tingled when she thought about it. He surprised her with his skill as a lover, discarding that uptight attitude along with his clothes. He reached her in ways she'd never been touched. Magic. Sheer physical magic.

Connie shivered though she was sweating from exertion. Ever since she returned from Vancouver she had been loaded with energy. She looked down at her body. It felt new and alive. Womanly and fulfilled. She felt complete. In many ways she felt empty without him, but in other ways she felt afraid. He'd made clear his feelings about marriage and a family. She'd never wanted one either. Could Weldon be the man who could change her mind?

Sadness washed over her, dampening her spirits and euphoria. Not likely. She had her work and he was back to chasing serial killers. Connie turned her bicycle onto the pier and stopped to chain it to a bike rack. As she straightened up, Lisa approached.

"Right on time for once," Lisa said.

"I can't believe I let you talk me into this," Connie groused.

"Connie, you insisted on coming with me to meet Tom."

She didn't apologize for wanting to meet the man who had captured her sister's attention, but it was safety that made her insist on coming. After what happened to Sandy and that weird Raven, Connie had become cautious. Perhaps this didn't constitute high risk behavior, since Lisa had been talking to Tom online every day. Connie's only conversation had been in the hotel room, but unlike the others in The Lair, he seemed very normal.

"Maybe one of the Romero sisters will be lucky

in love finally," Connie teased. It didn't look like she was going to be the one.

"Still haven't heard from the inspector?" Lisa asked.

Connie had told her she stayed with him in Vancouver, but she'd been reluctant to discuss what happened. She didn't want her sister's sympathy. Was that how Joy had felt? Unable to admit failure to her family?

"I think he's busy with that Slasher case," Connie said. "They found another body two days ago."

"I am so glad that Joy wasn't one of his victims. I hated thinking about her being killed by a butcher."

"Um-hum," Connie agreed. Neither mentioned the thought that a man they'd both trusted stood accused of killing her. Their father had gotten Ralph a lawyer before returning home, but no one was certain what would happen now. Ralph still protested his innocence.

She linked her arm through Lisa's. "Tell me about Tom. Do you know what he looks like?"

"He never sent a picture, but I sent him mine. He thinks I'm perky-looking."

They laughed. Lisa had been told that before because of her blunt hair cut and petite figure. Connie knew she detested the title and teased her with it whenever she got the opportunity.

Lisa had gone in a different direction today. She wore a cashmere sweater below her wool coat with a plaid burgundy skirt over boots. Her only accessories were a string of pearls and tiny earrings.

"Stop that," Connie said, jostling Lisa as she bit her lower lip. "You'll ruin your lipstick."

Lisa jerked Connie's arm as her eyes scanned the weekday crowd milling on the dock. "See that guy over there? Blue sweater, chinos, brown hair. I think that's Tom."

Connie followed her pointing finger. He leaned against the wooden rail looking out to sea. From the side he was nice looking enough if a little ordinary. His brown hair was thinning at the temples, but he had almost boyish facial features. Slim and not too tall, he was the picture of a computer geek. The perfect match for Lisa.

Lisa quivered with anticipation. "What should I do?" she asked in a squeaky voice, leaning close to Connie.

"Go say hello," Connie suggested, pushing her away.

The man turned toward them and his gaze fell on Lisa and then her. He looked somewhat surprised, eyes blinking rapidly, but he walked toward them.

"Lisa?" he said tentatively.

"Yes," she gushed and pushed Connie forward. "This is my sister, Connie."

Thin lips curled up into a very white-toothed smile. "Brought her along for protection, did you?" His voice was a little high, but not unpleasant. A sprinkling of freckles across his cheeks and nose gave him the appearance of a contemporary Huck Finn.

Lisa's cheeks turned a healthy pink at his comment and she released Connie's arm. "No," she said, attempting to laugh.

Connie could sense her sister's discomfort and jumped to her rescue before he labeled her a frightened nut case. "I made her bring me," she said.

"That's fine. I like meeting new people." He reached out and took Connie's hand shaking it with a firm grip. His boyish expression faltered. "I'm sorry about your sister and friend."

Connie stifled a gasp. Once again her younger sister had surprised her. She hadn't realized Lisa told him about Sandy and Joy.

"I was hoping Tom might help us," Lisa explained, as though she picked up on Connie's accusing vibes.

Connie summoned her brightest false smile and nodded.

Tom gestured toward the wooden pier. "Shall we walk? I like to come here and look at the water. It's so peaceful it can make you forget all the troubles of the world."

The thought was inviting, but she knew they could not fully enjoy nature while forgetting what was behind them—or what drew them together.

"You know I'm Sexy Lady?" Connie asked as they walked, the two women on either side of Tom.

"Lisa told me, but I had guessed there was something different about you."

How long had he known? He'd never let on—not like Raven. "Everyone is still going to that room?"

"A new room," he said. "I understand you think Raven is partly responsible for what happened to your sister even though her husband was arrested?"

"Ralph may be in jail, but he's not totally responsible," Connie said. "Raven had her addicted to that group instead of coming to her family with her problems."

"We considered ourselves family too," Tom said. "I feel I can tell those people anything. We're like a regular family, we talk, argue."

"But you don't know each other's names," Connie pointed out.

"Which is the beauty of the group. There are no prior judgments, no basing our feelings on class or education. We are simply the words we speak in that room."

His comments were similar to Raven's, but he was more convincing than the frightening dark man with his talk of aura and mystical spirits.

"Do you think you help each other?" she prodded.

Tom's nod was quick. He seemed sincere about what he was expressing, deep blue eyes filled with certainty. "I know what you're thinking. It's a room full of strangers. But we aren't strangers. We talk every day. I remember when your sister confided in us about her husband's affair. She said she couldn't talk to anyone. Her mother wouldn't understand and her sisters were busy. I felt bad for her. We all did. She was frantic at first. The other women told their stories, and the men chatted her up. I'd like to think we had done her some good."

Connie considered his comments and felt guilty for her earlier thoughts that the group had pulled Joy away from her and Lisa. They had pushed their sister away. Joy had called several times, but she'd put Joy off, promising to call back. She never had, and she didn't think Lisa had either. She glanced at Lisa, who walked with her head down, deep in thought.

"Your group tried to help her," Lisa said.

"Yes."

"Raven gave her personal attention." Connie couldn't keep the coolness out of her voice.

"We all did. I talked to her outside the room. We do that when someone needs help."

Connie was beginning to understand why Joy turned to the group. Her online friends were readily available every day, unlike her sisters. Perhaps Raven deserved an apology.

Lisa turned to Tom and gave him a halfhearted smile. "Thanks for being there for her. I'm glad she had friends."

"Except someone took it too far," Connie reminded them. "Someone began an affair with her. Do you know who Mike7445 is?"

He jerked back, looking surprised. "Mike? No.

He's been gone a while. I know he wanted to travel, so maybe that's what happened to him."

Connie considered that. Maybe he had traveled. Perhaps Joy sent him money so he could visit her.

"No one has heard from him recently?" she asked.

"He just disappeared one day."

"Like Little Bird," Connie said. "Except Little Bird had not disappeared. She was killed."

He blinked, looking surprised again, his face turning pink. "Well, yes."

"I'm sorry," Lisa said suddenly. "Connie's really gotten into this investigating thing."

"Yeah, so I noticed," he said, attempting a smile.

"Isn't it eerie to have three people in one group murdered like that?" Connie continued. "Little Bird, Joy, Sandy? Heck, for all we know, Mike is dead too."

"Your sister and Sandy have a connection. The other was sheer coincidence. But it's like we have a doomed family." He frowned, shifting uncomfortably. He glanced at Lisa with an almost silent look of appeal and Connie felt a twinge of guilt. This guy seemed so normal and here she was peppering him with all these strange questions.

"Let's stop talking about murders," Lisa urged.

Connie felt guilty for dwelling on the morbid topic. Lisa had wanted to meet Tom for social reasons, not to continue the discussion about Joy and Sandy.

"I'm sorry," Connie said, smiling at Tom. "Tell me about yourself, Tom. How long have you been in Seattle?"

"Just a few months," he said.

"Tom is a writer," Lisa said from the other side. As she gazed up at him, Connie could see a sparkle in Lisa's eyes. She liked this guy.

"Tell us what you're working on," Connie asked.

Tom nodded, and began to talk, directing most

of his comments to Lisa. Connie tuned out of the flirtatious conversation, although she enjoyed watching the interaction. She could imagine her sister being interested in Tom. He was bland, but pleasant. When they parted, he took Lisa's hand and shook it.

"May I call you?" he asked.

"Of course." Unspoken were the words that next time, Connie wouldn't need to be along.

As soon as he was out of earshot, and they began walking toward the bike rack, Connie turned to Lisa. "Well?"

"He's okay, I guess." Her face turned a healthy shade of pink as she smiled.

Connie started to laugh, but something else hit her. "Why did you tell him about Joy?"

Lisa's smile disintegrated. "We were talking so much, and I wanted someone I can trust. He's easy to talk to."

"Must be nice," Connie muttered, thinking of Mitch and their awkward parting.

"He misses Joy too. She was nice to him."

Of course, sweet, understanding Joy. And Connie had been as cool as DreamBaby.

Connie squeezed Lisa's arm as they reached the end of the pier. "I hope things turn out. I'll call you later."

Lisa headed for the parking lot across the street and Connie hopped on her bicycle and headed off along the waterfront. As she turned a corner, she looked up in time to see an overhead mirror. Coming up behind her was a burgundy van, moving at a fast clip.

She skidded to a stop and made a sharp right turn. As she pulled into a narrow doorway, the van leaped the sidewalk, also to the right.

If she had not seen the mirror and turned, the van would have hit her.

She pushed her bike into the door and glanced out, checking for a license plate.

The van pulled away, brakes squealing.

The rim where the license plate should have been was blank.

Chapter Twenty

The late afternoon sun stroked the inside of the apartment as Connie walked in the door and left her bike against the wall. She locked the door with shaking fingers and threw the bolt. She had taken the long way home but had not seen the van again. She had almost feared coming around the final turn and seeing it waiting on the corner, daring her to cross the street.

She wanted to think she was paranoid, but no one drove that badly. Should she call Ryan? Why would anyone want to hit her? Who was stalking her, and that seemed to be the case. Had that assault in Vancouver been a coincidence? Ralph was in jail. But that was presuming he'd been the person threatening her. She'd never been convinced of it.

So who was it?

Someone from the drug series? The man at the clearing? Did it go all the way back to that first attack in the hotel room? No one person could have so many close calls. Someone was clearly after her. She paced the loft, trying to decide what to do next. What could she tell police? And where? Here or in Vancouver? As she passed her answering machine, she saw a blinking red light that indicated she had messages.

She pressed the play button, hoping to hear Weldon's voice. She frowned at the deep voice of Will Lonetree. "Miss Romero? Could you please call me? I would like to talk with you about something unusual."

Unusual? Having no desire to talk to him,

Connie jotted down his number. The message button still flashed and she pushed it again.

"Connie, it's Dad." His voice sounded stressed and her heart skipped. "I just got a call from Ralph's lawyer. He says...well, Ralph told him he'd been seeing some woman. She was with him when Joy...was...well...in Vancouver. Do you know anything about this? Call me."

Connie stared at the phone. She and Lisa had never admitted to their parents what they'd learned about Ralph's affair. Had he been with Mary Sue Baker when Joy died? Was it possible that he'd been protecting her all along? Was that why he'd been acting so guilty with police?

A sudden knock at the door drew her up sharply. Connie jumped. She wasn't expecting anyone. The people at work were giving her space, and she had just left Lisa. She grabbed her aluminum tennis racket from beside her bike and walked to the door, holding it up as a weapon, ready to swat any intruder.

"Who is it?" she called.

"Inspector Weldon."

Connie didn't know if she wanted to kick Weldon or kiss him. She yanked open the door. "What are you doing here?" she blurted, heart quickening into a joyful tap dance.

His boyish grin turned the tap dance became a jackhammering. "I just happened to be in town. May I come in?"

"Of course." Trying not to sound too eager, she stepped back, lowering her tennis racket. Her hands shook and her knees grew rubbery. This was better than a phone call, but she felt like a mess, still in her sweatshirt and biking pants.

"What is this?" he asked, pointing at the racket.

"Protection," she admitted, with a sheepish laugh, waving it wildly. He caught it and she let him take hold of it. "I wasn't expecting anyone."

"You must swing a mean racket." He put the racket down.

Connie shoved her hair behind her ear, feeling warm all over. "You could have called," she said accusingly, though she wanted to grab him and hug him as hard as possible. He was very handsome in a pullover sweater, jeans, and a leather bomber jacket. She had never seen him dressed so informally.

"I wanted to surprise you," he said, shoving his hands into his pockets. "I've been in town on a stakeout."

"The Slasher?" she asked. "I heard he struck again."

"I can't discuss it." His green eyes grew clouded, as his smile lessened.

Connie regretted bringing it up. This was not a time to point out their differences. "I wondered how long before you realized you missed me," she said lightly. An electric tension sizzled between them. The hell with worrying about being in love or the future or even protocol and letting him make the first move. She stepped toward him, grasping his hand.

His smile returned, a handsome grin that jolted her pulse rate back into an accelerated rate. Touching him sent tingles rushing along her skin, especially when he squeezed her fingers in a possessive gesture.

"That's the only reason I haven't called, though. I haven't been able to."

Pleased by the explanation, Connie leaned forward. "Show me how much you missed me," she said in an attempt at a sexy growl.

He inhaled sharply and for a minute she feared he might push her away, but then she saw the sensuous flame that glittered in his emerald eyes. He drew her toward him and leaned over to kiss her.

His lips were warm, searching and the touch set her blood boiling. Her hands slid under his sweater to tease his warm bare skin.

He pulled back, chuckling. "You must have missed me."

A wave of embarrassment washed over her, and her cheeks grew warm. Was she blushing? "Am I being too forward?" she asked.

He stroked her cheek with a gentle finger that drew a quick intake of breath from her. He touched her hair, green eyes studying strands as though he'd never seen them before. "Not at all. I'm beginning to like women who go after what they want." He leaned forward and nibbled at her neck and she shuddered in his arms.

"Well, then, let me show you what I want." Her hand slid below his belt. If she feared her forward motions were too much for him, she discovered the hard truth. He wanted her. She pushed herself to him as her body came to life.

His hands slipped under her sweatshirt, caressing her bare skin, lighting little fires with each touch. His lips nibbled at her neck and she moaned in delight as his hands tugged away her sports bra and reached around to fill his palms with her breasts.

She unzipped his pants and slid her hand inside, stroking him, inflaming her own insides with her touches on him. And then they were yanking at their clothes in a frenzy of motions, pulling and peeling until the confining garments were gone.

They fell onto the sofa, and she welcoming him into her, lifting her legs around his hips to urge in farther inside, moving against him, harder and harder until they were both crying out with desire and finally, fulfillment.

****

Connie had never been to the Space Needle for

dinner, but this seemed the right occasion. It was a Seattle landmark, the symbol of the city's skyline together with Mt. Rainier. The restaurant at the top gave diners a panoramic view of the magnificent mountains and Puget Sound during the day and glittering downtown Seattle at night.

Weldon was very handsome as he sat across from her in a leather banquette. He wore a gray cashmere sweater, black leather jacket, and black slacks.

She had pulled from her closet a burgundy velour dress in a simple princess cut with a short, swingy skirt. Purchased for her office Christmas party, it fit her perfectly, displaying just enough cleavage to be inviting and showing off the lines of her breasts in enticing fashion. She wore it with a pearl choker and shimmering hose. She had taken special care to curl and pin up her hair leaving tendrils trailing around her neck. The shining of his eyes demonstrated his approval.

They couldn't have picked a better place for dinner. Outside, the downtown skyline glittered like jewels, a view that constantly changed as the restaurant revolved. Inside candles glowed on the tables and violin music played in the background. Was this magic spell how it felt to be in love? She felt like they were not just on top of the Space Needle, but the world itself.

The light from the candles glimmered in his eyes, and she recalled the fiery look of desire as he surveyed her naked body hours earlier when they moved from their frantic lovemaking on the sofa to a more sensuous session on her bed. They might still be there if she hadn't said she'd never dined at the Space Needle and he insisted on making a reservation.

"What are you thinking?" he asked.

"This is like a dream," she said, glancing

around.

"You look like you're on top of the world."

"I feel that way," she admitted with a giggle. "A perfect place for a perfect evening."

He held up his wine glass in a toast. "And perfect company."

"Yes, perfect," she agreed with a beaming smile. Perhaps this giddy sensation was how it felt to be in love. Wait until she called Lisa! Connie continued to study Mitch as they ordered and ate. He moved with such fluid motions, lean body tempting her to touch him. His long fingers twisted around the stem of the wine glass, and she thought about them skimming along her skin. When he smiled, she thought of his full lips on her breasts. She was so focused on his body, she realized she wasn't listening to him. All evening she had been thinking about the way Mitch made her feel physically instead of paying attention. She realized he'd just asked about her relationship with Joy.

"It wasn't that we didn't get along. We loved each other. She and I were opposite. She lived in a world of her family. I guess I didn't have much patience with her troubles. I should have been there for her. I guess that's what hurts so much."

"Don't think about it. Think about the present, the future."

The future. She took a sip of wine, wondering if he meant that the way it sounded. Could it be possible? The two of them? Making a life together? Until this instant the thought that they could make things work had not seemed possible, but now she knew where she stood. She wanted him, and not just for tonight or for the next time they could have sex together. She was in love with him. Yet Connie had never felt so helpless.

"I have a question," he said after a couple of seconds. He toyed with his wine glass as though he was trying to decide something.

"Yes?" she asked, excited and yet fearful all at once.

"We've never talked about if you were seeing anyone, eh?"

He said it with such question it was endearing. Her heart skipped, but she relaxed too. "I'm not. Though I did meet someone from that strange chat room," she said in a teasing tone.

His head jerked up, eyes wide and filled with fire. She was hoping to see jealousy, but instead he appeared to be angry. His firm jaw grew tense, rigid.

"That's stupid!" he said.

"Not at all," she replied defensively. "Tom is not like the others in that room. He's a normal guy. At least he makes sense. He explained the group as a family. It's not the same as Lonetree who thinks he has to enforce rules and play father. Tom sees it as a voluntary thing."

"I'm not talking about the group. I mean, meeting him. After what happened to your friend, weren't you worried?" Concern furrowed his brow.

Connie considered telling him it was Lisa's idea, but she didn't like his thinking she couldn't take care of herself. "We met in a public place. If he'd tried to get me, people on the waterfront would have seen him stab me or toss me off the dock."

"One of these days you won't be so lucky, eh?" he said in blunt disgust.

Visions of the burgundy van nearly hitting her and the mugging came to her. She had meant to tell him about the van, but now she feared he would take it the wrong way. She'd call Ryan in the morning. "This had nothing to do with luck. Tom was a nice guy."

"Your instincts aren't always right, eh? You were wrong about Ralph."

She bristled at his accusation. "He told his

337

lawyer he has an alibi. He was with someone, but I think he's protecting her."

He drew back, clearly stunned. "Have you told Case?"

"No, but I'm going to. According to Joy's journal, the one in that computer no one deemed important, Ralph was seeing Mary Sue Baker, a woman she worked with. Mary Sue is married. Maybe she's afraid to tell the truth because she might lose her husband. Heck, maybe she hired someone to get rid of Joy. Have any of you thought of that?"

Actually the thought struck her like a smack across the face as she spoke. Someone was still after her. Could it be that Mary Sue feared she might still be trying to prove Ralph innocent?

"Will Lonetree called and left a message for me today," she continued, though she had no idea why. "He has new information. Hell, I don't think this investigation is as cut-and-dried as you guys think. What if someone put that knife in Ralph's house to put the blame on him?"

Weldon looked away, studying the tablecloth, but the rapid movement of his eyes told her he was thinking through her words and weighing them carefully. "I wish you'd let police investigate this. You're not an investigator. Look at what a mess you've made so far."

Connie stared at him in horror. She could not believe he would say such a hurtful thing. "You don't need to remind me that I'm responsible in a way for Sandy's death," she said with a choked voice. "It's something I doubt I'll ever forget." Tears threatened, but she fought them back. She would not give him the privilege of seeing her cry, especially since he was waving his hands up and down, instructing her to lower her voice.

"I'm sorry," he said in a voice that bordered on a whisper. "That wasn't what I meant. I just think you need to be careful."

"Don't worry about me, I can take care of myself," she said.

"So you say," he replied curtly. "I'm not so certain."

Anger replaced the hurt. "Screw you," Connie said coldly. "I don't need any man who thinks I'm a helpless bimbo who needs a big strong hero to be her knight in shining armor."

"Maybe you don't need a man at all."

"Maybe not!" she replied hotly and he again waved at her to lower her voice. She did it, but she leveled him with a glare.

"I especially don't need someone who thinks they can come and go as they please without calling me. I'm not going to be used or sit at home waiting for anyone to come home." Connie knew she had gone too far immediately and regretted her words.

He grew pale and wiped his lips carefully and got to his feet. A nerve jerked on his lean jawline. The bill had come, and he signed it and picked up his credit card.

"You don't need to sit at home and wait for me. I'll get my things from your apartment and leave," he said coldly.

Connie watched him go through the tables, his large shoulders held high, moving with the athletic grace she had come to admire. How had they gone from being in love one minute to such a disaster?

****

Pacing the loft liked a caged tiger, Connie fought back a fresh bout of tears. The big room felt empty without Weldon. She took off her dress and started to remove her jewelry, and then noticed her answering machine was blinking again. She walked over and pushed the play button.

Another message from Lonetree. He needed to talk to her. She shook her head. She saw no reason to call him, especially this late at night.

Why had she let Weldon leave? She should have insisted on making coffee and maybe they could have discussed what was bothering them both. They had driven home in silence, and he put his clothes inside his bag while she stood by the windows looking out. Neither spoke, and he walked out without saying goodbye.

She put on her bathrobe, but she knew sleep would never come. The bed was a sad reminder of her glorious afternoon with Weldon. She could even sit on the sofa where they'd made love in a frenzy when he arrived. His presence filled the cavernous loft.

She poured a glass of wine and went to the computer. She wasn't up to talking to Lonetree, but perhaps he was online, and she could find out what he wanted. Raven didn't respond to her message, but as she was about to sign off, Tom sent a message.

LastDance: I enjoyed our meeting today.

SexyLady: So did I. Sorry if I was pushy.

LastDance: No problem. You love your sisters. You're keeping the name?

SexyLady: For now.

LastDance: You need a name that suits you.

SexyLady: Maybe. I don't think this one fit Joy.

LastDance: Let's not be judgmental.

SexyLady: No, I can't be. Not after the evening I've just had.

LastDance: Something on your mind?

SexyLady: Remember how you said the family helped you? I feel like that tonight. I need help.

LastDance: Tell me about it. Maybe I can help.

The letters pulsed on the screen, and she re-read them. Could he help? Was this what Joy had done?

She knew how her sister must have felt, filled with pain, hurt, and betrayal over her husband's affair. Tom was a stranger. How could she confide in him?

SexyLady: I don't want to burden you.

LastDance: We're friends. Think of me as your older brother.

SexyLady: Never had a brother.

LastDance: Then let me play the role. Tell me your troubles. Typing can be easier than talking.

Connie had not intended doing it, but as she began to type, she found herself pouring out her thoughts and fears about Weldon. Tom was understanding, asking questions, offering advice, until he came to the crux of the matter, a perception so simple she couldn't believe she hadn't figured it out for herself.

LastDance: You're afraid of commitment. Both of you. Neither one wants to make the move that puts your feelings on the line. Decide what you want, Connie. Then go for it.

She signed off with that thought on her mind. Perhaps she should call Mitch and let him know what Tom said, but she had already caused enough problems by mentioning his name. She should have made certain he knew Lisa was with her, that Lisa was interested in Tom. Would he understand? Or would he think she was just saying what she thought he wanted to hear? How would he react? Perhaps she should just let it go for now.

****

Mitch sat in the squad room, trying to concentrate on the report in front of him. The Blade was growing more brazen. Again he had struck during the day, snatching a woman from a nearly deserted car park. A man had heard the woman's shouts, and caught sight of the van disappearing out of the lot. Mitch felt powerless, helpless, unable to find the woman, knowing at this hour she was probably suffering. Hopefully the witness had been wrong. Hopefully the woman had not been screaming that her attacker was the madman.

He stared at the earlier witness report and that from the latest kidnapping. The woman had seen a black SUV. The man had seen more of a dark van.

The phone rang and he grabbed it.

Frank Case's voice came across the line. "I thought you should know that the case against Ralph Perkins is in danger. Connie Romero called me about his having an alibi, and we've been questioning the woman. This morning she admitted she was having an affair with Perkins and that she was with him when his wife was killed. She was with him the afternoon that other girl was killed too."

The air whooshed out of Weldon as though he'd been slugged. "What about the knife?"

"It's all we have now. Hopefully it will be enough, but Perkins swears he's never seen it. It's a brand sold only in the Midwestern United States, and even the in-laws say they don't recognize it. We can keep him in jail with the knife, but it may not be enough for a conviction if the woman provides alibis."

"He could have hired someone."

"He had no money. Paid killers don't work on the promise of an insurance policy. He was going into debt just to pay the bills and while his wife had money stashed, he wasn't aware of until the two sisters told him. I could tell he was hiding something, but now that we've learned about the other woman, I'm starting to have doubts."

Weldon sighed heavily. It wasn't his case, but disappointment flooded him nevertheless.

"Perhaps you should talk to the sisters again

about the other man and what they found on her computer."

"I've been thinking of that. I'm not re-opening the case, but perhaps a little more legwork is in order."

His pulse quickened. Maybe this was the opportunity he'd been looking for. "Do you want me to call Connie Romero? Do a little checking for you?"

"If you want. If you have time."

He didn't have time, he thought, as he considered the reports in front of him, but he still agreed. As he hung up, he muttered a curse under his breath. Weldon didn't know why he was so anxious to call her. Perhaps it was the way they had parted three nights ago.

Their argument as they left the Space Needle still grated on him. How could he have let the discussion degenerate so far? He basically blamed her for her friend's death, but that was not what he had been trying to say. Why couldn't he say the right thing to her? Why couldn't he tell her he wanted her to take care of herself because he worried about her so much? That he cared and didn't want to see her hurt?

And yet what purpose would it serve? Did he want to think of her sitting and waiting while he pursued another case, just as she had said she wouldn't do? Did he want the broken dinner dates or the accusations again as he'd once had from Wanda?

He enjoyed Connie's company, enjoyed her in bed, but was a relationship possible? Was he ready for that? He'd been thinking through the questions for days now, and come to no conclusion.

Thoughts of her and that man from the Internet came to him. He could imagine her exchanging witticisms, enjoying his company. Perhaps the man worked a normal job and could be there for the dinners, not disappear for days on end.

He punched in her home phone number. No answer, even though it was nearly eight. He tried her cell phone but it went right to voice mail. Where was she? Had she returned to the islands to be with her parents?

He called her house again, left her a message to call and then suddenly pictured her out with the Internet friend and added something else.

"One thing has been bothering me. For all your investigating, what do you really know about that Tom guy?"

The message was silly. Teenage preposterous. He needed to get over this infatuation or he'd never be able to work. Or was it infatuation? At times he feared he was falling in love.

But then as he looked down at the report from the latest witness, a chill ran over him. He dropped the phone and began digging through the piles of pages on his desk. The connection between victims. It was there. It had been there all along. The phone began to buzz in protest and he hung it up, barely remembering who he had been calling or why.

****

Connie made a face as she listened to Weldon's comments. She hadn't expected to hear from him, though he had been constantly on her mind the past two days in Bellingham. She and Lisa had finally told their parents what they knew, and now Mary Sue had broken down admitted being with Ralph. Her testimony might not totally clear him, but it cast doubt on whether he had killed Joy.

So had Lonetree. She'd finally called him from Bellingham.

"I tracked down Mike," he said. "It seems he moved to Portland to be with Kelly. She told her brother she'd fallen in love with a man she met on the Internet, and he was moving in with her. But then some other woman tried to take him away.

After she died, he discovered that his sister had been sending the Internet guy money. He also found hate notes on her computer from someone trying to lure the guy away by promising him even more money." He paused and cleared his throat. "I think we know that other woman was Joy. The brother thought this woman might have killed Kelly. I had to explain she was dead too."

His words flabbergasted Connie as nausea overwhelmed her. She could barely understand Joy seeing another man, but to battle over him to the point of sending him money or threatening notes to a rival? The thought sickened her. Ever since Joy's death Connie had been finding new, sad truths about her sister. At times she felt Joy had become a stranger to her, as unknown as the people in the chat room.

"Do you think...this Mike could have killed Kelly? Or Joy?"

"I don't know why. I'm going to talk to Sergeant Case and give him this information, but I wanted you and your sister to know."

Now that she was back home, Connie wasn't certain what she was going to do. If Ralph wasn't the killer, it brought back all her original questions and she still had no answers. She had not told Lisa about Mike. What if she tried to find him? What if he found her? If Mike was the killer, Connie couldn't allow him to take the life of someone else close to her. Yet she feared he was out there. Waiting somewhere in a burgundy van. At least she had not seen that damned van the past couple of days.

Chewing anxiously on a fingernail, Connie began to pace. She looked to the windows where a light rain had began to spatter against the glass. The night was as gloomy as her mood. She had been excited when she first heard Weldon's voice, but it sounded like a business call. There was no hint of anything personal in it, except the warning about Tom.

Tom. Now that was another story. The only person she'd confided in was Tom. What did she know about him? Maybe not a lot on a face-to-face basis, but online Tom was one of the most soothing people she'd ever met. For the past two nights he'd listened to her woes and offered tidbits of advice. She had not told Lisa they were talking as friends. She knew Lisa had also been talking to him on another level.

Signing onto the computer, Connie saw Tom was online as he usually was in the evening.

LastDance: Late night?

SexyLady: Just returned from Bellingham. I'm beat.

LastDance: Go to bed then.

SexyLady: They let Ralph out on bail. He might get off after all.

LastDance: Then who killed Joy?

SexyLady: I don't know. Maybe Mike. Or Raven. He's been pointing me at Mike.

LastDance: Is he?

She thought about whether she should admit that and decided against it. Tom was still too close to Raven and anything she might tell him would probably go back to the big man. For all she knew Tom had already told Raven she suspected him.

SexyLady: No.

LastDance: It could be Raven. He was jealous that Joy liked the others.

SexyLady: I've thought of that.

LastDance: Am I scaring you?

SexyLady: No, but I need to find out where Mike is.

LastDance: How will you do that?

SexyLady: I don't know. I hate to involve Lisa like I did Sandy.

LastDance: Have you told Lisa about this?
SexyLady: I haven't told anyone but you.
LastDance: Then don't tell her. I'll help. Let's not put her in danger.

That was considerate of Tom, but she hated to endanger him either and she told him so.

LastDance: I can take care of myself. I trained in the military. No slouch here.
SexyLady: Okay. I'll email you in the morning about all I've learned so far.
LastDance: Great. Goodnight, sweetie.

Sweetie. She looked at the close. It felt good to have someone call her that. Too bad it wasn't Weldon.

****

The next morning Connie typed a letter to Tom, explaining the notes from Joy and how she had been giving Mike money. Perhaps Lisa had told him most of it, but Connie was as thorough as possible. Maybe Tom could track down the elusive Mike. She sent the information to Tom before heading out for a morning walk.

For once a walk to the waterfront failed to engage her. She found herself constantly looking behind her, checking for the burgundy van. Every time someone came close to her, she pulled away. Would she always be afraid she was about to be assaulted? Perhaps she should see a victim advocate, or get therapy.

She returned home with a bagel and coffee, hoping to find voice mail from Weldon, though she'd had her cell phone with her.

"Just call him, dummy," she urged and then shook her head. Let him make the first move.

After toasting the bagel and lathering it with cream cheese and topping it with smoked salmon, she walked to the computer. Might as well check in. Connie flipped the on switch. The computer came to

347

life but the sign on screen did not come up. She flipped the switch to off and then back on again. The indicator lights came on but nothing showed up on the screen and the computer hard drive sounded like a Volkswagen bug trying to make it to the top of a steep hill.

"Damn!" she muttered. What a time for her computer to go on the blink. Connie had not replaced the stolen laptop—not after having two taken from her in the space of a month. She pounded the keyboard and jostled her mouse. Nothing did any good. What could be wrong?

She started to reach behind the terminal when her eyes were caught by a shiny object to the left of the monitor. The angel pin winked in the glow of the lamp.

Her heart skipped. Connie knew what it was, and she knew what it meant.

Chapter Twenty-One

Connie stared at the pin in horror, heart thudding so hard she felt she could hear it. She started to touch the gleaming object and then drew back as though it might be hot. What should she do? She needed to talk to Mitch.

Her shaking fingers punched his number into her phone. She whimpered as the phone rang. Once, twice, three times. No answer. When it went to his voice mail, she wanted to cry.

Drawing up her shoulders, Connie forced her voice to be as calm as possible. She left a message for him to return her call. No use frightening or upsetting him by telling him about the pin. What could he do anyway? He was in Vancouver.

Beside her the pin winked in the light, as though waiting to pounce. The significance of its presence reverberated around her like the aftermath of a knelling gong. The apartment was deathly still, but Connie turned her head from one side to the other, looking for anything out of place. Someone had gotten into her apartment. Who? How? Where were they now?

The door had been locked, and nothing else was disturbed. Connie had never been the neatest housekeeper—not like Weldon—but she would have noticed something out of order.

Her lips were dry, bordering on cracked, and when she tried to wet them, her tongue was dry too. Her throat grew tight and her pounding heart refused to slow. With trembling fingers she opened her desk drawer and removed a pair of scissors. If someone was in the apartment, they faced a battle. What did she have for defense besides the scissors? The tennis racket? Where was her can of pepper spray?

She needed to call Ryan or 911, but what could she tell them? Would they understand the significance of the pin?

The sudden ringing of her phone sent Connie leaping out of her chair. She grabbed it, hoping to hear Weldon at the other end. Tom was a welcome surprise. At least he was in Seattle.

"Oh, thank goodness," she said, pounding her chest to still her heart rate, voice high and excited. "I'm so glad it's you."

"That's quite a greeting. You sound upset."

"I have a pin. An angel pin. Like Sandy, like Joy!"

"A pin?" he asked, sounding confused.

"Like Joy and Sandy were wearing when they were killed," she said breathlessly.

"Calm down, it'll be okay," he said in a soothing tone. "Should I come over?"

"I...no! I need to get out of here. What if whoever left it comes back? Or is still here." Rolling her chair back against the wall, she let her gaze roam from one end of the apartment to the next, looking for any possible sign of movement.

"Maybe you should call 911."

"And tell them what? I found a pin?"

"Yeah. Okay. Have you called Lisa?"

"I don't want to frighten her. Besides, she would want to come over and stay with me. I don't think it's safe."

"Okay. Why don't you come here?" His comforting voice was having a steadying effect on her, and her rapid breathing was finally starting to slow.

"Call me right back on your cell phone," he

instructed. "Keep talking to me while you get out of there. That way if someone makes a jump or anything I'll know, and I can get police to you in seconds."

Connie hung up, and with the scissors tightly gripped in her hand, grabbed her purse. She kept looking around the apartment as she backed toward the door. The big room didn't offer many places to hide. Her closet door was shut, but in order to hide in it, a person would have to remove the clothes and shoes which littered the floor. She had been in the bathroom so she knew it was clear. All the same, Connie didn't breathe easier until she was in the hall, with her coat on and on the phone to Tom.

"I should call the police," she said as she hopped down the stairs, back to the wall. She held the phone in her left hand and kept the scissors poised for action in her other hand.

"We'll call them from here." His comforting voice was a relief. The man was proving to be good in a crisis. "When you get to your car, watch to make certain that no one follows you."

Thoughts of the burgundy van hit her hard. What if it was waiting on the street? She peered out the door, but the street was empty. Her car was in a garage across the street and she hurried to it, feeling safer once she was locked inside it.

"Here's my address," Tom said.

Connie nodded as though he could see her on the phone. "Are you sure about this? It could be dangerous, Tom. I don't know if I should involve you. What if something happens?" She thought of Weldon's accusation that she bumbled things. She could not afford to get another person hurt.

"I'll be fine," he reassured her. "You're the one in danger. Once you get here, we'll call police and let them deal with things."

"Good idea." Connie checked for the van as she

backed out and started down the street.

Tom remained composed, his steady voice a comforting beacon. "Now be careful as you drive. Watch the rearview mirror. If any car follows for more than a couple of blocks, turn off and see if they follow."

"Right," she said with a nervous laugh. "I feel like I'm in a teen slasher movie."

"Just remember the heroine always pulls through," he said.

Connie wasn't so positive, but she let him remind her of all the heroines who did dumb things and survived while she drove. The whole time she kept a close watch. With Tom skillfully directing her, she made it to his house without any problem.

He greeted her at the door and she flipped her phone closed with another giant sigh of relief.

"Thanks for letting me come over. I appreciate it. Shall we call police?"

"Sure. Where's the pin?"

Connie gulped, clapping her hand over her mouth as she realized what she had done. "I forgot the pin. It's still sitting on my desk."

A slight look of impatience crossed Tom smooth, boyish face. "Forgot it? But that was why you were coming over."

"Only part of the reason," she said, looking behind her. The street was empty.

"Come in." He led her inside and helped her remove her coat. His home was in an older section of the city, a brick structure with a pointed roof. The interior was gloomy, thanks to a preponderance of dark polished wood and darkly painted walls.

He gestured her toward a living room that screamed well-off bachelor. Black leather furnishings filled the room and one wall was taken up by electronic gear and a big screen television. "May I get you something to drink?" he asked.

Her stomach was too rattled. "I don't know that I could get keep anything down." She took several rapid breaths trying to calm down. She perched on the sofa, and tried to keep from chewing a thumbnail.

"Let me get you some water or club soda at least," he said. "You're all pent up."

"Okay, club soda."

He disappeared, and she rubbed her icy hands together trying to warm them up and stop the shaking. Her heart no longer raced, but she knew it would be a long time before her fear fully abated. At least she was safe for the moment. He returned with a tall glass with bubbles on the sides and a slice of lime at the top.

"Here you go. This will make you feel better." He sat on a chair opposite her.

Connie took a tentative sip. It was flavored with lemon lime but had the bitter after taste of something diet.

"Now what?" she asked as she set the drink on a glass coffee table. He reached over and picked it up, handing it back to her.

"You need to drink that. I put a touch of vodka in it to soothe your nerves."

She appreciated the effort, but liquor was not the answer. This was a time for clear-headed thinking. "I should call Lt. Ryan. He handled Sandy's case."

Tom sighed heavily, looking around the room as though seeking an answer. "You're right. Maybe I should get the pin."

Her breath caught. "Do... do you think it's safe?"

"I'll be fine. I'll call police on my way over and have them meet me there."

"I'll go with you," she said, lurching shakily to her feet.

He held out his hand, gesturing her to sit down.

"No, you shouldn't go back. As long as no one knows where you are, you'll be safe. Finish your drink and I'll be back in a few minutes with the police. Where are your keys? I'll put your car in the garage so no one can see it from the street."

"In my coat pocket." She wasn't certain about the idea. She couldn't take another death scene like Sandy's and she didn't want to be responsible for Tom getting hurt. Perhaps she should call Weldon again. He'd have some thoughts on what they should do. For once she felt like she was at a loss for ideas. Somewhere out there the killer was now focusing on her. How could she escape him? Tom was only a temporary answer.

"You wait here," he said with a comforting smile, flipping on the television set. "By the time this program is over, I'll be back with the pin and police."

Before she could protest, Tom was gone. She tried to relax, but found it impossible. The television program was annoying and she hit the remote control and turned it off. The silence was overpowering.

Connie took a sip of the drink and made a face. The diet taste was pronounced and vodka would cloud her thinking. Putting the glass down, Connie missed the coffee table, and the glass tumbled to the floor, spilling the drink. Luckily it fell on a throw rug under the table instead of crashing to the hardwood floor and breaking. The liquid formed a circle in the red rug that looked like a blood splotch.

Just what she needed, a cleaning bill. Lisa often laughed about her clumsiness. Maybe Lisa and Weldon were right. She did bumble around. Only luck had kept her from being seriously hurt so far.

Going to the kitchen, Connie found towels to sop up the liquid. The chore kept her busy physically, but it also gave her time to think. Who was the culprit? Mike? Ralph? He was out of jail. What if she had been wrong all along? What about Lonetree? Where was he? And what about Mary Sue? She knew about the pins. What if she'd been back there all along, pulling strings? Connie sighed. She wasn't certain she'd come up with a solution to her dilemma. She tried not to think that her life might depend on coming up with the right answer.

Maybe she should check Lonetree's whereabouts. Connie walked to the entryway to get her cell phone from her purse. She dug through it, but the phone wasn't there. Perhaps she had left it in the car. She started to get her keys from her pocket and remembered Tom had taken them.

She'd have to call from his phone and pay him back for making a long distance call. Starting toward the living room, she noticed a partially open door. Beyond it sat a computer on a desk. Maybe she would check to see if Raven was online instead.

Connie entered the room. Like the rest of the house it spoke of quiet elegance with dark wooden bookcases and a heavy cherry wood desk. A wall of books and boxes lined one wall, while another pile of boxes were stacked in a corner. Sitting at the desk, Connie started to turn on the computer and then spotted the phone. Without hesitation, she punched in Mitch's number. She'd pay for the call. This time Weldon's voice came on immediately.

"Mitch!"

"Connie, are you all right?"

"I...I got a pin," she cried. "An angel pin. Someone left it at my apartment."

"You haven't been investigating again, have you?"

"Not really. I talked to Raven, Lonetree. He thinks Mike, an online friend, did it, but we can't find out who that person is. Maybe it is Lonetree. Maybe he told me about Mike to send me in the wrong direction. I need to find out where Lonetree is. I was going to call him, but I called you instead." She was chattering, words spilling out like staccato gunfire.

"Calm down, Connie. I'll find out where he is. Don't worry. You stay put. Or maybe you should go to Lisa's."

"I'm at Tom's house. He went to get the pin and call police."

"Tom?" he sounded surprised. "What the hell are you doing there? What the hell do you know about him?"

It was like his message which asked the same question. What did she know about him? "He's helping me."

He muttered an off color oath of exasperation. "Don't wait for him to come back. Call police right now."

"He called already," she said, certain he would be at her house by now and in touch with them. "He and the police are on their way."

He inhaled sharply. "Connie...honey..."

Honey? The word coming from his lips sent her heart pounding and it had nothing to do with fear.

"I'm coming down there," he continued. "Don't do anything foolish, please." His voice was soft, almost pleading.

"I can take care..." Connie stopped as tears came into her eyes. She licked her chapped lips. Maybe she could take care of herself, but she wished he was beside her. She would have given anything for him to be with her, and not just for protection.

She bit hard on her lip to push back the tears. "Admit it," she said, trying to get a handle on her runaway emotions. "You're jealous because I'm here with Tom."

He inhaled sharply. "This isn't a joking matter."

"Isn't that why you left that message? Questioning Tom?"

"Damn you, Connie Romero," he said, but his voice was lighter. "Take care of yourself. I'll be there soon."

****

Mitch closed his cell phone and grimaced as he stared at the door to the Internet café. The answer to the Blade might be behind that door, but Connie needed him. He had to make a choice. His duty or the woman he loved. And he did love her. He knew that now. He'd known it every lonely minute since he'd last seen her.

Maybe there was a way around it. He'd call Seattle Police and get them to... he stopped. How the hell could he have made such a rookie mistake? He hadn't gotten her location. How could he send help if he didn't even know where she was? Quickly he hit redial on his phone.

The number was unknown.

Perhaps he could call Lisa. She might know where the man lived. He checked his contacts and found her name, but the phone rang several times and went to voice mail.

The door to the coffee shop opened and he recognized the owner whom he'd questioned earlier about Queenie Ambrose, a recent Blade victim, stepping through the door. He wore his coat.

"Wait, Mr. James. I need to talk with you."

The man's head jerked up. "Inspector, sorry, I'm in a rush. I gotta pick up my son."

"Can we talk just a second? I have a couple of questions, but I need to make a phone call first."

The man looked impatiently at his watch and shook his head.

Weldon closed his phone and put it into his pocket. Dammit, if he didn't do this now, another woman might die.

But then what about Connie?

****

Connie sat beside the phone, her hands no longer shaking. Talking to Mitch did that. And he was coming! She wanted Mitch. She loved Mitch and this time she wasn't going to let foolish arguments come between them. Maybe it wouldn't be so bad to let him take care of her—sometimes. Or she could take care of him. There were areas where she could help him. A partnership. Would that be so bad?

But she couldn't let down her guard until he arrived. This called for a level head, though she was afraid there had been more than a fraction of vodka in that drink. Her brain was beginning to fuzz over. Connie blinked, trying to clear her head. She needed to figure out who killed Joy and Sandy, and she must be close to unraveling the mystery or the killer would not have come after her. He would not have left that pin.

Raven? He was still suspect. Ralph? No. Why did Weldon keep casting doubts on Tom? Jealousy? She wanted to think that, but Tom had been in the area too, and he was the only other person besides Raven who knew what they were doing. What did Connie know about him?

She considered calling Lisa and changed her mind. She could not allow her sister to fall into danger. Maybe she should get online and see if Raven was around. At least if he was online it meant he wasn't in a car somewhere looking for her. Maybe he had information on Tom.

Tom's computer screen swirled with a screensaver, and she tapped the mouse. It brought up a desktop screen filled with folders. The guy certainly had lots of programs, but then he was a computer geek.

Connie found the Internet icon for the chat room and clicked to open it. She would have to sign on as a guest, so she lined up the mouse to the sign on button. It opened and a long row of screen names appeared. What the hell? Did he use all these? There had to be nearly a hundred names. She gasped and her breath caught as she recognized several. Below LastDance was DreamBaby.

What did that mean?

Next was JustMelvin, followed by DarkGhost.

Huh? The people from the chat room?

It took her a minute to realize what she was seeing. Hadn't Lisa said the Assembly group was a crew of people or the same person in one location? Was that what Tom was doing? Talking as several different people all at once? But why? And...

The next name on the list was Mike7445.

"Oh my God," she whispered.

Could Tom be Mike?

Could that be why they'd never found out who he was? Why change his name? The answer was simple. He didn't want to drop out of the group. He didn't want to lose his family.

Mitch's comment reverberated in the silent house. How well did she know Tom? She looked around the elegant room as suspicion took a cold hold on her brain. She fought it off. She was being silly, grasping at anything. He wouldn't have left her alone if he had anything to hide.

Yet why hadn't they been able to find out who Mike was? Even Raven couldn't find him. Had Joy fallen for Mike? Or Tom? What about Little Bird? Why hadn't Tom told the truth when she said she was looking for Mike? Unless he had something to hide.

Flipping off the Internet service, Connie went back to the front screen with faltering fingers. She shook her head as the screen swam in front of her. Was the room growing darker? She blinked, but her eyes were very dry. Looking at the many file folders, she tried to decide what to do next. They all looked innocuous. How angry would he be if she started being nosy? Why not find out the truth? He wouldn't be back for a while.

She clicked on a folder labeled "letters." A page filled with numbers and letters. From Lisa's comments about Joy's system she ascertained that the letters were initials and the numbers were dates. She called up one and found a query letter to a magazine. Another was to a credit company, asking for more time in paying off a loan.

A quick tap closed it. This wasn't good. She felt like she had when she went through Joy's diary. She was invading his privacy. She closed the file and studied the document folders. The initials JP leaped out at her. She clicked on it and found a series of files with dates from more than a month ago. She hesitated only briefly. She had already been nosy. What could one more letter hurt? Connie clicked on the icon.

Mike,

I need you now more than ever. I love you so much. Why won't you see me anymore? I'll leave him if that's what you want. Why won't you tell me what it is you want? I sent the money.

Tears flooded her eyes and a chill ran through her body. She didn't need to see the signature to know the letter was from Joy. She opened another blindly and in this one Joy was telling him she would be over that weekend with the money.

"Oh, hell," she whispered, aware of her quickened breathing in the darkened room. She closed the letter and went back to the front screen. Was it possible? But what other explanation was there?

Her gaze fell on a stack of letters on the desk. She thumbed through them. All were addressed to Mike Hardin in Illinois. Most of them were from credit card companies or collection agencies.

The reality of her predicament hit Connie with the force of a blow. Damn, she'd been sucked in, just like a heroine in a slasher movie. She had to get out of here. Rising to her feet, Connie contemplated her next move. She reached for his phone to call Weldon.

The line rang and rang. "Damn you, where are you?" she wailed as the line went to voice mail.

Should she call 911? But what could she tell them? She'd found out that the man she had come to visit was not who he said he was? She reached for the phone again. Lisa. She'd have her come over and pick her up and they'd hide some place until they could get in touch with Weldon.

Connie punched buttons frantically and as she hit the final one she realized she was so disoriented she had dialed Joy's cell number instead of Lisa's.

As she started to hang up, somewhere in the dark room, a song began to play. Her heart leaped to her throat and a chill ran down her spine as the tones of Beethoven's Ninth filled the room—the song Joy had on her cell phone.

Connie cried out as dropped the receiver. It clattered to the desk. Her hands were shaking uncontrollably and her breath was coming quick and loud. Moving on unsteady legs, she followed the sound to a closet. She yanked at the knob, but it was locked. Still the sound was unmistakable. She walked back to the desk, hung up the phone and the music stopped. Drawing a ragged breath, Connie dialed the number again and the song returned.

He had Joy's phone! What else? Her home computer? Maybe Connie's computer that had been stolen from the Vancouver hotel room? Or Joy's laptop that had been yanked from her shoulder in Vancouver? Had he feared what was on them? Connie dialed Lisa's number, but like Weldon, her sister didn't answer. She didn't leave a message.

Connie was on her own. She could call police.

They'd be there in minutes. No, they were already on their way.

"No, stupid," she whispered. Tom wouldn't have called them. Not if he was the killer. He'd told her that just to make her feel safe. Damn, her head was fuzzy. She shook it. That vodka had been a terrible idea, but now it made sense for him to give it to her. He wanted her fuzzy-headed.

She couldn't call police and wait. She might pass out before they arrived. Or he'd return. Wait! Her car was in the garage. She didn't have her keys, but she kept an extra set under the wheel well for when she got locked out. She'd leave and call police from a safe place.

Connie walked through the kitchen to the door Tom had taken to get to the garage. As she opened the door, she froze. In the garage, beside her car, was a dark van.

She blinked, eyes bleary. What color was it? She fumbled at the wall until her fingers located a light switch. Fluorescent light bathed the garage, and the color was unmistakable. Burgundy.

Her stomach churned with anxiety. The blocks were falling into place. This was like a bad dream where she stumbled from one predicament to the next. All her doubts were gone. She crossed to the back of the vehicle. No license plates.

Kneeling on the cement floor, Connie fumbled under her tire, but her extra set of keys was not there. She walked back to the kitchen door, which had closed behind her. She turned the knob. Locked. She pounded on the door and searched frantically around her for an opener for the garage. It was an old house and an old garage. The doors looked like they opened on their own. She went to the doors and pushed. They refused to move.

Maybe there were keys in the van. She'd drive the damn thing through the doors if she had to! The ignition was empty as she climbed inside, but there was a gray pouch on the floor. Maybe it had keys? She unzipped it and it tumbled from her hands. A long flat gold object flashed in the overhead light. She pulled at it and it flicked open. It was a long blade, the sort of razors used in the early part of the century. And it was very sharp.

Oh no! Could that be? Weldon called the serial killer who dumped his bodies in Stanley Park, the Blade. Was it possible? As though it might harm her, she closed the blade. She started to drop it back into the pouch, but slid it into her pocket instead. If Tom or Mike or the Blade or Slasher or whoever the hell he was tried to come after her, he had another thing coming!

She twisted in the seat to see if she could find something in the back to help her open the damn garage doors and she nearly fainted.

Tied up in the empty back of the van was Lisa, a tiny pin on the yoke of her sweater.

Chapter Twenty-Two

Connie gasped and climbed over the seat. Lisa lay slumped on the floor, eyes closed. He'd killed Lisa! And she was next. She slid along the floor to her sister and felt for a pulse under her neck. To her relief she felt a faint thump. She was alive! Connie pulled out the razor and used it to cut Lisa's bindings on her hands and feet.

Lisa's eyes fluttered, but they didn't open. She patted Lisa's face and began rubbing her cold hands to get the circulation going.

"Lisa honey, it's Connie. I'm here. We're going to get through this, baby, I promise. Mitch is coming."

Could he get there soon enough? Connie looked around fearfully. How soon before Tom returned? Damn! How could she have been so stupid, one of those women who don't do the most logical thing?

"Too stupid to live," she muttered as she and Lisa often chastised feisty heroines on television.

She hadn't been thinking straight. Tom said he put a spot of vodka in the drink, and recalling the bitter taste, she realized that wasn't what he had used. He'd put in something else, something that had set her head spinning. If she'd drunk more as he urged, she probably wouldn't be thinking at all, No wonder he hadn't minded leaving her alone. He figured she'd pass out on the sofa and he could tie her up and put her here with Lisa once he got the pin.

Lisa moaned and Connie tapped her sister's slack face. "We're going to be okay."

As she began to stir, Connie tugged at her limp

body. Maybe she could get Lisa out of the van and out into the street. She was too heavy to carry, but Connie struggled until she half dragged Lisa to the back door. Just as Connie started to push on the door's latch, it flew open, and she nearly tumbled out.

Tom stared in at her.

"Well, well, the Romero sisters," he said in a cool tone, unlike the pleasant voice she knew so well.

"You did it," Connie said. "It's been you all along."

At his smirk and knowing nod, she screamed as loud as she could, her cries reverberating around the garage. A hard slap cut her off, sending her toppling backward. Her head collided with something hard and stars erupted in the blackness behind her eyes. She tasted blood.

"All your banshee screaming won't work this time. This garage is concrete and well-sealed. So is the van." He shoved her back and climbed inside and closed the door.

She blinked, trying to clear her head, but he suddenly yanked her forward. She tried to struggle, but he caught her hands.

"You're more trouble than you're worth. I should have taken you down that first time in Vancouver. Left you dead in that hotel room."

"I called Weldon," she blurted. "He's calling Case. They're on their way."

"From Vancouver? Pardon me if I don't believe you, but if they were coming, they'd be here already. They have no idea who I am. And you'll never tell them."

"Lonetree," Lisa mumbled.

"Mr. Voodoo?" he laughed harshly. "Uh-uh. Always so in control, but he has no idea either. I was really running that room."

"Lisa figured you out," Connie challenged. "She

found you, like Sandy."

"Like you were about to," he said with a grim smile, blue eyes glacial.

"Mike," she spat. "Or should I call you The Slasher?"

"You can call me anything you want, but you won't tell anyone. I'm going to make certain of that this time." He moved toward her and she inched away, until her shoulders hit the back seat of the van.

"You're going to kill us, aren't you? I knew that when I saw the pin."

His smile grew sinister. "Not kill you. You and your sister are going to have an accident and drive into a lake. There have been too many murders."

"Tell me, Tom. If we're going to die, I want to know what this was all about," she said, summoning the remainder of her courage.

"I wanted friends," he said in a strangely calm voice as though they might still be at the pier watching ferries and seagulls. "They threw me out, because of Joy and Kelly flirting and fighting. It was my family, and I was ejected. So I came back."

"As Tom?"

"Only outside the chat room. I took on other names inside. So I could control who got to stay or go."

Raven had guessed something was wrong. With his advanced powers of perception or whatever he had, he would find Tom, though it would be too late for her.

"But Joy? Kelly?"

"Kelly wasn't who she said she was. She claimed to be an heiress. I moved to Portland believing her, thinking I could settle in and write. Hell, she could barely pay rent."

"And Joy?"

His shrug was unapologetic. "She said she would

366

make millions from the real estate or her writing. But Kelly didn't want to let me go. Her dying was a mistake. It just happened..."

He shook his head, eyes growing glazed. "But it felt good. Holding that power—the power of life and death." He looked at his hands as though they held magic answers.

"So you became the Slasher?" she questioned as the horror of what he was saying sent bile rising in her throat.

His voice was calm and that only made him more terrifying. "No one knew. Vancouver is in another country. I could go back and forth, and no one guessed. I made a mistake trusting Joy. She sounded enthralled with the idea of killing someone. She wanted to write about it. We were going to do it together. She asked me about killing her no-good husband and his girlfriend so we planned it together, like a murder mystery. Then I discovered she was never going to be rich either. I tried to make her let me go, but she hung on even though she knew what I was doing. So I tested her. I told her where I'd be that day. When she got there, I showed her my latest lady and found out that she hadn't believed what I'd been telling her. She thought it was a damn story we were making up together. When she saw the truth, she panicked. I had to stop her. To be free."

"You'll never be free," she croaked.

He looked at her accusingly. "This is your own fault. Why couldn't you let it go? If you'd given up when police arrested Joy's husband, that would have taken care of everything."

Lisa moaned again and he turned toward her. Connie took advantage of the situation to fumble in her pocket again for the blade. Sensing her movement he whirled back around and grabbed for her. She slapped at his hands, but a powerful lock caught her around her wrists and he yanked her forward. Hadn't he said something about military training? He pinned her arms against her side, but she managed to kick at his face. She heard a crunch and his startled curse. She twisted around to aim another kick at him, but a blow to the side of her head rocked her and then there was only blackness.

****

Connie woke to the sound of moaning. Her head pounded like a gong. She tried to move and realized rope bound her hands and ankles. She blinked, but she couldn't see anything. She was in total darkness, lying on her side. She smelled rubber and what?

She twisted and her fingers touched canvas. What? Where was she? She fumbled in the darkness with the canvas, outlining a bag—a canvas bag with the raised letters of Pacific Northwest News. It was the emergency bag of clothes she kept in her car trunk. No wonder it was so dark. She was stuffed in the trunk of her car. She kicked her foot and the moan came again. She'd hit flesh.

"Lisa?"

"Connie?" she croaked. "What…where are we?"

"In my trunk. Tom put us in here."

"Why?"

Connie couldn't explain about Joy falling for Mike. Like their older sister, both had fallen prey to his shows of understanding online. He pretended to be their friend, while all he wanted was to see how much the sisters knew. They had been so busy blaming Will Lonetree they'd refused to see what was right before their eyes.

"Will he kill us?" Lisa asked breathlessly.

"He's…The BC Slasher. He's already killed Joy, Sandy, even that poor Kelly Penrose and all those other bodies in the park. Yes, he intends to kill us."

"It's my fault," Lisa said. "I found him."

"No, I got us into this when I decided to

investigate Joy's death."

"Will Lonetree knows, or at least he guessed."

"What?"

"I talked to him last night. He had done more research on that list of people and discovered some of the names on it were fake identifications. Like Tom. Stupid me, I didn't believe him. I thought... I could talk to Tom and find out... I should have called you but I didn't want to put you in danger."

Tears slid into Connie's eyes. She had not wanted to endanger Lisa. They had not gone to each other and now they could end up paying the ultimate price. She should have trusted Weldon when she found the pin. She loved him, and she'd never get a chance to tell him. She'd foolishly put up barriers and now he would never know how she felt.

"What's Tom going to do?" Lisa asked.

"He said it has to look like an accident. He mentioned something about putting us in a lake."

"Oh, God. Help!" she screamed.

"Stop. This place is concrete and I don't want him to open the trunk and gag us. Sooner or later he's going to take us out of here to stage his accident. Once we're on the road we can scream or kick the trunk every time he stops."

"Are you sure he's the Slasher?"

"I saw the blade..." Connie stopped. Wait! She had it in her pocket. She twisted, trying to reach it.

"What are you doing?" Lisa protested as Connie accidentally kicked her.

"I have the blade in my pocket. Can you get to it?" She squirmed toward Lisa's voice.

"We're a team," Lisa mumbled, and wriggled up beside her. Together they worked, trying to get into the proper position so Lisa could reach the blade. Finally, Lisa issued a small shriek of triumph. She pressed the flat blade into Connie's hands.

From outside the trunk came the sound of the

garage door opening.

"Can you move?" Connie whispered as she wriggled to grasp the blade and get it open.

"A little."

"Pull on that blade with your fingers. Maybe we can open it and cut the ropes."

"I can't grasp it. My fingers are numb."

"You're doing fine," Connie said, but she didn't think they'd make much headway at this rate. Sooner or later he would have to untie them. He couldn't toss them into the water this way and hope for a decision of accident. Maybe they could fight back somehow. If they could only get that damn blade open.

From outside came footsteps again. The trunk popped open. She blinked into a flashlight.

"I thought I heard something." She heard an unmistakable rip and tape was clamped over her mouth. He did the same to Lisa's. The trunk slammed shut and the jolt sent the blade tumbling from her hand.

Lisa reached for her hand again, but Connie's fingers were empty. She squeezed Lisa's hand and her sister whimpered and moved in the darkness, fingers scratching in the darkness.

Connie waited for the car to start, but instead heard a car engine and the slamming of doors. Then she heard something wonderful.

Weldon's voice. He'd come to find her! How did he know where Tom lived? She couldn't hear what they were saying until she heard Weldon's voice right outside the trunk.

"What are you doing with Connie's car, eh?" he asked.

"She...uh...left it when her sister picked her up. She thinks someone is after her."

Lisa was breathing hard and something cold came against her wrist. Lisa had the blade open.

Connie pulled and tried to guide Lisa to the ropes on her hands. She worked her hands against the blade, feeling the ropes loosen slightly. She tried kicking, but couldn't get enough room for a good blow. Connie renewed the struggle to free her hands. If only she could pound on the trunk and let Weldon know where she and Lisa were.

She couldn't hear the voices anymore and then she heard the sound of a car engine. Weldon was leaving!

She twisted her wrists and her hands came free. She took the blade from Lisa and cut the bindings on her feet. Suddenly her cheek brushed against something. At first she recoiled in fear. Then she realized what it was. The emergency release for the trunk! She remembered showing it to Lisa when she changed the tire.

She grasped the release and tugged as hard as she could. She'd never seen the damn thing work. She didn't even know if it did, but the trunk flew open. She gasped in terror as her eyes fell on Tom's shocked face. He turned quickly to close the garage door as Weldon's familiar gray car pulled away.

Connie's muscles ached but she launched herself out of the trunk, flinging herself at Tom. She collapsed onto her side and they both saw the razor on the ground. Tom reached for it, but Weldon seemed to come out of nowhere, kicking it away. His next kick caught Tom in the chest as Tom turned away, taking only a glancing blow. Tom aimed a punch at Weldon's face but he deflected it in a move so fast Connie barely saw his arm shift. Weldon retaliated with a blow to the side of Tom's face, sending him to his knees.

Connie started to breathe sigh of relief, but she saw Tom's eyes focus on a tire iron near his hand. She rolled forward, kicking the iron away. Her other foot connected with Tom, tripping him as he fought to rise. He grunted and stumbled, collapsing onto her. Pain wracked her side, but she kicked at the hard body with as much force as she could, hearing him groan and curse as her blows struck home. She squirmed, thrashing against him with legs muscled from her bike riding, stopping only when the body was lifted from her.

Weldon yanked Tom to his knees, jerked his hands behind him and expertly cuffed him.

For an instant nothing happened. Then she saw Will Lonetree appear in the door way. Oh, damn, was he in on it with Tom? She cried out and rushed toward him, but Weldon caught her.

"Whoa, easy. He's with me."

She turned to Weldon then, collapsing against him, tears flooding her eyes. "Damn," she muttered. "Sometimes I can't take care of myself."

****

In the distance came the sound of sirens and beside her Lonetree was pulling Lisa from the car and helping to take off her ropes and the tape from her mouth.

He turned to Connie. "So you think I'm a killer," he said with a grim smile.

"I'm sorry," she said, looking for Mitch. After her crying outburst, he had calmed her and she pulled free, feeling self-conscious at her behavior. Now she found him examining the inside of the van, while Seattle police officers swarmed the area around them.

"Luckily Inspector Weldon didn't agree with you," he said.

"How did you find us?"

His eyes went to Lisa. "Your sister's not the only one who's a master of tracking people down." He touched Lisa's bleeding head, and then pulled a red scarf from around his neck and touched it to her head.

Connie looked over the car roof toward Weldon. Their eyes met.

"Wait there," he ordered before he walked with Tom toward a Seattle police car.

Like an obedient puppy, Connie didn't move. Her knees were shaking too badly. Beside her, Lonetree had seated Lisa on the edge of the trunk and was checking on her cut.

"Is she okay?" Connie asked.

"Just a scrape. Head wounds bleed more. The ambulance is on the way."

Connie leaned over and hugged her sister's quaking body. "It's gonna be okay, hon."

Lisa smiled wanly. "Teamwork," she said, waving a small fist.

"I'll always be there for you," Connie promised, catching her fist and squeezing it as tears edged into her eyes. "We'll always talk and never let anyone come between us. That's a pledge."

Lisa nodded, pressing her shaking lips together, her own eyes watery.

An ambulance zoomed around the corner, and Lonetree put his arm protectively around Lisa and helped her toward it.

Weldon came around the side of the van. He stopped a foot from Connie, shaking his head. She chewed on her lower lip. When the trunk had popped and she flew into Tom, she had seen the pale fear on Weldon's face. Whether the stern inspector would admit it or not, he had been worried about her. He cared about her. Loved him maybe? It didn't matter. She loved him and she was going to make certain he knew it.

"Your investigating days are over," he said, but despite the hard tone of his voice, a small smile tugged at the edges of his lips.

Connie started to protest, but tears flooded her eyes and a lump closed her throat. She nodded, lifting her hand toward him, finding her voice, even if it was squeaky. "I suppose. But I think that's the blade you've been looking for."

He nodded and then took her hand and held it almost primly. "I can see you'll need a lot of watching to keep from falling back into bad habits," he said, his smile widening.

"Not from just anyone," Connie replied coyly. She pointed toward the ambulance where Lonetree was supervising Lisa's care. "I think Lisa has a fan. How did you link up with Raven?"

Weldon squeezed her hand. "He called me. I had made the connection of the Blade victims and an Internet café and then there was a complaint about a van that sometimes parked near it. I'd talked to the café owner before but he kept saying it was a black van. A new witness said he'd thought it was a very dark, almost midnight burgundy."

"Burgundy?" she looked back at the van.

"You must have seen him in the park. Spooked him. I went back to the café today to see if the owner might have seen a burgundy van, but I didn't get to talk to him. You called. And while I was deciding whether to head down here or go back and talk to the owner, Lonetree called. I'd asked him about the Internet café and if there was some way to figure out who the girls were talking to. Our computers came up empty, and I'd given him the girls' email addresses. Somehow he looked them up and found they'd all been talking to Mike Hardin. The same Mike Hardin from his Internet chat room."

"He figured that out?"

"Yep. He was quite helpful. We'd never have made it if he hadn't found the address. We sent police by while we were flying down in a chopper, but Hardin claimed Lisa had picked you up. They were waiting for a warrant when we arrived."

Connie looked down at their joined hands. There

was so much she wanted to say, but the words wouldn't come. "I never knew you were such a macho guy. I saw the way you punched that guy out. What a Rambo."

He shrugged. "You're pretty damn resourceful yourself. It's a trait I value. Something that is very necessary for someone I'd love. I do love you, by the way."

Tears flooded her eyes. She might be resourceful, but she was also emotional at times. Like now. She jerked her head up to him. "I love you, too, Mitch."

He nodded and squeezed her hand. "I thought so. I hoped so."

"Sometimes I like having someone take care of me. Not that I need it."

"Truce?" he said, grinning at her. "I have some paperwork to finish, but then I'll come to see you. Will you wait? We have a lot to talk about."

Connie could have drowned in the love she saw in his sea green eyes. "I'll be waiting. I'll always wait for you." Then, as if the moment had grown too serious, she couldn't resist teasing him. "And we can talk, but then I want you to teach me some of those kung fu moves."

He leaned forward and kissed her softly on the lips.

"Inspector," she chided, acting shocked. "In front of your fellow officers?"

"In front of the whole damn world," he said.

A word about the author...

Becky is an award winning former broadcast journalist who is now writing romance and romantic suspense. Her first published romance novel, LOVE ON DECK, was an Aspen Gold finalist and she contributed a short story to TROUBLE WITH ROMANCE, which was a 2007 New Mexico Book Award finalist in the anthology category. She is also published in non-fiction. She co-authored the book, 10 STEPS TO CREATING MEMORABLE CHARACTERS, which is a workbook for writers. She and one of the co-authors are currently working on a follow up book on plotting. In her free time she teaches online writing classes.

Visit Rebecca at www.rebeccagrace.com

Thank you for purchasing
this Wild Rose Press publication.
For other wonderful stories of romance,
please visit our on-line bookstore at
www.thewildrosepress.com

For questions or more information,
contact us at
info@thewildrosepress.com

The Wild Rose Press
www.TheWildRosePress.com

Other suspense-filled Roses to enjoy
from The Wild Rose Press

DON'T CALL ME DARLIN' by Fleeta Cunningham. Texas, 1957: Carole faces not only censorship but mysterious threats and a fire-setting assailant. Will the County Judge who's dating her protect or accuse her?

~from Vintage Rose (historical 1900s)

SECRETS IN THE SHADOWS by Sheridon Smythe. Lovely widow Lacy had taken in two young children—and the rambunctious little angels wasted no time getting her into trouble with Shadow City's new sheriff...

~from Cactus Rose (historical Western)

SOLDIER FOR LOVE by Brenda Gale. An award-winning novel set on a lush Caribbean island. As CO of the American peacekeeping force, Julie has her hands full dealing with voodoo signs and a handsome subordinate.

~from Last Rose of Summer (older heroines)

TASMANIAN RAINBOW by Pinkie Paranya. A concert violinist grapples with remote ranch life, intrigue and the mystery of a missing diary, the peril of a flood in which all could be lost, and the undeniable attraction of the man who would do anything to protect his son.

~from Champagne Rose (contemporary)

THAT MONTANA SUMMER by Sloan Seymour. Samantha has everything but love. Dalton has only one thing on his mind: land. Neither wants to be a summer fling or be stalked by a mysterious attacker.

~from Yellow Rose (contemporary Western)

A CHANGE OF HEART by Marianne Arkins. Jake Langley returns to Wyoming to find more than changes at the family ranch. Discovery of a well-kept secret sets duty against heart's desire, changing hearts and lives forever.

~from Yellow Rose (contemporary Western)

DRAKE'S RETREAT, by Wendy Davy. Maggie needs a place to hide. Drake's Retreat, deep in the Sierra Nevada Mountains, is the perfect solution. But she has to convince the intimidating resort owner to let her stay.

~from White Rose (inspirational)

www.ingramcontent.com/pod-product-compliance
Lightning Source LLC
Chambersburg PA
CBHW071112290626
47170CB00018B/248